Intimate Strangers

Susan Lewis is the bestselling author of *A Class Apart, Dance While You Can, Stolen Beginnings, Darkest Longings, Obsession, Vengeance, Summer Madness, Last Resort, Wildfire, Chasing Dreams, Taking Chances, Cruel Venus, Strange Allure, Silent Truths* and, most recently, *Wicked Beauty*. Having spent many years in Los Angeles she now lives in Wiltshire. Her website address is www.susanlewis.com.

Acclaim for Susan Lewis:

'Mystery and romance *par excellence*'
Sun

'Susan Lewis strikes gold again . . . gripping'
Options

'Spellbinding! . . . you just keep turning the pages, with the atmosphere growing more and more intense as the story leads to its dramatic climax'
Daily Mail

'Will keep you guessing till the last page'
19

'Erotic and exciting'
Sunday Times

INTIMATE STRANGERS

Susan Lewis

arrow books

Published by Arrow Books in 2004

1 3 5 7 9 10 8 6 4 2

Copyright © Susan Lewis 2003

Susan Lewis has asserted her right under the Copyright, Designs and
Patents Act, 1988 to be identified as the author of this work

First published in the United Kingdom in 2003 by William Heinemann

Arrow Books
The Random House Group Limited
20 Vauxhall Bridge Road, London, SW1V 2SA

Random House Australia (Pty) Limited
20 Alfred Street, Milsons Point,
Sydney, New South Wales 2061, Australia

Random House New Zealand Limited
18 Poland Road, Glenfield,
Auckland 10, New Zealand

Random House (Pty) Limited
Endulini, 5a Jubilee Road, Parktown 2193, South Africa

The Random House Group Limited Reg. No. 954009

www.randomhouse.co.uk

A CIP catalogue record for this book is
available from the British Library

ISBN 0 09 945329 0

Typeset in Palatino by Palimpsest Book Production Limited,
Polmont, Stirlingshire
Printed and bound in Great Britain
by Cox & Wyman Ltd, Reading, Berkshire

To Mum and Dad

Acknowledgements

An enormous thank you to Pallavi Sohonie for guiding and inspiring me through the Indian scenes, the characters and their plight. Rarely has anyone been so helpful or insightful. Thank you, Pallavi, thank you.

Once again I thank my friends Andrew Solum and Stephen Kelly for their generous hospitality while I was researching the Docklands. Also Brian and Valerie Sidaway for all the help they gave me on the island of Hydra. And I'd like to thank Sarah Shelley for introducing me to Cinnabar Wharf – a great location.

Love and thanks to my dear friend Chip Mitchell for the title, *Intimate Strangers*. And more love and thanks to Gene Franklin Smith, for unfailing support, friendship and advice, not just for this book, but for them all.

Chapter One

Some said there was no such thing as coincidence, but even when viewed in the light of all that was about to happen, Sherry MacElvoy could find no other way of explaining it. A wedding invitation and a suicide note turning up on the same day. Neither sender knew the other, so if there was a hidden message in the timing, or even in the bizarre extremes of subject, it certainly wasn't coming from them.

It was the middle of the afternoon and Sherry, to whom both letters were addressed, had just popped downstairs to stretch her legs and pick up her mail. After a brief chat with Bob, the porter-cum-security guard, who was trying with small success to look more important than bored, she avoided the lift again and started back up the two flights of stairs to her river-view flat. As she reached the second landing, she tore open the large white envelope addressed in artful black script. The invitation was embossed in platinum and every bit as elegant as she might have expected.

1

Melinda and Edward Forbes
are happy to invite

Miss Sheralyn MacElvoy

to celebrate the wedding of
their daughter
Laurie Jane Forbes
to
Elliot Francis Russell
at
St John the Baptist Parish Church
Tremmington, Nr Windsor
on
Saturday 12th August
at
4.30 p.m.
Reception to follow
at
The Gables House
Tremmington

She read it through, then closing the front door she returned to her desk, which was in front of the high counter that formed a bar between the neat, well-equipped kitchen and spacious sitting room. As she sat down she binned the small blue airmail letter, written in an all-too familiar hand, as though it were of no more importance than the accompanying bundle of junk mail. Today, the mystery and synchronicity of both turning up in the same delivery failed to make its mark. That would only come later.

Going back to her computer Sherry finished the article she was writing for a new teen magazine, and after emailing it to the editor, she picked up the wedding invitation again and wondered what the emotions inside her were really saying, for they didn't feel readily identifiable.

Tilting her head out of the rogue ray of sunlight that was falling through the window, Sherry let her gaze drift from the card and felt the pleasure of receiving it stealing quietly through her. She hadn't known Laurie for more than a few months, so it was quite an honour to be a part of the big day, even though Laurie had already told her she would be. Almost as soon as they'd been introduced, by the flamboyant and delightful Rhona, Laurie's best friend, and Sherry's next-door neighbour, Sherry had sensed a kind of connection between them that Laurie herself had actually given voice to, just a few weeks ago. They didn't see each other often, Laurie was always so busy, but whenever they did get together it felt as though they'd known each other for years.

Returning her eyes to the card she allowed them

3

to focus, then defocus, first on Laurie's name, then on Elliot's. It was easy to picture them, vibrant, ambitious and unstoppably successful in their exclusive world of investigative reporting. Laurie was blonde and feminine, with intensely intelligent eyes and a wonderfully infectious laugh, while Elliot was tall, dour, impatient, his dark eyes lancing their subject in a way that could reduce even the most powerful to nervous incompetence – and frequently did. He wasn't an easy man, nor, unlike Laurie, was he blessed with any obvious charm or good looks, but professionally he stood head and shoulders above almost anyone else in the field.

Resting her head on one hand, Sherry slid her fingers into the crinkly mass of her dark bobbed hair. Thanks to the girlishness of a small, upturned nose and the shrewdly playful light of forget-me-not eyes, her large, almost sloppily arranged mouth was an attractive imperfection. The freshness of her pale skin and crimson-smudged cheeks was accentuated by the cool white of her smile. She was neither tall, nor exquisitely shaped, though her breasts were delectably full and her waist quite tight. Her hips were undeniably round, which might not have mattered so much had her legs been just a few inches longer. In a couple of months she would be thirty-one – thirty-one and still as single as her first bed.

How fortunate Laurie was, she reflected. Not only did she have her own TV documentary programme, but she had managed to find someone like Elliot, who inspired in Sherry a deep-rooted sense of what a man should be, supportive, respectful, attentive, powerful and loving. When thinking of him she slipped with ease into her uniquely private game of comparisons, where she saw him, in a musical sense, as Wagnerian, full of passion, mystery and high drama. The rugged planes of an unknown African land also came to mind, with the uncompromising angles of modern structures and cubist art. His colours were darkly purple and blue and grey. He was the sun around which his own world turned; the storm that wreaked havoc on abusers of power and the masters of crime.

And Laurie? How did she see Laurie? That was easy too, for Laurie was morning sunshine streaming through trees; birds singing at the start of spring. She was a Puccini aria; a crisp white wine on a hot summer's day. If she were a city she'd be Paris. As a flower she'd be a stargazer lily, elegant and fragrant, and leaving a mark on anyone who touched her.

Sherry hadn't often come across two people who seemed in such contrast to each other, yet who were in fact so right for each other. It was, she had to confess, how she'd once felt about her and Nick. In their case she'd turned out to be wrong. She wasn't this time though, for no-one could ever mistake how much Laurie and Elliot loved each other. Though they both fascinated her, it was Elliot's type of success Sherry coveted more, and even dared, on occasion, to dream of achieving, for she was much more interested in the lengthy and often dangerous undercover investigations he and his skilled team of researchers undertook than she was in the flashy TV fame that

Laurie enjoyed and handled so well. On a few occasions Laurie had invited Sherry to join the programme that she and her partner Rose produced, but Sherry had always shied away. Elliot's covert operations held much more appeal. She'd actually visited his offices, just along the river in Canary Wharf, with Laurie a couple of times, but she hadn't yet summoned the nerve to admit how interested she was in joining the team – which was just as well, for considering the kind of journalism she was involved in now, they'd probably laugh.

Sighing, as much with frustration as with fatigue, she propped the invitation against a small stack of filing trays, and was about to go and pour herself another coffee when the telephone rang.

'Sherry Mac,' she answered.

'He called!' the voice at the other end announced. 'Last night, about ten o'clock. You're amazing. How do you always get these things right?' It was Anita Gruber, a successful psychotherapist and good friend, though not in that order. It was impossible not to warm to Anita, mainly because she was so disarmingly honest about her own faults, and so shockingly inept when it came to navigating her way through love's cruel tricks and extremely bad jokes. There was a certain comfort, Sherry often thought, in knowing that someone who got it so right for others could still be human enough to get it so wrong for herself. And Anita could be quite spectacular when it came to getting it wrong.

'So what did he say?' Sherry asked, dismayed by the envy stirring inside her, for it was utterly misplaced in this context, since she had zero desire to be involved with a man less than half her age, which was no bad thing in her case as it would be illegal. In Anita's it was just plain weird, for she was an attractive, intelligent woman of forty-two, and the boy who hadn't yet got the key to the door was a silver-spoon-fed jerk who emanated from the elite world of Chelsea Mondays-to-Fridays and Gloucestershire at the weekends. 'No, don't tell me, he needed his nappy changed,' she quipped.

'Funny,' Anita responded drily. 'Actually, he said he was missing me. Did you write his script, by any chance?'

'I come up with better lines,' Sherry countered.

As Anita laughed, Sherry could easily picture her small dark features, as spritely as a Gluck sonata, alive with happiness and relief that the boy had finally picked up the phone to call her. Dear, kind-hearted Anita, she just got walked over every time. 'So what was his excuse for not calling for two weeks?' Sherry enquired.

'He's been to France and Germany, on a buying trip. Apparently he picked up some fantastic bargains . . .'

'Spare me,' Sherry interrupted. 'If there's one thing I'm less interested in than the boy himself, it's his tawdry antiques.'

Again, Anita only laughed. 'That's what I love about you, Sherry,' she responded, 'you always say what you think. If only more of us had your courage. Anyway, holding out, not calling at all, just as you advised, definitely worked. He's absolutely dying to see me, he said, so do you think it's OK if I just give in, and go?'

'If you haven't already said yes, you're not the Anita I know.'

More delighted laughter. 'You know, he might be young and a bit lacking in finesse when it comes to seduction,' Anita chirruped on, 'but he's something else between the sheets. So firm, and eager to learn. I'm just afraid, when he's not with me, that he's out there teaching his own generation.'

'Do you care?'

'Of course. I'm extremely fond of him. If it weren't for the age thing I could get serious.'

'There's always an excuse,' Sherry reminded her. 'They're either too young, too old, too married . . .'

'I know, I know, and it's all down to a fear of intimacy and a lack of self-worth. I'm the therapist, remember. I just wish I didn't feel as though he's managed to get the upper hand in our relationship so soon. He should be the one waiting for my calls, not the other way round.'

'He would be, if you weren't so keen to play the victim. You can't stand it if anyone treats you well. I swear you actually get off on insults and abuse.'

'Text-book MO for someone with no self-worth,' Anita responded chirpily. 'You see how well we both understand me? Anyway, as I said, you were absolutely right about when he'd call. It's no wonder we all come to you with our relationship problems.'

'Anita, any idiot knows that as soon as you stop calling a man he'll get straight on the phone,' Sherry retorted. 'I just wish you'd take the rest of my advice and dump the creep, because I can't

8

imagine why you'd want to spend even another minute with someone who tells you outright that he doesn't want to be seen in public with you because you're too old.'

'It was a joke. You had to be there,' Anita informed her.

'For God's sake!'

'OK. OK. You're right, I should have more willpower . . .'

'Self-respect,' Sherry corrected, and quickly added, 'Oh sorry, there goes my other line, I'll get back to you later.'

As she disconnected Sherry felt her spirits take a sudden downturn, and deciding to let the other call go through to the machine she put the phone down and stared glumly at the window. Sometimes, she was thinking, it was hard to deal with how much time she spent alone, working here at her computer, most of her contact with the outside world coming only through email or by phone. She longed to get out there more, perhaps then she'd have a love life to talk about, even if it was as disastrous as Anita's. She might even have a partner to take to Laurie and Elliot's wedding. Just think how wonderful it would be if she were able to take Nick. But that was never going to happen, so she quickly closed off the thought, and tried not to mind that Laurie hadn't even thought to ask if she'd like to bring someone along. Why would she? She'd never known Sherry to have a partner, didn't even know Nick van Zant existed, at least not as a part of Sherry MacElvoy's life. Anita did, but they'd never discussed him in any detail. What was the point?

9

It was over now, and nothing was ever going to change that.

Feeling slightly more in need of a fortifying vodka than a mere mug of Nescaff, she got up and wandered into the kitchen. It was only four in the afternoon. Resorting to alcohol now, to buoy herself up, would be like offering an oar to a drowning man – it might keep him afloat for a while, but with no boat or land in sight, what was the point? A chocolate biscuit? There were, of course, none in the cupboard, she didn't dare to allow such malicious hip-inflaters into her super-market trolley, never mind into the flat. In fact, there was nothing in her cupboards at all to offer even a moment's bodily delight, with the exception of a vibrator, and she definitely wasn't in the mood for that.

After making yet another coffee, she carried it into the sitting room where the week's news-papers were strewn about the carpet and sofas, and a startlingly garish collection of paintings flashed around the walls. They were her own work, created several years ago, when she'd first come back to England. They'd been a release of sorts, a way of expressing what she'd felt inside when she'd been unable – or perhaps unwilling – to find the words. She wondered idly what Anita would make of their shapes and colours, were she to admit the works were hers, but even though Anita was a therapist, not an analyst, she still wasn't about to invite any kind of probing into a part of her past that had been buried a long time ago. It might be like exhuming a body and finding it wasn't actually dead – or worse, discovering it had now acquired an agenda.

Remembering the blue airmail letter that had arrived with the invitation she grabbed up the waste basket and took it out into the hall to empty down the chute. She hadn't even opened the envelope. There was no need; she knew who it was from, and more or less what it would say. She wished Aunt Jude would stop forwarding the letters, but since her aunt didn't feel she had the right to discard someone else's mail, it was left to Sherry to do it instead. She hadn't read one in a long time, and had no intention of doing so ever again – unless the person sending them was finally prepared to tell the truth, and if that happened she'd find out soon enough, without reading the letters.

During the next ten minutes her phone rang at least as many times, bringing a flurry of requests from editors who'd left vital column inches to the last minute and were now looking to the ever-resourceful Sherry Mac, or, more accurately, one of her many aliases, to fill the gap. She usually obliged, occasionally with an original concoction of her own, or just as often with an adroitly reworded piece of scuttlebutt that she'd accessed from the Web. The ethics of it didn't bother her particularly – after all, journalists were writing the same stories day in day out, the world over, and invariably got their information from each other, which meant that someone, somewhere, was no doubt recycling her material too. The Chinese whispers element of it might be an interesting aspect to pursue were any of it related to serious news, but since none of it was, she preferred to focus what spare time she had on writing a follow-up novel to the one she'd had published – under a pseudonym – a year ago. The book hadn't been a success, so she was still dependent on her journalistic skills for an income. Not that she was complaining, for under a variety of pseudonyms she was much in demand, since she was fast, witty, reliable and could turn her hand to almost anything. She even had her own columns in a couple of magazines – Dear Molly in one of the glossies, and Helena's Beauty Tips in a teen weekly – as well as a regular commitment as a TV reviewer for one of the tabloids. Occasionally she even contributed to the arts pages of a Sunday supplement and an upmarket monthly, and in the past couple of years she'd become a much-sought-after holiday relief for three named columnists whose style she could easily mimic.

Hearing a familiar voice coming from her answerphone she quickly snatched up the receiver. 'Rhona!' she cried. 'Are you back? Where are you?'

'I'm in the flat next door,' Rhona replied, managing to sound droll, distracted and bored all at the same time. 'Have you got your invitation?'

'Yes. Did you?'

'Have,' Rhona corrected. 'We say, have, not did.'

'Who's the we?' Sherry laughed. 'I'm the Brit here, remember. You're the Greek.'

'Half. And I came here at the age of three, which was about the time you deserted, I believe. No, your blood might be British, my sweet, and you might live here now, but in your soul, your heart and your lamentable, though occasionally entertaining, vernacular, you are as American as a class action lawsuit. Now hang up, I'm coming over.'

As Sherry put down the phone, her spirits were already lifting. There were few people in the world she enjoyed more than Rhona, whose life was as bizarre as a Fellini movie, and whose tongue was as wicked as her soul was gentle and true. Everyone loved Rhona, and Rhona, in her uniquely disdainful way, loved them all back.

'Have you spoken to Laurie today?' Rhona demanded, sweeping in through the front door and heading straight for the kitchen. 'Vodka tonic? Or are you back on the wagon?'

'What do you mean back? I was never on it. And no, I haven't spoken to Laurie today. Why?'

'I think we should start measuring her pre-wedding stress on the Richter scale,' Rhona quipped. 'Another flaming row with Elliot this morning, which has already been made up, I'm told, but now she's gone whizzing off to follow up on some lead she's just been given on a story and he's royally pissed off, apparently, at being left to carry on moving into their new place alone.'

'God, my life feels so dull,' Sherry groaned. 'What I wouldn't give for a good row, a new place or even a whizz off.'

Rhona grinned. 'Here's a vodka instead,' she said, passing her a glass. 'So apart from no rows, new pads or whizzes off, what's been happening with you these past two days?'

Sherry sighed. 'I could make something up, I suppose, it would certainly be more interesting and in some way salve my ego.'

'Have you been anywhere? Seen anyone?'

'Too busy. Too many deadlines. But I spoke to

13

Anita just now. My friend, the psychologist . . .'

'Of course. How is she?'

'As unbreakably cheerful as ever, but I did my best.'

Rhona spluttered with laughter. 'Is she still seeing the young boy you told me about?'

'I'm afraid so.' Sherry shook her head in dismay. 'You know, sometimes it really seems to get to me, the way she lets him treat her so badly. Not only him, everyone she meets.'

Rhona's dark eyes were long and lazy, her full mouth curved in a teasing smile. Like Sherry she was neither tall nor slim, nor was she breathtakingly beautiful, but her sumptuous olive-toned flesh and shameless sexuality had caused many an intelligent man to lose contact with all but one part of his brain. 'Anita's on her own journey through life,' she said gently. 'You shouldn't let it affect yours.'

Sherry crooked an eyebrow. 'Isn't that the truth?' she commented wryly.

Rhona took another sip. 'But it's not really about Anita, is it?' she challenged.

Sherry had been about to wander back into the sitting room, but stopped in surprise. 'Isn't it?' she countered.

Rhona merely looked at her.

Sherry took a breath, then, laughing and shaking her head, she continued around the bar to go and stand in front of the rain-speckled French windows. The plants on the balcony outside looked bedraggled and sad, the wrought-iron table and chairs glistened wetly in the late afternoon sun. She started to speak, but instead took

14

a generous mouthful of her drink, while gazing down at the flat grey surface of the river.

'What is it?' Rhona prompted. 'Something's been bothering you for weeks, it seems to me, so it's time you got it out.'

Sherry's eye was caught by a police launch as it sped round a bend in the river and headed down towards the pier. Emergency sirens wailed in from the distance, an invisible lasso of sound, snagging her attention and drawing it to an imagined crime or catastrophe. Inwardly she shuddered. 'I'm fine,' she responded, turning round. 'Apart from the time of the month.' Her eyes showed a quick flash of impatience. 'All right, if we're getting to the truth here I suppose it's about jealousy, because at least Anita manages to get a boyfriend, which is a damned sight more than we can say about me. I mean, when did you ever see me with anything even approaching a man? It's been seven years, Rhona. Can you imagine that? Seven years and nothing to itch. No relationship, no affair, no passing flirtation, not even a one-night stand. Yet here I am, Dear Molly herself, giving all this dazzlingly insightful advice to the emotionally screwed-up and downtrodden, which for some weirdly perverse reason seems to work, when I can't even get started. I mean, tell me, when does my door ever get knocked down by a panting Lothario who can't get enough of my irresistible bedroom technique? Can you recall the last time I got swept across the Continent in a frenzy of unbridled passion? Do you see any fresh flowers in this apartment not bought by me? Any Tiffany jewels nestling between my breasts? A globe waiting to be spun for me to stop with my finger to decide my next vacation?'

'All right, that's enough about me, let's get back to you,' Rhona quipped, coming round from the kitchen to perch on the edge of the desk.

Sherry laughed. 'But it's all true,' she cried, going to slump down in an armchair. 'There's never a man in my life and anyway, the only ones worth having are already taken, meaning what's left is like rummaging through an end-of-season sale and finding all the goods are damaged. Or, more accurately, like looking through God's over-crowded attic of embarrassing mistakes.'

Rhona choked on a laugh. 'You're too harsh,' she accused.

'So speaks the woman with the fantastically rich lover who picks up her every bill, satisfies her every whim, rips off her lace panties and gives her a thousand orgasms, before jetting back to his exotic Middle Eastern palace, where he has to make do with phoning you three times a day and sending you so many flowers you can't breathe at night. Has he been invited to the wedding, by the way?'

Rhona nodded.

'Is he coming?'

'I think so.'

'So I'm the only one who doesn't get to take a partner?'

Rhona frowned. 'Have you got someone in mind?'

'No.'

'There are sure to be plenty of single men there. Elliot's got a lot of friends. They'll be turning up from all over the world.'

'I'd rather have Elliot.'

Rhona laughed and got to her feet. 'The way he's been behaving lately Laurie might just be happy to hand him over. Which reminds me, she's changed the time for this evening. She wants us there at seven thirty now, instead of seven. Apparently Chris and Rachel are in town, so they're coming too. You've met them before, haven't you?'

Sherry nodded. 'Yes. A couple of times.'

'Of course. OK. I'd better go and call my mother back. I'll give you a knock around seven and we'll go upriver to the new Laurie and Elliot pad together.'

After Rhona had gone, Sherry stood for a moment, unsettled by the emotions the last few minutes had stirred. There were times, like now, when all the empty spaces in her life seemed to join together in a circle around her as though to isolate her from the rest of the world. Not so far that she couldn't see it, but far enough for her to feel cut off from it. No parents, no partner, no children. Why did these things happen so easily for other people, and not for her? She didn't understand it. Every day millions of women around the world fell in love, got married, had babies. Why was it so difficult for her? What made her different? Why was she always alone?

The only answers were those she didn't want to face, they hurt too much, so returning to her desk she attempted to lift her mood by concentrating on one of her more frivolous columns. And the thought of spending an evening at Laurie and Elliot's was quite pleasing too, so why waste time on worrying about aspects of her life that could never be changed?

Chapter Two

Laurie Forbes's dark blue eyes were gazing intently into the exquisite face of a young Indian girl. As the girl spoke, her words came in breathy, broken sentences, conveying at least some of the terror that was making her hands clasp tightly together, and her eyes constantly dart to the door. She spoke in her own language, while the doctor, seated the other side of the desk, translated in his gentle, sonorous tone.

They were in his first-floor surgery, over a newsagent's in London's East End, where a few minutes ago he'd let Laurie in through the back door so she could meet and speak to this tragic young girl. After the girl's first visit here, the doctor had contacted Barry Davidson at the No Sweat action group, fearing, if he went direct to the police, that even more harm would come to the girl – and others. In turn, Barry had got in touch with Laurie, knowing this would be an issue she'd feel very strongly about, and would almost certainly want to get involved in. He couldn't have been more right, since Laurie and her producing partner, Rose, were already investigating a human-trafficking chain running from the Asian subcontinent into the UK, and this case was showing all the signs of being at least one small part of it.

Though there was no visible evidence of what the girl had suffered, Laurie knew that beneath the soiled and ragged sari she was wearing she had been so hideously abused that it was agony for her just to move.

'Ask her,' Laurie said, 'if she has any idea who the man was who did this to her.'

Dr Patel shook his head. 'She told me on her first visit,' he said, 'she doesn't know who he was. She was taken by car to the place where it happened. I believe there was more than one man.'

Laurie looked at him, then returned her eyes to the girl. 'Who drove the car?' she said.

'A man she simply calls the driver.'

Laurie leaned forward and lifted the girl's hands into her own. 'Daya,' she said softly, knowing that the only word she'd understand would be her name, but it was the tone of her voice that mattered – she wanted the girl to know she could trust her. 'We need you to tell us where you live. Where they are keeping you.'

The beautiful face turned to the doctor as he translated. She answered quietly and briefly.

'She doesn't know,' Dr Patel said.

Laurie looked at her helplessly.

'She has no point of reference,' the doctor explained. 'She's probably blindfolded whenever she's taken outside, not allowed to see where she's

19

going.' He spoke to Daya, putting the suggestion to her, then nodded. 'Yes, that's what happens,' he told Laurie.

'The woman who brought her to you,' Laurie began.

'She'll be back any moment,' the doctor warned. 'She mustn't know you're here.'

'I understand, but you must ask *her* how Daya got these injuries.'

'I have already done that. She says the girl fell onto a sewing machine.'

Laurie winced at the lie. Then, seeing the girl was watching her, she softened her expression again. 'Are there others?' she asked. 'Is it just you they're keeping locked up?'

Daya's large brown eyes watched the doctor's lips as he spoke. When she turned back to Laurie her own were full of fear, but they didn't waver as she answered the question.

'There are others,' the doctor translated. 'Thirteen women and . . . there are children too. She has a sister, she says, who came with her from India.'

'How did they get here?' Laurie said.

The doctor asked. 'By boat and then by lorry,' he answered.

The girl carried on speaking. Laurie watched her lovely face, held her delicate hands and felt an almost overwhelming urge to pull her into her arms and take her home.

'Some of them got left behind in India,' the doctor was saying, 'and some others were taken off the boat in another place. She doesn't know where. When they started out there were many of them, she says. Men and women, but mostly women. She doesn't know what happened to everyone else. She only knows about those who are with her now.'

'If only she knew where that was,' Laurie muttered. She looked at the doctor. 'Is she going to be all right? Does she need to go to hospital?'

'She should, but Mrs Ghosh, the woman who brought her here, has forbidden it. I could overrule her, of course, but I'm afraid of putting Daya, or those with her, into any more danger.'

'She will recover though, won't she?' Laurie said, squeezing Daya's hands. 'Her injuries will heal?'

The doctor nodded.

'Tell me more about this Mrs Ghosh,' Laurie prompted, thinking how dearly she'd like to get her hands on the woman who, a few minutes ago, had gone down to the street for a better mobile phone connection. Barry was at the other end of the call, so time was precious, the woman would be back any second. 'Had you ever met her before she brought Daya here the first time?'

'No,' the doctor answered. 'She called my receptionist . . .' He stopped as Daya began to speak. After listening he turned his solemn eyes back to Laurie.

'She has a daughter,' he told her grimly. 'She is afraid for her . . .'

'You mean here?' Laurie cut in, her heart starting to thud. 'In England?'

The doctor began to put the question but was cut off by a sharp knock on his door. It was the signal, from his receptionist, that Mrs Ghosh was on her way back. 'You'll have to go,' he told Laurie.

21

'Use the back stairs, and please don't do anything without speaking to me first.'

Swallowing her frustration, Laurie grabbed her bag and quickly took out a card. 'Here,' she said, pushing it into Daya's hand. 'If you can, call me. Tell her to call me,' she said to the doctor. 'I want to help you. Please don't be afraid.'

'Quickly,' the doctor said, opening the door.

On impulse Laurie hugged the girl, then slipped out through the door into the passage beyond. The stairwell was an obstacle course of old mail and newspapers, but she barely noticed as she ran swiftly to the bottom and burst out into the sunlight behind the old Victorian building on Whitechapel's New Road.

Barry Davidson was waiting, his mobile phone still in his hand. 'Sorry,' he said, 'I think she started to get suspicious. I had to let her go.'

'It's OK,' Laurie assured him, as they began winding through the back alleys. 'The girl's terrified, that much is clear. I'm not sure what's going to happen to her now, I'll call the doctor later.'

'Did you find out where they're keeping her?' he asked, sticking a cap on his nearly bald head to protect it from the sun.

'She doesn't know. Apparently, there's a group of them, women *and* children.'

'Children,' he repeated. 'Shit, we've got to go to the police.'

'I don't think the doctor wants us to yet. He probably already told you, he's afraid if this Mrs Ghosh and her bosses get wind of a police investigation, they'll just dispose of the women and we don't even want to think about how they'd do that.

Ditto press investigation, which is why we'll have to tread very carefully now.' She glanced at her watch. 'Listen, I'm sorry, but I have to go,' she said, hailing a passing cab, 'we've got friends coming round tonight.'

'You only moved in two days ago,' he laughed in surprise.

'Tell me about it.' After giving him a quick hug, she jumped into the taxi, gave the driver her address, then took out her mobile to call her partner, Rose.

By the time she got to Butler's Wharf, on the south side of the Thames at Tower Bridge, she'd fully updated Rose on her meeting with Daya, had taken a call from her closest friend, Rhona, which hadn't turned out to be quite as welcome as Rhona's calls normally were, and she was now, as she summoned the lift to take her up to the fourth floor, talking to her mother about what kind of flowers they should have at the church.

'If you don't like my choice, then you choose,' she snapped as she pushed the button to go up.

'I'm not saying I don't like your choice,' her mother replied, 'I'm just saying we could do with more colour.'

'Then get more colour.'

'I will. I just need you to tell me what you'd prefer.'

'I don't know. I'm not an expert on flowers.'

'We need to get this sorted out, Laurie.'

'I know, Mum, and we will. I'll call you back when I've had a chance to decide.'

'There's not just the church, there're the tables at the reception . . .'

'Mum, I can't give you an answer now, because

23

I don't know what flowers I want. So I'll call you back, OK?' and before her mother could say any more she clicked off the line and began digging around in her bag for her keys. It was too much, just too much, trying to organize this wedding, move into a new apartment, uncover some monstrous human-smuggling chain, and work out how to find and rescue a group of helpless young women without getting them killed in the process. She was going to go mad – either that, or no, she was just going to go mad.

'Hi! Anyone home?' she called out as she let herself into the luxurious converted-warehouse apartment.

'Over here,' Elliot responded, from where he was putting together a coffee table in front of the wall of windows that looked out over the river and Tower Bridge.

'Everything all right?' she asked, dropping her bag and retying her hair as she picked a path through all the boxes.

'Sure, why wouldn't it be?' he retorted.

Biting back a sarcastic response, she said, 'We need to get some of this cleared up before everyone comes tonight. That looks good,' she added, as he stood back to survey his handiwork.

She waited for him to look at her, but he didn't. 'So, anything happen while I was out?' she asked.

'Not especially,' he replied, starting to clear up the tools he'd been using.

Dragging her eyes away, she looked up at the railings of the mezzanine where a workman was applying a second coat of stain. 'Any messages?' she asked Elliot.

'They're on the pad.'

Going to the large, glass-topped counter that was between the brand new Poggenpohl kitchen and Radiata pine bar, she checked the list, decided everyone could wait, then went to start sorting out some of the boxes. The fact that he hadn't asked anything about her interview with the Indian girl was beginning to rankle, but she was prepared to wait, maybe it would be forthcoming at some point in the next hour or so.

Silence prevailed for at least another ten minutes, by which time the workman had gone and so had her patience. 'I hope your mood's going to improve by the time everyone gets here,' she commented tartly. 'If you go on scowling like that you'll scare them all away.'

Elliot's dark eyes flicked in her direction. She was dragging a heavy box across the designer-cracked concrete floor towards the entrance hall, where a door opened either side into each of their studies.

'Don't bother to help,' she told him. 'I can manage.'

Lifting a box onto the bar, he started to break open the sealing tape.

A moment later she reappeared from her study and stood with her hands on her hips, glaring at him. Her blonde hair was tumbling out of its knot again, her lovely face was flushed red with anger. 'That,' she snapped, pointing to the room in the opposite corner, 'is yours. I'll leave you to sort it out.'

Still he made no comment, merely continued unravelling the bubble wrap that was protecting the glasses, while gazing blindly at nothing.

Wanting desperately to slap him, she somehow managed not to, and looked round for something else she could move without his help. Spotting a plastic sack full of pillows that needed to go up to the mezzanine, which would soon be a luxurious master suite, she grabbed it in both arms and started up the spiral staircase. It was time to get ready for the evening anyway, so she'd stay up there, out of harm's way, or another furious row was certain to break out, and they'd had enough of them lately.

Dumping the pillows on the queen-sized mattress that was currently serving as their bed, she kicked aside a pile of clothes and stomped into the bathroom. It was childish to cry, but who cared? She was tired, stressed, and sorely tempted to walk out of this dream apartment right now and leave him to deal with the whole sodding mountain of moving in himself.

'Bastard,' she seethed into the mirror. '*You could try a bit harder to be helpful,*' she screamed out loud. '*It's your bloody apartment too. And your wedding, in case you'd forgotten.*'

Silence from downstairs.

Struggling hard with the urge to go and fling something deadly down on his head, she cupped her hands under the cold tap and splashed water on her face. She'd calm down in a minute, she just needed to breathe deeply, dab her face with a towel, and concentrate on something soothing and peaceful and totally unrelated to the nightmare her life was turning into. The trouble was, no matter where she went in her mind, all roads seemed to lead back to the monster downstairs, whose long silences and moodiness these last few weeks was driving her crazy. Though she knew what was behind it, she was finding it increasingly hard to be understanding or sympathetic. Right now, in fact, she was feeling a good deal closer to murderous than selflessly supportive.

Snatching the band out of her hair, she began to undress. A shower might help, and a full-strength Martini followed by a nice, mellowing trip into marijuana nirvana, if anyone was thoughtful enough to bring some along.

Starting to relax at the mere thought of imminent rescue, she was on the point of running the water when she heard the phone. Immediately she stiffened. *Don't let it be my mother. Pleeeease don't let it be my mother.*

'It's Sherry,' Elliot shouted.

Untold relief. 'Tell her I'll call back. Is she still coming tonight?'

'Yes. She wants to know if we need anything?'

'You mean apart from marriage guidance, or boxing gloves?' she muttered under her breath. 'Ask her to pick up some salsa and chips from the Mexican deli she told me about. And anything else she thinks we might like.'

She listened to him relaying the message, and felt annoyed by how pleasant he was to Sherry. He even managed to laugh at something she said, which was considerably more than he'd managed for her these past few days. After hearing the phone go down she turned the power jets on full. Thank God Sherry was coming tonight, she usually managed to put everyone in a good mood,

27

and Chris Gallagher would be there too, one of Elliot's favourite people since he'd been involved in the Phraxos scandal that was still, in spite of the investigation being over, dominating Elliot's life, so with any luck the evening could turn out well. On second thoughts, the last thing she wanted was Elliot dwelling on that blasted scandal any more than he already was. And where was her head about Sherry? Only an hour ago Rhona had called to inform her that Sherry was hurt she hadn't been invited to bring a guest to the wedding, so Sherry was hardly going to be in a good mood with her either. At the time of Rhona's call Laurie had uttered a few catty remarks that she deeply regretted now, for Sherry certainly didn't deserve them. Though, in her own defence, Laurie had to point out that since she'd never seen Sherry with a man, and since Sherry hadn't mentioned a word about wanting to bring someone, it was hardly surprising she hadn't thought to add the option.

'I'm sure she understands that,' Rhona had said. 'I think it was just the reminder there was no-one that hurt.'

'Jesus Christ, if I have to consider the petty sensitivities of every bloody person who's being invited to this wedding I'm going to end up in the nut house,' Laurie had cried.

'I know it's nerves talking, so I'll forget you said that,' Rhona responded. 'She's not making a fuss . . . This is just me . . .'

'OK. OK. So what do you want me to do?'

'Actually, nothing. I shouldn't even have brought it up, so let's change the subject.'

They had, but Sherry's call just now was making Laurie feel guilty all over again, because the truth was, she *had* thought of putting 'Sherry + guest' and had decided not to, mainly because it had seemed almost spiteful when she knew very well that Sherry didn't have anyone to bring. Now it appeared that no matter what she'd decided she'd been destined to hurt Sherry's feelings, which was the last thing she wanted when she was so fond of Sherry – in fact much fonder of Sherry than she was of certain other people she could mention right now!

Feeling the water starting to massage at least some of the tension from her shoulders she closed her eyes and continued to think about Sherry, who, she and Rhona had often agreed, was a bit of an enigma, for as much as they genuinely liked her, and had welcomed her into their lives, they knew very little about her. Of course, Sherry was always saying that there was nothing to know, just that she'd grown up in the States, had moved back to England seven years ago, after her parents died, and now her only family was an aunt living in Somerset. The rest, i.e. her career, where she lived and who her friends were, was an open book that made rather dull reading, she'd quip, and her love life was much the same, except it had no story at all. But apparently there had been a man, because she'd once mentioned him to Rhona. It was some-one she'd been quite serious about, she'd said, until they'd broken up, which had been around the time she'd left LA. He was a journalist, by all accounts, whom she'd met while he was in California covering a story. Rhona couldn't remember his name, and Laurie hadn't liked to ask, since Sherry had never mentioned him to her.

Finding her thoughts moving on to Sherry's wonderfully poetic way of seeing the world and the people in it, Laurie's eyes started to shine with irony, for she felt very far from anything even remotely as romantic as a Puccini aria, or morning sunshine streaming through trees. However, thinking of Sherry and her unique way of connecting people to places, art, nature, music, food, or whatever came to her mind, almost always had a calming effect. She really was an unusual person, and had added a whole new dimension to their group of friends since she'd moved into the flat next door to Rhona.

Abruptly remembering that there was a good chance she'd be moving in next door to Sherry if things didn't start improving with Elliot, she quickly rinsed off her hair and reached for the conditioner. She'd stayed with Rhona once before when life had become intolerable with Elliot, so she could always do it again, and God knew the prospect of having fun with Rhona and Sherry was a lot more appealing right now than having to put up with Elliot's silences and her mother's hysteria for the next eight weeks.

Stepping out of the shower she wrapped a towel round her hair, and grabbed another as she wandered back into the bedroom where she glanced over the railing to see what was going on below. There was no sign of Elliot and she wondered with a moment's unease if he'd gone out. He'd done that a few times lately, not saying where he was going, or when he'd be back – nor was she entirely sure where he went, though she guessed it was to his office. Hearing his voice she realized he must be on the phone in his study, so she carried on with what she was doing and tried not to read anything into the fact that he'd taken the phone out of earshot. It probably had nothing to do with being secretive, just that there was something on his computer that he needed for the call.

A few minutes later she heard him coming up the stairs. Immediately she turned her back so she wouldn't have to look at him. OK, she wasn't helping matters behaving this way, but for God's sake, he wasn't the only one round here who was all stressed out over the happy day, nor was it her damned fault that things had turned out the way they had with the Phraxos business.

'I'm sorry,' he said.

His voice was both gruff and tender, and feeling an instant melting of hostility she turned to face him. Then she loved him completely, for he'd read her mind and brought her up a Martini. 'Me too,' she said, taking the drink. She looked up into his shadowy face, so austere yet reassuringly familiar that her heart caught on another wave of love.

'It's not you,' he told her.

'I know.' She smiled crookedly. 'At least, I hope not.'

A flash of impatience showed in his eyes, then was gone. 'You know what it's about,' he said.

After sipping her drink she put it down on the box that was serving as a nightstand, and looked at him again. 'You have to let it go,' she told him gently. 'There's nothing you can do about it, and you're becoming obsessive.'

'If you don't have anything more helpful to say than that, say nothing,' he retorted tersely.

'Elliot, you didn't have a choice,' she cried. 'As governments they're infinitely more powerful than you, and you have to accept that.'

'I took the money. They *bought* my silence.'

'Then give the damned money back, if that's how you feel. But you still won't be able to tell the story, so stop doing this to yourself.'

His face was paling as the anger that was never far from the surface lately started to return. 'OK, I'll just forget the fact that certain individuals in both the British and American governments are actively involved in promoting war on innocent peoples . . .'

'It's not as simple as that!'

'. . . for the sole purpose of making the defence industries even richer than they already are, and grabbing as much oil, or minerals, or territory for themselves as they can, and I'll concentrate instead on this ludicrous circus of a wedding that you're dragging me into. In the grand order of things I guess it comes above genocide and wholesale corruption.'

Laurie's mouth was open. 'How dare you?' she seethed. 'You bastard! No-one's forcing you into this, least of all me, and if you think it's all so bloody ludicrous, then why don't you just call the whole damned thing off?'

'Don't tempt me.'

'That's it!' she raged, slamming down the towel. 'I've had enough. I can't take any more of you.

I'm calling my mother now.' Grabbing the phone she started to dial.

'Stop it! Stop!' he barked, snatching the receiver from her hand. 'I'm sorry. I shouldn't have said that. I didn't mean it. I just . . .' He put the phone down. 'I'm sorry,' he repeated.

Still shaking she stooped to pick up the towel. As she started to walk away he turned her back and pulled her into his arms.

'I shouldn't be taking this out on you,' he said. 'I know it's not your fault, and you deserve better.'

Putting her arms around him she rested her head on his shoulder. 'I understand why you're angry,' she replied. 'I am too.' She looked up at him. 'Everyone is who worked on the story, but there's nothing more we can do.'

He gazed long into her eyes, clearly wanting to vent more anger, but in the end, all he said was, 'What time is everyone arriving?'

'In about half an hour. I should dry my hair and start preparing some food.'

He nodded and let her go. 'I'll take a shower, then I need to call Max.'

As he went into the bathroom Laurie sat down on the floor in front of a mirror that was propped up against the wall and began to brush out her hair. She was bothered by how often he was calling Max lately, for Max was the American journalist he'd worked closely with on the Phraxos affair. She just hoped they weren't cooking up some way of thwarting the agreement they'd made with the British and US secret services not to reveal what they'd learned, because she didn't even want to think about what the consequences might be to them personally, never mind everyone else, if they did.

An hour later everyone had arrived, including Chris Gallagher and Rachel Hendon who'd driven up from Cornwall that morning. It was largely because of Chris and Rachel that Laurie was cooking pasta at home, for the attention the couple received when out in public was as intolerable as the snide comments that frequently appeared in the press the following day, about the 'surprisingly short time' it had taken Rachel to get over the untimely death of her Cabinet Minister husband, and how 'very accommodating' it had been of Chris's wife, a fairly well-known actress, to meet with a fatal accident a mere few months after. The insinuations were clear, even if the accusations weren't.

'You look fantastic,' Laurie commented, as Rachel wandered into the kitchen to join her, her short, shaggy dark hair framing her face in a way that made her seem much younger, and more frivolous, than she actually was – rather more like the TV news producer she'd been before marrying Tim Hendon. 'Motherhood definitely agrees with you. How is the love of my life?'

'Adorable – and loud!' Rachel replied, cocking an eyebrow.

Laurie grinned. 'Is he six months yet?'

'Almost, and already trying to walk. I've left him at my sister's tonight. Much like his father, he'll enjoy all the female attention.'

Laurie continued to smile. It was good to hear Rachel talking about Charlie's father in such a natural way, though Laurie knew that she was still far from over the terrible tragedy of his murder, and the investigation that had followed, for it had totally torn her life apart. It was how she and Laurie had become friends, since Laurie had helped to uncover the truth behind the murder.

'So how are things going with you and Chris?' she asked Rachel, pouring more wine into their glasses.

'OK, I think,' Rachel answered with a smile. 'We're still taking it slowly, but he's wonderful with Charlie, and we're spending so much time at his house, down in Cornwall, that I'm thinking of renting out my little cottage.'

'You'll always have takers in us,' Laurie commented, beginning the hunt for a garlic press. 'So how long are you going to be in London this time?'

'Chris is arranging an exhibition of Andraya Sorrantos's paintings so it could be a while.'

'Is this an artist I should have heard of?' Laurie asked.

'She's Brazilian and her work is amazing, if you like that sort of thing, which both Chris and I do. She's arriving next week, from Rio, staying in an apartment belonging to the Brazilian Embassy, then we'll probably take her down to Cornwall for a quick weekend's break before things really hot up.'

'Lucky her,' Laurie commented, glancing over to where Elliot and Chris were standing in front of the picture windows quietly talking. 'I could do with a spell in Cornwall myself right now,' she said. 'Elliot's really uptight. He can't let go of the Phraxos story. He's desperate to get it out there.'

35

'I know, Chris told me, and to be honest, I understand his frustration. I even feel it myself. So does Chris.'

Laurie wasn't surprised by that, for Chris had been more involved in the Phraxos Special Project than any of them, though the actual details of his undercover role were still, for most, as secret as the project itself. 'What's happening is unconscionable,' Laurie stated. 'There's absolutely no way to justify it, and of course the public should be told, but if any of those defence industries start going down as a result of the exposure, which they inevitably would, it wouldn't be long before the entire world markets began to collapse and that would be . . . Well, it would be catastrophic. Everyone will start going under, and it certainly won't help save the innocent lives that are being sacrificed for profit in godforsaken parts of the globe, if anything it'll make it worse.'

'And Elliot knows that, which is why he won't break the agreement,' Rachel reminded her.

Laurie stared down at the garlic she'd just squashed. 'Actually, I think it's the fact that he took money for his silence that's really bothering him,' she said, scooping it into a pan and watching it sizzle. 'Or maybe it's the dread of marrying me.'

Rachel's eyebrows shot up as she chuckled.

'You think I'm joking,' Laurie responded, 'but if you heard some of the rows we've been having lately . . .' She broke off as a howl of laughter whooped up from the sitting room. 'What's going on over there?' she called out when she could be heard.

36

Rose Newman, a handsome, middle-aged woman with neat greying hair, and a smile that totally lit up her normally serious expression, got to her feet and wiped a tear from under one eye. 'Sherry's being outrageous,' she answered, going to the bar to refill her glass.

Sherry's expression was a picture of innocence.

'Even for her,' Rhona confirmed, from where she was sitting cross-legged on a downy cushion.

Sherry shrugged, and Laurie laughed. They were all, by now, quite familiar with Sherry's ability to shock them into laughter with unexpected turns in a conversation.

'I wish we could get her to join our team,' Rose commented, as she carried an empty wine bottle into the kitchen. 'Can't you persuade her?'

'I've tried, but you've heard what she says: she doesn't like the limelight, and she values her independence.'

'Sounds wise to me,' Rachel commented, popping a couple of baguettes into the oven to warm up. 'So what are you two working on at the moment?'

'Human trafficking and forced prostitution,' Rose answered.

Rachel turned to Laurie in surprise. 'That's a bit involved when you've got a wedding coming up, isn't it?' she commented.

'I'm helping out with the research, and taking care of the London end of things,' Laurie replied. 'Rose is on the globetrot.'

'Have you told Rachel about the girl you spoke to today?' Rose asked.

Laurie shook her head, then merely listened as

Rose filled Rachel in on the developments of the day. Since Rose was so much more experienced at production, and so level-headed in her approach to the world's horrors, she almost never failed to give Laurie a rational and helpful perspective on what they were dealing with, and now was proving no exception. On the other hand, however, Rose admired Laurie's passion, and even encouraged her impulsiveness, which was probably what made them such a great partnership. Laurie could just wish that once in a while Rose didn't remind her quite so much of her mother.

'So you've got no idea where these women are being held?' Rachel was saying.

Laurie shook her head. 'The only address the doctor has is a garment workshop, just along the road from his office. Barry Davidson, the chap who tipped me off about her, has checked the place out, but there was no sign of any women working there at all.'

'Do you know who owns it?'

'Some character by the name of Eddie Cribbs. I don't know much about him yet, but I will.' As she spoke she was seeing Daya's face in her mind's eye and sorely wishing now that she'd given in to the impulse to bring her home. God only knew what might have ensued if she had, but surely anything would be better than leaving the girl to a fate that might very well be worse than death. 'She was so tiny,' she said. 'So fragile. It makes me feel sick to think of her little body being hurt and abused like that.'

'What's your next step?' Rachel asked.

'I'm not sure yet. She says she has a daughter,

but we've yet to find out whether the child's here, or back in India.'

'Is that where you're going?' Rachel asked Rose.

Rose nodded. 'If the child's there I doubt very much we'll find her, but who knows. Even if we don't, there are plenty like her.'

'Isn't that the truth,' Rachel murmured, recalling her own trip to India and how devastated she had been by the plight of abandoned children. 'So Laurie misses out on the exotic hot spots this time around?' she said, attempting to lighten the moment.

'Not exactly,' Rose replied with arched brows. 'She's got a honeymoon coming up, remember?'

'Of course. Do you know where you're going?'

'Bali,' Laurie answered. 'I've always wanted to go, and now Elliot's a very rich man he's splashing out on three weeks in one of the Amman Resorts. Let's just hope he forgets to pack his conscience.' She glanced over at him again and felt her heart tighten with the desire to be there now, away from all that was going on here.

Feeling her eyes on him, Elliot turned towards her and winked. It made her smile, which was a relief, since he was all too aware of how poorly he'd been doing in that department lately. He was briefly tempted to break off his conversation with Chris and go over to her now, if only to stop her thinking they were discussing the Phraxos affair, which, in fact, they weren't. However, the current topic wasn't one he wanted her to know about either.

'Frankly, I think it's a great idea,' Chris was saying, following the progress of a loaded barge as it chugged downriver. 'And it'll be a terrific investment too. The big question is, how much do you want to spend, because I have to warn you, old chap, Andraya's paintings don't come cheap.'

Elliot glanced at Laurie again. 'Let's wait until after she's seen them,' he said. 'I have to be sure it's something she'll want. If it is, I still want to keep it as a surprise.'

'Of course. No problem. I'll set up a private viewing for you, before the official opening. They're due to arrive next Monday. So's the woman herself. Now there's an exhibition, if ever I've seen one. I'll say no more than that, but remember, you were warned.'

Elliot grinned. 'I'll bear it in mind,' he responded, watching Sherry as she caught the tea towel Laurie threw at her. He'd heard the comment Sherry had made, how he and Laurie couldn't take their eyes off each other, and Sherry was right – though perhaps not for the reasons she was thinking.

'Are you all right?' he suddenly heard Chris saying. 'You seem a bit . . . distracted.'

Elliot shook his head. 'I'm fine,' he answered. 'Just not enjoying this forced sabbatical. I need to be working.'

'How long are you taking off?'

'A year. I've just been contracted to do a book, did I tell you?'

'No. That's great news. I don't imagine it's going to contain anything about Phraxos though.'

'It's tempting, but if I did, they wouldn't publish it.'

'Of course not.' Chris's handsome face turned as grim as Elliot's.

40

'Come on,' Elliot said, slapping him on the shoulder. 'If we stand here much longer Laurie'll start getting edgy, and we don't want to spoil the evening.'

A couple of hours later, they were all seated around the large glass dining table, plates empty, candles burning down, and the rest of the room still in splendid disarray around them, as they bantered back and forth about anything that came to mind, though mostly about the wedding. Even Laurie, Sherry noticed, who'd seemed so tense earlier, had finally managed to lighten up, and the looks going between her and Elliot now appeared far less spiked with annoyance, or resentment, than they had before they'd sat down. For her part Sherry couldn't remember when she'd last felt so relaxed and happy – maybe it was the last time she'd spent an evening with them all, for they were starting to feel rather like family now, and she could hardly express how much it meant to her to be a part of their lives. Given a little more wine she'd probably start gushing it all out, so maybe she should do everyone a favour and call a halt now. To her dismay, as Elliot finished topping up her glass she hiccuped, and everyone burst out laughing.

'Was that me?' she gasped, in mock horror.

'How much have you had?' Rhona laughed.

'The same as everyone else.'

'Then you're drunk. Whoopee. I love it when you're drunk.'

'I don't know what you mean,' Sherry protested, and with a broad grin she took a generous sip of wine.

Rose was watching her as closely as her slightly blurred vision allowed. 'What I want to know,' she said, saluting Sherry with her glass, 'is why an attractive young woman like you shuts herself away and never seems to go out on dates. No, no, I don't want to hear some rubbish about how there are no decent men, or you never get time, because it's all bollocks, excuse my language. I think you're hiding something from us, Sherry Mac, and my guess is it's a mystery lover. So now, out with it. Who is he? What's his name? What does he do? Tell us everything.'

Laurie was staring at Rose in astonishment, for it was hardly her style – at least when sober – to blunder into someone's private life like that. On the other hand, she was fascinated to see how Sherry handled it.

In true Sherry fashion, she took it on masterfully, assuming a befuddled sort of Mata Hari expression, while slouching one arm across the back of her chair and stroking the stem of her wine glass. 'What makes you think there's only one?' she drawled.

As the laughter and applause died down, Rose said, 'OK, then which one are you bringing to the wedding?'

Laurie flinched.

Sherry continued her enigmatic smile. 'If I tell you, it won't be a surprise,' she responded smoothly.

'So there is someone?' Rose challenged.

'I didn't say that.'

'But there is. There has to be.'

Sherry's head went to one side as she toyed with

the idea of making something up, just to entertain them, or perhaps actually telling them about Nick. After this much wine, she'd probably end up making a fool of herself, and wanting to drown herself in the river the next morning, so maybe not, particularly while Elliot was listening. She would do better to try and dazzle him into realizing what a valuable addition she would make to his team.

Too late, for Rhona was already saying, 'There used to be. Who was the guy you told me about? The journalist. I'm trying to remember his name.'

The natural colour in Sherry's cheeks was deepening, but she was quite pleased the decision had been taken out of her hands, for in her present mood she quite wanted to talk about Nick. Indeed, why keep him a secret? There was no shame in everyone knowing that she had mattered to someone once, even if it was an embarrassing seven years ago. 'It's Nick van Zant,' she answered, casting a glance at Elliot.

He frowned in recognition. 'I know that name,' he said. 'Isn't he with the *New York Times*?'

'That's right,' she replied, feeling ludicrously important by association. 'At least, the last I heard he was.'

'He's English,' Rhona informed everyone, seeming to think it mattered.

Elliot nodded. 'I remember reading some of his reports from Afghanistan. And Iraq. War's his thing, isn't it?'

'It is now', Sherry replied. 'But when I knew him he was still US based, covering crime, mainly.'

'So what happened?' Rose wanted to know.

Sherry shrugged. 'Nothing much really,' she responded mildly. 'We actually only spent a month together, the summer before I left California . . .'

'She's going to make light of it,' Rhona protested. 'It was huge. The big love of her life, even if it did only last a month.' She looked at Sherry and signalled for her to continue.

Sighing, but secretly delighted by the interjection, Sherry said, 'OK. It's the only time in my life I've been with someone and felt such an amazing sense of something being right. It was easy. We were so in tune with each other we hardly needed to ask any questions. It was as though we already knew everything about each other, but still we couldn't get enough of each other. We laughed, we talked, we made love, we explored places neither of us had ever been, both physically and mentally, we admitted things we'd never admitted to anyone else. You know how it is, when you feel like that, you just don't hold back. There's no need to. If you're meant for each other, which was how we felt, what's the point in playing games, or pretending?' She glanced at Laurie, pleased by her rapt expression. Then the corners of her mouth turned down. 'There was only one dark spot in the dream,' she continued, 'because, of course, there always is, one obstacle that stood in our way, and made it all completely impossible . . . Actually, in his case there were four obstacles . . .' She counted them off on her fingers. 'A wife, a daughter, a mother and a religion.'

Elliot's surprise showed. 'Religion?' he echoed.

'He's Jewish, and though it's not a particularly big deal for him, it is for his mother.'

44

'But Jews divorce,' Chris said.

'Not when they're afraid it'll kill their mother – and when their daughter means everything. To be honest, if he didn't feel that way about his daughter, he wouldn't be the man I thought he was. So we had our month together, and then . . . Well, he went back to New York to rejoin his family, and I came here, to England.'

'But you still saw him, after you came here,' Rhona reminded her.

'Not very often. It was around then that he got his first break as a war correspondent, so I saw him a few times when he was passing through, en route to the Middle East, or Africa, or wherever.'

'Are you ever in touch now?' Rose asked.

'No. After the first few times in London we agreed it couldn't go on. His situation wasn't going to change, and it was too painful for us both every time he left. I wasn't getting over it, I just kept hoping and praying that something would work out, but I had to make myself stop, because the only way we could be together was if his mother were to die, or worse, his daughter, and I could hardly hope for that.' She shrugged and threw out her hands. 'So, that's it. He's an incredible man, an impossible act to follow, which is why I'm sitting here on my own tonight, because I've never found anyone who could match up. So how sad is that?'

'You know, I'm sure I've met him,' Elliot said.

Sherry's heart turned over. Maybe she shouldn't have got into this after all. 'I'd say it was quite possible,' she conceded.

'Don't you ever feel the urge to get in touch?' Laurie asked.

'No,' she lied. 'What's the point? It can't go anywhere.'

Laurie glanced at Elliot, as though in some way he might be able to fix it. Then her eyes closed as his mobile started to ring. *Please don't let it be Max,* she was thinking, as he got up to answer. The evening had been going so well, she didn't want anything to remind him of Phraxos again. But it was Max, and as he disappeared into his study to take the call, she could feel the tension that had built in her earlier starting to return.

'I don't know how much more of this I can take,' she muttered to Sherry as they carried dishes through to the kitchen. 'He's obsessed with this damned Phraxos thing and to hell with everything else, including the fact that we're supposed to be getting married.'

Sherry looked at her in surprise. '"Supposed,"' she echoed. 'You're surely not having doubts, are you?'

Laurie sighed, heavily. 'No. Of course not. I just wish he'd show a bit more interest, that's all.' She turned to Sherry and gave her a wry, affectionate smile. 'Let's have lunch this week, shall we?'

'Sure. Give me a call when you can make it.'

'I think that's yours, Laurie,' Rhona called out, as another mobile started to ring.

'Can you see who it is?'

'No number,' Rhona told her, looking at the read-out, then clicked on to answer. 'Hello, Laurie Forbes's phone.'

'OK, who wants coffee,' Laurie shouted, rummaging around for the cafetière. 'I'm really sorry he cut off your story about Nick so abruptly,' she said to Sherry. 'And I'm not much better, am I? Already going on about myself.'

'It's not a problem. The story's not exactly new and I was finished, anyway. Where's the coffee?'

'Good question.'

Rhona came to the counter with the phone. 'I think he said his name was Barry,' she said, passing it over. 'It's not a great connection.'

Taking the phone Laurie turned aside and blocked one ear. She was already experiencing some concern as it was late for Barry to be calling. 'Hello?' she said. 'Is everything all right?'

'Sorry to interrupt,' he replied, 'I know you've got guests, but I thought you'd want to know . . . I've just had an extremely interesting call warning me to stay away from the doc and the workshop, if I know what's good for me.'

'Do you know who it was?'

'I'd guess at one of Eddie Cribbs's people, the bloke that owns the workshop.'

'What did you say?'

'I told him we wanted to know where Daya was, so's we could get her the treatment she needs. And I was told we wouldn't ever see her again, no-one would.'

Laurie felt suddenly sick. 'What does that mean?' she said.

'Probably what you think. Seems they've found out she talked. Don't ask me how, but if this bloke's to be believed, she ain't going to be talking again.'

Laurie's eyes were large as she saw Daya's lovely face in her mind, those little hands, the bird-like body, the hidden, unthinkable injuries. Why hadn't she taken her? Why hadn't she just acted

47

on her instinct and to hell with what came later? It could never be worse than this.

'You still there?' Barry said.

'Yes.'

'I better let you go now. We'll talk in the morning.'

Laurie's face was pale as she clicked off the line.

'Laurie?' Rose said, noticing. 'Are you all right?'

Laurie's eyes came up. 'It's Daya . . . They found out she talked. Barry thinks they've . . . got rid of her.'

'Oh my God,' Rose murmured.

Laurie dashed a hand to her head. 'It's my fault,' she murmured. 'I should have. . .'

'It's *not* your fault,' Rose cut in, getting to her feet. 'You were trying to help.'

Laurie looked at Elliot as he came out of his study. 'What is it?' he said, surprised by the silence.

'It's the Indian girl Laurie spoke to earlier,' Rose told him.

His expression was blank. 'What about her?'

Rose glanced at Laurie as she said, 'We're thinking the worst.'

His eyebrows went up. 'Oh,' he said flatly.

Suddenly Laurie lost it. 'Oh!' she seethed, flinging the phone against the wall. 'Is that all you can say? The wretched girl's probably dead. It could be my fault, and all you can say is, *oh!*'

'What the hell do you want me to say?' he shouted back. 'I don't know her. You don't even know any details . . .'

'How do you know? You haven't even asked. No! Don't say any more. Just don't say anything. You're not interested in anything I do, so I'll deal

48

with the fact that a poor, defenceless young girl has probably been dumped in the Thames, or buried in some concrete, thanks to me, while you . . .'

'Laurie, we don't know that for certain,' Rose interrupted, attempting to calm things down.

'Nor does he. But what the hell would he care anyway? It's all about him these days. Him and that fucking project that's going to get us all killed if he doesn't damned well let it go.'

Elliot was striding towards her, and grabbing her he pulled her across the kitchen, into the utility room. 'Stop it!' he growled, holding her tight. 'Just stop. The Phraxos affair is over. We're not doing anything to break the agreement, so stop getting yourself worked up like this.'

Sobbing almost uncontrollably she covered her face with her hands and sat down on one of the boxes behind her. 'I love you,' she choked. 'I love you so much, but I'm so afraid.'

'There's nothing to be afraid of,' he told her sharply.

'Isn't there?' She looked up at him. 'Are you sure about that?'

It took several moments but finally his expression started to soften. 'I'm sure,' he said, and kneeling down in front of her he held her hands in his. 'It's going to be all right,' he told her gently. 'I promise. Everything will be all right.'

She wanted to believe him, with all her heart she wanted to believe him, but though the words rang true there was something in his tone, or maybe it was in her instincts, that was telling her that it – whatever *it* was – was going to be anything but all right.

Chapter Three

'Sherry? It's Aunt Jude. How are you, dear?'

Sherry's fingers paused in their race over the keyboard. Aunt Jude. Warm, mellow, Aunt Jude. A box of soft-centred chocolates; sunlight on a cloudy day; the scratchy sound of a seventy-eight record; the feel of safety on a stormy night. Always a reminder of the past.

She continued to type, speaking into the headset. 'I'm fine,' she answered fondly. 'How are you?'

'I'm well. I've been thinking about you, and reading your columns. They're always very good.'

'Thank you.' Sherry swallowed. She loved her aunt, but sometimes there was a part of her that wished she didn't exist. 'I'm going to try to get down there to see you in the next couple of weeks,' she said.

'That'll be nice. You know how we love to see you. Uncle John's taking care of your vegetable patch. We've got some nice spring onions coming through at the moment.'

'My favourite,' Sherry replied. 'How are the tomatoes doing?'

'Should be a bumper crop this year. We'll probably have to give some away.'

'The neighbours'll be pleased.' There was a pause as she tried to think of something else to say.

Eventually her aunt said, 'Did you get the letter, dear?' It was what this call was really about.

'Yes,' Sherry answered.

'Did you read it?'

'No.' She took a breath. 'I'm really sorry, Aunt Jude. I wish . . .'

'Don't apologize, dear. I understand. But I thought you should know, I had a call last night from Bluebell's . . .'

'I don't want to know, Aunt Jude. I really don't.'

'I think you should, dear. There's been a suicide attempt. I think that's what the letter was about. It was a pity you didn't read it.'

Sherry's breath had stopped at 'suicide'. Now her heart was pounding, as grotesque and horrific images stampeded through her mind.

'It wasn't successful,' Aunt Jude continued.

Sherry was barely listening. She was mentally focusing on the letter now, imagining that flimsy blue rectangle tumbling down through the chute, to join the pile of trash below. It seemed a metaphor of what might have happened to its writer if the suicide attempt had succeeded.

'Sherry? Are you all right? Are you still there?'

'Yes. Yes,' she answered, quickly collecting herself. 'I'm sorry, Aunt Jude,' she said abruptly. 'I wish I could stay and talk, but I have to meet someone at one, and it's almost that.'

51

'All right, dear. If you need to talk, you know where I am.'

After ringing off Sherry instantly blanked the call from her mind. She'd had plenty of practice at doing that over the past seven years, so it wasn't difficult now. In fact, the more time that passed, the more expert she was becoming. It was a survival technique, a necessary function for a mind that would never be able to bear the horror if it hadn't found a way of detaching, even shutting down completely on events that would forever remain irreversible – unless the truth was finally told. But Bluebell wouldn't do it. The suicide attempt had just shown that she was prepared to go to her grave with what she knew.

After finishing the article she'd been composing before the call, she attached it to an email, and was about to rush out the door when someone rang the bell downstairs. The sound made her jump, proving the call had left her edgier than she'd want to admit, but it would fade, it always did.

'Hi, it's me! Anita!' the voice announced over the intercom. 'Can I come up?'

'I'm on my way down. Give me two minutes.'

When Sherry emerged onto the street it was to find Anita clad in her usual professional black and looking fit to burst. 'I'm so excited, I just had to tell someone,' she gushed, combing her hands down either side of her long, dark hair.

Sherry stooped to check the tubs of geraniums that sat either side of the main door. 'What's happened?' she asked.

'The *boy* has paid back the money he owes me.'

Sherry blinked. A cause for relief, certainly, but for such untold pleasure? 'I'm very happy for you,' she responded, giving a wave to one of her elderly neighbours who was sitting on a bench just inside the park opposite.

'Well, it's all down to you,' Anita informed her, falling in beside her as she walked. 'I've been following your advice and now I've virtually got him eating out of my hand. I mean, he really cares about me, I know that, but it's time he realized it too, and I think he's starting to.'

'What advice was that?' Sherry said, mystified.

'I read it in your column. Let him think there might be someone else on the scene and if he's really interested you'll see things starting to change.'

Sherry blinked again. This was like teaching a nuclear physicist how to add up. 'I don't know what to say,' she finally murmured.

'Me neither,' Anita cried, throwing out her hands. 'But it's fantastic. It works.'

Sherry stopped and eyed her warily. 'You're kidding me, right?' she said.

'No. I've got the cheque here, in my bag.'

Deciding the only sensible response was to stop and smell the roses outside Boodle's, the restaurant, Sherry was about to walk on when the owner carried out a blackboard showing the day's menu. They exchanged pleasantries, Sherry praised the flowers, then glanced at her watch.

'So where are you going?' Anita asked, her heels wobbling slightly as they continued along the cobbled street.

'I'm meeting Laurie at the Grapes.'

'So how is she?'

'Stressed.'

'Hardly surprising. Are you going to the wedding?'

'Yes. Alone, of course.'

'You'll meet someone there.'

'I thought you were a psychologist, not an astrologist?'

Anita chuckled and allowed a few moments to pass. 'So are you still smarting about revealing all at dinner the other night?' she teased.

Sherry grimaced and laughed. 'Don't remind me, because yes, I am. Not that I actually revealed *everything* . . .'

'When do you ever?'

'I just told them about Nick, that's all.'

'Which is nothing to be embarrassed about.'

'Except it's seven years out of date. I could have better used the time to try and impress Elliot into giving me a job.'

'I don't understand why you've never asked Laurie to put in a word for you.'

'Because she's offered me a job herself, and it would be a bit of an insult, wouldn't it, if I said not with you, but with your boyfriend. Soon to be husband. Actually, she might even get the wrong idea. Anyway, right now it's a moot point, because she's so snowed under I've agreed to help her out with the story she's working on – which is why we're meeting for lunch. If it weren't for that, I'd invite you to join us.'

'It's OK. I was only passing. I've an appointment at one thirty.' She threw Sherry a sidelong glance. 'Is that a relief?' she challenged softly.

Sherry's head came round. 'What do you mean?'

Anita only smiled, then quickly threw out an arm to hail a passing cab. 'I'll call you later,' she said, embracing her. 'Have a good lunch.'

As the taxi pulled away Sherry was left staring across the street towards the large, curved windows of Laurie's office, where Rose and two of the production team were clearly visible. Anita's comment was still echoing in her ears, causing her to wonder if she was being too exclusive about Laurie and Rhona, and not including Anita enough. If she was, she should try to do something about it, because she definitely didn't want to hurt Anita's feelings.

Waving back as Laurie signalled for her to go on into the pub, she turned to push open the door and stepped into the hot, smoky mayhem. After managing to secure them a table, at the river end of the bar, she ordered herself a tonic water and started to study a menu she knew almost by heart. She'd got no further than piemash and chips when Laurie slumped down in the chair opposite.

'Thank God,' she gasped, sounding breathless. 'It's a madhouse over there with them going away at the weekend, and everything else in my life in a state of uproar. I almost wish I was going with them, but don't tell Elliot I said that.'

Sherry grinned. 'Things still tense?' she said.

'I'm told it's normal in the lead-up to a wedding. Oh Jack, my hero,' she declared, as one of the barmen brought her a vodka and tonic.

'Well, if it's any help, you're looking pretty good,' Sherry told her, as they clinked glasses.

'I've lost weight. About seven pounds, apparently, which is not sitting well with the dressmaker.' She laughed and growled. 'Is there no-one I can please at the moment?' she cried. 'What with her, Elliot, my mother, my father, the vicar, Rose . . . Just thank God for you, agreeing to help out on this story. Elliot said you would.'

Sherry's eyebrows rose, as her heart gave a beat of pleasure. 'He did?'

'It was his idea, though I can't imagine why I didn't think of it myself.'

'I never thought he took me seriously as a journalist.'

'Then you're wrong, because he's got a lot of respect for you. We all have. Just because you seem determined to hide your light under the fluff that pays you so well, it doesn't mean we don't see what you do from time to time in the more serious press. So, believe me, we're pretty aware of what you'd be capable of, given half a chance, which Rose and I have long been willing to do.'

Sherry's eyes were shining.

'The point is,' Laurie continued, 'we feel we can trust you. That's a big plus in anyone's book, especially in this field.' She cast her a teasing look. 'We can, can't we?'

Sherry laughed delightedly. 'A hundred per cent,' she assured her. 'And I'm touched to have earned such confidence. I promise it won't be misplaced.' Was this a good time, she wondered, to mention her interest in joining Elliot's team? Maybe not, but she was certainly being presented with a perfect opportunity to prove herself, thanks to Laurie, for whom she felt so much affection just then it was hard to hold it back. Looking down at her glass, she picked it up. 'So how's the bridegroom doing in the stress department?' she asked, feeling it time to get off the subject of herself.

Laurie sighed and groaned. 'I honestly don't know what's going on with him,' she answered. 'He keeps disappearing. Either into his study, to the office, or to heaven only knows where. He's supposed to be writing a book, for God's sake. The publishers have advanced him a fortune.'

'So what do you think he's up to?'

'I've got no idea. It's just not like him to be this . . . secretive, at least not with me.' She took another gulp of her drink. 'You know what I'm starting to think? That he doesn't want to go through with this wedding.'

Sherry rolled her eyes. 'Somehow I knew you were going to say that,' she responded, 'and I'm telling you now, you're wrong. Of course he wants to go through with it – he's just being a man. Most of them hate weddings, especially Elliot's type, but that doesn't mean he doesn't want to marry you.'

'So should I call the wedding off, tell him we'll go away somewhere, just the two of us, no fuss?'

Sherry shrugged. 'What about your mother? She'd be devastated.'

Laurie shuddered and covered her face with her hands. 'It's a nightmare,' she wailed. 'An utter bloody nightmare. I've never felt so strung out. I'm just not myself. Something's going on somewhere, in my psyche, in the stars, that's making me feel as though . . .' Her breath caught on what almost sounded like a sob. She looked at Sherry, her eyes suddenly swimming in tears. 'I keep wishing Lysette were still alive,' she said, haltingly. 'Well, of course I wish she were alive, how could I not . . . But if she were, would Elliot and I . . . ? No, don't let's go there. Lysette's gone, and though I sometimes feel like she took half of me with her, I have to accept that's what it's like being the twin of someone who ended her own life.'

Sherry's heart was filling up with this second tremendous honour Laurie was paying her, in discussing a matter that was so intensely personal and obviously still painful. However, providing comfort and understanding was something she was very skilled at. 'This is a very emotional time,' she said gently, covering Laurie's hand with her own. 'It's natural that you'd be thinking about your sister now, and feeling this way.'

Laurie nodded and took a deep breath. 'Has Rhona ever told you what happened?'

'Some of it, not all.'

'She used to be Elliot's girlfriend, did you know that?'

Sherry nodded.

Laurie's eyes went down as she swallowed the rising lump in her throat. 'She called me, the night he finished their relationship,' she said hoarsely. 'She needed me then, but I wouldn't let her come.' Her mouth trembled. 'I can hear her voice now,' she whispered, 'begging me, *please, Laurie, please, I have to see you,* but I wouldn't give in. I couldn't. It felt wrong to be comforting her, when I knew I was in love with him myself, and the truth was, I wanted their relationship to end. She didn't know that, at least I don't think she did. I didn't want

her to be hurt, obviously I didn't . . . I loved her
. . . She was the world to me. Oh God, it was such
a mess, Sherry. You can't believe how awful it was.
He told her there was someone else, and for one
crazy, awful moment, I thought it might be me.
But it wasn't. He'd told her that because he
couldn't think of another way to make her accept
it was over.' After a moment her head came up
and she tried to force a smile. 'I miss her so much
. . . So much, I can't put it into words. Yet sometimes I wonder if she's looking down on me and
hating me for what I'm doing, marrying Elliot,
taking what was hers . . . But if you knew her,
Sherry . . . She was an angel. She could never hate
anyone, especially not me. We were so close. It was
as though I lost a part of myself when she went
. . . Oh God, I'm sorry, I can't seem to stop crying.'

'It's all right,' Sherry assured her. 'I felt the same
way when my parents died. And if you want to
cry, just cry.'

Laurie looked at her, her eyes showing gratitude. 'How do you get over it?' she asked brokenly.

Sherry sighed. 'The truth is, you don't, really,'
she answered. 'You just learn how to live with it.
Does Elliot ever talk about her? Do you know how
he's feeling now?'

'Not really. We used to discuss it, but it
happened three years ago. Life moves on.'

'Did you have any counselling at the time?
Either of you?'

Laurie shook her head. 'No. Did you, when you
lost your parents?'

Sherry nodded. 'I was almost forced into it. Thank
God. I'm not sure I'd be sitting here, otherwise.'

'What happened to them, exactly? If you don't mind me asking.'

'They were killed in an air crash. It was my father's plane . . . They were on their way back from San Francisco. I was driving out to the airfield to meet them . . .' She paused for a moment. 'We were very close. I was an only child, and it was so sudden. I just couldn't come to terms with it. One day they were there, the next they were gone, and there was just no way of ever getting them back. It must have been the same for you, with Lysette. Probably worse, with you being twins, and because of the way you lost her.'

Laurie nodded and looked down at her hands. 'It's not a competition though, is it?' she said softly. 'However it happens, it's devastating, and it never really seems to go away.' After a moment she blew out some air, and attempted a smile. 'Sorry, I didn't mean to load all that on you.'

'Please don't apologize. I'm glad you felt able to. You should probably try to discuss it with Elliot though, if you can.'

A glimmer of irony broke through in Laurie's eyes. 'Dear Molly,' she teased. 'But I'll bear it in mind. For now, though, I think we should decide what we're going to eat, don't you?' She looked down as her mobile started to vibrate across the table. 'Rachel,' she announced, reading the number on the display. 'Do you mind?'

'Of course not,' Sherry answered, waving her on.

Taking the phone out onto the balcony, where it was easier to hear, Laurie clicked on the line. 'Hi. How are you?' she said, feeling suddenly annoyed with herself for just abandoning Sherry, when this probably could have waited.

'Great,' Rachel answered. 'Up to my eyes with the exhibition. The invitations should go out by the end of the week, I hope you're coming.'

'You can count on it.'

'Good. Andraya, she's the artist in case you'd forgotten, arrived yesterday, so we thought we'd have drinks for her on Friday. Just a few close friends and some very rich people. Nothing formal. Can you make it?'

'I'll check with Elliot, but I don't think it'll be a problem.'

'OK. Everything all right with you two now?'

'I think so. Listen, I'd better go. I'm in the Grapes and we're not supposed to use mobiles.'

'How is she?' Sherry asked, as Laurie came back.

'Enjoying getting involved in Chris's world, by the sound of it. They're having drinks on Friday for the Brazilian artist Chris is promoting, and wanted to know if Elliot and I could make it. So, have you chosen?'

Sherry passed her back the menu. 'Bangers and mash for me,' she said.

As Laurie went to the bar to order, Sherry gazed absently towards the window. The top of a mast was just visible as a yacht glided down the river. It was a part of being single, she knew that, not being invited to those intimate little gatherings, but that didn't make it any the less hurtful.

'OK,' she said briskly, as Laurie returned to the table. 'Time to get down to business.'

'Absolutely. Where do you want to start?'

'How about the missing girl? What was her name again?'

'Daya. No more news, so we still don't know if she really is missing, or if it was something Barry was told to make us back off. I called this Mrs Ghosh, at the garment factory, yesterday – the garment factory that Barry discovered employs no female workers, remember? What a nasty piece of work she sounds. Obviously she couldn't deny she knew Daya, after she'd taken her to the doctor, so she spun some story about the girl doing some casual work from home when it was needed.'

'Did you get an address?'

'Yes. It's near Brick Lane. Barry's checking it out, but don't hold your breath. It's almost bound to be number six, Blind Alley.'

'What about the girl's injuries? Did you ask how she'd come by them?'

'Yes, and wait for this, she said Daya was carrying a sewing machine down the front steps of her house, slipped and fell onto the machine. That, according to Mrs Ghosh, was how she came to be so ripped apart inside. Can you believe it? "We do our best for these girls,"' Laurie said, mimicking Karima Ghosh's Indian accent, '"but they are very clumsy. I take her to doctor, and now we have to buy new machine. We won't be employing her again."' Laurie shook her head in disgust, and her spirits seemed suddenly to sink as she looked down at her drink. 'She's dead,' she said, bleakly. 'I just know it.'

Since Sherry had no idea whether or not that was true, she merely said, 'What about the factory owner? Eddie Cribbs? What have you managed to find out about him?'

Laurie's tone took on an ironic lilt as she said,

'He's your regular twenty-first-century gangster, by all accounts. Which means all the old clichés, nightclubs, betting shops, car lots, etc, but apparently we can add to that the wonderfully useful euphemisms of import/export, Internet trading, stocks-on-line, an executive travel club, and several different varieties of adult entertainment. There's a lot more, Barry said, but he's still working on it. The man's definitely into prostitution, through his strip clubs and probably through the Net too. In fact, there doesn't seem to be much he isn't into.'

'Have you tried talking to him?'

'Not yet. At this stage Barry's advising strongly against it. Even calling Karima Ghosh could have put those women in serious jeopardy, he says, as if they aren't already.'

Sherry lifted her drink, and took a few moments to mull over what she'd learned so far. There was no doubt the thrill of the chase was starting to build, but she was determined to remain rooted in the seriousness of it, rather than get carried away by the excitement. 'Did you tell this Mrs Ghosh who you were?' she asked.

Laurie nodded. 'I'm not sure whether I should have, but if she found my card on Daya, which she could have, she must have been expecting the call. It would account for how prepared her story was.'

'Has Barry given you any kind of profile on the factory?'

'Half a dozen workers, all men, all legally here. Everyone's paid above minimum wage, though only just, no real health and safety issues. Bit of a model workshop, actually, by East End rag-trade standards.'

'What about the customers? Do we know who they are?'

'Some of the smaller high street chains. Sunday markets, independent clothing stores, that sort of thing.'

'Then it could be an idea for someone to pay Mrs Ghosh a visit, posing as a buyer. If nothing else, we could get a look at the woman, and a feel for who she is and what the workshop's about.'

Laurie nodded. 'It's probably the only way, because neither of us is going to pass as an immigrant, so we can't join the workforce, and no-one there is very likely to talk to the press, it would be more than their job's worth, if not their life, so we can't go that route either . . .'

'And since they know Barry and you're too easily recognizable, I guess that leaves me.'

Laurie cast her a look.

Sherry laughed. 'You've been leading me up to this,' she accused.

'Guilty. You know I'd do it myself though, if I could.'

'Of course, but you can't, so that's settled. Presumably Barry can connect me with someone who has a market stall, or small dress shop, who can show me the ropes.'

'I'm sure he can. But we also need to find out how these women are being smuggled into the country. Our best source for that is obviously the women themselves, which brings us right back to how the heck we're going to find them.'

Sherry looked round as their order was shouted

from the bar. 'We will,' she said confidently as she rose to her feet.

When she came back again Laurie said, 'I just hope I'm not dragging you into something we're both going to end up regretting, because we're heading for some pretty rough terrain, that's for sure.'

Sherry's voice was loaded with irony as she said, 'Well, at least it's taking your mind off everything else.'

'Oh God,' Laurie groaned, her shoulders sinking as her appetite fled.

Sherry chuckled. 'Sorry. I shouldn't have reminded you. But come on. You'll get through this. All of it. The story, the wedding, the doubts, the fears . . . You can deal with it, and I'm here to make sure you do.'

Chapter Four

Neela Kumbhar lay very quietly under her blanket. The thin mattress beneath her was pushed up against the wall, where clumps of paper hung down, and big swathes of damp made shapes like the clouds. Next to her Bhanu Ganesh lay snoring. Neela knew she had to be careful of this woman. She told things to Mota Ben – the boss lady – that got the rest of them into trouble.

All the women were careful of Bhanu, they had learned to be during the terrible journey here. Bhanu had hated Daya, Neela's sister, right from the start, because Daya was beautiful, and Bhanu was disfigured by the *jellan* – the burning jealousy inside her. Now Bhanu hated Shaila, Daya's daughter. She hated Neela too.

Neela wanted to cry, but she had learned not to. During the journey, on the boats, and then in the lorries, she had been beaten for crying, and for being hungry, and for needing to urinate. Handfuls of her hair had been torn out when she'd let her bowels go. She couldn't help it. She couldn't hold

66

it in any longer. But she wasn't the only one. Others had done it too, until finally they had lain there, limp, exhausted, squashed into boxes, and suffocating in the stench of their own bodily waste.

The smell here was like that, but not so bad. They had big white urns to pee in and a chain to pull that washed it away. At home they had squatted over a hole in the ground. At least then they knew where it went. Here she was afraid it might come back in their food, or out of the pipes with the water.

England was a bad place. A very bad place. Their uncle, Achal Kumbhar, had told them it was good, but he was a cruel man who had beaten them all the time, and he had always lied. Their father, his brother, was dead, so was their mother, and when Daya's husband had died too, the care of them all had fallen to Achal. He was a poor man. How could he be expected to feed so many? They would all starve. Women were a curse. As a widow Daya would not be allowed to remarry, so she could not be given to another man, and no-one would ever want Neela because of the hideous mark on her face.

When the men had come to take them they had only wanted Daya and Shaila. They didn't want Neela. At sixteen she might be young and ripe, but the purple scar over the side of her face and down her neck made her ugly. Ugly ones were no good to them, they'd said. Uncle had told them that if they didn't take Neela they couldn't take Daya and Shaila either. They could have Neela for free, but she had to go too. In the end the men had given her uncle many *taka*, then they had taken them away. In England they would have food to eat, Uncle had told them, and they would be rich, because in England everyone was.

Now Neela worked the sewing machines to repay the *taka* Uncle had been paid. Daya had been made to repay another way.

Little Shaila moved in her sleep, turning her skinny body into Neela's. Neela held her close. Since Daya had gone Neela's young heart had been overflowing with fear. Daya had taken care of her and Shaila, because Daya was strong. Now it was Neela's turn to be strong. The other women said Daya was never coming back, but Neela told them it wasn't true, because she didn't want Shaila to think that. In her heart, though, she knew it was true, because Daya had spoken to someone outside. They had been warned not to do that. Daya hadn't wanted to, but the Englishwoman who'd been waiting with the doctor had said she wanted to help.

In her dreams Neela imagined the Englishwoman coming to save them, but it was only a dream. They were never going to leave here now, there was nothing they could do to break free. The doors were locked, the windows were blacked. The only time anyone left their eyes were made blind, so they couldn't tell where they were, except at the top of a staircase, in a big room where rats poked about in the gloom.

Holding her niece's little body close she began murmuring a prayer to Ambamata. She kept her voice low so that Bhanu would not hear. She didn't want Bhanu to beat the child, nor her either. It was Bhanu who had told Mota Ben that Daya had spoken to someone outside. She'd seen Daya showing Neela the card the Englishwoman had given her. Bhanu had snatched it away and handed it over to Mota Ben.

Lorries thundered past. A cat screamed like a child in pain. Across the room someone was quietly sobbing. Despair hung in the air like cobwebs. After a while the big steel door was unlocked and Charu, one of the girls, returned to her bed. Shaila woke up and turned her big brown eyes to Neela. In the moonlight she was so beautiful it caused a pain in Neela's heart, for Neela had learned that, here, it was not good to be beautiful. Somehow she had to get Shaila away.

'Don't be a fool,' Ekta Mittal had said, when she'd told the older woman that they must try to escape. 'If the English find us they will put us in prison.'

'But why?'

'Don't you understand? You're no-one now,' Ekta had told her bitterly. 'You don't exist any more. None of us do.'

Neela felt as though she existed, but she wished she didn't.

Laurie was standing in the doorway of Elliot's study watching him as he worked on the computer. Bags of groceries were lying on the floor behind her. She'd hoped he would help her carry them through to the kitchen, but apart from a quick hello when she'd come in, he hadn't looked up.

It wasn't anger she was feeling, or unease, but more a mix of the two, as she tried to pinpoint when she'd first sensed this distance creeping between them. In truth, she couldn't even be sure it was real, though it certainly felt that way now. A sudden fear of losing him engulfed her, yet she didn't really think it would happen. They belonged together, and not even this irrational anxiety could make her stop believing that. It was just that lately he seemed to be closing her out in a way he never had before.

'You're planning to publish it on the Web, aren't you?' she suddenly stated.

He looked up in surprise. 'I didn't realize you were still there,' he said.

She wanted to ask if he'd prefer her not to be, but she was determined not to row. 'Aren't you?' she pressed.

'The Phraxos story?'

'You know that's what I'm talking about.'

Turning back to the computer, he saved what he'd been doing, then got up from his chair. 'I imagine that needs taking to the kitchen,' he said, indicating the shopping.

She glanced round at it, then back to him. 'You realize it'll still get you into trouble,' she said. 'They'll know where it came from, who was behind it . . .'

As he looked down into her worried face he seemed slightly puzzled. Then his expression softened as he appeared to take on board how difficult she was finding this. 'I'm not publishing it on the Web,' he told her gently. 'Nor am I planning to do anything else with it. OK, I won't deny that I want to, but I know what would happen if I did, so does Max, which is why we're letting it go.'

He started to smile as her eyes bored into his, as though seeking more reassurance.

'You just have to accept that it isn't easy,' he said, pulling her into his arms. 'I still get mad as hell about it, and I hate the way I allowed myself to be bought off. But I know very well that making any of it public could have even worse consequences than we want to imagine, so please stop worrying. All I was doing then, when you came in, was roughing out a first chapter for my memoirs.'

At last the irony in his voice seemed to soothe her tension, while the feel of his embrace began restoring a sense of their connection. 'I don't know what's the matter with me,' she sighed. 'I seem to be having such a hard time trusting anything lately. I'm so edgy. So . . . full of doubt. Not about us, but about . . . well, everything else, it would seem.'

'And I haven't helped.'

She tilted her face up to his. 'You do still want to get married, don't you?' she said.

He smiled and touched his mouth to hers. 'I wouldn't have asked you if I didn't,' he said.

'But I asked you,' she reminded him.

'So you did. But as I recall, I already had the ring. Now, I know we probably don't have time for this,' he continued, starting to unbutton her blouse, 'but I'm sure Chris and Rachel won't mind if we're a little late.'

A couple of hours later, still flushed from the pleasure of their lovemaking, and feeling much more relaxed than she had in weeks, Laurie pressed a path through the guests in Rachel's

Hampstead sitting room to where Rachel was chatting with a prominent politician. Clearly she was exploiting the wealthy and influential connections she'd made through her marriage to Tim Hendon, and why not? It was what this gathering was all about, introducing the artist to her potential clientele – and there were more than a few in the Cabinet, and the House, who probably felt they owed Tim Hendon's widow a favour or two.

Seeing Laurie heading her way, Rachel politely excused herself, and drew Laurie into a warm embrace. 'You look wonderful,' she told her. 'Positively glowing.'

Laurie's eyes were mischievous. 'I'll leave you to guess why,' she responded. 'But I mustn't hog you. I just wanted to say hi. It's an impressive gathering.'

'Andraya Sorrantos's paintings have impressive price tags,' Rachel informed her. 'They command a small fortune in Brazil and Germany, though Chris isn't sure he'll be able to match up when she's not actually known here. We'll have to see. He's already talking to someone in New York about showing her there, regardless of how well it goes here.'

'So where is she?' Laurie said, sipping her champagne and looking around.

Rachel slanted her a glance. 'Still upstairs,' she answered. 'It had the audacity to rain on her as she was coming from the car to the front door, so she needs to repair the damage.'

Laurie's eyebrows rose. 'How much damage can be done in a twelve-foot sprint?'

'I don't think Andraya actually sprints,' Rachel

72

replied in a tone that made Laurie laugh. 'But I wasn't about to argue. She's been up in my bedroom for over half an hour, and no-one but Chris is allowed in.'

'Which is presumably where he is now?'

'No. He's over there, talking to Elliot. Have you seen the catalogue, by the way? They've done a fabulous job. There's a pile of them on the coffee table. Take as many as you like and give them to as many rich people as you know.'

'What are the paintings like?'

'If you're into surrealism, you're going to love them. Think Dali, Kahlo, a bit of Kandinsky, but don't quote me, as she likes to consider herself unique. Chris is absolutely blown away by her talent, and I have to confess, they work for me too. Utterly mesmerizing. Which is pretty much how I would describe the woman herself, when she's not being a royal pain in the ass. And speaking of the devil . . .'

Laurie turned round, and was about to take another sip of champagne when her hand stopped mid-air and her eyes widened in surprise. 'My God,' she murmured, for Andraya Sorrantos, with her luxuriant black hair, sleepy dark eyes and wide, shiny mouth wasn't just the quintessential Brazilian bombshell, she was the full-blooded embodiment of a true sex-goddess. Her skin was the colour of dark honey, her eyes glowed like amber, while her delectably wide, full lips oozed the kind of promise that could fulfil any man's dreams.

'Quite something, isn't she?' Rachel responded.

'You're not kidding,' Laurie replied, experiencing

more ripples of amazement as a brief gap in the crowd allowed her a full-length view. 'Don't they have vests in Brazil?' she said, gazing at the gossamer-fine black top that clung tightly to the magnificent voluptuousness of two brazenly naked breasts.

Rachel chuckled. 'Watch all the repressed Englishmen,' she whispered. 'When they're talking to her their eyes won't drop below chin level.'

Laurie watched as Chris went to greet her, and began introducing her round. 'You're right,' she laughed. 'Anywhere but. Oh my God, I swear old Robert Ryan isn't just blushing, he's actually trembling.'

'A lot do.'

Laurie was transfixed. 'I can't wait to see how Elliot reacts,' she murmured, casting a quick look in his direction. 'Who's that he's talking to now?'

'Felicity Barr. She's a top QC, and second cousin to our estimable PM. Terrifying individual, reminds me of my old headmistress.'

'And just how impressed is *she* going to be by Andraya's little exhibition?' Laurie couldn't help wondering.

'Andraya doesn't care much what women think,' Rachel informed her.

'Now why doesn't that surprise me?'

Still fascinated, Laurie watched the Amazonian sex-goddess, who was almost as tall as Elliot, move from one guest to another, greeting them all with a deeply seductive smile, while stroking her glossy hair and licking those wickedly pouting lips. When she finally reached Elliot, his expression showed little more than politeness as he took the

bejewelled fingers she was offering. He said something neither Laurie nor Rachel could hear, but
whatever it was it made Chris chuckle and
Andraya appear pleased. Her reply caused Elliot
to smile as he dutifully brought her hand to his
lips. His eyes, Laurie noticed, had resolutely
remained above the chin.

'Typical of Elliot not to be embarrassed,' Rachel
commented. 'Chris is much the same, though I
know he loves it. Show me a man who wouldn't,
and in Chris's case he's ecstatic, as it's virtually
guaranteed to get them all back for the real
exhibition.'

'It'll get the press in too,' Laurie said, wanting
to laugh as Elliot winked in her direction.

The performance was so compelling that Laurie
merely continued to watch, marvelling at the
wonderful shamelessness of the woman whose
breasts formed such truly delectable mounds of
caramel flesh, with big maroon nipples protrud-
ing like plums from the peaks, that even Laurie
could feel herself being turned on by them. Were
they real? she wondered. They couldn't be, for as
stunning as Andraya was, she had to be at least
forty, and the stupendously jutting pair now heading Laurie's way seemed as impervious to grav-
ity as their owner did to modesty.

'Andraya,' Rachel crooned, kissing the air either
side of Andraya's cheeks.

'Rachel, such a lovely party,' Andraya responded
in an exquisitely accented drawl that Laurie could
just hear Sherry describing as gallons of rich, dark
chocolate pouring all over the naked genitals. 'Such
fascinating people.'

'I want you to meet Laurie Forbes,' Rachel said. 'She's a very good friend of mine.'

Andraya's bewitching eyes slanted in Laurie's direction. 'You mean Laurie, of Elliot and Laurie?' she murmured, raising an elegant hand. 'Chris has told me about you. Are you not soon to be married?'

'We are,' Laurie replied, looking at the hand. Surely she didn't expect her to kiss it! 'It's a pleasure to meet you,' she said, touching the tips of Andraya's fingers.

'Your fiancé is an interesting man,' Andraya remarked.

'I think so,' Laurie responded. And after a pause, 'May I say, that's an extremely eye-catching top you're wearing.'

'Mm.' Quite suddenly Andraya's smile was so dazzling that Laurie actually blinked. 'Ah, a joke,' Andraya purred. 'Very good. Very droll.' She was already turning away.

As she went Laurie cast a look down at the ankle-length skirt she was wearing. It was slit up the back to way above mid-thigh, and hugged her shapely bottom so lovingly that there was not the slightest chance she was anything but naked underneath. 'Does she always dress like that?' she asked Rachel.

'Not quite as outrageously, but she's usually got something on show. Thigh, cleavage, navel. I don't actually think she can help it, it's just the way she is.'

Laurie looked at her again, and was just beginning to feel extremely dull by comparison when Elliot murmured in her ear, 'You've got much better tits.'

76

Spluttering with laughter, she turned to look up at him. 'You think so?'

'I know so.'

Standing on tiptoe she whispered something she knew would turn him on. His eyes darkened, and she felt herself moving closer to him.

'OK, I know no-one else exists for you two these days,' Rachel cut in, 'but you could at least say hello, Elliot.'

Grinning, Elliot swept her into an embrace. 'Great party,' he told her. 'And the catalogue is superb. Chris tells me you were in charge.'

'Pff,' Rachel scoffed. 'He let me think I was, but he doesn't let go of the reins. Have you seen the real thing yet? And I don't mean the artist, I mean her paintings.'

'I saw a few when they were being unpacked the other day,' he answered. 'They're pretty spectacular.'

'Any of them take your fancy?'

'Can't afford them. And I won't be crass enough to ask if there's a discount for friends.'

'Which is his way of asking,' Laurie chipped in.

'If you were serious about buying, I'm sure there would be,' Rachel told him.

'A three-week honeymoon at an Amman Resort, an apartment overlooking Tower Bridge, and a woman with extremely expensive tastes in interior design, is about as far as I can stretch,' he said ruefully.

'Oh come on, the smaller ones start at a quarter of a million. I'm sure that's in your budget,' Rachel teased.

'A quarter of a million!' Laurie cried. 'They must be good.'

'They are,' Elliot assured her. 'Now, can I get you ladies a refill?'

'There should be a waiter going round with a tray,' Rachel responded, trying to spot someone. 'Ah, there he is.'

As Elliot went off Rachel turned back to Laurie. 'Have you had a second fitting for the dress yet?'

'We went yesterday. My mother wept – and I have to confess, so did I. It's beautiful. I can hardly wait for Elliot to see it. Actually, the worst is going to be my dad, because he'll probably cry too when he sees me. Just thank God he's so mad about Elliot, or he might not let me go.' She glanced impishly up at Elliot as he passed her a glass of champagne.

'What was that?' he said.

'OK, I'm going to leave you two lovebirds alone to go and do my hostessing bit,' Rachel told them. 'Let's have lunch next week, Laurie, if you've got time.'

As Rachel slipped into the crowd Elliot put an arm round Laurie's shoulders. 'How long before you think we can go?' he murmured.

She looked at him in surprise. 'Bored?' she said.

'A bit. Actually, I don't feel too good. I've had a blinding headache all day, and it's starting to come back.'

She frowned. It wasn't like him to be ill, even if it was just a headache. 'I'd say another half an hour should do it,' she responded. 'Can you last that long?'

'I think so.' He looked across the room, and

78

keeping an arm around her, he steered her towards George Herbert from *The Times*. 'I suppose we need to be sociable,' he murmured, 'though frankly, I just want to get you back into bed.'

It was strange, Laurie thought, when finally they were in the car heading home, how nothing had happened during the last half an hour to make her mood change, at least nothing she could put her finger on, yet she was aware of feeling edgy and uncertain again. She glanced over at Elliot. His mind seemed to be elsewhere, though his hand was on hers, and sensing her looking he gave it a squeeze. She cast her thoughts back over the evening, wondering if it was their second encounter with Andraya that had unsettled her, but if anything she'd actually warmed to the woman as she'd confessed to feeling nervous about the upcoming show, and had managed to sound genuinely pleased when Laurie had suggested she join her and Rachel for lunch in the week.

'I'll tell you my secret,' Andraya had whispered, easing Laurie aside. 'I am very intimidated by the English. You are all so proper, so superior. Never do I find it easy to make friends when I come here. I show my breasts, because the men, they like it, and because it help to sell my art, and they are beautiful part of me. I know that, and I am not ashamed of them, but I know this shocks you.' She smiled right into Laurie's eyes. 'Thank you for not letting it stop you to be my friend.' Which just went to show that even someone as beautiful and successful as Andraya wasn't without their insecurities, so maybe they were a normal, even necessary part of the human psyche.

Her thoughts moved on to Daya. She'd give almost anything to know where the girl was now. The sick feeling of being to blame if something terrible had happened to her began twisting its way inside her again. She wondered if any of the people they'd just left behind at the party had any idea what it was like to be displaced and dehumanized, the way Daya, and millions like her, were being displaced and dehumanized every day. And if they did, would they care?

In her mind's eye she pictured Daya and Andraya – two stunningly beautiful women, even similar-sounding names, yet how different their worlds. And how appalling, she thought, to be charging a quarter of a million pounds or more for a painting which was no damned use to anyone, except to fill up a space on a rich man's wall. What a difference a sum like that would make to the life of someone such as Daya.

She considered mentioning her thoughts to Elliot, but he seemed so engrossed in his own world that he probably wouldn't welcome the intrusion. She wished that didn't annoy her, but it did, because it made her feel shut out again, and she resented it. Worse was not knowing how to handle it, because this never used to happen between them. They could go for hours without speaking, and still feel as close as ever, but it didn't seem to be like that any more.

As he pulled the car to a stop in the underground garage she turned in her seat to look at him. 'How's your headache?' she asked.

'Much better, thanks.' To her surprise he reached over and drew her into his arms.

'I love you,' she told him, looking up into his eyes.

For a while he just continued to look at her, searching her face almost as though imprinting it on his mind. Then, kissing her again, he said, 'I love you too.'

Chapter Five

The big problem with dreams, Sherry always found, was how wretched they could make you feel in the morning, even the good ones. Actually, especially the good ones, because realizing that it was something illusory that just popped in to show you how fantastic it could all be if only you had your way, then vanished again like some half-baked genie – all promise and no delivery – was about as welcome as being woken up by twenty volts. However, this morning, lying there in the first rosy glow of a rather lovely sunrise, she was still enjoying the after-effects of the night's adventure, even daring to believe that at least a part of it might actually transform itself into reality. And who could say, maybe it would. Dreams could be premonitions, everyone knew that, so why not believe?

A cloud drifted across the morning sun, turning her bedroom a pinkish grey. She shifted restlessly. Ominous signs were definitely not in the plan right now, so rolling on to her side she went back to the soothing promise of her dream. Actually, now she came to think of it, it wasn't quite as perfect as she'd thought, and the part where her father had shown up in a growbag – *a growbag* – was weird indeed. But that was only to be expected from an encounter with the unconscious. It was what her father had said, from inside his growbag, that really mattered.

'You see, you believed, you trusted and it's all happening now in just the way you wanted.'

Certainly Nick coming back into her life, which was what had happened in the dream, would qualify for her dad's cheesy prediction, as would Nick's surprise to discover just how much he still loved her. In fact, she could – and would – run that part over several more times before moving on, because what came next, or at least after the most amazing orgasm that she could swear had really happened, was a tad disturbing. Not that she put any great store by the way faces changed in a dream, because they generally did, and it wasn't as if Elliot's had replaced Nick's before the big moment, because it hadn't, it was just starting to feel, in the cold light of day, as though she'd somehow betrayed Laurie, which was absolutely the last thing she wanted to do. OK, it was true, she found Elliot attractive, what woman in her right mind wouldn't? He was everything she could ever want in a man, or he would be if Nick van Zant didn't exist. But then there was the little problem of neither man being free, so it just went to prove what a sad person she was, that she built her dreams around total futility. Show her something she couldn't have and she'd fixate to the exclusion of all else. And in case she should ever be in any doubt of that, she only had to count up the years she'd nurtured this almost laughable yearning for Nick to remind herself just what a no-hoper she was.

So much for bloody dreams, she thought, flinging back the duvet and getting out of bed. Hearing the phone on her desk, she decided to ignore it and went to answer the front door instead.

'What the heck are you doing up at this ungodly hour?' she demanded, as a bleary-eyed Rhona, still in her dressing gown, stumbled her way in.

'I'm out of coffee, and I'm meeting an author at nine to take him on tour. Oh God, why do I do it?'

'You mean work? Or drink?'

'Can we put some toast on? I'm starving. Ah, coffee,' she gasped, almost falling on to the pot.

'It's cold,' Sherry warned her, taking a loaf from the fridge. 'But we can soon make fresh.'

Rhona was in no mood to wait. She was already filling a mug and popping it into the microwave. 'So where's the tour?' Sherry asked.

'Manchester, Leeds, Edinburgh, Dublin. All madly exotic. However, I talked to Amon last night, and he's got some spare time coming up, so we might take off to Granny's villa for a couple of weeks. Do you know, we haven't had a holiday for at least three months?'

Sherry was aghast. 'I can't imagine how you've managed to survive,' she cried.

'Me neither,' Rhona said, seriously, watching the seconds counting down.

Popping the bread in the toaster, Sherry said, 'I take it you mean the villa on Hydra?'

'The very same. Granny's going to be in Rome visiting her sister, Great-Aunt Kristina, so there's no chance of her turning up. She adores Amon, of course, but we hardly want her hanging around when she's such an embarrassing flirt. She had a boob job, by the way, did I tell you?'

'Your grandmother had a boob job!'

'I know, hideous, isn't it, but Mummy assures me they look quite good. I'll take her word for it and pray the old trollop doesn't insist on flashing them the next time I see her. Have you spoken to Laurie, by the way?'

'Not this morning. Why, has something happened?'

'I don't think so, unless we count you helping out with this story, saint that you are. She's invited me to join you all for lunch with this Andraya creature by the way. I won't be around, sadly, because the woman sounds a delight. In love with her own tits as well as her art.'

'A recipe for blinding success, if you ask me,' Sherry commented. 'Are you going to be around next week for the show?'

'I don't think so. I should be in Greece by then.'

Sherry was looking at the time. 'I've got an appointment with Laurie's contact at eight thirty,' she said, 'so I should start getting dressed. The toast'll be ready any second, help yourself to more coffee, and if you're gone by the time I come out again, don't worry, I'll keep everything watered while you're away. And don't forget to call now and again – my thrills might be vicarious, but they're the only ones I get.'

An hour later Sherry was hurrying up the steps

of Aldgate East tube station rapidly pressing Laurie's number into her phone. She still had a few minutes to spare before the action-group guy turned up, so please God let Laurie be at home.

'Sherry, hi!' Elliot said, sounding genuinely pleased to hear her.

'Hi yourself. How are you? I had a dream about you last night.'

'How was I?'

'Sizzling, but don't let it go to your head. Now, is Laurie there? I need to speak to her, pronto.'

'You've missed her, I'm afraid. She's gone to pick her mother up from the station and her mobile's right here in front of me. Anything I can help with?'

'Not unless you know the name of the guy I'm supposed to be meeting. It's the one who's been working with her on this story about the Indian women. It's gone clean out of my head, and I can't find it in my notes.'

'It's Barry Davidson,' he told her. 'You'll like him. He's a good cockney lad.'

Shouting over the wail of a police siren as it sped past, she thanked him and had just rung off when a slender man with a mere shadow of hair on his scalp and a neat gold ring in one ear came loping up the steps behind her.

'Sherry?' he said, holding out a hand to shake.

'You must be Barry. Good to meet you.'

'Laurie not turned up yet?'

'She can't make it, so I'm afraid it's just us.'

'That's cool. She's told me all about you. Welcome on board. The house we want isn't far. Can't guarantee anyone'll be in, there hasn't been the last two times I tried, but it's definitely the address Karima Ghosh gave Laurie for Daya.'

'Is the doctor expecting us too?' she asked, as they started along Whitechapel Road with its iron-grilled shopfronts, dilapidated, soot-blackened buildings and litter-strewn pavements.

'He is. Not for another half an hour though.'

'If it's OK with you, I'm going to ask him to go over everything again, as though I know nothing,' she said. 'That way I should get a clearer picture.'

'No problem. He's a decent bloke. You'll like him.'

A double-decker bus roared past, drowning her next words. She waited for the noise to fade, then said again, 'Tell me more about the owner of the workshop, Eddie Cribbs.'

'First up,' he answered, 'it's not wise to mention his name too loud round here, you never know who's listening. He's a big noise, with big ears and more reach than BT. But to answer your question, he's a bit different to the crime bosses of old, in that he's into protection, gambling, prostitution and all the rest of it, but he's also, I have on good authority, heavily into computers and the Internet. Runs all kinds of porn sites, might even be into filming the stuff, I don't know. He has a right upscale suite of offices over in Canary Wharf that they call the control centre, which seems about right considering how many people he has working for him.'

'It's a lot?'

'You could say that, but like anyone in his position, he's got his core team. Or his board of directors, is what I think he calls them.'

'Any idea where he lives?'

'He's got a couple of places, but his wife and daughter are in a dirty great big mansion out in Epping Forest. The daughter goes to some fancy boarding school down in Kent. Here's where we turn,' he said, grabbing her elbow and tugging her round the corner into Brick Lane, where the local merchants were rolling up their shutters and opening up shop for the day.

Sherry smiled at one or two as she passed, and was pleased to be smiled back at, big, white-toothed grins and even an occasional traditional bow. 'Have you come across anything about Mr C. that puts him in line for people-smuggling?' she asked, as they turned another corner.

'Not specifically, but it's the in thing these days. Everyone wants a piece of the action, or everyone in his sort of world, and I can't imagine someone like him being left out in the cold.'

'What about the Turkish and Albanian gangs that are supposed to be controlling it in the UK?'

'Can't answer that. Maybe he's in bed with them, or maybe he pays them to stay off his patch. No doubt he'll have something worked out. Here we are, this is where Daya's supposed to live.'

Sherry stopped outside the red-brick terraced house with white lace curtains at the downstairs windows and peeling yellow paint on the front door. There was nothing at all to make it stand out from any others in the row, though she noted immediately the inconsistency with Karima Ghosh's story – there were no front steps to this one, or any of the others, that Daya could possibly have fallen down. In fact the houses opened right on to the pavement. A stupid mistake, but a fortunate one for them.

As Barry knocked she looked along the street to where a woman in traditional Moslem garb was loading boxes into the back of a car, and an elderly Asian man in a pristine white kurta and embroidered cap was hobbling along on a stick and the arm of an obliging young woman. Her mind was just drifting back to last night's dream when Barry said, 'Bloody hell, someone's there.'

Sherry turned and watched as the door creaked slowly open. A portly, middle-aged Indian woman, who barely reached Barry's waist, appeared from the darkness. 'Yes?' she said, looking both cross and alarmed.

'We're looking for Daya,' Barry stated. 'We were told she lives here.'

The woman's eyes narrowed suspiciously. 'Who told you?' she demanded.

'Her boss, at the workshop. Mrs Ghosh.'

The woman's eyes moved to Sherry. 'Is Daya here?' Sherry asked, stepping forward.

'No. Her father take her back to India. She have arranged marriage. A nice boy. Good family. She's not here any more.'

Well isn't that convenient, Sherry was thinking. 'But she did live here?' she said.

'Yes. She lived here.'

'We wanted to make sure she was all right,' Sherry explained. 'We were concerned, after she went to see the doctor.'

'She fine. She good now. I tell her you come,' and stepping back into the shadows she closed the door.

Sherry turned to Barry, eyebrows raised. 'Well,

I wonder how much she was paid to say that?'
she mused.

'A couple of hundred would probably have
done it,' he responded. 'She didn't even ask who
we were.'

'No. She was determined not to let us in either.
Do you think she's hiding something in there?'

'I doubt it. She probably just wanted to get rid
of us, before she said something she shouldn't.'

When they reached the end of the street Sherry
took out her mobile to update Laurie on what had
happened. Getting the voicemail she left a
message, while swerving to avoid a couple of boys
zooming by on their bikes.

They were early arriving at Dr Patel's surgery,
which was on the first floor over a newsagent-
cum-grocer's shop, and behind a scratched,
panelled door that provided a barrier between the
evocative aroma of Indian spices drifting around
the stairwell, and the unmistakable smell of disin-
fectant. The reception area was small and stuffy,
with an assortment of old-fashioned toys stored
in one corner, and a few women's magazines piled
on a table.

'This way,' a querulous-looking receptionist told
them, holding a door open. 'The doctor's free, so
he can see you now.'

As they walked in Dr Patel was already getting
to his feet. He was a small man with a neat mous-
tache and weary brown eyes that despite their
troubles managed to exude a comforting amount of
warmth. 'I am pleased to meet you,' he told Sherry,
shaking her hand. 'Please, come and sit down.'

Sherry sat in the chair he indicated, while Barry

pulled another alongside. 'You can ask the doc what you like,' he informed her. 'He's OK with answering.'

Sherry's blue eyes followed the doctor as he returned to his own chair. Why was she suddenly thinking about Elliot and Nick, she wondered. Where was her focus? The dream was over. How did she want to begin this?

'Has there been any more news on Daya?' she asked.

The doctor shook his head solemnly. 'I am very worried what might have happened to her,' he confessed. 'As I told Barry here, there's a chance she could be on her way back to where she came from, which is probably the best we can hope for.'

Barry told him what had just happened at the address they'd been sent to.

The doctor absorbed it, but his only comment was, 'Let us pray that is true.'

'If she has a daughter, she could already be married, which would make a nonsense of what we've been told,' Sherry said.

The doctor nodded agreement. 'But we have no way of knowing the truth,' he said.

Sherry opened her notepad. 'If she is on her way back to where she came from . . .' She looked up. 'Do you know where that is, exactly?'

'She is from Gujarat. Her language is a form of Gujarati. There are many Harijans there.'

'Harijans?'

'It is one of the lower-caste people. They used to be called the Untouchables. I'm afraid, if she disappeared, here, or in Gujarat, there are not many who would miss her.'

91

Untouchables, for God's sake, Sherry was thinking. How could any human being in the world be untouchable? 'Have you ever treated anyone else for the same kind of injuries?' she asked. 'I mean from that workshop?'

He shook his head. 'It is the only time anyone has come here from that workshop.'

Sherry was about to ask another question when he said, 'Before we continue, I think I should tell you that I have had a visit from someone who didn't give his name, but he told me if the police came asking questions about Daya I was to contact him immediately. He left an envelope. Inside was two thousand pounds and a telephone number.'

Sherry's eyebrows went up. 'Subtle,' she commented. 'What did you do with it?'

'It is here, in my desk.' He reached into a drawer and slid the envelope across.

Sherry opened it, leafed through the twenty-pound notes, then made a note of the phone number. To Barry she said, 'Has anyone told the police?'

'Not that I know of,' he answered.

She turned back to the doctor. 'What about the little girl?' she asked. 'Daya's daughter? Laurie said she mentioned her just before she had to leave. Did you manage to find out any more, such as whether the child's here or still in India?'

'I'm afraid I did not get the chance. I believe her sister is here though.'

'Younger or older?'

'I don't know.'

'Well, what we do know,' Sherry said, 'is if Daya

92

is only twenty, her daughter must be very young.'

He nodded agreement.

'OK,' she said, getting ready to take notes again, 'I've read Laurie's notes, and we've discussed it quite a bit, but if you don't mind I'd like to go over it all from the beginning, starting with when Mrs Ghosh brought Daya in here, the first time.'

As he talked she wrote quickly, listening out for anything Laurie hadn't already told her, but on the whole the accounts were the same, with the exception of the fact that Daya was due to come back to have her stitches removed on Thursday of next week.

'It'll be interesting to see if that happens,' she commented, looking up.

'I doubt it,' the doctor replied. 'But if it does, I'll be sure to let you know.'

'Thank you,' she said. 'And what about your mystery visitor who wants to know if the police come calling? Are you going to tell him you've spoken to us today?'

'No-one has made that request, so I will keep it to myself,' he replied, standing up as Sherry and Barry got to their feet.

After saying their goodbyes Sherry led the way back down to the street, where she waited for Barry to fall in beside her. 'So it seems they've been in touch with the doctor, and with you, but not with Laurie yet,' she said. 'Why do you suppose that is?'

'Messing with the press,' he replied, 'it'd be like waving a red rag. No, it's us what'll get leaned on, to stop us giving you any co-operation. But don't let it go to your head, because if they need to get heavy with Laurie, or you, take it from me, they will.'

Laurie was on the phone to Rachel, talking about Andraya, when Sherry walked in with Barry. The office was considerably calmer than usual, with everyone else being away in India, so there was plenty of room to sit, and even a half-full pot of coffee on the machine.

'It's fine by me if she can't make lunch today,' Laurie was saying as she waved Sherry and Barry in.

'But can you do it tomorrow?' Rachel asked. 'She really wants to meet you again.'

'Why? I thought she didn't like women?'

'It seems she's taken to you.'

Laurie screwed up her nose. She could think of others she'd rather impress, but it was flattering, she supposed. 'Make sure she knows I don't have any money,' she warned. 'Or not enough to reach her prices. Anyway, who's the private showing for, that she's had to cancel out on us?'

'No idea, Chris didn't say.'

'Tell him to make a note of what she wears. I'll be dying to hear. Sherry's just walked in, I think we can put her down for a couple of the big ones. What are they, a million and a half apiece?'

'Not quite. Tell her her invitation to the show is in the post, and thanks for reminding me. Don't tell her I forgot.'

'Sure. I'll ask her if she'll do a piece on the show. She's still got her contact at *Vogue*, haven't you, Sherry?'

Sherry nodded, giving no indication of guessing what was really going on.

'Yes, I'm sure she'd love to join us tomorrow,' Laurie added, 'if she's free. Lunch tomorrow?' she said to Sherry.

Sherry shrugged. 'Why not?'

'All right, I have to go,' Laurie said to Rachel. 'Let's talk in the morning to decide where to meet.' As she rang off she turned to prop her feet on an open drawer and picked up her cup. 'OK, I got your message about the arranged marriage,' she said, as Sherry handed Barry a coffee then sat down with her own. 'You'd have thought they could come up with something a bit more original, wouldn't you? Anyway, what did you think of the doctor?'

'I think he's honest, trustworthy,' Sherry answered. 'He didn't tell me much that I hadn't already heard from you, but I'm glad I met him.' She glanced at Barry. 'I think we're probably all agreed,' she said, 'that there's some kind of clandestine workplace where our friend Mr Cribbs is housing – or I should say, exploiting – a group of illegal immigrants.'

'And given the nature of Daya's injuries,' Laurie responded, 'we're in no doubt of how he's exploiting them.' To Barry, she said, 'Has Sherry told you she's offered to go and meet Mrs Ghosh, as a buyer? She's just going to take a look around, get a feel for the place, and the woman. Do you know someone with a boutique, or a market stall, who can lend her some cover?'

'Probably,' he answered. 'I'll make some enquiries.'

'You know, I saw a documentary about this sort of thing once,' Sherry said, appearing slightly strained. 'Illegal immigration, forced prostitution . . . What's done to those women is so horrendous . . . We saw that with Daya, so what I'm saying is, in some cases they're not used as regular prostitutes, they're given to the perverts, the really sick bastards who should be locked up and never let near a woman.'

'And there could be a child involved here,' Laurie said quietly, hating every thought in her mind now.

'Maybe even more than one,' Barry added.

'I really think we should get the police involved,' Sherry said.

'I agree,' Laurie responded.

'I'll go over there myself, when we've finished here,' Barry said. 'But we have to remember, all we've got at the moment is an Indian girl's mysterious disappearance – and we're not even sure about that, since we didn't even know where she was in the first place . . .'

'The doctor treated her injuries,' Sherry reminded him.

'They've got an explanation for how she got them, and while she's not here, who's going to question it? Who even cares? I mean, really.'

Sherry looked at Laurie. 'We do,' Sherry answered, 'and I for one am totally committed to finding these women.'

'Me too,' Laurie agreed.

They looked at Barry. 'You know this territory far better than either of us,' Laurie said. 'Can we count you in?'

'I wouldn't be here if you couldn't,' he replied. 'I was just giving you the lowdown on how the Old Bill's likely to view it.'

'Sadly, you're probably right,' Laurie sighed, 'but try talking to them anyway. And as for the three of us, we should start by agreeing that no matter what aspect of this any of us is working on, at any time, we must remember always to keep the others informed.'

Sherry and Barry both nodded.

'Can I use this computer?' Sherry said, swivelling round to the one in front of her.

Laurie waved her on. 'Do you think you can find out the registration number of Eddie Cribbs's car?' she asked Barry. 'There's a private detective Elliot sometimes uses who we can put on his tail.'

'I'll get on to it,' he said. 'But you won't ever catch the bloke within a mile of those women, take my word for it.'

'I don't disbelieve you, but it could lead to something, so it's worth a try.'

After he'd made a note for himself, Barry glanced at Laurie. 'Leaping ahead,' he said, 'what if we find these women, what then?'

'A lot could happen between now and then to determine that,' Laurie answered. 'We just need to make sure we don't do anything to get them whisked out of the country, or worse, before anyone can get to them.' She turned to Sherry. 'What are you doing there?'

'Reading about Harijans,' Sherry answered, her eyes still glued to the screen. 'Hari means god, and jans means people, so I guess you could call them God's people. It was a name given to them by

Mahatma Gandhi, it says here. However, like the good doctor said, they're also known as Untouchables, because their occupations, such as cleaning toilets and carrying night soil, makes them so. They're deemed the lowest of the low. So what I'm thinking is, that Mr Cribbs, or someone representing him, could be taking advantage of the social chaos in Gujarat, which still has major problems after the massive earthquake a couple of years ago, and with all the Hindu-Moslem fighting that goes on in that state, plus the poverty, starvation, corruption . . . Frankly, if you're of the lower caste no-one's even going to notice if you disappear, never mind care.' She looked up. 'They're so poor they'd probably do anything for their next meal, and if someone's offering to give them a better life . . .' She shrugged. 'There are all kinds of scenarios here. He could be paying someone to kidnap them, or their families could even be selling them.'

Laurie was looking at Barry. 'You seem worried,' she told him.

'I am,' he confessed. 'The whole thing bothers me, and before we go any further I just want to be sure that you two really know what you're getting into here, because the kind of blokes we're talking about, the Eddie Cribbses of this world, and all the nasty little scum involved with him, they're not the types to piss around. It's not a game to them – or maybe it is, I don't know. What I'm saying is, they just won't put the same kind of value on your life as you do, and that's putting it mildly.'

'He's right,' Laurie said gravely, turning to

Sherry. 'This is showing all the signs of becoming extremely dangerous, so if you want to reconsider . . .'

Sherry was shaking her head. 'I understand what we're getting into,' she interrupted, 'and I'm with you all the way.'

Laurie's eyes moved back to Barry. 'You were right to spell it out like that,' she told him, 'because it's easy to get carried away and forget the reality. So none of us should ever take our safety for granted.'

'Or underestimate their potential for evil,' he added.

There was a solemn pause as they all digested that, then Sherry glanced at her watch.

'I'm afraid I have to abandon you now,' she said. 'One of my other aliases has a deadline to meet.'

Laurie opened her diary. 'All right. So let's keep in touch, all of us,' she said, 'and meet again on Friday, unless something comes up to make it sooner.'

Elliot's expression was unreadable as his eyes absorbed all the fantastic detail of the large, flamboyant canvases that formed the major works of Andraya Sorrantos's collection. For the purposes of this impromptu private showing, they were propped up against the whitewashed walls of Chris's secure warehouse in West London, and even amongst the ladders, torn packaging and wooden crates they had arrived in, they still managed to exude an exotic and even erotic power that was every bit as commanding as the artist herself.

He hadn't expected her to be here, and wished she wasn't, for it was extremely disconcerting to have her watch his every move, and wait, with an almost naked hunger, for his response. Since Chris had gone into the office, neither of them had spoken, though he was intensely aware of her presence, could feel it almost as though it were touching him, yet she was more than ten feet away, standing in the stark rays of sunlight pooling through the open delivery-dock door. By the standards of the other night she was modestly dressed, in a white tie-front shirt, and white jeans. There were no buttons to the shirt, it plunged straight to her navel; the jeans were so low they didn't come anywhere close. Her raven hair fell in thick, soft waves around her shoulders.

He could hear the muted sound of Chris's voice as he spoke on the phone. He thought he could also hear Andraya breathing, but maybe not. He moved on to the next painting. It was smaller than the rest, yet somehow more vibrant.

'I knew the other night that we would meet again,' she said finally, in her throaty accented voice. 'Did you not feel it too?'

He made no response, yet now she had voiced it, he realized that maybe he had felt it. It was hard to know, when he was standing here, almost drowning in the sheer sexual force of her.

Her smile was catlike as she began sauntering towards him, the golden flesh of her belly gleaming as if wet. 'Have you made your choice?' she said. 'Which painting would you like for your bride?'

'I think this one,' he replied, pointing to the one at his feet.

She stopped beside him. 'It's a good choice,' she responded, without looking. 'You must love her very much.'

He didn't reply. She was too close, but he didn't move away.

Her smile grew. 'She would never know,' she murmured.

He stared into her eyes, understanding exactly what she meant.

She laughed, and leaning forward touched her tongue to his lips.

For several seconds he did nothing, merely allowed her to kiss and lick him, until finally his hand circled her neck and he eased her away. 'I'll see you at the opening,' he told her, and turning to the door he walked out to his car.

After Sherry and Barry had gone Laurie spent the afternoon downloading as much information as she could find on the Scotland Yard website about organized crime in the East End, forced prostitution and human trafficking. Her research took her to dozens more websites, and by the time she was ready to leave she had to confess Barry's warning was feeling more ominous than ever. Not that she was deterred, but she was concerned enough to print some of it out to take home to show Elliot. He had a lot of valuable contacts in the East End whom she could probably take advantage of, and she wouldn't mind hearing what he had to say about the human-trafficking element of the case, because that was almost certainly where the nastiest characters were going to turn up.

After packing the printouts in her briefcase she

was just starting to lock up when Stan, the private detective she wanted to tail Eddie Cribbs, rang back.

'Don't want to discuss this geezer on the blower,' he told her, 'so we should meet.'

'Where? When?'

'Wednesday. Blind Beggar. Eight o'clock do you?'

'That's fine.'

As she rang off Laurie couldn't help wondering if there was any significance to the choice of venue, since it was the site of a famous Kray brother shooting back in the Sixties. Dismissing the thought, she called Elliot to let him know she was on her way. The machine was on, so guessing he was working, she left a message, continued to lock up then walked down to the pier to take the river bus home.

By the time she got off at Tower Bridge clouds had come in and a fine drizzle had started. She glanced up at the windows of their apartment, but there was no sign of any lights. It still wasn't quite dark enough though, and besides, Elliot's study was the other side of the building. Hurrying her pace she descended the steps on the south side of the bridge, turned left into the narrow cobbled street of Shad Thames where upmarket estate agents, vintners and restaurateurs had set up shop, then let herself into the discreet lobby of their luxury block.

'Hi! I'm back!' she shouted, opening the front door.

No reply.

'Elliot! Are you home?'

Still no reply.

Sighing, she closed the door and went to dump her briefcase and jacket on one of the sofas. 'Where are you?' she grumbled aloud as she began dialling his mobile. 'I thought you were going to be here.' She'd just made the connection when she spotted a note on the kitchen counter.

'You've reached Elliot Russell,' his recorded voice told her. 'Leave a message and I'll call you back.'

'It's me. Where are you?' she said, picking up the note.

As she clicked off she began to read. By the time she finished alarm was forming an unwelcome presence in her heart. *I won't be back tonight,* he'd written. *There's no need to worry. Everything's OK. I'll call you in the morning.*

Chapter Six

Neela's sari was soaked in sweat. Her hair clung to her skull like an inky black veil. She was deafened by the sound of the machines. Her fingers were sore; the fabric coarsened her skin and clogged her breathing. The smell burned her throat and made her want to choke. The frightened faces around her were kept lowered as busy hands worked, stitching, pressing, folding. Fraying black cloth covered the windows, lights hung like stalks from the ceilings, thick bare wires entwined with cobwebs, steel ducts and gurgling pipes. There was little air and the heavy work left no time for the daily *puja*. Their mattresses lay abandoned. A small other world of despair, lying alongside the one they were in now.

Neela fed the sleeves through. The needle punched up and down. The machine vibrated through her limbs. At her feet, hidden beneath the table, was Shaila. She was holding a woollen doll that one of the girls had brought back from doing the things Neela didn't want to think about. Shaila understood that she had to keep quiet, stay out of sight. She never moved from Neela's side, slept always in her bed now.

Neela moved her leg, using it like an arm to embrace her niece. She looked down at the little dark head and felt so much love and sadness she couldn't bear it. She wanted to grasp her, but instead she looked quickly away. Someone was coming.

The big iron door that led out to the stairwell creaked open, then clanged shut again. Neela kept her eyes down, didn't even look up as Rupa came to sit at the machine facing hers. No-one spoke. They just kept on working. Eventually Neela stole a glance at Rupa. Rupa's eyes were empty. They had done evil things to her, so her spirit had fled. Neela lived in terror of losing her spirit too.

Later, when the work was finished and they had returned to their beds, Ekta, who was old and kind, held Rupa's spindly body in her arms and rocked her as she sang. Neela held Shaila and listened to the words. Shaila had hardly spoken since her mother had gone. Neela had told her it was best not to talk. That way, she prayed, they would forget she was here.

When it was dark Mota Ben returned with two others, bringing pails of food. They left it inside the door and went away again. It was animal flesh. Mota Ben was cruel in her kindness of feeding them, because she knew they were forbidden to eat meat. But they were so hungry they forced the food down, dipping in with their hands and pushing it into their mouths. If it made them sick, and they couldn't work, Mota Ben would beat them.

Charu was the only one who liked to work, not with the machines, but with the men, so they had taken her away. Now they said she lived in a place where she could drink and eat all she wanted, and sleep on a bed that was soft. They said she danced for the men and made enough money to send home. They said Daya was with her, because Daya was a good girl who understood what the men wanted. Neela knew that wasn't true. Daya would never have left her and Shaila.

Shaila was the only child here now. When they'd first come there had been thirteen women and three children. Now Daya and Charu had gone, the other children had been taken away two days ago. They still hadn't come back. Neela listened as the mothers wept and begged, but Mota Ben wouldn't say where they were. Neela heard some of the women talking, saying things she didn't want to hear. She kept her hands over Shaila's ears and hummed louder and louder so that Shaila wouldn't hear either.

As they lay down to sleep Neela knew the wicked Bhanu was watching them, but she didn't look back. Earlier Bhanu had tried to push them from the food so she could have their share, but Ekta had told her to leave them alone. Bhanu didn't always listen to Ekta, but tonight she had.

The next day Mota Ben came to the workshop, lifted Neela's face and sneered in disgust. Neela's head dropped down. The mark was her curse and her salvation. A moment later terror stilled her heart. Mota Ben was stooping to look under the table. Shaila shrank back against Neela's legs. Mota Ben grabbed the girl and yanked her out. Neela

wrapped her arms round Shaila's little body. Mota
Ben slapped Neela's face. Neela held on tight. Mota
Ben slapped Shaila, slapped them both. Neela clung
even tighter. The other women continued to sew.
Machines pounding, irons hissing. No-one would
rescue them. No-one could. Bhanu watched. Ekta
prayed. Shaila's terror sank into Neela's skin.

An hour later dry sobs still whimpered from
Neela's throat. Her head was bent over the
machine, her fingers continued to shake. Shaila
was at her feet, her small body limp in exhaustion. Mota Ben had gone. Rupa's place was empty.
Today the gods had been kind to Neela and Shaila.
Tonight Neela would give Bhanu their food.

Laurie was sitting at one of the garden tables
outside Jamie's Wine Bar with Sherry, Rachel and
Andraya, looking as agitated as she felt. Just thank
God for the bright sun, so she could hide her red,
swollen eyes behind dark glasses, because nothing she'd tried before coming out could disguise
their devastation. In fact she almost hadn't come,
but the need to slam out of the flat and leave Elliot
wondering where the hell she might be now had
been too overwhelming.

'So what time did he come back this morning?'
Rachel was asking, as a waiter adjusted their
parasol.

'About ten. And to be frank, I almost wish he
hadn't. We had a terrible scene, I even hit him . . .'

'But where on earth did he go?' Rachel said.

'You try asking him,' Laurie snapped. 'Maybe
he'll tell you, because he sure as hell won't tell me.'

'So what did he say?' Sherry prompted.

'*Nothing!* He won't say where he went. "It doesn't matter," he says. "I'm back now, so let's just forget it."' Repeating those words made her want to scream, which she would have done were they not in a public place.

Andraya's feline eyes were watching her closely. 'Is there another woman?' she asked, picking up her wine glass.

Laurie flashed a look in her direction. Under any other circumstances she'd never have blurted out her troubles in front of a stranger, especially one whose shining beauty and indecently exposed cleavage was drawing so much attention, but she was still so wound up about Elliot failing to come home all night that she just hadn't been able to hold back.

'Of course there isn't,' Rachel answered for her. 'It's got nothing to do with that.'

'Then what is it to do with?' Laurie cried. 'You say he wasn't with Chris. No-one at his office knew where he was . . .'

'Can they be trusted to tell you? If they knew?' Andraya asked.

Though it was a perfectly reasonable question, Laurie wished she'd shut up and mind her own business. This had nothing to do with her, so why didn't she just flash her tits a bit more to satisfy the rubbernecks who were trying to get a better look, and let Laurie talk to Sherry and Rachel? 'I think they were telling the truth,' she answered, forcing herself to sound calm. 'They really didn't seem to know where he was.'

'I don't understand, how can he just not say where he went?' Sherry persisted.

108

'Well he's managed it. He didn't want to discuss it, and nothing I said was going to make him.'

Andraya's throaty voice exuded pity as she said, 'Then I think there can be no other explanation. There is another woman, so you must follow him, and if you find he is cheating . . .' Her smile turned malicious as she used her elegant hands to mime a castration.

Laurie glared at her in anger and despair. This woman knew nothing about Elliot, so she had no right even to offer an opinion, especially one that was so ludicrously soap opera and uninformed. There was nothing straightforward about Elliot, he didn't conform to generalities or typical male behaviour, which was largely why she loved him so much – and detested him too when she ran up against it like this.

'There's no-one else,' Rachel repeated firmly, obviously sensing the need to get Andraya off the subject.

Sherry said, 'Where is he now?'

'At home. Or he was when I left.'

'I'm sorry,' Andraya said, shaking her head. 'A man with a secret is a man not to be trusted. So I say either you follow him, or you let it go and forget it happened.'

Thankful for the waiter's interruption as he came to take their orders Laurie reined in her temper again, mumbled something about a salad, then gazed off past the other tables towards the river. No matter how irritated she might be by Andraya's advice, she knew, at least to some degree, that the woman had a point, because she certainly couldn't go on tearing herself apart like this. However, the very idea of having Elliot followed was absolute anathema. Surely to God their relationship had to be based on trust, or it just wasn't worth having. But the alternative, of letting go and carrying on as though nothing had happened, was hardly acceptable either.

Feeling herself getting worked up again, she took a large gulp of wine. She hated the direction her thoughts took then, but there was no holding them back. She was due to meet Stan Bright, the private detective, later. Was there some kind of synchronicity going on here, that Andraya's suggestion should come at a time when events were already lined up to make it happen? But no, she could never ask Stan to spy on Elliot. They knew each other too well. It would be wrong, and totally unfair of her to ask Stan to divide his loyalties like that.

When the waiter had gone she turned back to Andraya, feeling she had to say something. 'We're getting married in less than two months,' she reminded her. 'It's a hell of a time to start having issues with trust.'

'Which is why you must get them resolved,' Andraya told her gently. 'And maybe you should give him a taste of his own medicine; stay out for the night too, let him wonder where you are.'

Sherry's eyebrows went up. So did Rachel's.

'No! It's just games, and I'm not getting into it,' Laurie responded.

Sherry and Rachel nodded agreement.

'Now let's change the subject,' Laurie said. 'We don't want our whole lunch taken up with this.'

110

'But, Laurie, my dear friend,' Andraya said, refusing to be put off, 'love *is* a game, so if you want to win, you must learn the rules.'

Feeling it was time to step in Sherry said, 'I'm going to presume, Andraya, that you're someone who's an expert on these rules, and I've got no pride here, I readily admit I'm a disaster at the game. So please, start teaching.'

Rachel laughed. 'You're the one who's paid to give such advice,' she reminded her.

Sherry was incredulous. 'Look at this woman, then look at me,' she demanded. 'Whose advice would you want?'

Andraya's laughter rang with false modesty as she said, 'Believe me, it takes a long time and many mistakes to learn what is needed, but you can begin by understanding the power of surprise.'

'Yes?' Sherry prompted.

Andraya smiled.

'What kind of surprise?' Sherry persisted.

'Why, the kind only a woman can give a man, of course.'

'Of course,' Sherry agreed. Her eyes flicked to Rachel. If Rachel knew, she wasn't letting on. Nor, it seemed, was Laurie, but at least she seemed to be enjoying the moment.

Andraya continued. 'You must also discover the way of making him feel as though he has captured the only woman in the world that every other man wants.'

Sherry's expression turned comical. 'Forgive me for saying,' she responded, 'but looking like you it wouldn't be hard to make a man feel as though he had something every other man wanted, because basically he would have. So I think we have to take another tack here. Maybe you can tell us about the most difficult man you ever found to seduce, and how you eventually managed it?'

Laurie stifled a laugh. Only Sherry could be this blunt and not cause offence.

Andraya's eyes were alive with humour.

Sherry waited – and waited. Then it dawned. 'Of course, you've never found it difficult, have you?' she said. 'Silly me.'

'Oh but I have,' Andraya assured her.

'Then how did you finally get him?'

'You're assuming I finally did.'

'If a man has ever resisted you, then I'm going to feel a lot better about myself,' Sherry told her frankly.

Both Rachel and Laurie burst out laughing.

'Have you ever been married?' Rachel asked her, topping up their wine.

'Twice,' Andraya answered. 'My first husband I loved very much. Very, very much.'

'So what happened?' Sherry wanted to know.

Andraya's golden eyes were mournful. 'I met the man who was to become my second husband,' she sighed, tragically.

Laurie choked on her drink.

'So what happened to the second?' Rachel said, patting Laurie's back.

'He died,' Andraya answered.

'Oh, I'm sorry,' Rachel said, instantly sobered.

'On stage, in a Rio nightclub,' Andraya added.

Everyone looked confused. 'You mean he was an actor whose show didn't go well?' Sherry said.

'No. I mean he was shot. He was on stage at

112

the time, singing with a friend of ours who is very good musician.'

To the others' relief their food arrived at that moment, for not one of them could think of a suitable response. They'd just got settled and ordered another bottle of wine when Sherry's mobile started to ring. Reading the incoming number she knew she should let it go through to the voice-mail, but something compelled her to take it.

'Aunt Jude, how are you?' she said, feeling as though a cloud had passed over the sun.

'I'm well, dear. How are you?'

'Great. I'm having lunch with some friends, next to the river. Is it a lovely day with you too?'

'Yes, it is. I just wanted to call to see how you are.'

Anxious about where this might go, Sherry excused herself and got up from the table. 'I'm fine, really,' she told her aunt, starting down to the river wall.

'I'm glad. I was a little worried after our last conversation.'

Of course, Sherry had known she would be, which was why she should have called back by now, but she'd been busy and she just wanted to forget the issues her aunt kept raising. It wasn't fair to be so selfish, though, so bracing herself, she forced the question her aunt wanted to hear. 'Has there been any more news?'

'I received a letter from Bluebell this morning . . .'

'I don't want it. Please don't send it.'

'It was for me, dear.'

'I don't want to know what it said.'

113

'Are you sure?'

'Positive.' She took a breath. This was hurting her aunt and she knew it, but nowhere near as much as it was hurting her. 'Look, if the suicide attempt failed,' she said, sounding both angry and conciliatory, 'and she still won't tell the truth, there's really nothing else to discuss, is there?'

'She did tell the truth, Sherry. At the time . . .'

'No! You don't know what happened, you weren't there.' It was as though her heart was trying to explode from her chest. The world around her had started to swim, as the confusion became too intense to contain. She couldn't deal with this now. She never could again. It was over. Her parents were dead. She would never see them again, so why couldn't it all go away?

'Sherry?'

Sherry stared blindly across the river to where the sun was glinting off the houses on the facing bank. It was as though she had been sucked into another world, where everything looked the same, but was in some strange, Dantean way entirely different.

'Why don't you come down for the weekend?' Aunt Jude said. 'We can talk. I'll show you the letter . . .'

'I can't. Not this weekend,' Sherry answered. She turned and looked back at her friends sitting round the table. Andraya was in Rhona's place, but it didn't matter. Rhona would be back, and Andraya was welcome. This was Sherry's life now, with the people she cared about and who cared about her. What Aunt Jude was trying to discuss had nothing to do with them, and nothing to do with her now either.

'I'll let you get back to your lunch,' Aunt Jude said, a note of resignation in her voice. 'You know where I am if you need me.'

As she rang off Sherry tilted her head down, counted to five, then brought it up with a smile.

'Andraya's about to tell us how the private showing went yesterday,' Rachel told her as she rejoined them.

Andraya's laugh was infectious. 'It is supposed to be a secret,' she reminded Rachel.

Rachel's smile dropped. Dear God, she hadn't realized it was Elliot they were talking about. 'Then maybe it should stay that way,' she said quickly.

'No, I think we can share with friends,' Andraya said, picking up her glass.

Rachel glared her a warning.

Andraya only smiled. 'Eduardo Olivieri is our secret buyer,' she announced. 'He has purchased already two of my best works to add to his private collection. He has also invited me to his home in Tuscany to help him decide where they should hang – once the show is over, of course.'

Rachel breathed again.

'I find Señor Olivieri to be a very wonderful man,' Andraya continued. 'He has the most refined tastes, as most Italians do. We talked for many hours on subjects that interest us both. I believe we found much pleasure in each other. Yes, I think I will enjoy my time at his Tuscan home.'

Not wanting to be the one to ask if his refined Italian wife was going to be there too, Sherry listened to the rhapsody a while longer, then turning to Laurie she whispered, 'I'm meeting

115

someone with a fashion shop over in Spitalfields later. She's going to turn me into a buyer. Do you want to come?'

Realizing she was being offered a distraction from more turmoil over Elliot, Laurie smiled her gratitude. 'Thanks, but I should go home. Running away from this isn't going to get it sorted.'

'There'll be an explanation,' Sherry assured her.

'Of course, but will it be one I want to hear?'

Andraya suddenly said, 'Laurie, I want you to be my guest of honour at the show next week.'

Laurie blinked, then looked at Rachel.

'Yes. That is settled,' Andraya declared. 'Rachel, we must make certain not to forget. Laurie is to be my guest of honour.'

Laurie almost laughed, for Rachel's expression showed just how delighted she was with her new role of personal assistant. 'Does something special happen for guests of honour?' she wanted to know.

Andraya frowned. 'I am not sure,' she confessed, 'but we will think of something, no?'

'A free painting,' Sherry suggested.

Andraya didn't seem averse. 'Maybe. As a wedding gift,' she said. 'We shall see,' and with her eyes still on Laurie, she picked up her glass and drank.

Stan Bright, the burly, broken-nosed private detective, was already waiting when Laurie joined him at the Blind Beggar that night. To her surprise, just setting eyes on him caused a surge of affection to rise up in her, for knowing this big, gruff ruffian of a man was in the world somehow made it seem a safer place.

'I got you a white wine, is that all right?' he said in his gravelly cockney voice as she sat down.

'Perfect,' she assured him. 'So how are you?'

'I'm all right. Elliot not with you?'

She shook her head and sipped her wine. 'He'll be here in about half an hour, to pick me up,' she answered, already feeling nervous about it, for she hadn't seen him since she'd stormed out before lunch. They'd merely spoken on the phone, when he'd called to let her know he'd be at his office if she needed him, otherwise he'd see her later, as arranged.

Stan put his pint down, and folded his big arms across his chest. 'So how you been keeping, girl? I hear you's getting married.'

She nodded and smiled.

'Got yourself a good bloke in Elliot,' he told her. 'One of the best.'

'That's what he says about you.'

He grinned, showing his East End dentistry, which consisted of several more gaps than teeth.

'So how's business?' she said.

'*Comme ci, comme ça,*' he replied in a terrible French accent. 'What about you? What's all this about Eddie Cribbs?'

'Do you know him?' she asked.

'Not personally. Know a bit about him though. Got to take some of it with a pinch of salt, but whichever way you angle that bloke, ain't no way he's ever going to be up for no sainthood.'

'Tell me more.'

As he mulled it over, he downed half his pint, then wiped the back of one huge hand across his mouth. 'It's all different now,' he said. 'Computers

117

is what changed it. And drugs.' He sniffed. 'Weren't like it in my day. Bit of Mary-Jane, or LSD, never did no-one much harm, but the stuff they got going round now . . .' He shook his head. 'They say Cribbs is into it all. Smack. Crack. Jacks no-one never heard of before.' His sunken eyes suddenly narrowed. 'I hope that's not what this is about. You want to pull him for drugs, then you might just as well go down the Co-op and pick out your coffin now.'

'No, it's not about drugs,' she responded. 'It's about illegal immigrants.'

He jutted his bottom lip out as he thought. 'Got some boobies working for him, has he?' he said. 'Can't say I'm surprised.'

'We think they're probably all women, and he's using them for prostitution.'

He nodded. 'Suits his MO.'

'He could even be involved in the actual trafficking,' she said carefully. 'We don't know for sure.'

Immediately his face darkened. 'Now that's an area you definitely don't want to get into,' he warned.

'We want to find these women,' she said. 'The traffickers we'll leave to the police.'

'Might not be as easy as that.'

'I know, but we still want to find them. We think he's got them holed up somewhere, maybe in a hidden workshop, some derelict council block or warehouse . . . They could be anywhere, but they're definitely here, in the East End.'

'And that's where I come in? You want me to see what I can find out?'

She nodded. 'So far, all we know is that a young Indian girl was taken to a doctor to have some internal injuries treated, and the address given was Cribbs's workshop on New Road. We've spoken to a couple of the workers there and no-one knows anything about her.'

He sniffed and drank more beer.

'We're afraid she might be dead,' she added.

'What makes you say that?'

She explained about the call Barry had received after her brief meeting with Daya, when he'd been told no-one would ever see Daya again.

'Mm,' Stan grunted. 'Don't sound too clever, do it?'

'He's almost certainly using them for prostitution.'

He grimaced and scratched his jaw. 'Geezer's got strip clubs full of pros what know their stuff,' he said, 'so why would he be needing a bunch of boobies who know nothing? Probably can't even speak the lingo.'

'If they're illegal, he can use them for anything,' she pointed out. 'I mean, *anything*.' She paused to let it sink in. 'It's possible he's got children there too,' she added.

Disgust immediately registered in his watery eyes. 'Gives me the right hump, that sort of thing,' he grumbled. 'If I found out it was true, I'd kill the bastard meself.'

She took out her notebook. 'Here's the registration number of his Jag,' she said, tearing out a page. 'It's dark blue, apparently. I know he's probably got more than one car, but it's a start.'

'What am I supposed to do with that?' he said, confused.

'Follow him?'

He chuckled. 'Following the likes of Eddie Cribbs round in his Jag ain't going to get you nowhere but Harrods Food Hall or Royal Ascot on Ladies Day,' he told her. 'He has people working for him who handle all the dirty stuff. Take it from me, if he does have a bunch of women holed up somewhere, you won't catch him anywhere near it. The only place you'll find him is in his fancy offices over there in Canary Wharf, twiddling about with his computers and running the world.'

'So what do we do?'

'You leave it to me, that's what you do. And make bloody sure he don't get wind of what you're up to, cos whether or not any of this is true, he's not going to be a happy bunny having his business poked into.' He nodded towards the door. 'Here's the bridegroom just come in.'

Laurie's heart turned over as she looked round to see Elliot winding his way through the bar towards them. It had been a long time since she'd reacted that way to seeing him, and she could only wish it wasn't happening now.

When he reached their table he made to kiss her on the mouth, but she turned her cheek. Maybe he could carry on as though he hadn't vanished for an entire night without explanation, but she couldn't.

'Stan,' he said, shaking the big man's hand. 'Gorgeous as ever, I see.'

'I do me best. How are you, son? Back from the dead, I hear.'

Elliot grinned. 'That was a while ago.'

'Well, it's been a while since I saw you. What you having?'

'I'll get . . .'

'My shout. What you having?'

'Half of bitter.'

As Stan went off to the bar Elliot pulled up another chair and sat down next to Laurie. 'So, is he on board?' he asked.

'I think so.'

'Good. It'd be tough to pull off something like this without him.'

She nodded and drank the last of her drink. 'So how were things at the office?' she asked, trying not to sound uptight.

'Pretty normal. Murray thinks the headaches I've been getting are due to pre-wedding nerves.'

The idea seemed so preposterous for someone like him that she couldn't help but laugh. Just as funny was the image of Murray, his office manager, fussing around like an old hen. 'Did he have any suggestions how to deal with them?' she asked.

'He said I should be kind to myself.'

Despite herself, she laughed again. 'So how are you getting on, being kind to yourself?'

His eyebrows went up. 'I don't quite have the hang of it yet, I was hoping you could help.'

Immediately her humour vanished. 'If this is your way of trying to make me forget about last night, it's not going to work,' she snapped.

They didn't speak again, merely sat in awkward silence until Stan returned with the drinks, when they carried on talking about Cribbs and the illegal immigrants. Fortunately she managed to remain professional enough, in front of Stan, to listen to Elliot's input and was even

121

able to speak to him civilly, until finally it came time to leave.

'You only have to tell me where you were,' she said tightly, as he drove them back along Whitechapel Road. 'I don't see what the problem is, unless you've got something to hide.'

'I told you. I needed some time to think.'

'About what? I mean, if you're having second thoughts . . .'

Sighing, he indicated to go left, then turned on to the Tower Bridge Approach.

'I might find it a bit easier if you'd tell me where you actually spent the night,' she said, through her teeth.

'OK. I was at the Chelsea Hotel.'

She turned to him, amazed that he'd actually answered, when earlier he'd refused to. 'Who with?' she suddenly demanded.

There was a moment's silence as shock registered with them both, for though she'd never actually suspected him of being unfaithful, and wasn't even sure she did now, the question had come blurting out from somewhere, and to her horror, it was being met with silence.

She waited, so fragile and so still she might shatter into pieces. *Oh my God*, she was thinking. This couldn't be true. It couldn't be happening.

'I was alone,' he said finally.

Relief almost made her choke, but it was short-lived, for now the suspicion had taken root . . . 'Then who did you meet there?' she said tartly.

'No-one.'

'Why should I believe you? How do I know you were even there?'

'Call the hotel. The reservation was in my name.'

'Which means nothing. You could have done that to throw me off the scent and stayed somewhere else entirely.' She wasn't sure why she was doing this, but the words just kept coming.

'I could, but I didn't,' he said.

'*Are* you seeing someone else?' she demanded, her eyes bright with fear, her voice sounding shrill.

His tone was incredulous. 'Of course not. For God's sake, Laurie, do you seriously think I'd do that to you?'

'I don't know. I never imagined you'd disappear for a night then refuse to tell me where you were.'

'I've just told you.'

'But not *why* you were there.'

He took a breath, let it out slowly, then pressed the remote to open the underground parking.

'I'm sorry, but if you don't tell me what's really going on, I'm calling off the wedding,' she said rashly. The words echoed in their own horror. She immediately wanted to take them back, but it was too late now.

After pulling into his parking spot, he switched off the engine and turned to face her. 'I swear to you, nothing is going on. There's no other woman, I just needed some space for a while, so I took it.' She started to speak, but he continued. 'OK, I didn't handle it well, and I'm probably not now either, but you know how bad I am at these things. It doesn't mean I don't love you, it just means that I needed some space.'

A part of her wanted to go on fighting, needing

to make him understand that it wasn't all right to disappear like that, but another part just wanted an end to it, a return to how they were before. 'Why didn't you just say that in the first place?' she said. 'Why keep it a secret, where you were?'

'I guess I don't really have a good answer for that,' he said. 'But I didn't mean to hurt you. I swear, that's the last thing I want to do.'

She gazed anxiously into his eyes, certain he was telling the truth, that he didn't want to hurt her, yet knowing too that he was still holding something back. She wished she knew what to say, how to get inside his head so that she could find out what it was, but even if she could did she really have the courage to hear it? She looked down to where her hands were bunched in her lap, and heard Andraya's words echoing in her mind: *'Have him followed . . . A man with a secret is not to be trusted.'*

Feeling his hand on the back of her neck she turned her face into his shoulder and started to cry.

'Sssh,' he whispered, stroking her hair. 'It'll be all right.'

'Will it?' she said, looking up at him.

He smiled and used a thumb to wipe away her tears. 'Of course,' he said, and kissed her on the mouth.

'I wish the wedding was over,' she said miserably. 'The stress is killing me.'

He laughed. 'Come on, I'm 'ank Marvin, me,' he said, mimicking Stan's accent and lingo. 'Let's pick up something from the Chop House, then maybe we can rehearse the honeymoon night.'

Chapter Seven

It had taken Sherry all of one minute to decide that Karima Ghosh was very possibly one of the most unpleasant characters she'd ever had the misfortune to meet. Even the most condescending editor, in a world full of condescending editors, couldn't match this pompous ice queen for sheer dislikability, and not many were cursed with such foul breath either. It was an abomination, particularly in a woman whose middle-aged face still bore the residue of an earlier beauty. Now her features were cramped in a mask of sourness and resentment, with a sharpness to them that was actually quite scary.

Twenty minutes or more had passed since she, as Tara Green, fashion buyer, had entered the four-storey building on New Road, and climbed the most putrid of stairwells, which appeared to be used for anything from dossing to shooting up, or even for letting go of bodily waste, to this large, desolate workshop. It was on the first floor, over a rank of partly derelict, partly run-down shops, with dull concrete floors and walls, exposed over-head pipes netted by cobwebs, cracked, painted-over windows and a sad-looking workforce of six, all Asian and all male. It was a depressing place indeed, with no colour except in the boxes of cotton reels and bolts of fabric, though even they were dreary, and no sound apart from the staccato bursts of machines. No-one spoke or looked up from their work, not even when Karima Ghosh addressed them. After going through the many racks of clothing that were stacked up along one wall of the workshop, like carriages in a siding, Sherry and Karima Ghosh returned to the office to write up 'Tara Green's modest order. As she waited Sherry looked around at the steel-grey filing cabinets, the scratched wooden desk, the handwritten notes pinned to a board, the old-fashioned Rolodex, the shelves of directories and fabric swatches, wondering if in there somewhere she might find some evidence of a secret work-force, a hint of the existence she was here to prove. Since she could hardly rummage through with the dreaded Ghosh woman right there, she directed her gaze out of the office window to watch the men at their machines. She wondered what their lives were really like, working in this sweatshop, living in a country that wasn't their own, struggling to speak a language they barely knew. It couldn't be easy, though she didn't imagine for a minute that their boss, the woman sitting in front of her now, in her bright yellow sari and exotic red dot, could have cared less if she tried.

'There, you can authorize,' Karima Ghosh stated, turning the order pad round for Sherry to see.

Sherry looked it over. Half a dozen strapless dresses with matching bolero jackets and four evening tops with faux-fur trim. Hideous, but cheap enough not to make too big a dent in Laurie's budget.

'When can I expect delivery?' she asked, after signing the order.

'We don't have much work on at the moment,' Karima Ghosh informed her. 'It could be done in two weeks, if you're prepared to pay more.'

Sherry smiled sweetly. 'Let's keep the price the same, and do it in two weeks,' she said, handing over a freshly printed business card. 'I'm told Mr Cribbs's workshop has a reputation for fast turn-around, as well as quality and reliability.'

The mention of her boss added an even flintier edge to Karima's tone as she said, 'You were told correctly.' Then after a pause, 'May I ask who recommended us?'

Sherry wrinkled her nose. 'You know, I talked to so many people before I drew up my shortlist, I can't actually remember now. But I'm sure I can look it up, if it's important.'

Karima's eyes returned to the order book.

'I was hoping,' Sherry continued, 'to meet Mr Cribbs. I always like to know who I'm doing business with.'

Karima's head came up, her eyes gleaming like a cobra's. 'I am in charge of the workshop. All the business is done through me.'

Sherry cocked an eyebrow. 'I could be putting a lot more orders your way, if my plan to join with a national chain comes off. Do you think you could cope?'

'It would depend on the quantities, but these are not prosperous times for our industry, so we can always get the workers.'

'How many workshops do you have?' Sherry enquired.

'Just this one.'

'Oh? I thought Mr Cribbs had two or three.'

'You are mistaken. There is only this one.'

Sherry was still smiling benignly. 'OK. Well, I guess I should be going,' she said smoothly. 'Please mention to Mr Cribbs that I'd like to meet him,' and before the woman could respond she was heading back into the workshop.

As she passed through all the workers' heads stayed down, eyes fixed on the hems and seams they were pushing through the loudly thumping machines, but she knew they'd hear as she turned round and called back to Karima, 'Are there no women working here?'

The reply took a moment to come. 'No. This is all the staff we have at the moment.'

'Pity,' Sherry responded. 'I'm looking for a girl to do alterations at the shop. If you hear of anyone . . .'

Karima was coming towards her. 'Here is a copy of your order,' she said, handing her a pink sheet.

Sherry took it, wanting to kick herself for such a stupid oversight. She was about to thank her when her mobile rang. To her surprise, the readout told her it was Elliot. She'd call back once she got outside. Shaking Karima Ghosh's hand, she said, 'Thank you, it was a pleasure.'

As she left Karima Ghosh's eyes stayed with her, watching until the door swung closed behind her, then, scowling at a worker who was re-threading his machine, she went over to the window to look down into the street. A moment later Sherry emerged from the building, took out her mobile and started to dial. Not until she had turned the corner on to the main road did Karima Ghosh return to her desk and pick up her own phone.

'Hello,' she said to the voice that answered. 'It is Mrs Ghosh. Please inform Mr Cribbs that I would like to see him.'

'Is there a problem?'

'I am not sure.'

'Hi, Elliot? Did you call me?' Sherry was saying into her phone.

'Yes. Where are you?'

'I'm . . .' She drew back and grimaced at a cloud of fumes blown out by a bus. 'I'm on Whitechapel Road,' she answered, after the roar died down. 'Sorry about the noise. Is everything all right?'

'Everything's fine. I just thought . . . Well, I'm not sure you'll want to know this . . . Laurie said you probably would, but . . .'

'Know what?' she cut in, with a tremor of unease. 'What's happened?'

'Well, after the other night, when we were talking . . . well, I ran into Nick van Zant earlier. At Davey's.'

Sherry stopped walking. She knew she'd heard right, knew too that she should respond, but for the moment she didn't know how to. Nick was in London. Here, in this city, this very minute, and he'd spoken to Elliot. A rush of emotion made her feel dizzy but she quickly suppressed it. She needed to remind herself that this was only a co-incidence. He hadn't come looking for her, so giving rein to any amount of elation could easily prove embarrassingly premature. 'Did you . . . ? Did he . . . ?' She wasn't sure what she was trying to say. 'How is he?' she finally managed.

'He seems fine. He said to say hi.'

Her name had been mentioned. What had they said? The possibilities made her heart start to thud, for Nick being here, knowing all he did . . , 'Is that all? Didn't he say anything else?' she asked.

'Plenty, but not about you, I'm afraid. There were other people around.'

It was the answer she wanted. 'I'm about to go into the Underground,' she told him. 'Thanks for letting me know.'

The train journey back to her flat didn't take long. When she got there, she closed the door behind her and went to stand in the middle of the room. Part of her wanted to whoop with joy, but she continued to remind herself that this was just a chance meeting, that she shouldn't start reading things into it that were only going to crush her later, for it was highly unlikely that anything in Nick's life had changed.

Putting a hand to her head, she took a breath and blew it out slowly. Then she started to laugh, softly, as though chiding herself for being foolish enough to think that he'd have blurted out anything about their past to someone he'd just run into. He was far too discreet, would never discuss it with anyone, she was sure, unless she'd already told them herself. But the events of that time, what had happened to her parents, and how Nick himself had come to meet Bluebell . . . She'd tried desperately to close herself off to all this since the day she and Nick had parted and she'd left Los Angeles, but that had been a heartbreaking time, while this . . . This wasn't, and still smiling, she let the past fade to where it belonged, and began to picture him at Davey's, meeting Elliot.

It was a pleasing image, for they were as tall as each other, with as commanding a presence, though while Elliot was dark, Nick was blond and had much finer features. It made her feel warm inside to recall how handsome he was with his liquid, laughing brown eyes, intense frown lines, and the hard, wide mouth that lit her up inside when he smiled. How had he felt, she wondered, when Elliot said he knew her? What had gone through his mind? It was impossible to know, but he surely must have felt something. Had he told Elliot how they'd met? Her heart twisted. No, of course he hadn't, because Elliot had already told her, they hadn't discussed her at all.

After opening the French windows to let in some air, she spent a few moments checking her plants, inhaling their scent and feeling the pleasure stealing all the way through her. Then she went to play back her messages, unable to stop herself thinking how wonderful it would be if his voice was amongst them. Of course, it wasn't; she'd moved from the last address he'd had for her a long time ago, and she couldn't imagine Elliot giving him her new one without permission. She wondered if he'd asked. If he had Elliot would surely have told her.

'"He said to say hi."' She could hear Nick

saying it, see him, even, his tousled head tilted to one side, his rich brown eyes showing his surprise at hearing her name. A moment's unease stole through her as she wondered how long he was here for. There was every chance he'd be gone again tomorrow. Her eyes closed at the prospect, for she knew already that it would feel as though he'd abandoned her again. Since the last time she'd done all she could to shut him out, refusing to torment herself by following his career, or even writing him letters she knew she'd never send. Even so, it hadn't stopped her imagining or hoping that one day . . .

As the minutes ticked by she allowed herself to think about him more deeply than she had in years. She wondered if he ever thought about her, and if he did what the thoughts were. Did he still have feelings for her, or had his died a long time ago? He'd never really spoken about his feelings, which had sometimes worried her, but she still had the letters and postcards he'd sent, reminding her of things they had done together, places they'd been; he wouldn't have done that if he hadn't cared.

They'd packed so much into that one short month. She smiled to recall the crazy, laughter-filled drive they'd taken up the California coast to Monterey and Carmel in an open-topped Mustang. They'd stayed at the most romantic cliff-top inn where they'd made love in a four-poster bed until they couldn't make love any more. No man had ever made her feel like that before, and none had since. He was so passionate and demanding, yet gentle and attentive. Even the

132

male scent of him had driven her wild, and the long lovers' looks into each other's eyes were as potent as an intimate caress.

When they'd returned to LA they'd filled their days with long, rambling walks through the Malibu mountains, or picnicking in the canyons, or sipping cocktails at the beach. She remembered only too well the roadside café they'd stopped at one day for fresh shrimp and Chardonnay. It was when he'd told her he never wanted any of it to end, and she'd cried, and next day he'd bought them two tickets to Hawaii. She still had the shell necklace he'd given her during those perfect, but heartbreaking last four days.

She swallowed and breathed in deeply. It was all a long time ago and nothing in the world could make her want to sit here reliving that dreadful goodbye again. It was enough to know it had been as hard for him as it had for her, though he'd had his wife and family to go home to, and by then she'd had no-one.

The phone rang on her desk, making her jump. She knew it wouldn't be him, but it seemed her hopes had a life all their own. She looked at the answerphone and waited.

'Hi, it's Laurie. If you're there . . .'

Sherry lifted the receiver. 'I'm here,' she said. 'And still in shock.'

There was a smile in Laurie's voice as she said, 'I hope we did the right thing in telling you. It just felt wrong to keep it from you, especially as Elliot's going to meet him again.'

Sherry's heart turned over. 'I didn't know that,' she said.

'It's next week, I think. They're having lunch.'

Sherry wasn't sure how she felt about that – thrilled at the length of Nick's stay, yet afraid of its potential to hurt.

'So, will you get in touch?' Laurie asked after a pause.

Sherry's breath caught. 'No. I mean, I can't. I don't have his number . . .'

'Elliot probably does.'

This was going too fast. 'No,' Sherry said, shaking her head. 'It's not a good idea. He's married and I just don't want to go there again.'

Laurie's tone was tender as she said, 'You're right, it just seems such a shame when you felt so strongly about each other.'

Sherry swallowed, and, to her embarrassment, when she tried to speak she found herself close to tears.

'What are you doing?' Laurie asked. 'I can come over if you like.'

'It's OK. I'm fine. Up to my eyes, actually. I've got a couple of deadlines to make for tomorrow, so instead of sitting around here like some lovesick schoolgirl, I should fill you in on my meeting with Karima Ghosh.'

'OK, but if you change your mind . . .'

'I'll call, don't worry. And thanks.'

'You're welcome. Now, before you get going, have you looked at your email in the last couple of hours? I sent you a news release from the National Crime Squad about a dawn raid they carried out in Bedford this morning. Apparently they've arrested six people on charges connected with the illegal entry of immigrants into the UK.'

Sherry's interest was immediately perked. 'Any names?' she said, turning on her computer.

'Not yet. I'm waiting for a call back from my contact at the Yard. I know Bedford isn't East London, but it could still be connected. It's a long shot, of course, but did you happen to see any signs of anything at the workshop that might in some way relate to this?'

'Not a thing. Everything looked perfectly normal to me, if you can call what I saw normal.'

'So what happened?'

'Apart from almost being asphyxiated by Mrs Ghosh's halitosis, I've put in the first order, which should be delivered in two weeks. I also requested a meeting with Mr E.C. himself. Mrs Ghosh didn't seem terribly up for that, so whether or not she passes the message on, we'll see. She's nobody's fool though, that's for sure. And the guys in the workshop are scared stiff of her.'

'What do you hope to achieve by meeting E.C., if you can pull it off?'

'I'm not sure yet. I just wanted to see how she'd react to the idea. I'll call her again in a few days to see what she has to say for herself.'

'With any luck Stan might have come up with something by then. Rose and the crew are getting some good stuff their end, apparently. She called about an hour ago, from Bombay, sorry, Mumbai. They're flying up to Gujarat tomorrow to see what they can find out, and shoot some footage of the Harijans in their own environment. Barry's dropping in around six to give me an update from his end, so if you can join us . . .'

'I thought we were meeting in the morning.'

'Oh sorry, I had to cancel. It's the vicar's turn to get stressed out by my mother, so I have to go and calm him down.'

'OK, I'll try to get there at six, which means I should go now or I won't make it.'

After she rang off Sherry went online to retrieve her email, then called up an article she'd been working on for the past few days about celebrity obsession. It was hard to keep her mind focused though, and it wasn't long before she found herself wandering back out to the balcony and staring downriver towards Canary Wharf. Was Nick still there somewhere, she wondered. She liked to think he was, though of course it made little difference, for however much she fantasized about a phone call, a blissful reunion, a magical disappearance of his family, it still wasn't going to make it real. The only reality was her, standing here now, torn between a powerful longing to see him again, and an encroaching sense of dread of what could happen if she did.

Eddie Cribbs was sitting on a bar stool in the smoky lounge of one of his strip clubs, rolling a double shot of Wild Turkey around the ice in his glass, while watching Karima Ghosh's colourful sari retreat into the darkness. He was a large man, just shy of six feet and sixty years. His thick, sandy hair waved like dunes over his scalp, thinning slightly at the crown and curling raffishly at the neck. His sharp brown eyes were set too far apart, his skin was pale, flecked with shapeless freckles, his mouth was large with a fleshy lower lip that drooped down over his chin like a hook. Though by no means handsome, he considered himself a man of style, with his hand-tailored suits, cashmere turtlenecks and dandyish silk scarves. His pinkie ring and crucifix were twenty-four carat gold, as were two of his teeth.

Right now he wasn't too pleased with the way things were going in his life, in fact not pleased at all. First, he'd got a phone call at seven this morning telling him about the police bust in Bedford, which, though it had nothing to do with him directly, was definitely not good news for anyone in the same game. It was a small world, and none of those Albanian bimbos they now had in custody could be relied on not to blab what they knew about other networks. Then he'd received the glad tidings that one of his major substance-suppliers had had his boat impounded by the French coastguard so the next delivery was up the Suwannee, and now Karima comes to express her concern about some buyer who turned up at the New Road workshop yesterday. Not that this buyer had barged in without an appointment, or was missing any credentials, it was just that something about her had made Karima uneasy.

'She wasn't the normal type of customer,' she'd told him. 'She had more class, and an accent that sounded American. I've got no reason to link her to Barry Davidson, and she's definitely not the reporter Daya spoke to, because we know that was Laurie Forbes. I just think we should check she really is who she says she is.'

'Have you rung the shop she came from?' he asked.

'Yes. She wasn't there, but they confirmed that she's one of the owners.'

'OK, give me the details, I'll put someone on it.'

Still gazing absently at the staircase Karima had just ascended connecting the underground club to the sex shop above, he lifted an arm to summon Frank, his driver. Karima wasn't prone to over-reaction, she was a shrewd, efficient manager whose instincts he trusted like his own. So, if Karima had a bad feeling about this buyer who'd expressed an interest in meeting the big boss, he had a bad feeling too.

'Go after Mrs Ghosh,' he said to Frank. 'Make sure she gets back to the workshop safe. Take the Nissan, then hang around for a while, see who's coming and going.'

As Frank left Cribbs knocked back the rest of his Scotch, put his glass down for a refill and surveyed the room. Normally, at this time of day, the club was closed, but after this morning's double fiasco he'd put the word out that he wanted a meet. Not at the offices because the auditors were in, but here at the club. Over the past hour the senior members of his board had been steadily arriving, turning up in anything from chauffeur-driven Rollers to beaten-up Fords. As a bunch of suited executives they could have belonged to any bank, or government office – and some did – except Happy, so named for the scar that had turned his mouth into a permanent grimace, and Gentle George who no-one could mistake for other than what he was, an ex-champion boxer.

Eddie glanced at his gold Rolex. It was just after three, but he wouldn't get heavy with anyone for being late, traffic in London was a bastard these days, and they were all busy men. Besides, no-one was dumb enough to miss the hour out of disrespect.

He sipped his drink and idly watched one of the girls as she jotted down a fresh order for the group at Perry Boon's table. He was a good bloke, Perry. The best right hand Eddie had ever had. Talked with a fucking ridiculous accent, like he had something stuck up his arse, and made them all cringe when he laughed, but no-one knew computers like Perry. And not many could be trusted like him either.

'She's new, isn't she?' he said as Gentle George came to join him at the bar.

George glanced over at the waitress serving Perry. She was petite, blonde, with big blue eyes, a pointy little chin, waif-like shoulders and the biggest pair of knockers he'd seen at the club in a long time. 'Can't say I've seen her before,' he said. 'Regular Shirley Temple.'

Eddie chuckled. 'Good pair of threepennies.'

'Ass ain't bad either,' George responded, looking at her reflection in the floor-to-ceiling mirror behind her.

'She dance, or just a waitress?'

'I'll find out.'

Eddie put a hand on his arm. 'No rush,' he said. 'She's busy right now.'

At the sound of someone clattering down the stairs they both looked up. It was Danny Boy, the East End kid with movie-star looks and, so they said, a cock the size of a stallion's. He was a kid to watch. Bright, ambitious, cunning like his old man, who had very sadly passed on after a run-in with the Turks when they tried to move in on his patch. That was the official version – only Eddie and Gentle George knew what had really happened, that Danny senior had done a deal with the Turks and was about to start selling out big time until George got wind and, under Eddie's instructions, put a stop to it. Course, Danny Boy didn't know that, he was only party to the official version, so he hated those Turks with a vengeance now. This was no bad thing, just as long as his hatred was better controlled than the rampant urges of his dick.

'Mr Cribbs, Eddie,' the boy said, attempting a nonchalant swagger as he approached. 'How are you, sir?'

'I'm all right, Danny,' Eddie told him.

Danny's anxious eyes scanned the room.

Eddie watched him, fondly remembering himself at twenty-five, twenty-six, when he'd first been inducted into the inner circle of his mentor. Those were the days. He could do no wrong then. He hadn't done much wrong since, either, because his mentor was long gone, despatched direct from Her Majesty to his Maker, and there had never really been anyone to challenge Eddie for the turf he'd left behind – until the foreign bastards started moving in, but he'd found a way of dealing with them that seemed to work all round. At least for the time being.

'Now there's an impressive pair,' Danny commented, noticing the waitress as she came towards them. 'Wouldn't mind getting stuck into them.'

Eddie didn't respond.

140

The waitress set her tray on the end of the bar where she gave the barman her order. When she looked up she seemed surprised, and vaguely self-conscious, at finding herself the focus of Eddie Cribbs's attention. Eddie felt a stirring in his loins. Shy tarts always did it for him, even if it was an act.

'By the way,' Danny said, 'I saw your Penelope the other day, out shopping with your missus. Beautiful girl. A real sight for sore eyes. Must be right intelligent, with all that education you're giving her. It's a good thing, education. Got a lot of respect for intelligent women, me.'

George's eyes closed.

Eddie's smile was pleasant as he looked down at his drink. 'Is that a fact?' he said.

Danny nodded. 'A lot of respect,' he echoed.

George was bracing himself. Poor kid had no idea.

'You like intelligent women?' Eddie said.

'Oh yeah.' Danny's laugh was starting to turn nervous as he glanced at George.

George said nothing.

Nor did Eddie.

Danny shrugged and attempted another laugh. 'What?' he said.

Eddie turned on his stool so that he was facing out into the club. Over the next few seconds, as though some kind of signal had gone out, silence began to spread.

Danny's survivals were starting to kick in, but he didn't know what to do, had no idea what he'd said wrong. 'What?' he said again.

When everyone was quiet and looking their

141

way, Eddie said, 'Danny boy, I want you to go and stand in front of that mirror over there.'

Confused, Danny only looked at him.

Using one large hand Eddie gestured in the direction he should go.

Danny looked at George, then at the others.

No-one spoke, or moved.

With an awkward sort of bob from one foot to the other, Danny stuck his hands in his pockets and did as he was told.

'Face it,' Eddie called out. 'Turn round and face the mirror, there's a good lad.'

Fear was starting to show in Danny's eyes as he did as he was told.

'OK. Now pull your trousers down,' Eddie said.

Danny froze. 'What?'

'You heard.'

Danny's eyes moved round all those in the reflection. Everyone was watching. They all knew what was about to happen, he could tell, and it wasn't going to be good.

'I'm waiting,' Eddie told him.

Danny's fingers were shaking as he unbuttoned his jeans and began sliding them down over his legs.

'Your pants too,' Eddie said.

Danny's face was turning white, but there was no way he could refuse, when the whole board was there to make sure he didn't. 'This is embarrassing, Eddie,' he said, trying to keep it light.

Eddie waited.

Danny pushed his pants down.

'Now, son, I want you to take a good look at your dick,' Eddie told him. 'A real good look, because it's the last time you're going to see it.'

Danny's face went slack with horror as a titter of amusement threaded round the room. 'No, Eddie,' he cried. 'You don't mean that. I didn't do nothing. I . . .'

'Are you looking?' Eddie cut in. 'I hear it's been good to you, so tell the poor little bloke a fond goodbye.'

More laughter.

Danny turned round, his eyes stricken with terror. 'Eddie, just tell me what I did and I'll make good.'

'I don't hear you saying goodbye,' Eddie responded.

'Please,' Danny begged. 'You can't chop me cock off. I need it. I'm still young . . .'

'Come over here,' Eddie said.

Danny shrank back.

'Help him, someone.'

Danny tried to run as Happy and Gentle George began closing in.

'Eddie. I'm begging you,' he sobbed. 'Don't do this. A bloke ain't a bloke without his cock.'

Harry and George had him under the arms.

'Eddie, please,' he implored as they half-walked, half-carried him to the bar.

Eddie waited for him to get there, then waved George and Happy out of the way.

Immediately Danny dropped to his knees. 'I'm begging you, Eddie,' he gasped, clasping his hands together. 'I'll do anything, just let me keep me cock.'

Ignoring the sniggers, Eddie leaned forward until his nose was almost touching Danny's. 'Don't

you ever mention my girl again, do you hear me?'
he snarled. 'Am I making myself clear? The likes
of you aren't fit to lick her shoes clean with your
fucking ass-wipe tongue, never mind utter her
precious name. So you see her again, you pluck
out your eyeballs, do you understand? You pull
out those minces, erase all your filthy thoughts,
and just make sure you keep that randy fucking
dick inside your strides, because I'm telling you
now, if you don't, you'll be singing fucking soprano
at next year's Midnight Mass. Now get up.'

Shaking with as much relief as fear, Danny stag-
gered back to his feet and yanked up his jeans.
'I'm sorry,' he mumbled. 'I'm very sorry. It won't
never happen again. Never, I swear.'

'Good boy.' Eddie got up and walked over to
one of the tables. 'Right, I reckon we're about ready
to get this meeting under way,' he declared, sitting
down. 'We'll start with what happened in Bedford
this morning. Perry, you manage to find out any
names yet?'

'Only three and none of them have ever done
any work for us.'

'Which don't mean they know nothing about
us. What about the other three?'

'I've got everyone working on it. They'll call on
the mobile as soon as there's any news.'

Eddie nodded. It didn't pay to get angry or
impatient in this game. Perry and his team knew
the score. If there were any links to the people-
movers working for him they'd have to shut everything down, PDQ, and that wouldn't be good. 'OK.
Give us an update on where the latest shipment
is at,' he said.

As Perry began filling them in on the progress of a Latvian freighter carrying a thousand passengers, three hundred belonging to them, for sale in Hamburg and other German cities, Danny stood sweating against the bar, still too shaken up to take much of it in, or even to notice the great tits that had just bobbed their way over to him. The waitress was asking him if he was all right, but he didn't answer. No way, José. Pussy was the last thing on his mind right now, he didn't even want to look at it, never mind talk to it.

'Can I get you a drink?' she said.

He shook his head, his eyes still fixed on Eddie.

'My name's Cheryl,' she told him.

Why the fuck couldn't she just go away?

'Let me get you a drink.'

'Oi! You!' Eddie suddenly shouted.

Cheryl spun round.

'Leave the boy alone. Can't you see he's trying to concentrate?'

Her eyes went down. 'Sorry,' she mumbled, and keeping her head bowed she walked back to her tray of drinks.

Eddie waved Danny over and told him to sit.

Perry carried on with his brief.

A couple of minutes later, after Cheryl had delivered drinks all round, Eddie leaned over to Danny and spoke quietly in his ear.

Danny got up, too fast, too eager to please.

Eddie winced as the chair crashed to the floor.

Anxiously, Danny picked it up, then crept quietly over to Cheryl. 'Mr Cribbs wants to see you after the meeting,' he told her.

She glanced back over her shoulder. With her

peachy complexion and baby-blonde curls she barely looked sixteen, though Danny knew she had to be at least two years older, because Trevor, who ran the club, was a stickler for his girls being the right age.

'Of course,' she responded. Then, tossing her hair over one shoulder, she glanced down at his crotch. 'I'm glad he let you keep it,' she whispered mischievously.

Not wanting any reminders, or even to register her come-on, Danny quickly returned to Eddie's table and sat down.

'So apart from being quality, did Karima say why she had a problem with this buyer?' one of the board was asking.

'The problem comes as much in the timing as the type,' Eddie replied. 'It's less than a month since Doctor Patel got in touch with Laurie Forbes from the press . . . Has that been taken care of, by the way?' He was looking at George.

'We're keeping an eye on it,' George assured him. 'But we're sticking to our policy not to mess with the press unless forced.'

Eddie nodded. 'So we want this Tara Green checked out,' he said. 'Perry, get someone on it.'

Perry pushed horn-rimmed spectacles higher and made a note. 'Are you going to meet her?' he asked.

'When I know more about her, and if I think it's worthwhile,' Eddie replied, waving Cheryl over to the table. 'Meantime, I want to know about anything, or anyone, that turns up anywhere they shouldn't. Get me a refill,' he told her, passing her his glass with one hand while fondling her bottom with the other.

'You know, it just occurred to me,' George said, 'that Stan Bright's done some work for Laurie Forbes in the past. And her boyfriend, whatever his name is.'

'Elliot Russell,' Eddie informed him. 'So what are you saying?'

George shrugged. 'Just that I saw him upstairs, doing a bit of shopping, a couple of days ago. Could be nothing, but . . .'

'Don't treat anything as nothing,' Eddie cut in. 'Find out what Stan the man's up to, and Perry, get someone on the Tara Green case now. She's making me very nervous all of a sudden, and I don't like people who make me nervous.' His eyes moved to Danny and he grinned. 'Do I, Danny?' he said.

Chapter Eight

Just no way in the world was Sherry going to embarrass herself, in the middle of this celebrity-packed art show, by blurting out a confession that Andraya's magnificent million-dollar paintings were reminding her of her own, but they were. Bold, brash, garish. Amorphous explosions of colour erupting from the heart of structured forms, such as animals, trees, birds, and humans. Vast shocking works that enlivened the white walls they hung from, and challenged the viewer's senses like a fast-moving dream. At least that was how Sherry was seeing them, she hadn't heard anyone else's interpretation yet, but since the collection as a whole was entitled Mesmerics she assumed her reaction wasn't entirely out of tune with her fellow guests', or indeed with the artist's intent.

Keeping a safe distance from those she knew, she skirted the edge of the crowd, sipped her champagne, and faded out the constant burble of sound. Though her expression was calmly reflective and curious, inside she was madly intrigued, for she knew only too well the inner demons that had driven her to tear apart established forms that way. So had it been the same for Andraya? Were these paintings a form of exorcism for her too? Was the size of them a measure of how great her suffering had been? If it were, then she'd certainly known a great deal worse than Sherry, for not even the largest of Sherry's efforts could match up to the smallest of Andraya's.

However, as the initial surprise began to wear off she started to feel faintly ridiculous, for there was, in fact, no real likeness to her paintings at all, except perhaps in the jarring blends of colour here and there, and the hugeness of aggression some of them exuded. She had simply been shaken back to the time she'd used this medium to help rid herself of all the pain and hate she was feeling. It didn't mean Andraya shared the same turbulence, or even anything like the same experiences. Andraya's life and complexities were her own, depicted in abstract brilliance on these walls, while hers remained behind the closed doors of her flat, and buried in the shadowy depths of her past.

'Here I am, your date for the evening,' Anita cried, sweeping up behind her. 'Sorry I'm late. I got caught in traffic. How are you?'

'Great,' Sherry answered, as they embraced. 'Or maybe I should say bedazzled.'

Anita gazed up at the towering masterpiece beside them. 'Awesome,' she mumbled.

'So come on, what are they saying?' Sherry prompted. 'What do they tell us about Andraya, apart from the fact she's sublimely gifted?'

149

'I don't know if I'd even dare to go there,' Anita replied with a baffled tilt of her head.

Sherry grinned. 'OK, then how's the boy?' she asked as they moved on. 'Where is he?'

'You'll be pleased to hear I've dumped him,' Anita declared. 'It's a shame, but, well, let's put it this way, plenty going on in the basement, but nothing in the loft.'

Sherry spluttered with laughter. And that was that, she was thinking. So typical of Anita, mad about a man one day, forgotten his name the next. 'Does that mean you've met someone else?' she ventured.

'Possibly. I'll let you know when there's more to tell.' She was watching Laurie, who was laughing at something Elliot was saying. 'Now that's how I want to look,' she said wistfully. 'Loved and in love.'

They raised their glasses as Laurie waved out.

'She's radiant,' Anita declared. 'And Rachel Hendon's glowing like some heavenly body too. Just look at her. What must it be like to have a relationship that works? Not only are my own affairs disasters, my entire life is riddled with other people's screw-ups, which could be the reason I can't get it right. There's no role model there. I'm saturated in human misery, because whoever goes to see a therapist when they're on a roll? All I get are the saddos in search of someone else to blame for their pain and ghastliness – mother, father, inner child, God – or the suicide junkies who blame themselves, but never quite manage to carry out the deed. It's no wonder I'm such a failed human being.'

Sherry's laugh was weak. 'Hardly,' she commented, inwardly flinching at the mention of suicide. Since she'd found out Nick was in London, she'd been thinking more about Bluebell than she'd ever want to, and this was the kind of reminder that she could do without.

'Oh God, is that my phone?' Anita grumbled, fishing around in her bag. 'Yes, it is. How embarrassing. Everyone's looking, but *I'm on call*. I'm a doctor. This is my emergency number.' Finding it, she put it to her ear and turned away from the crowd. After listening for a few seconds, she interrupted the caller. 'Hang on, I'll have to go outside. Sorry,' she said to Sherry. 'I'm on the suicide shift tonight, and someone's having a problem. I might be back, if not, explain for me.'

As she disappeared Sherry drained her glass and grabbed another from a passing tray. After downing half of it she looked around for someone to talk to, and found herself quite impressed by the number of celebrities and high-flying politicians the event had brought out. Now she was paying attention she was amused by the way the journos were sidling into star-studded photographs, eager for the world to know they were on the A list, which was certainly where this showing ranked. She could just see them tomorrow morning, preening with self-importance and pleasure as they scoured the papers in greedy search of themselves hobnobbing with London's *crème de la crème*. The greatest kudos, she imagined, would be achieved by occupying a space next to the artist herself, whose totally transparent cream trouser suit with its tantalizing swirls of sequins and beads was every bit as much a source of fascination as her remarkable talent. Right now she was standing between Chris and Elliot, facing a battery of cameras and managing to make a standard shot of an artist with her dealer and a potential client look like a smouldering moment of foreplay. It was no wonder the woman was so successful, when she was as brilliant at packaging and marketing herself as she was at creating her art.

Deciding to go and join Laurie, Sherry was just starting to squeeze a path through when Anita came back.

'Emergency over,' she declared, looking round for another glass of champagne. 'I managed to talk them down.'

Sherry's eyes simmered with irony. 'Good,' she commented. 'Let's go and talk to Laurie.' She didn't need to know the details of an aborted suicide attempt, nor did she really want to hear any more about the next easy conquest on Anita's busy dance card.

'At last,' Laurie cried, as Sherry reached her. 'I've been trying to work my way over to you. Anita. How lovely to see you again. How are you?'

'Wonderful, thank you,' Anita cooed, kissing her on both cheeks. 'No need to ask you the same, one look at those eyes is answer enough.'

Laurie laughed. 'So what do you think of the show?' she asked. 'Who are you writing this up for, Sherry?'

'*Elle* actually,' Sherry answered. 'And I can't decide whether to focus more on the artist or the art. The trouser suit's going to provide a nice little

152

intro with some kind of parallel to the Emperor's new clothes, I just have to figure it out. God, I wish I had her courage.'

'I wish I had her figure,' Anita stated.

Sherry laughed. 'So what's your take on the paintings?' she asked Laurie.

'I love them,' Laurie answered. 'But listen,' she went on, taking Sherry's arm and drawing her to one side, 'Elliot had to bring his lunch forward with Nick, so it happened today.'

Sherry's heart missed a beat. 'Really?' she said, feeling her face draining of colour. Then, realizing they were shutting Anita out, she quickly drew her in. 'It's OK, Anita knows about Nick,' she told Laurie.

'She only told me yesterday that he was in London though,' Anita chided.

'So what happened at the lunch?' Sherry asked, already sensing something had.

Laurie's eyes were shining in a way that didn't seem to be heralding bad news. Even so, Sherry was hardly daring to breathe. 'Apparently his wife left him about three years ago,' Laurie said softly. 'She went to live in Boston with some multi-millionaire businessman and took his daughter too. And now . . .' she squeezed Sherry's hand, 'Nick is moving back to England.'

Sherry almost felt as though she'd been struck. Or maybe she wanted to faint. Her head was spinning, her insides were in turmoil. She had to be dreaming, she just had to be. Nothing ever happened that perfectly, not for her, anyway. 'What about his mother?' she said, her voice sounding strangely distorted, at least to her.

153

'I don't know, she wasn't mentioned. But isn't that amazing about his wife? He's free now, so maybe you two . . .'

'No, don't even say it,' Sherry cried, covering her ears.

Laurie laughed. 'It's high time something worked out for you in the love department,' she told her, 'and if you ask me . . .'

'No, don't,' Sherry protested, starting to feel drunk on all the hope that was flooding in. 'Oh my God,' she laughed, putting a hand to her mouth. 'This is too much. It's just too much. Is he divorced, do you know? What about someone else? He's sure to have met someone else by now. If you knew him . . .'

'Tell you what,' Laurie cut in, 'why don't we go and rescue Elliot so he can tell you everything himself?'

Sherry was on the point of going with her when she suddenly stopped. 'No! No!' she exclaimed, pulling Laurie back. 'We can't just go up to Elliot like this. It looks . . . *childish*.'

'Oh come on. He won't mind.'

Sherry could feel herself shaking, and was half afraid it showed. 'No,' she said as firmly as she could. 'And not in front of Andraya either. It's her night. We can't start talking about other things when she's the star turn.' Visions of her own paintings were racing through her mind again, and for one fleeting moment she wanted to run. It was all too much, first this peculiar reminder of her own past through Andraya's art, the obscure mentions of suicide, now Nick being free . . . Or possibly free . . . It felt hard to breathe all of a sudden. She needed some air. 'I'm going to the Ladies,' she said, blinking as a series of flashbulbs went off nearby.

Laurie was about to follow when Rachel called out to her. 'Come on, you should be in this,' she told her.

'It's all right, I'll go with Sherry,' Anita assured her.

Laurie shrugged apologetically, and went to join the group around Andraya. After the photographers moved on to snap the other guests, she said to Elliot, 'I've just told Sherry about your lunch with Nick. Did he say anything about being involved with anyone else now?'

'No. Just that his wife had left him.'

'What about Sherry? Did he mention her at all?'

Elliot shook his head. 'Not that I recall.'

Laurie glanced in the direction of the Ladies.

'What are you looking so worried about?' he said, shouting over an explosion of laughter nearby.

'It was just weird, Sherry's reaction,' she said. 'I got the impression she wants to see him again, but . . .' She shrugged and shook her head. 'I suppose she's just nervous. It's been a long time.'

Elliot's eyebrows went up. 'I imagine the real challenge now, if they do get together,' he said, 'is whether he'll live up to the image she's created in her head, because memory has a peculiar way of altering perspective and reinventing the facts to how we want them to be, rather than how they actually were.'

Laurie's eyes widened, then standing on tiptoe so her lips were against his, she said, 'You know, it's one of the things I love most about you, how you never cease to impress me. So now, impress me again, and tell me whether we should try to get them back together, or just let fate take its course.'

After taking a moment to kiss her, he said, 'Fate gets my vote, and she's coming this way.'

Laurie turned round.

'Sherry, hi,' Elliot said, pulling her into an embrace. 'Are you buying, or just looking?'

For once she was lost for a witty response, though Elliot didn't seem to notice as someone chose that moment to drag him away.

'Are you OK?' Laurie asked her.

'Sure, I'm fine,' she responded.

In the background Anita was shaking her head, denying it. 'Maybe you should have something to eat,' Laurie suggested, wondering what had been said in the Ladies.

'Actually, I think I might leave now,' Sherry said. 'I've got enough to conjure a thousand words. If they want any more I can always get it from Rachel.'

Laurie was now more concerned than ever. 'Why don't you come over to the office tomorrow?' she said. 'We need to discuss our next moves in the immigrant story.'

'I'll check my diary,' Sherry replied, hugging her. 'Say goodnight to Elliot, and Chris and Rachel. Tell them it's a wonderful exhibition.'

'I will,' Laurie assured her.

As she started towards the door Laurie put a hand on Anita's arm and held her back. 'What's going on?' she asked.

'She's afraid,' Anita answered. 'I think we both know that she's never stopped loving – or at least wanting – that man, and now I guess, if they do get together, she's going to find out whether or not it's been the same for him.' Her eyes seemed to increase in intensity. 'After seven years, and all the heartache she went through, I'd say that was pretty scary, wouldn't you?'

Laurie nodded and let her go. There was more to it though, she felt certain, but catching Andraya fixing Elliot with her brazenly seductive eyes again, she decided to make her way back to Elliot's side, wanting to remind the Brazilian beauty that this one was already spoken for.

Neela was screaming, but only inside her head. No sounds were coming out. Her body ached with holding it back, her fear was like an evil spirit come to devour her. She felt nothing but dread, like the gnawing beaks of vultures picking over what was left on the bones.

On a mattress nearby Parvati was whimpering, her face turned into Ekta's soft body, her limbs quaking with fear and despair. The others lay in the darkness and listened. No-one moved. No-one spoke. Parvati's daughter had been gone for more than a week and there was still no news. Earlier Parvati herself had been taken to the same man who had hurt Daya. Parvati's injuries were not as bad as Daya's, but still she must see the doctor. Ekta was insisting. Mota Ben said she would take her tomorrow.

Neela held Shaila close and prayed incessantly to the gods that their turn to go with the men would never come. But it would, as sure as the dawn, for they were the only two who had not yet been chosen, saved so far, Ekta said, by her disfigurement and Shaila's age. Shaila was so little. Only just six. Neela wanted to run away, to run and run and get them as far from here as she could, but how?

She pressed a fist to her mouth. No-one must hear her crying. She must be as silent as the thoughts in her head, as careful as the rats who came to find food. She was not brave in her heart, or beautiful in her face like Daya, but she was clever in her mind to remember things even when she'd been told to forget them. She remembered the name of the doctor Daya had seen, and the name of the Englishwoman who had given Daya a card.

Feeling Shaila snug in her arms Neela waited for another wave of terror to pass as she thought of what she must do, and how she must do it. If she got hurt, the way Daya and Parvati had been hurt, Mota Ben would take her to the doctor. It was the only way she could think of to get word to someone outside.

Eddie Cribbs rolled off the young body he'd been pounding for the past ten minutes and looked at his watch. He was feeling good, but not as good as he'd hoped before getting her over here. There was always too much to worry about, and sex was only a brief distraction. One he enjoyed, it was true, but as soon as it was over all the problems started coming back.

'Was that OK for you, Mr Cribbs?' the girl next to him said.

'Yeah, now be quiet, I'm thinking.'

They were in the private quarters of his eleventh-floor executive suite in Canary Wharf, which had been done up to act as an independent studio flat complete with kitchen, bathroom and good-sized bedroom. The grand office the other side of the double doors was from where he governed his empire, and beyond that was Perry's large department of highly skilled and extremely highly paid computer experts. Since the firm had put these kids through university, taking care of every expense and providing the kind of lifestyle anyone but a moron would become addicted to, their loyalty was pretty much bagged. Certainly no-one had failed a security check yet, and since the fate of anyone who did was widely known, failure was unlikely. They didn't take too many chances though, and things were only revealed on a basis of need-to-know.

Beside him the phone rang.

'What?' he grunted into the receiver.

'You wanted a call after twenty minutes,' Perry reminded him.

'Oh, yeah, right.' He swung his legs over the side of the bed. The girl beside him was forgotten. 'What's happened, anything?' he wanted to know. 'Anything on Bedford?'

'Not yet. The interrogations are still going on, we're told, but so far no awkward connections seem to have been made. The latest cargo is on schedule. I've just wired funds through the usual route to cover the next leg of the journey. So everything's cool there.'

Eddie could feel his headache coming back.

There might be no connection, but the ongoing interrogations were making him nervous. 'We're ready to dump the cargo at a moment's notice?' he asked.

'If it proves necessary, everyone's primed.'

'Good. Anything else I need to know?'

'The results have just come in on the fashion buyer you wanted checked out. Turns out she's a reporter.'

Eddie's face darkened. 'I knew it. *I fucking knew it*. Has anyone spoken to her yet?'

'No. We're waiting for instructions from you.'

'Reporters are tricky bastards,' he snarled, 'you sort one out and you get the whole fucking pack on your ass. Do we know if this one has a connection to Laurie Forbes?'

'Her flat's a stone's throw from Laurie Forbes's office, so I wouldn't be surprised.'

'Shit! The last thing we need is Forbes and her fucking boyfriend sniffing round our affairs,' Eddie growled fractiously. 'Have you checked if this reporter . . . What's her fucking name?'

'Sherry MacElvoy.'

'Do we know if she's spoken to the doctor?'

'Not yet.'

'Then find out. Pay the man another visit, put on a bit more pressure. Has he got kids?'

'Three.'

'Then he's ours. Make sure he forgets he ever heard of our workshop, and if he's told anyone about the stupid bitch we had to get rid of he's going to suddenly remember it was a mix-up. Read me? And don't leave his office without the necessary files. If they're on computer get them erased. Send the Tomkins boy, he always handles those things right.'

'No problem. Do you want to relocate the women?'

Eddie thought. 'If necessary, yes. Remind me how many there are.'

'Eleven adults, and one kid now, which reminds me, I had a call earlier from Karima. Our headmaster friend's been on again, wanting a rerun with the woman we had to dispose of.'

'Well he's out of luck there, isn't he, perverted bastard. Fucking glad I was never in his class at school. What did she tell him?'

'That he had to have someone else. He's OK with it, apparently, but we're probably going to need another doctor. One we can put on the payroll.'

'This should have been thought of a long time ago,' Eddie growled. 'It's these kinds of mistakes that are going to end us up in deep shit, and that isn't somewhere we want to be, Perry.'

'No, of course not. It'll be sorted. The taxi's just arrived for Cheryl.'

'Who?'

'The girl you've got in there with you.'

'Oh, yeah, right.' So that was her name, it had slipped his mind.

After ringing off he padded over to the bathroom and turned on the shower. The reflection in the mirror told him he really had to lose some weight, or his doctor's predictions of trouble were going to start happening.

'You getting up now?' she said, coming to stand in the doorway.

161

He turned to look at her and remembered why he liked her. There was a cute, virginal sort of look about her, with her Cupid's bow lips and Shirley Temple curls, which, when put together with those enormous knockers, reminded him of the first girl he'd ever poked, when he was fifteen and she was . . . Shit, she'd been twelve.

'Your taxi's downstairs,' he told her. 'Time to run along.'

'Are you sure?' she said, coming to rub herself against him.

'Yeah, I'm sure. But you can come back tomorrow, around the same time.'

Her face lit up. 'Really? That's great.'

His eyes narrowed. What was she after, that she wasn't already getting, he wanted to know.

As he went to get in the shower, Cheryl returned to the bedroom and began picking up her clothes. As she dressed she was humming tunefully to herself, and glowing with triumph, for this was exactly why she'd got a job at the club, to get in with Eddie Cribbs, and look how long it had taken her. Less than a week. Plus, it had turned out to be a lot better than she'd expected. A bit of oral, then straight for the missionary – and now he'd already invited her back. Just wait till she told the other girls, they'd be sick as parrots, because normally, according to them, his MO was to get someone over here, screw her once, then toss her back in the pile, like he was marking his territory, or sampling the goods, making sure the quality was OK. It was rare, almost unheard of, for anyone to get invited back again, she'd been told, and now she, little Cheryl Burrows, had pulled it off without even trying. She could hardly wait to see their faces, especially Suzy's, the stuck-up bitch of a star dancer – she was going to be *sooo* flipped off.

Still humming softly, she hooked her bag over one shoulder and strutted proudly out of the room. Everyone in the offices would know why she was here, what she'd just been doing, and she was happy for them to know. They'd probably start treating her with a bit more respect once they registered how often she was coming, but for now she was OK with their furtive glances and smothered giggles. Perry was all right though, a real gentleman was Perry, walking her down to the cab like this. It didn't occur to her that he was making sure she left the building without any impromptu stop-offs or detours, or idly lifting a document or two. But she wasn't into spying, she was only into her own thing, which was getting to be Eddie Cribbs's number one girl. And there was no doubt about it, in her mind at least, she was off to a good start.

Chapter Nine

There was nothing to prepare Laurie for what was about to happen – no stirring of an instinct, no strange feeling of premonition, not even a fleeting sense of something being not quite right. In fact, as she descended the steps from Tower Bridge and turned under it towards the cobbled street of Shad Thames she was feeling on top of the world. It was just before six in the evening, the sun was still high, and noisy groups of office workers, drinking cocktails and smoking cigarettes, were spilling out of the restaurants and bars on the ground floor of their apartment block. She was suddenly seized with happiness, for the past two days with her parents had gone blissfully smoothly, the latest fitting for her dress had moved her to tears again, as she imagined Elliot turning to watch her come down the aisle, and now she could hardly wait to see him to show him just how much she'd missed him while she was gone.

As she let herself into the flat the phone started to ring. 'Hi! I'm back,' she shouted, closing the door.

There was no reply, which surprised her, for she'd just spoken to him, as she was crossing the bridge, so he must be here.

'Elliot,' she called out, from the bottom of the stairs.

No reply.

Deciding he must have popped down to the convenience shop – or florist – she dumped her overnight bag ready for him to carry up, then went to glance through the pile of mail he'd left on the kitchen counter. She should probably check her messages, both here and at the office, but she wasn't in the mood to deal with work right now, so deciding to leave it until later she went upstairs to freshen up a bit before Elliot came back.

It wasn't until she was replacing her toothbrush in the holder that it struck her something wasn't quite right. Frowning, she looked at the place where Elliot's toothbrush normally was, but for some reason wasn't. She opened the cabinet to see if it was there, but all she discovered was another empty place, this time where his shaving gear should be.

Feeling an unsteady beat in her heart, she dabbed her mouth and hands with a towel and went to check his closet. At first it didn't appear that anything was missing, but on closer inspection she realized there were gaps. Starting to turn cold she reached up to open an overhead cupboard. His suitcase was gone.

Shock jarred through her body. This was crazy. She'd only spoken to him a few minutes ago. He couldn't have just run out the minute he put the phone down.

Hearing the front door slam she rushed to the stairs. She was halfway down when he walked into the sitting room. There didn't appear to be anything different about him, except there was. It was the way he was looking at her.

'What – what's going on?' she said, her voice an unsteady echo in the strangeness. 'Where have you been?'

'Just down to the car,' he answered.

'Why? Where are you going?'

He didn't answer.

'Your things have gone,' she said, trying to stay calm. 'Are you going somewhere?'

He dashed a hand through his hair, and averted his eyes. When he looked at her again she wanted to put up her hands as though to stop what was coming. 'I'm sorry,' he said quietly. 'I can't go through with it, Laurie. We can't get married.'

She could feel his words coming at her, as though from a distance. They weren't real, yet the room was tilting and she was starting to shake. 'What do you mean? I thought . . .' She clasped a hand to her mouth as a sob cut her off. 'Everything's arranged. The invitations are out.'

'I'm sorry,' he said again.

She stared at him, knowing what he was saying, but unable to understand.

'Chris is letting me use the flat over his gallery until I can sort something out,' he told her.

The blow was still coming, an inexorable, invisible force that seemed to be hitting every part of her. She continued to stare at him, not wanting to believe this was happening, trying to wake herself

166

up from the dream. 'Sort what out?' she finally said.

He swallowed hard. 'Somewhere to live.'

'But you live here. We live here. We've only just moved in.' She was starting to panic. This was the man she loved, they were getting married in less than four weeks. He couldn't be leaving like this. He couldn't mean what he was saying. 'Why?' she heard herself suddenly cry. 'What's happened to make you decide this?'

'Nothing. It's . . . I'm . . .' He broke off, not sure how to continue. 'I just can't go through with it.'

Her mind was moving in too many directions, trying to find the right words, something, anything that would make him take back what he was saying, feel another way. She was too confused, too afraid. 'Is this why you've been spending so much time with Chris?' she demanded. 'You've been discussing it with him, before discussing it with me?' Then the truth suddenly hit her with a blinding clarity. 'Oh God, this is about Phraxos, isn't it?' she cried. 'You're ending our relationship, cancelling our wedding even, so you can be free to break your agreement with the Government.' Even as she said it she was praying it was true, because she could live with that far more easily than she could with the alternative, that he just didn't want her any more. 'That's what you've been talking to Chris about, isn't it? You can't let it go.'

'Actually, we've been arranging your wedding present,' he told her. 'I've bought you one of Andraya's paintings.'

She could only look at him. That was nothing

like what she wanted to hear, and she didn't know how to respond.

'I still want you to have it,' he said.

As the awfulness of it all sank into her, her eyes started to dilate with anger and pain. 'And that would be to salve your conscience, would it?' she said bitterly. 'You think a painting's going to make you feel better?'

He continued to meet her gaze, letting the silence build around them until she almost couldn't stand it. Panic was squeezing her so hard now that for one dreadful moment she thought she was going to scream or throw herself at his feet and beg. 'Why?' she said, her voice shredded with despair. 'Just tell me why.'

He took a breath to speak, then looked away.

'Is there someone else?'

'No.'

'Then *why*?'

'Because you deserve someone who loves you the way you should be loved,' he said softly.

The implications of that rushed at her so hard that she took a step back and sank down on the stair behind her. 'You're saying you don't love me?' she whispered. 'That it's all been a lie?'

'No. I do love you, just not the way . . .'

She waited, but he didn't finish. 'Not the way I love you,' she said for him, her lips hardly able to shape the words.

His eyes went down and he shook his head.

Her chest felt horribly tight. Her eyes were bulging, as her heart thudded a terrible beat. She had to make this stop. She couldn't let him go. He meant everything to her. She loved him more than her own life. Without him there would be no point to her life. 'Elliot,' she said, as tears began rolling from her eyes. 'Elliot, please don't do this.'

He came to the foot of the stairs and reached for her hands. 'I'm sorry,' he whispered, pulling her into his arms. 'I wanted it to work, more than anything, I wanted it to work.'

'But it can,' she said, her voice muffled by his shoulder. 'We can make it.'

He just went on holding her, listening to her cry and feeling very close to it himself. 'I'll get us a drink,' he said, after a while. 'I think we need it.'

As he walked to the bar she remembered her plans for a romantic evening at home. That seemed such a long time ago now, something that had happened in another place, another life. She was still dazed and disbelieving, unable to accept that suddenly, out of nowhere, her whole life was falling apart. Yet she must be connecting with it or she wouldn't be trembling like this, or so torn between anger and fear.

He put their drinks on the coffee table, and waited for her to come and sit next to him. 'There'll be a lot to sort out,' he said, taking her hand, 'but we don't need to discuss it tonight.'

Denial was pressing down on her like a fist. She couldn't think about tomorrow, couldn't even bear to think about tonight. 'How long . . . ?' she began. 'When did you know . . . ?'

Understanding what she was asking, he said, 'I'm not sure. A few weeks . . .'

The words swept her into another current of shock. 'You knew all that time you didn't love me, and you never said anything?' She took her hand away. Images of what had happened in that time were flashing before her, intimacies they'd shared, plans they'd made. It wasn't making any sense. It was all wrong. She had to wake up, get out of this nightmare.

'I kept thinking it would pass,' he said, 'that it would all come right again . . .'

'But it hasn't?'

He shook his head.

She wanted to die. She didn't want to go any further with this, she just wanted to die. 'Were you afraid to tell me because of Lysette?' she said after a while. 'Did you think I'd do the same, is that why you've waited this long?'

When he didn't answer she turned to look at him. 'It is, isn't it?' she said brokenly.

'I admit, it was a concern,' he replied.

Tears began falling on to her cheeks. 'Well, I can understand that,' she replied, 'you wouldn't want two sisters' deaths on your conscience, would you? One is bad enough, I'm sure.' She covered her face with her hands. 'Now I know how she felt,' she choked. 'Now I know what it was like for her when you told her you didn't want her any more. God, you're such a bastard.' Her head came up, her eyes were bright with pain, her lips twisted with the effort to stop crying. 'What the hell is it with you?' she demanded. 'Just what gives you the right to do this to us? You've devastated my family once. My sister's dead! She killed herself because of you, so how the hell do you think my parents are going to cope with this?'

His face was taut, his eyes were heavy with the pain he felt too. 'Believe me, I've thought about

170

that,' he told her, 'and all I can say is I just wish to God this wasn't happening.'

'But it's you who's making it happen!' she cried. 'No-one else. Just you. We don't have to break up. We can still get married. I love you, Elliot, and it'll break my parents' hearts if you do this. You know that. They can't go through it again, not after Lysette.'

'But you're not going to kill yourself,' he told her.

She turned away, too bewildered and angry to get any more words out, too full of resentment to give him the reassurance he was seeking.

A horrible silence followed. 'Just tell me the truth,' she said brokenly in the end. 'Is there someone else, and you're too afraid to tell me?'

'No,' he answered.

Her eyes fell away and came to rest on his hand as it covered hers.

'I'd give anything for this not to be happening,' he told her softly, 'but I can't live a lie. I care about you too much to do that to you.'

Care, not love. She got up and walked over to the window. The sun was almost ready to set now, the lights of Tower Bridge and the buildings on the opposite bank were starting to come on. A barge and a tour boat were passing on the river, the sound of laughter rose up from the restaurants below. It was another world, one that had somehow remained the same while hers was shattering into pieces. She thought of the next few hours, the emptiness he would leave behind if she let him go, the fear, the utter devastation of their dreams . . .

171

Long, agonizing seconds ticked by. She heard him get up, and terrified he was about to leave, she spun round. He came towards her and pulled her into his arms.

She clung to him, sobbing. 'I can't bear it,' she gasped. 'I love you so much, Elliot. Please . . . Please don't do this.'

He continued to hold her, stroking her hair and feeling her tears dampening his shirt. 'I'm sorry,' he murmured. 'I'm just so sorry.'

'We belong together,' she said, looking up at him. 'You know we do.'

His only response was to gaze sadly down into her face as she continued the desperate search for words to change his mind. 'You'll meet someone else,' he told her softly.

'*No!*' she raged, pushing him away. 'How dare you say that? I don't want anyone else. I want you. For God's sake, you don't seem to understand what you're doing, what this means to me. I love you, Elliot. You're everything to me, so how can you stand there saying I'll meet someone else? Don't you care? Doesn't it hurt you to think of me with another man?'

'Of course it does, but if it's someone who can give you . . .'

'*Don't* talk about what I deserve again,' she seethed, her eyes flashing with fury. 'I don't want to hear it. It's pathetic. It's you pretending to be some kind of worthless bastard . . . Well it's what you are, so you don't have to pretend.'

His eyes reflected her torment as he looked back at her.

'Stop it!' she cried. 'Stop looking at me like that.

172

If you don't want me, then just go. Get out of here. But before you do, maybe you'd like to call my parents and explain why you're doing this, see if you can make them understand why you're destroying their other daughter now.'

'It's not . . .'

'Maybe you'd like to call everyone else and tell them there's not going to be a wedding,' she shouted. 'Yes, you do it. You tell them that you've decided you don't love me any more, and probably never did. I don't see why the hell I should do it.'

'Laurie, listen . . .'

'No!' she cried, raising her arms as he tried to hold her again. 'I don't want you to touch me. I don't want you near me any more.'

He stood looking at her as she buried her face in her hands. She turned her back and let her head rest against the window. He lifted a hand to touch her, but let it drop again. He didn't want to leave her like this, but there was nothing he could do to make it any better. In the end, he went over to the table, picked up his keys and started towards the door.

Hearing it open she spun round. 'Elliot,' she sobbed.

He stopped and turned back.

'Please don't go.'

He took a breath.

'Please. Don't leave me yet.'

His head went down as he took another breath. 'I'm sorry,' he said. 'I never wanted to hurt you like this.'

As the door closed behind him she felt an

unbearable panic rise up inside her. She had to go after him, she just had to. She started to run, then stopped. She turned round, clasped her hands to her head and began sobbing again. 'No, no, no,' she cried. 'Please, no. This can't be happening. I can't bear it.'

Sherry was settled in for the evening, curled up in an armchair, a balmy night air drifting in from the river, and a favourite CD playing softly in the background, when the phone started to ring.

Reaching behind her, she scooped up the receiver. 'Hi, are you back in London now?' she said, certain it was Laurie calling to set a time to meet in the morning.

There was a pause before the voice at the other end said, 'Yes, but I think you could be mistaking me for someone else.'

She was suddenly very still. Even if he'd spoken only one word, she'd have known it was him. 'Nick?' she whispered.

'How are you?'

She took a breath. *Oh my God, it was actually him.* She'd imagined this call a thousand times in the last week, but only now did she realize that she'd never really dared believe it would come. 'How did you get my number?' she said, feeling the delayed reaction of her senses starting to kick in.

'From Elliot Russell. Do you mind?'

'No. No, of course not. He told me you were in town.' She was trying desperately to think of something to say, anything that would sound at least halfway intelligent, but her thoughts were moving headlong into chaos and she was starting to shake.

'I'm going to be here a while,' he told her. 'I was hoping we could meet up.'

'Yes. Yes of course.' *Well done, Sherry, on the scale of cool you've just scored a humiliating zero.* 'Let me check my diary. When's good for you?'

'Any time. Friday?'

'Yes, Friday looks good.' She hadn't even reached for a book. 'Would you like to come here? We could have a drink, and maybe go to one of the restaurants nearby.' Oh God, what if he hadn't meant dinner?

'Sounds perfect. Now all I need is your address, and I'll come by, shall we say around seven?'

A few minutes later she was standing next to the phone, her hand still on it as she stared at nothing in a daze. She wasn't entirely sure now what she'd expected if he called, but this was definitely qualifying for one of her wildest dreams. She was actually going to see him on Friday – today was Monday – and she wished to God Rhona was next door, because she was absolutely going to burst if she didn't tell someone. She was on the verge of calling Anita when the phone rang again.

She stared down at it. What if it was him, having second thoughts? *For God's sake, Sherry, pull yourself together.*

'Hello?' she said anxiously into the receiver.

'Sherry. It's Laurie . . .'

'Laurie!' she cried, seized by relief and euphoria. 'What amazing timing. I've just heard from Nick. We're meeting on Friday.'

'Oh, that's great,' Laurie mumbled. 'I'm really pleased for you. How is he?'

175

Sherry paused. 'Are you all right?' she said, frowning. 'Have you been crying?'

'Oh Sherry,' Laurie choked, unable to hold it back. 'I'm sorry. I don't mean . . .'

'Laurie, what is it? What's happened?'

'It's Elliot . . . He's . . . called off the wedding.'

There was a moment's stunned silence before Sherry said, 'Are you at the flat?'

'Yes.'

'I'm on my way.'

It was now the early hours of the morning. Laurie's face was a ghostly mask in the semi-darkness, her eyes staring blindly into nothing. She looked completely worn out, and would, Sherry guessed, soon be able to sleep.

It had been a while since either of them had spoken. They were simply sitting quietly now, stilled by creeping exhaustion, numbed by the shock of what had happened.

Laurie looked down at her empty glass and felt the dread of it all rising up in her again. While waiting for Sherry she'd called Elliot's mobile and left a message, but he hadn't called back. Did he have any idea how much that hurt? Did he care? She was sure he did, but somehow that made it worse. She pictured his face, tried to read his mind, went over and over all they had said. Then the thought of what it would be like the next time she saw him tore at her heart, for it was a scenario that consisted of two strangers dismantling their lives, breaking it all apart to go their separate ways.

Sherry looked at her.

'Why do we do this?' Laurie said dully. 'Torment

ourselves with just how awful things are going to be?'

'I don't know,' Sherry answered. 'But if you can stop, it'll help you to get through the next few hours much easier than if you keep doing it.'

Laurie tried to smile.

'You've got no idea what's going to happen next,' Sherry reminded her. 'You don't even know what tomorrow's going to bring, so somehow you have to just focus on now.'

'Except now's not so great either, is it?' Laurie responded, rubbing her hands over her eyes. 'I'm so tired, but I don't think I can sleep. I just want to sit here waiting for him to come back, even though I'm terrified he won't.'

'Well, probably not tonight, anyway,' Sherry said.

Laurie's eyes were wide like a child's as she watched Sherry get up and stretch out her limbs. 'Are you going?' she said.

'No. I was just thinking, why don't I get a couple of blankets? We can sleep here, on the sofas.'

Laurie's heart recoiled from the horror of why it was necessary, though she was grateful to Sherry for understanding how hard it would be for her to go to bed tonight. 'I can't believe that it's really going to end,' she said, her voice starting to shake. 'It's not, is it? Please tell me it isn't. We're so much a part of each other's lives. How can he just walk away like that?'

'He might not,' Sherry answered. 'He could just need some time to think, to come to his senses and realize you really are who he wants.'

Laurie looked away. The fact that he could be in any doubt was maybe what hurt most of all, for she'd truly believed he loved her as much as she loved him. 'Why hasn't he called back?' she said. 'I left a message . . .'

'He'll call tomorrow, I'm sure.'

Tears began filling her eyes again. 'How am I going to tell my parents? I'm dreading it. They're going to be as upset as I am, and I don't know if I can cope with that.'

'You're tired now,' Sherry reminded her. 'You'll feel better when you've had some sleep. I'll go and get those blankets.'

As she went, Laurie curled up on the sofa and held herself tight, until the thought of him in Chris's apartment, alone, without her, made her suddenly sit up again. She couldn't lie there with the pain of it, she had to move around, as though she could somehow escape it.

She was standing at the window when Sherry came back, staring out at the night. 'You've been through this,' she said quietly. 'Please tell me what I have to do . . .'

'Come on,' Sherry said. 'We can talk again in the morning.'

'You give all this advice,' Laurie reminded her. 'You tell people how to deal with their pain . . .'

'Ssh,' Sherry interrupted, and gestured for her to sit down. 'It's a little advice column, nothing to be taken too seriously.'

'But you know,' Laurie said. 'You've been there. You've had to deal with so much yourself. The death of your parents. Nick leaving you . . . Tell me again what he said when he rang.'

'Tomorrow,' Sherry insisted. 'I'm much too tired even to think about it now, and so are you.'

178

Later, with the lights turned off, they both lay under their blankets, eyes closed but neither of them sleeping yet. Sherry listened to the uneven sound of Laurie breathing, and could almost feel her fear. The irony of Nick's return to her own life, while Laurie was having to contemplate the nightmare of Elliot's departure from hers, wasn't lost on her, though she didn't want to believe that would happen. Elliot might just wake up in the morning and realize what a monumental mistake he was about to make. She hoped to God he did, because she knew from experience that the kind of pain Laurie would suffer if he didn't was so devastating that it was a miracle anyone ever got through it. Somehow they did, usually with the help of close friends and family, which was why Sherry was here now, and would be for as long as Laurie needed her.

After a while she realized Laurie had finally fallen asleep, so she turned her thoughts back to Nick, and smiled into the darkness at the wonderfully warm glow it gave her inside. She knew time should have lessened her feelings, but after hearing his voice tonight she didn't think it had. She had to remind herself, though, that in many ways he was a stranger now, made familiar by memories and dreams, but a stranger nonetheless. It was hard to think of him that way though, for it simply wasn't how he felt. His dark moody eyes, his deep melodic voice, his wit, his charm, his readiness to take on any challenge, or to help anyone in distress . . . He was a unique and fascinating man whom, in her heart, she felt she knew almost as well as she knew herself. No, he could never be a stranger.

Gazing into the silvery moonlight pooling around the room, she let her mind slip back to those wonderful balmy California nights, the flicker of candlelight in a secluded garden and the buzz of crickets in the darkness. To the Hawaiian dancers in a tropical sunset; waves washing gently over their feet as they strolled and kissed; waterfalls crashing into rock pools as they swam. She could hear him laughing and sighing with pleasure, could feel the touch of his hand on hers, the whisper of his breath on her cheek . . . Then her eyes closed as a dark cloud seemed to threaten her happiness, and fear began tightening her throat. So much time had passed, so many things had changed, could they really go back? She didn't possess the kind of will-power it would take not to try, but it was going to open up so much, so very much, and if it didn't work out how was she ever going to bear losing him again?

It was a little after nine when Laurie woke up, slowly, groggily at first, until with a horrible, sickening jolt everything came rushing back. 'Oh no,' she groaned, turning her face into the pillow.

'I won't ask how you're feeling,' Sherry said from the kitchen, 'I can guess. All the vodka won't have helped, either.'

'You're right about that,' Laurie said, throwing off the blanket and swinging her legs to the floor. 'How did you sleep?'

'OK. I've just been downstairs to get some croissants and coffee. Are you up for it?'

'The coffee, yes. I don't think I can eat anything.'

Sherry didn't press it, she knew food was the

180

last thing anyone wanted at a time like this, but later she would insist, because no way was Laurie going to be able to handle anything with her physical energies down. Stamina and practical thinking were called for now, and though Laurie might believe herself incapable of either, Sherry was here to remind her she wasn't.

'I don't suppose he's called,' Laurie said, as Sherry brought her coffee round.

'It's still quite early,' Sherry replied.

As Laurie took the coffee she could feel herself starting to break up inside. 'I'm sorry,' she said. 'Oh God, what a mess. I'm so pathetic . . .'

'Not pathetic,' Sherry responded gently. 'You're still in shock, and it's better to let it out, so cry all you want.'

Laurie smiled and wiped her eyes with the back of her hand. 'Thanks for being here,' she said. 'I'd probably throw myself off the roof if you weren't, but suicide's not something I should joke about, is it? Not in my family. Oh God, here I go again,' she said as more tears welled up. 'Am I ever going to stop?' The thought of Lysette was overwhelming her now, and waking up with this awful disruption in her life was making everything worse, because she shouldn't be sitting here with Sherry like this, it wasn't what happened in the morning. Elliot should be here, poring over the papers or talking on the phone. Oh God, where was he? What was he doing now?

Sherry sat quietly with her own thoughts, still trying to decide the best way to handle this. Of course, there was always a chance it would work out and he'd come back, but if Elliot really meant

181

what he'd said, that he didn't love her the way he should, then they had to face the fact that he probably wouldn't return. It was the negative aspect that Sherry had somehow to prepare Laurie for, because the positive needed no help, but how on earth did you ever prepare anyone for the fact that she was about to go through hell? She had no real answer to that, though she did know that right now shock and denial would be providing their own form of assistance. It was like a dance, she thought, or a grotesque pantomime, the good guys and the bad guys, hope and strength versus fear and despair. In a week or two the bad guys would be dominating the stage, which was when things would really get tough. In other words, it might be bad now, but if Elliot didn't come back it was going to get a whole lot worse.

However, anything could happen between now and then, so deciding to deal just with the present, Sherry said, 'After you've had a shower and made yourself presentable, we should work out what you're going to do today.'

Laurie shrank back. 'I can't do anything until I've spoken to Elliot,' she protested.

'OK, then we'll put that top of the list. Call Elliot.' She made it sound as though she were writing it down. 'What are you going to say?'

Laurie started. 'I don't know. I haven't thought about it yet. I suppose I should ask if we can meet and talk.'

'Why not *tell* him you want to talk?'

Laurie looked uncertain, until a glimmer of humour broke through the doubt. 'OK. I'll *tell* him,' she said. 'What next?'

'You need to decide what you want to talk about.'

'Well, us, of course.'

'What about you?'

Laurie frowned. 'What's happening. What we're going to do.' Her heart twisted – she was already talking as though he wasn't coming back.

'I'm just trying to make you see that you don't have to be the victim here,' Sherry said. 'You can take charge. Let him think that you're willing to go along with what he wants . . .'

'But I'm not.'

'I know, but if you make a show of accepting his decision, and let him think he's doing the right thing, there's a very good chance he'll start to doubt himself.'

Laurie had to take a moment to think about that. 'You mean if I allow him to leave me, he won't want to.'

'Possibly. You know what they say about setting someone free if you want them to come back.'

Laurie looked decidedly dubious.

'All right, I can see we need to take this more slowly,' Sherry smiled. 'So why don't we start with the shower?'

'What about the phone call? Can't I make that first?'

'If you like.'

Laurie reached for the phone, horribly aware of the mayhem that had started up inside her. 'I just tell him I want to talk?' she said, looking at Sherry.

Sherry nodded. 'Don't get into anything else.'

'Can't I ask him how he is? How he slept?'

183

Though Sherry wanted to say no, she realized it was too harsh, too soon. 'OK,' she relented. 'Just try not to get emotional.'

At that Laurie stopped dialling and laughed. 'You're not serious, I take it.'

'I am, but I can see I won't win.'

Laurie was still laughing, despite the tears that were blurring her eyes. 'Oh God, why is this even necessary?' she wailed. 'Why isn't he here?' A moment later his voicemail picked up the call. 'Shall I leave another message?' she said as the message played.

'OK.'

'Hi, it's me,' Laurie said into the phone. 'Can we . . .' Her eyes flicked to Sherry. 'I want to talk. Please call me.' Only as she rang off did she realize how hard she was shaking. 'How was that?' she said.

'Not bad.'

'I should have told him I loved him.'

'You should get in the shower.'

Laurie took a breath and let it out slowly. 'The shower,' she repeated, feeling the memories of things that had happened even in that small room starting to crowd in on her. 'OK. I'll just pretend he's away on an assignment.'

'That should do it.'

Half an hour later Laurie came back down the stairs, looking so lost that Sherry wanted to hug her.

'Has he called?' she said.

Sherry shook her head.

Laurie looked down at her hands and swallowed hard. 'I'm sorry. I shouldn't be doing this

184

to you,' she said. 'I'm being so pathetic, and you've got your own life to get on with.'

'Don't worry about me. I'm fine,' Sherry assured her. 'Rachel's on her way over.'

'You've spoken to her?'

'She called just now to see how you are. I guess, as he's in Chris's flat, Chris must have told her.'

Laurie looked around, tried to hold it together, but suddenly couldn't. 'This is really happening,' she said brokenly. 'People know. Oh God, Sherry, he really means it.'

Sherry went to hold her, wishing she could find the words to stop the hurt, but there were none. It was a horrible, terrible thing to go through, and nothing, but nothing ever made it feel better. There were just pauses in the intensity, moments when you could cope, until the ones when you couldn't came back again.

'Is there any more coffee?' Laurie said finally.

'It's just brewing. I hope you don't mind, but I called Rhona.'

Oh God, it was getting worse. She didn't want anyone to know, it made it too real. 'What did she say?'

'That you'll probably be back together by the end of the day, if not, by the end of the week.'

Laurie felt a lift in her heart and smiled. 'Typical Rhona,' she said, loving her.

Sherry nodded. There was no reason to tell her that Rhona had also said she'd be home on the next plane if Sherry thought it necessary. They'd left it that Sherry would call again later in the day, when she had a clearer idea of where things might be going. She just wished she could say she had a good feeling about it all, but the truth was she really didn't.

Going into the kitchen to take charge of the coffee, Laurie said, 'Did Rachel say if she's seen Elliot?'

'No. She just asked how you were, and if it would be OK to come over.'

Laurie continued pouring the coffee, put a few plates in the dishwasher, wiped down the counter tops, then suddenly stopped, as the thought of the honeymoon swept in from nowhere and took her breath clean away. She looked at Sherry. 'I can't do this,' she said. 'I'm sorry, I just can't. He's got to come back. Please tell him, he has to.'

'It's all right,' Sherry assured her. 'Just breathe. Let the feelings happen and breathe. It'll pass.'

Laurie was shaking her head. 'I can't . . .'

'Yes you can. Now come on. Breathe in to the pain, out with joy. In to the pain, out with joy.'

The doorbell rang.

'Just stay there,' she told Laurie. 'Keep breathing.'

As she opened the door Sherry's fingers were crossed that it was who she was expecting. Finding herself confronting an elegant, older woman with the same vivid blue eyes as Laurie's, she said a silent prayer of thanks and smiled. 'Come in,' she said. 'She's through there.'

At the sound of footsteps Laurie looked up from behind the kitchen counter.

'Hello, darling,' her mother said.

Laurie's eyes were wide with shock. 'Mum,' she murmured. 'What – what are you doing here?'

'Sherry called me,' her mother answered.

Laurie's eyes moved to Sherry. For a moment, she hardly knew what she was thinking, until she realized that Sherry had read the situation perfectly, for her mother was the very person she needed to see right now. She started to speak, but the words were swallowed into a sob. 'I'm sorry,' she choked. 'I'm so sorry. I don't want to do this to you, not again . . .'

'Sssh, sssh,' her mother soothed, going to take her in her arms. 'Don't you worry about me. Or Dad. We'll be fine. You just let us worry about you and how we're going to sort this out,' and catching Sherry's eye she smiled her thanks.

Close to tears herself, Sherry left quietly, and went to summon the lift. She'd wait downstairs for Rachel, explain what had happened, then they'd probably go and have coffee and discuss what they could do to help Laurie through this, and what might really be going on with Elliot.

As she reached the lobby her mobile started to ring. Looking at the readout she saw it was Barry Davidson and clicked on.

'Sherry?' he said. 'I got Stan Bright here, Laurie's private detective. He needs a word.'

'With me?' she said, surprised. 'OK. Put him on.'

A moment later Stan's gruff voice came down the line. 'I'm not going to beat about the bush,' he told her, 'it's not my style. Someone's having you watched, and it don't take no genius to work out who.'

Sherry's heart gave a thud of unease.

Stan was still talking. '. . . so you better presume they know who you really are by now. Your cover

187

was too thin, girl. It won't have taken the likes of them more than five minutes to crack it.'

Apart from feeling naïve, Sherry was horribly unnerved. 'What about Laurie?' she asked. 'Is she being watched too?'

'I don't think so. It was you what went round there, so it's you they're interested in. You should watch your step, especially once they find out their workshop's been broken into.'

Sherry's eyes widened. 'How do you know that?' she said.

'Because it was me. I went in last night to take a look around. There weren't no sign of the women we're looking for, but I reckon they was there, locked away in an upstairs room, probably up until a couple of days ago.'

'What makes you say that?'

'There was some old mattresses, a veil sort of thing, like an Indian woman would wear, a hair-brush, some female stuff, you know, the monthly kind, and a couple of sewing machines what are in working order.'

Sherry took a moment to digest this, then sounding gratifyingly firm, at least to herself, she said, 'OK, we need to meet. Laurie won't be able to make it, but I'll get the keys to her office and see you there in an hour. Barry too if he's free.'

As she rang off she could feel the adrenalin kicking into her system. She hated to be opportunistic, but there was no denying this could be a perfect chance to prove herself, not only to Laurie, but to Elliot too. Whether either of them would notice, being in such emotional turmoil, was debatable. However, equally, if not more important, was finding those women, for after meeting Karima Ghosh, and learning even what little she had about Eddie Cribbs, there was no doubt in her mind that they desperately needed to be found.

Chapter Ten

'Her name's Sherry MacElvoy, known to her friends as Sherry Mac,' the smart middle-aged woman stated. 'She lives on the second floor of Dunbar Wharf, in Narrow Street, no husband or boyfriend, no family at all, in fact, except an aunt who lives in Somerset. She's British by birth, but grew up in California, which is what gives her an American accent. The California connection is extremely interesting, and could possibly prove useful should she become too troublesome. You'll find the details on page two of the dossier. She writes under a dozen or more pseudonyms for a dozen or more magazines and newspapers, and has never, according to our investigations, worked in the fashion world at any time in her life.'

Eddie Cribbs was sitting at the head of the conference table that stretched across the south side of his executive suite. With him were his right-hand men, Perry Boon and Gentle George, along with Julian Godfrey, the firm's senior solicitor, Will

Grossman, the chief accountant, and Jenny Cox, the firm's Head of Data Accumulation and Analysis. It was Jenny, with her trace of a Mancunian accent, who'd just read aloud from the report one of her hand-picked team had delivered that morning.

'We can also now confirm,' Jenny added, 'that there is a connection to Laurie Forbes. She was followed to Laurie Forbes's flat in Butler's Wharf two nights ago, where she remained until just after Laurie's mother arrived the following morning. After that she met with Rachel Hendon, widow of Tim Hendon and ex-ITV news producer, while Laurie left with her mother to go to Windsor, where she still is. As you may already have read in the papers, Elliot Russell has apparently called off their wedding, which, as far as we're concerned, could have the twin advantage of removing him from any investigation she's involved in, as well as possibly putting her out of action for a while.'

'Or she could bury herself in work,' Perry pointed out. 'Which might make her worse.'

Jenny nodded. 'We'll be keeping an eye on her,' she assured him. 'For the moment though, our chief concern is Sherry MacElvoy. She doesn't have Laurie's reputation for digging out the truth, but that doesn't mean she's not capable, in fact we should presume that she is.'

'Why's she writing under pseudonyms?' Eddie wanted to know. 'What's the matter with using her own name?'

'I don't have an answer for that yet, but we're checking into it.'

Eddie sniffed, and sat back in his chair. 'So,' he

said, taking off his glasses and wiping them with the end of his tie, 'since we don't want to get involved in offing a member of the press and all the shit that would entail, we've either got to find a way of convincing them they're up a dead-end street, or we're going to need someone on their team to keep us abreast of what our new friend, Sherry MacDonalds, is up to.' He put his glasses back on and cast his eyes around.

'Trying to talk them out of it never works,' Julian Godfrey said.

'Never,' Eddie agreed. 'So, who have we got who can help us?'

'To date, Sherry MacElvoy's always been a one-man band,' Jenny told him, 'and Laurie Forbes's team is too tight to penetrate.'

'What about the Barry Davidson fellow?' Perry ventured. 'He's the one who tipped the press off in the first place. He's bound to be working on this with them, so we just persuade him it'll be in his best interests to keep us informed of developments.'

Eddie gave that some consideration, then glanced towards his desk as his secretary's voice came over the intercom.

'Your three o'clock's arrived, Eddie,' she told him. 'I've put her in the flat.'

He frowned and looked at Perry for enlightenment.

'Miss Burrows?' Perry guessed.

Still nothing.

'From the club?'

'Oh yeah, right.' He leaned back and shouted towards the speaker. 'I haven't got much time,' he

192

told his secretary, 'so tell her to have everything ready.'

'Will do,' came the reply.

Jenny was typing fast on her laptop. 'I'm just calling up our profile on this Barry Davidson,' she informed Eddie. 'He's a bit of a do-gooder around the East End, so I know we've got something.'

Eddie nodded. 'Right. So how are we going to persuade him to switch teams, is what I want to know. Is he married?'

'Just give me a sec,' Jenny replied. A beat later the information was there. 'Not married,' she answered, scanning it quickly. 'But he does have a girlfriend, who works for the council, and a mother who lives in Bethnal Green.'

'Father? Brothers?'

'Nothing here.'

'Does the mother live alone?'

'Yes.' It was the kind of information that had an accumulation priority.

'Then she's our ticket. Get someone to turn her place over, scare her a bit, then drop in for a chat with Sonny Jim. He'll get the message.' He turned to Perry. 'Has the doctor been taken care of?'

Perry nodded.

'Have we found a replacement yet?'

'I think so. We'll just have to rein in our headmaster and his chums, until it's properly fixed.'

Eddie turned to his accountant and lawyer. 'I hear you used a few of the boobies for a party the other night. Any good?'

'Not bad,' Julian replied.

'I hope you paid the going rate, it's a good little

earner, that one, and we don't want to be cheating ourselves now, do we?'

'I gave us a discount,' Will confessed. 'Not a big one, but it generated some interest among the guests for future use, so it should pay off nicely.'

Appearing pleased with that, Eddie moved on to other business. 'Right, let's have the low-down on how the crack boys are doing, after the cock-up with the last shipment.'

'Everything seems to be getting back on track,' Perry answered, 'pardon the pun. Not too big a loss. Nothing we can't recover from.'

'When's the next one coming in?'

'Friday. By plane. We've got the usual operators on standby at Stansted.'

'Quantities. Value. Expected profit,' Eddie prompted.

Will passed him several sheets full of figures and began going through them, while the others reshuffled their papers ready to move on to their next items of business. It was Perry who had details of the human cargo due to arrive at its destination in less than ten days, and he knew already that Eddie wasn't going to like what he had to report on that. Apparently what should have started out as one thousand bodies on the good ship *Tonna Maru* had, he'd now been informed, been closer to thirteen hundred, because some tosser in a turban – crew? captain? – had thought they could make a few bob for themselves. Now, due to overcrowding, lack of food, insanitary conditions, etcetera, etcetera, they had twenty or more stiffs on board that had to be disposed of before the cargo could land in Hamburg.

It was past four o'clock by the time Eddie brought the meeting to a close, by which time his expression was a dark, brooding study of a man with too much on his plate. But when had it ever not been like that? There were always problems, they always got sorted, he'd just feel a bit happier in himself if this press thing could be got rid of.

'This Sherry Whatever-her-name-is,' he said, turning back as he was about to leave.

'MacElvoy,' Jenny supplied.

'You mentioned she had an aunt.'

'In Somerset.'

He nodded. 'Might be worth bearing in mind,' he said.

In the private apartment just along the hall, in accordance with instructions, Cheryl was undressed and ready to go the minute Eddie came in. The longest he'd kept her waiting so far was three and a half hours, which was why she'd brought the latest copies of *Hello!* and *OK!* with her today, and a Walkman so she could practise her routine. Two weeks it had taken her to be promoted from waitress to dancer, which was a record in the club's history, and had been so successful in putting Suzy-Woo's nose out of joint that if the stupid cow didn't stop bitching and trying to stir up trouble, Cheryl was going to work on Eddie to get rid of her altogether.

Yawning, she shifted her position on the bed and carried on reading the paper his secretary had brought in a while ago. It was an early edition of the *Standard*, which she didn't normally go in for, but she was right into this story about the reporter,

Laurie Forbes, who'd been dumped by her boyfriend, another reporter, six weeks before they were supposed to get married. Poor cow. Must be broken-hearted, getting elbowed like that, and then to go and have it gossiped about in all the papers . . .

Hearing the door open she gasped and quickly covered herself with the paper.

Eddie grinned.

She looked up at him from under her lashes, and coyly let the paper go so he could see her boobs. He loved it when she acted shy like this, and she was getting quite good at it.

'Sorry I kept you waiting,' he said, closing the door.

'Oh, that's all right,' she assured him. 'I don't mind.'

As he came over to the bed he was loosening his tie.

She kept her head down, and arms pressed into the sides of her boobs as though attempting to cover them, but only succeeding in pushing them together and making them look bigger than ever.

'Trevor tells me you're turning into a good little dancer,' he said, sitting on the edge of the bed to remove his shoes.

'I'm glad he thinks so,' she answered softly.

'Do you enjoy it?'

She hesitated. 'Yes, but . . .'

'But what?'

'Nothing.'

'Come on, out with it.'

'Well, it's the other girls . . .'

'Take no notice of them. You're my girl, so that

gives you special status. You just make sure you don't go upsetting the punters, that's all.'

'Oh, I'd never do that,' she promised.

'And I don't want you going with them either.' He thrust a hand between her legs. 'This is all mine, right? You can dance your little ass off, shake your tits about, do whatever the hell you like, but no-one gets to touch, except me. You got that?'

She nodded and gazed at him with big, girlie eyes. He'd laid the rules down before, but she liked hearing them again. It reaffirmed her special status, as he called it.

'There is just one little thing though,' she said in a tiny voice.

'What's that?'

'Well, because the other girls get to go with the punters, it means they make a lot more than me, and . . .'

He started to laugh. 'You're a foxy bint,' he told her, chucking her under the chin. 'Find out how much the top earner's getting and we'll double it. How's that?'

Her eyes opened wide. 'Oh, Eddie, Mr Cribbs,' she gushed.

'You can call me Eddie.' Then, after thinking about it, 'I quite like the Mr Cribbs too, so you can keep it.' He tilted her face up and turned it from side to side to get a good look. 'I can see straight through you, I hope you know that,' he told her. 'But I like you, and I'm always generous with the women I like.'

She looked back at him with wide, innocent eyes.

He grinned. 'That's my girl. Now, let's put the paper away and . . .' He broke off as he noticed the picture of Laurie Forbes staring out of the open pages. 'What the . . . ?' he growled. 'Is that woman fucking haunting me, or what?'

Confused, Cheryl looked down at the paper, then started as he grabbed it and bunched it into a ball. 'On your back, girl,' he commanded, tossing the paper on to the floor, 'and let's get on with what you're here for.'

'Honestly, I think it's a great idea,' Sherry was saying to Laurie on the phone. 'Even if you only go for a few days, the break is bound to help, and I can manage things here.'

'But I feel like I'm leaving you in the lurch,' Laurie protested, sounding very much as though she had a cold, though Sherry knew better. 'It should be my responsibility . . .'

'Don't worry about me. I'll cope. You just go and relax with Rhona on that sunny Greek island.'

Laurie fell silent, then in a slightly wavering voice she began going over all the reasons again why she didn't want to go to Hydra.

Sherry glanced at her watch. Normally she'd be happy to talk as long as Laurie needed to, but this evening she couldn't. Her heart skipped a beat at the thought of why – Nick was due in less than two hours, and she still had so much to do she was afraid she wouldn't be ready in time. However, she knew what it was like to be in Laurie's shoes, so she couldn't just cut her off.

'I don't want to be that far from him,' Laurie was saying. 'I know it doesn't make any sense, but he can't be feeling good about any of this, and if he does want to talk . . .'

'Have you heard from him yet?' Sherry asked.

'No, he still won't return my calls. I don't understand it. It's just not like him to behave like this.'

'Has Rachel seen him?'

'No, but he's still at Chris's flat, over the gallery.'

Sherry was shaking her head in bemusement. 'What the heck's going on with him?' she murmured, almost to herself. 'It makes me wonder if his mind's as made up as he said, hiding away like this. It could be he needed to clear the decks completely in order to think straight.'

'Or that he thinks there's no more to say. That it'll just drag everything out, make it even more painful and difficult, if we keep discussing it.'

'Even if you're right,' Sherry said, clicking her mouse to send an email, 'there are still things to sort out. I take it the flat is in both your names.'

'Yes, it is, but don't let's go there. I can't bear to think about having to pack it up and divide . . .' After collecting herself she said, 'Sorry, I . . . This isn't getting any easier.'

'Don't apologize,' Sherry told her softly. 'It's still very early days. How are your parents dealing with it?'

'Much better than I expected. You were right to involve them, being here reassures them I'm not going to do the same as Lysette. My dad left a message for Elliot yesterday, but he hasn't heard back either.'

'What about going round there?'

There was a spark in Laurie's voice as she said, 'I'm not chasing him. He's the one who did this. If he wants to talk he knows where I am.'

Knowing there was no point getting into the

contradiction, or the pride that was probably already falling apart, Sherry said, 'Do you want me to go, see if he'll talk to me?'

'Thanks, but no. Chris is going to try. It's more likely he'll talk to him.' There was another pause, and her voice became strained again as she said, 'It's hard to imagine what's going through his mind, whether he cares about what he's done, if he's just managed to cut off completely . . .'

'Men have different ways of dealing with things,' Sherry reminded her. 'We all do. Just give him a little more time.'

'That's what my mother says. I wanted to send out the cancellation notices today, which I suppose was a kind of F you gesture to him, but she thinks we should wait another week.'

'I agree. There's no rush, it's been in half the papers anyway, so it's not as if people don't already know. And if he does change his mind . . . Oh hang on, I'm waiting for a call from Barry Davidson, I'd better see if that's him.' Quickly she switched lines. 'Hi, Sherry MacElvoy.'

'Sherry, it's Nick.'

Her heart jumped. Nick. It seemed like a dream, even a trick. 'Hi,' she responded warmly, though it had taken a mere split second for her to start bracing herself for the let-down she just knew was the reason for this call. 'How are you?'

'Great. Looking forward to seeing you. Can we make it eight fifteen instead of eight? I'm running a bit late.'

'That's perfect for me,' she replied, almost unravelling with relief. 'Eight fifteen. I'm on the other line, so I'll see you then.' She switched back to Laurie. 'Sorry about that. Are you still there?'

'Yes. Was it Barry?'

'No. Actually . . . it was Nick.' She waited a beat. 'I'm seeing him tonight.'

'Are you serious? Why didn't you say something before? I've been rattling on about myself . . .'

'There's nothing to tell – yet,' Sherry cut in. 'I'll fill you in tomorrow. I should go now though, to start getting ready.'

'All right, but before you do, what news on the women?'

'There's still no indication of where they might be now,' Sherry answered, 'but we're working on it.' It would take too long to get into that right now, and, with everything else she had going on, Laurie's attention span wouldn't cope. Nor, come to that, would hers.

'What about Barry?' Laurie said. 'Has . . .'

'Listen,' Sherry interrupted, 'you can't deal with any of this right now, so just let it go. I'm on the case, Stan and Barry are too, so you go to Hydra, get some sun on your skin and Rhona wisdom in your heart, and I'll fill you in on it all when you come back.'

'What about Rose and the crew?'

'I'll keep in touch with them and deal with whatever comes up, if anything does. Now, I'm really, really sorry, but I have to go.'

Though she felt bad for cutting Laurie off, the phone was hardly down before she was grabbing her purse and dashing out to the wine shop to pick up an expensive Pinot Noir, then on to Waitrose for a smoked salmon roulade, Earl Grey tea and crispy croissants (just in case). Next stop was the florist for a lavish bundle of lilies, the dry cleaners for the three outfits she'd selected to choose from, then a quick stop-off at Hilda's to buy scented candles. If anyone was following her she caught no sight of them, and though she was still unnerved by the prospect she'd decided, for the moment at least, to take the attitude that she'd been through enough in her life to withstand a little stalking.

Two hours later she was standing in front of her bedroom mirror, feeling even more nervous than she'd expected. Her hands were actually unsteady, and her eyes reflected an anxiousness she was finding hard to disguise. Though she'd told herself a hundred times that this shouldn't mean so much, she couldn't help it, it just did. However, she looked lovely. Her skin glowed, her soft crinkly hair cascaded down over her neck, and the miraculously slimming white jeans and sparkly lavender top were, she thought, just right for the occasion – not too dressy, but not too casual either.

Still not quite able to believe this was happening, she dabbed on a little more perfume, then went back to the kitchen to continue preparing the hors d'oeuvres. Ten minutes to go. Her mouth was turning dry and her heart was constantly fluttering, so she poured a small glass of wine in the hope it would help. After taking a mouthful she searched out some matches and went to start lighting the candles. It didn't matter that it wasn't dark, candlelight always lent a glow of intimacy to a room. The French doors stood open on to the balcony, allowing the warm evening air to drift in with the scent of the flowers. The sound of a speedboat racing down the river grew, then faded into the distance. In the quiet that followed she heard the murmur of her neighbours' voices on the balcony below. She gazed out at the sky. It was a clear, pale blue, too early yet for the first glow of a sunset to stain it with pink.

The music she chose was from the Forties and Fifties, classic blues – ballads she and Nick had danced to on moonlit evenings during the short, precious summer they'd shared. Would he want to be reminded? She felt fleetingly unsure, until the opening bars of 'Misty Blue' floated from the CD. How could he object to such beautiful songs, or think her sad for trying to recapture something that had been lost a long time ago?

Wandering out onto the balcony she gazed down at the river. She felt so apprehensive, and yet so happy, to know that in less than ten minutes he would be here. Though she was trying hard not to expect too much from tonight, it was impossible to stop imagining a future she'd hardly even dared think about for so long that the dreams should have faded by now. But tonight they seemed more vivid, more alive and maybe even more possible.

With a tremulous smile she turned to the nasturtiums spilling down over the sides of a large clay pot. Next to them were bright pink and lavender fuchsias mingling with tall purple and white delphiniums and orange hibiscus. The scent of a white flowering jasmine, climbing a wooden trellis, mingled with the pungency of fresh herbs.

She adored her little garden, unsophisticated

and cramped as it was. It reminded her of the one she'd grown up in, with its agapanthus and birds of paradise, iceberg roses, peonies, palms, yuccas and jade. Her mother had tried so hard to keep it all alive, tying, pruning, planting and feeding, but she'd never really had the knack. Long spells of neglect would turn the garden into a wilderness, until suddenly one day they'd jump in the car and go off to the nursery to buy big, colourful replacements, to start all over again.

Then, for a while, everything in their garden would be beautiful and right, full of sunshine and fragrance, a place where hummingbirds and butterflies flitted and fed. It was as though their garden had been a metaphor for their life, which, Sherry knew, was why she cherished and tended her flowers with such care now. She couldn't bear anything to die, for it reminded her too much of things she'd rather forget.

At last the doorbell rang.

As she crossed the sitting room she felt almost nauseous with nerves. She had the odd, disconcerting feeling that her paintings were watching her, gathering like ghosts from the past to see what she would do now. Nick knew everything – he was one of the few people who did – which was why she was experiencing this strange sense of being both here in the present, and back there in the past.

After pressing the buzzer to let him in, she quickly checked her reflection in the mirror, felt relieved and surprised to see how calm, and even pretty, she looked, then pulled open the front door. She could hear the lift rising. Her heart was in her throat. She wanted to weep, run, reach for more wine . . . She stayed where she was, and waited for the lift door to open.

As he stepped out she felt almost light-headed. It really was him. After all this time he was actually standing right there, smiling, and holding an enormous and exquisite bunch of wild flowers.

'Hi,' she said softly, her own smile starting to grow.

'Hi yourself,' he responded. His dark blond hair was pushed back in the same way it had always been, slightly too long, straight, a wayward strand dropping over his brow. There was the odd hint of grey in it now, and more lines around his deep brown eyes. There seemed a harder set to his jaw, yet his smile was as compelling as the warmth and charisma he exuded.

'You haven't changed,' he told her, his eyes almost seeming to touch hers with their gaze.

Irony filled her smile. 'You have, but for the better,' she told him.

He laughed and threw out a hand. 'You always did manage to come up with the better lines.'

As they laughed his eyes remained on hers. 'It's good to see you,' he said softly.

'You too.'

Holding the flowers aside he stooped to kiss her lightly on the mouth. 'Sherry MacElvoy,' he said.

'Nick van Zant,' she responded.

His eyebrows went up, and blushing slightly she looked at the flowers. 'For me?'

'Of course.'

'Then we should put them in water.'

As she walked back into the flat he closed the

front door, and came into the kitchen behind her. She turned to glance at him and loved him just for being there and managing to look as though he belonged.

'Your favourites, if memory serves me correctly,' he said, watching her unwrap the flowers.

She smiled. 'Actually, wild flowers were my mother's favourite,' she gently responded.

His eyes closed. 'I'm sorry.'

'It's OK.'

After a pause he said, 'That was stupid of me. I . . .'

'Honestly, it doesn't matter.' She turned so he could see her smile. 'Look, I'm not upset,' she said, her eyes twinkling with humour.

He dashed a hand awkwardly through his hair, then smiled too. 'A great start, van Zant,' he muttered.

'Forget it,' she chided. 'Now, would you like some wine? I've opened a bottle of red, but there's white if you prefer.'

'Red is fine.' Seeing the bottle next to an empty glass, he picked it up and started to pour.

'Mine's in the sitting room,' she told him.

Carrying the bottle through he topped up her glass and went to stand at the open French doors. 'This is a great place you've got here,' he declared. 'A river view. And flowers. Always surrounded by flowers. How long have you been here?'

'Nine, ten months. I've become very attached to it, so I'll probably stay.'

'Do you still have the house in LA?'

'You mean my parents' house? No. I sold it a few years ago. I couldn't imagine ever going back, so there seemed no point in keeping it. What about you? Elliot mentioned something about you returning to London.'

He drank some wine and turned back into the room. 'It's why I'm here,' he told her. 'I'm going to be looking for a place, and I'm talking to a few people. I'll probably go the freelance route though. I've done my time on staff.'

She glanced up from where she was arranging the flowers and said, 'Could you move those on the coffee table, I want to put the ones you brought there.'

Picking up the vase he breathed in the scent of the lilies and said, 'Didn't your father used to call you Lily?'

She looked up. 'Yes, he did,' she replied. 'I'm surprised you remember.'

He also seemed surprised. 'Sheralyn Lily MacEvilly,' he said.

'Now Sheralyn MacElvoy,' she responded, carrying the fresh vase round to the sitting room and setting it on the table. 'My friends call me Sherry Mac.'

He watched as she stood back to admire the display, then passing her wine, he clinked her glass with his own. 'Here's to Sherry Mac,' he said.

As they drank their eyes remained on each other's, and she wondered again how real this was. 'Shall we sit down?' she said, gesturing towards the sofa.

As they sat she offered him the plate of hors d'oeuvres.

'So, tell me about you,' she said, as he took a slice of smoked salmon roulade. 'What have you been doing all this time? I was trying to remember when we were last in touch. It must be more than six years.' Of course she knew exactly when it was, but she wasn't going to admit it, unless he did.

'Can you believe so much time has gone by?' he murmured, and sipped his drink. 'So much has happened. For you too I guess. You've got quite a career going, I'm told. The last time I saw you, you were almost ready to give up on London and go back to the States.'

She rolled her eyes. 'Is that what I said? Idle threats, because I'd never have gone back, not then, or now. I was probably just feeling frustrated, wanting it all to happen immediately, not giving it any time to come together. You were a great help to me then, with all the contacts you gave me over here, the doors you opened. I've got a lot to thank you for.'

'It was my pleasure,' he said, raising his glass. 'I tried to keep up with what you were doing, but all those aliases . . .'

She chuckled. 'They keep me more or less anonymous, which is how I want to be. Unlike you,' she added, teasingly. 'Your name is always cropping up somewhere, usually in the most dangerous spot on the globe. Tell me about when you were shot in Afghanistan.'

'Actually, it was Pakistan,' he corrected. 'We were just crossing over the border. I got hit in the wrist. But it only skimmed. I don't even have a scar there now. I'm amazed it even made the news.'

She looked at the hand he held out and wanted to touch it. 'I missed your postcards when they stopped coming,' she said lightly. 'It used to make me feel important, to get mail from the great Nick van Zant.'

'Not so great,' he grimaced. 'And I never felt good about that, the way I just stopped writing and calling. I shouldn't have done it like that. I just didn't know how else to do it.'

For a fleeting moment the warmth drained from her smile. She'd become so used to her own version of events now – how they'd made a pact not to see each other again, because their feelings were too strong and the partings too painful – that she'd actually forgotten how it really was. But he was right, he had just cut her off with no word or warning, and at the time it had totally torn her apart. She looked down at her drink. It seemed strange that she could have forgotten that now, but the mind had many different ways of coping, one of which was creating a less painful reality.

'Were you OK?' he asked.

'Of course,' she said, looking up.

He still looked troubled. 'But after what you'd been through, to just cut out on you like that . . .'

Her eyebrows rose playfully. 'I managed to survive,' she said lightly.

His head was tilting to one side as he cast his mind back. 'I'm trying to remember exactly when you left California,' he said. 'Was it immediately after that summer?'

She nodded. 'More or less. After we flew back from Hawaii, and you had to go straight on to New York . . . It was a couple of weeks after that. I closed up the house and came here to England to stay with my aunt.'

'Of course. Your father's sister. In Somerset. That's when you did these paintings.'

She followed his gaze around the walls.

'I remember now,' he said, 'how much they shocked me when I first saw them.'

'I remember that too,' she smiled. 'You helped me to hang them in my first flat, here in London. You were the only one who seemed to see what I saw in them. No-one else has since. People don't even seem to notice them much. Well, they're not particularly good, I'm not even sure why I've kept them, except I suppose they serve as some kind of reminder that if I could get through that I could get through anything. Or maybe they're a reminder that nothing could ever be as bad again. Whatever. At the time it was a way of expressing what I had going on inside, getting it all out, like some kind of exorcism. And I needed it back then – a lot.'

'That's true,' he said softly. 'How are you dealing with it all now?'

'In many ways it feels like a bad dream,' she answered, her eyes starting to drift. 'Something that never really happened. I've tried to cut all contact with everyone from that time, though I still get the occasional letter.'

He was watching her closely. 'So you've never seen her since?'

She shook her head, and looked at him again. 'It's amazing what we manage to come through, isn't it?' she said. 'Eighteen months of pure hell, then along comes you.' Her eyes were taking on a playful glint. 'My very own hero.'

There was no answering light in his eyes as he

said, 'Who happened to be married and broke your heart all over again.'

'It wasn't intentional,' she reminded him, 'and, like I said, I survived. Mainly thanks to Aunt Jude, who put up with me and my nightmare paintings for six months or more, before I finally got myself together enough to start calling the numbers you'd given me in London. You used to call me every week then, to see how I was doing. Do you remember that?'

He nodded.

'I used to live for those calls. They made all the difference at a time when I kept wondering if there was any point in going on. You always managed to persuade me there was, even though I knew we, you and I, could never work out. It didn't stop me hoping, of course, but I gradually got used to the fact that it wouldn't happen. Then one day, out of the blue, you called up and told me you were right here in London. I hadn't seen you since we'd left Hawaii, and suddenly you were here.' She didn't tell him how, at the time, she'd thought he'd left his wife, that he'd come because being apart from her had been too much to bear. It was a long time ago and there was no point now going back over her terrible crash into despair when she'd learned she was wrong. 'Do you remember that tiny bedsit I used to have, in Chiswick?' she said. 'Where we first hung the paintings?'

He frowned.

'You mean you've forgotten our little love nest!' she cried, eyes dancing. 'It was on the High Road, over a Chinese restaurant. You came there at least three times.'

'I remember the paintings,' he said. 'Are you sure it was Chiswick?'

'Of course. Then I moved to Wandsworth.'

His expression remained uncertain, telling her he'd forgotten that too.

She laughed and flicked him to cover the disappointment.

'My memory is useless,' he confessed. 'I know we stayed in touch, and obviously that we saw each other here in London . . . But the details . . .' He shrugged and apologized. 'I remember our summer in California though,' he said, his voice softening, 'and those few wonderful days in Hawaii.'

'Well there's a relief,' she responded.

He smiled. 'It was a very special time.'

'It was,' she agreed, her tone less dry now. 'One of the most special times of my life.' She looked down at her glass. 'It was difficult too. I mean for you.'

'For us both. But I have no regrets. I guess you do, but . . .'

Her eyes came up. 'Not about us,' she said. 'I'll never regret that.'

As they continued to look at each other he raised a hand to touch her face.

'They say,' she whispered, 'that someone always comes along when you need them most. You were there for me then.'

'I'm glad,' he said gently. 'And I'm glad I've found you again now.'

A faint colour rose in her cheeks and she watched his hand as he reached for more wine. 'So tell me,' he said, refilling her glass, 'has there been anyone since? I mean, anyone serious? Are you seeing someone now?'

'No, I'm not seeing anyone now,' she said. 'What about you? I heard about your wife. I'm sorry.'

He put the bottle back on the table. 'It hasn't been an easy time, that's for sure,' he said. 'For ages I kept thinking I could persuade her to come back. I'd always managed it in the past, but this last time . . .' He shrugged. 'Her mind was made up. She wanted to go and nothing I said was going to make her stay.'

Confusion was making Sherry blink. Hadn't he always wanted his wife to go? Wasn't he only in his marriage because his religion, commitments, conscience wouldn't allow him to leave it? The way he was telling it now didn't make it sound that way at all.

'How long ago did she leave?' she asked.

'Three years.'

Three years. And in all that time he'd never come to look for her.

'It's taken me until now to accept that there really is no hope,' he was saying. 'This other guy, the one she left me for, Gavin Sutherland . . . He's rich, well connected and I guess *there* most of the time, which I almost never was.'

Her smile showed only sympathy and understanding, though inside she was feeling something else altogether. 'What about your daughter?' she asked.

A softness came into his eyes. 'Julia? She lives with them, of course, but I see her a lot. She's coming over next week to help me find a flat.'

'How old is she now?'

'Thirteen, going on thirty. She's a good kid. That was the hardest part, losing her. And my mother, of course. She died around the same time Trudy left.'

'I didn't know that,' she said. 'I'm sorry.'

He was looking into her eyes in a way that seemed to make her heart beat harder, but as he started to speak his mobile rang. 'Damn thing!' he laughed, taking it out of his shirt pocket. 'I meant to switch it off,' and without checking who it was he did just that. 'So,' he said, turning back to her, 'where were we? No, tell you what, how about we continue this over dinner? Are you hungry?'

'Sort of,' she lied. 'I take it you are.'

'Ravenous.'

As she went to close the French doors she was still feeling disturbed by how they didn't seem to be remembering things in quite the same way. It was almost as though he'd considered himself as much a friend as a lover, when, to her mind, that couldn't have been further from the truth. He was talking as though only her heart had been broken, when she'd felt certain that he'd been as deeply affected by their break-up as she had. Or was that just what she wanted to think? Had she managed to convince herself of his feelings in the same way she'd convinced herself they'd made a pact not to see each other again? But no, she knew very well what had happened between them, how hard he had found it to go on to New York when they'd left Hawaii. Maybe this was a case of him creating his own scenarios, altering his memories in a way that would help diminish his guilt for the

214

way he'd cut her off, just as she'd altered hers to ease the pain of her loss.

By the time they'd strolled along the river walk to an Italian restaurant the sun was starting to set, and they'd fallen into an easy, light-hearted banter that was much more reminiscent of the earliest days of their relationship than the difficult, sensitive times that had followed. On this safer ground she could feel the powerful attraction between them beginning to work its magic again, almost as though they were being given a chance to start over.

'I'm remembering now,' he said, after they'd been seated at a patio table under a tree, 'how easy you are to be with. You always were.'

'You're pretty easy yourself,' she responded, picking up a menu, 'so I think you have to take some of the credit. Or maybe,' she added, 'we're a couple of old souls who've known each other for centuries and have come back to spend some time together again.'

He smiled. 'I like that,' he decided. 'It's how it feels, that we've known each other for a very long time.'

Her eyes were shining with laughter. 'So I wonder who we were in our past lives and what stories we shared?' she teased. 'And are we here to resolve something, or continue it, or to do something of profound significance in the world, before moving on?'

'Any of the above will be fine by me,' he grinned, glancing up at the waiter as he passed him the wine list.

After they'd ordered he switched the subject

215

back to her career, and the choices she'd made since they were last in touch. 'You were destined for great things,' he told her earnestly. 'I always felt that. I know you'd hardly had a chance to get going when your life fell apart, but talking to you after it had happened, spending time with you then, and now – you have an insight, a feel for people and events . . .' He was shaking his head. 'The kind of stuff you're doing now . . . It's not who you are. You could make a name for yourself getting involved in things that really matter, and you know it.'

'Well thank you for those few kind words on my contribution to everyday life in our congenitally screwed-up society,' she responded, raising her glass.

'Come on, you know what I mean.'

'Yes, of course I do,' she said, putting her glass down. 'But the person you knew back then . . . I was so young. I still didn't know how hard it was all going to hit. I had no idea the damage wasn't going to confine itself to then, that the repercussions were just going to go on and on . . .'

'But it was a long time ago. They've got to have faded by now. And it wasn't your fault, what happened. You've got no reason to . . .'

'Before you go any further,' she interrupted, 'you were there in Hawaii when that woman snatched her little girl away. You heard what she said. "Don't go near those people, they're bad." Of course she meant me, not you, because she recognized me from the news.'

'She was just ignorant.'

'And I've since learned that there's a lot of

ignorance out there, because believe me it wasn't the only time it happened, nor was it the worst. There's a stigma attached to being who I am, and you don't want to know how cruel some people can be. It was one of the reasons for coming here, to England. It was a chance to start again, and if I just kept a low profile, changed my name slightly and made sure I didn't put it out there too much, there would be less risk of some curious hack going and digging up a past I just wanted to leave behind. And it's working. No-one here's ever really heard of John and Isabell MacEvilly, or their daughter.'

'But even if they had, it doesn't make you any less than who you are. You've got nothing to be ashamed of.'

'Yes, I have. OK, I know you don't think so, but I do, and that's what matters. I don't want it all being raked up again, fingers pointing, comparisons being drawn . . . It's not who I am now.'

'But if it's holding you back professionally . . .'

'It's a small price, and occasionally I do get to work on the kind of things that fire me up and I feel to be worthwhile. In fact, right now I'm working on a story with Laurie Forbes. Do you know her? She's Elliot Russell's . . . Well, she was his fiancée until a week ago.'

'I read they'd broken up,' he said. 'What happened?'

'I don't really know. He said he didn't want to go through with it, but whether he actually means that . . . They were due to get married in a month.'

'That's got to be tough,' he commented. 'On them both.'

'I don't suppose he mentioned anything to you,

when you met?' she ventured. 'Something that might throw some light on why he's backed out now?'

He looked surprised and shook his head. 'He didn't even mention her,' he replied, 'not even to say he was getting married.'

'What about the stories he's working on? Did he tell you anything about them that could suggest going undercover, or running some kind of risk that for some reason he wouldn't want Laurie to know about?'

'Nothing like that,' he answered. 'In fact, I didn't get the impression he was working on anything in particular, except a book he's been commissioned to write.'

'Mm, it's weird,' she commented. 'I just don't understand it.'

He pulled a sardonic face as he looked at her. 'You know, us men are pretty uncomplicated in comparison to you women,' he said, 'so dare I suggest it might be just what he says, that he doesn't want to go through with it?'

She was shaking her head. 'I think there's more to it,' she responded. Then, eyeing him meaningfully, 'I'll take issue on the men being uncomplicated remark another time, because you're not getting away with it.'

He grinned. 'Somehow I didn't think I would, but now, you started to tell me about the story you're working on with Laurie – what was her name again?'

'Forbes. It's a double-edged issue of human trafficking and forced prostitution that we suspect is operating in the East End of London.'

He immediately looked interested, though definitely wary. 'That's some pretty rough territory you're getting into there,' he commented.

'Believe me, I know, though I have to confess I'm enjoying – if that's the right word – the challenge of being involved with something really serious for once.'

'How far into it are you?'

'Hard to say, really. Currently we're trying to track down a group of low-caste Indian women, possibly children too, who we believe are being held against their will and used to service the needs of perverts and paedophiles.'

Disgust curled his lip. 'It goes on, of course,' he said, 'we all know that, especially via the Internet. Who's running this particular operation, any idea?'

'Someone by the name of Eddie Cribbs.'

He shook his head. 'Name doesn't ring a bell.'

'He's your typical modern-day gangster,' she told him. 'Runs everything from his smart offices here in Canary Wharf, never soiling his own hands, apparently, he's got an army of minions to do that for him. Amongst the many fronts he uses is a small garment factory, here in the East End, which is where we believe he was keeping the women until recently.'

'Does he know you're on to him?'

'Probably. My cover, as a fashion buyer, was too thin, I've been told. I don't think it helped, either, that when I went to the workshop I expressed a desire to meet the boss. Not the smartest opening move I've ever made, but it definitely seems to have got things moving.'

'In what way?'

'In that they had me checked out, and that the women have been moved. A guy called Barry Davidson, from a local action group, and a private detective, Stan Bright, are working with us, though I'm not sure what role Laurie's going to play in the coming weeks. If things don't get back on track with Elliot she could be tempted to throw herself into it as a means of distraction, but I'm not sure that's a good idea. She won't be thinking straight, because it's not possible to at a time like that, and even if she were she might be tempted to take too many risks.'

'And that's not something you can afford with these people,' he said gravely. Appearing thoughtful, he took a sip of wine. 'If it weren't for Julia coming over,' he said, 'I'd offer to help out, but I've promised her no work the whole time she's here.'

Her eyes widened. 'I wasn't hinting,' she assured him, 'but thanks for the thought anyway.'

'I could probably come up with a few names though, people who've got an insight into that world.'

'That would be great,' she responded.

He nodded, and sat back as their food arrived. By the time the waiter had finished with his pepper mill, bread basket and need to know if everything was OK, the thread of the conversation had been lost, and Sherry didn't try to find it, for she was quite keen to try again with matters slightly more personal.

As it turned out though, this didn't happen, for once he got talking about the stories he'd been covering in the past few years she was so fascinated, and had so much to ask, that she didn't want him to stop. Besides, there was no rush, for the way things were going there seemed little doubt they'd be seeing each other again, so there would be plenty of time to talk about personal matters. And what was to be said, really, when the chemistry was right there, as potent as it had ever been, in the way they were looking at each other, becoming engrossed in whatever the other had to say, the physical responses that were shooting to various parts of her body. So she was more than content to listen to the inside stories of events he'd become involved in, not only because his passion for journalism went so to the heart of who he was, but because it went to the heart of who she was too.

Later, as they walked, hand in hand, back to her flat, slightly tipsy and seeming perfectly in tune with the romance of the darkening summer night, he said, 'You know, I've been thinking about this human-trafficking story of yours. There's someone I want to put you in touch with who might be able to help. She's New York based, but she's worked on a couple of cases that have involved just this sort of thing.'

'Who is she? A reporter?'

'No, a lawyer. I haven't seen her for a while, but I'm sure she'll be willing to talk to you, give you the kind of MO she's come across with the Cribbs type of operator. I can't imagine it would be much different here to the way it is in the States.'

'That could be really helpful. What's her name?'

'Elaine Sabarito. She's someone I got involved

with after my wife left. We lived together for a while, but it didn't work out. We broke up about nine months ago, on good terms I'm glad to say.'

Though she kept smiling and walking, inside Sherry was reeling. He'd been involved with someone else since his wife left? Someone he'd been serious enough about actually to live with?

As they arrived outside her apartment block she gently withdrew her hand and began searching for her keys. 'It's been wonderful seeing you again,' she said, with a politeness that seemed ludicrously at odds with how things had been a few minutes ago. 'I've had a lovely evening.'

'Me too,' he responded, apparently unfazed.

Was he expecting to come up? It was what she'd hoped for, but now with the spectre of Elaine Sabarito looming over them it didn't seem such a good idea.

'Can I see you again?' he said as she looked up at him.

'I hope so,' she replied. She was thinking now of the croissants and waking up alone in the morning. Saying goodbye at this point in the evening wasn't what she'd planned, it really wasn't what she wanted either.

'I'll call you tomorrow,' he said, pulling her into his arms.

She tilted her face for his kiss. When it came the potency of it stole through her so magically that she'd already taken breath to ask him up when he said, 'I had a great time. It's really good to see you again.'

'It's good to see you too,' she whispered.

Smiling, he touched a finger to the tip of her

nose, then turning on his heel he started down the street to his car.

A few minutes later she was inside the flat staring down at the flowers he'd brought, trying to connect with what had happened, and the way she was feeling. Much of the evening had been wonderful and romantic: he'd said so many things that had melded so easily into her memories and made her feel certain it had all been special for him too. Yet there was no denying those jarring moments when she'd realized how differently they'd felt.

In the end she turned off the lights and went to bed. It would all, she told herself as she gazed into the moonlight, look quite different in the morning, from the small mistake with the wild flowers, to the inconsistency of their memories, to the shock of Elaine Sabarito. So instead of wondering if she'd just been rejected, down there at the door, she should relax and fall asleep thinking about nothing more than how truly wonderful it had been to see him again.

Chapter Eleven

Barry Davidson had no doubt, as he worked to repair the damage to his mother's two-up two-down terraced home, what it was all about. His mum thought it was a random break-in, kids who had nothing better to do than rob and terrorize old ladies, but it wasn't as simple as that. It was probably better for her to think it, though. Less complicated, and less frightening than knowing someone was putting the squeeze on her boy.

Bastards! He'd kill 'em if he could get his hands on 'em. She was seventy-four years old, for God's sake! What chance did she stand against two thugs in leather jackets, with crow-bars and steel-capped boots? She'd been terrified out of her tiny. They'd just burst in, taking the front door right off its hinges, and started smashing the place up. Chairs, the sofa, the table where she'd been filling out her lottery ticket, the sideboard where she kept her best china, her ornament cabinet – it was all over the place. The kitchen cupboards had been ransacked, the bin upended.

The place was a bloody mess, and all the time it had been happening she'd cowered in a corner behind the telly, trembling for her life. They didn't care that she had a dodgy heart, and even if she didn't she was too old and too frail to fight back. She wasn't even steady enough on her legs to go down the corner shop without her Zimmer, which, as it happened, they'd smashed up along with everything else. Fucking bastards! They were too fucking cowardly to come and do his place over. They had to pick on a defenceless old lady, who'd suffered an asthma attack after they'd gone and had ended up being rushed to hospital.

Just thank God for Nosy Nance who lived opposite, otherwise the police wouldn't have turned up when they did, and then the ambulance might not have got there in time. Nance had seen the thugs breaking in, and had dialled 999 straight away. She could be a pain in the arse, could Nance, but it wasn't the only time she'd been on the ball for an emergency in the street.

His mum was still in hospital, but he should be able to pick her up later today. She was insisting on coming back to her own home, which was why he was here with his mates, doing his best to fix it up. She could be a stubborn old cow at times, because, God knew, he'd practically begged her to come and stay with him. Not her, though. This was her home, where she'd lived since she got married, and no thieving little villains were going to drive her out now. She'd get her pension again next week, so the money they'd taken would be replaced, it just meant she'd go short for a bit, but it wouldn't be the first time. She'd survive.

As he picked up an old photo of her and his dad he looked down at their smiling faces and wanted to weep. What the hell was it all about? These were decent, honest people, who'd give you the clothes off their back if they thought you were worse off than them. They'd never done anyone any harm, but his dad had been killed by a drunk driver ten years ago while on his way to pick up a neighbour whose car had broken down, and now his mum was being turned into a victim again because of the help her son was trying to give to those who needed it. Yeah, God. What the hell was it all about? You tried to do some good in the world, and this was what you got.

'Not as bad as it looks,' one of his mates said, coming in from the kitchen. 'Not much breakage, more chucking stuff about really. We should have it all back together by the time you bring her home.'

As it turned out his mate was more or less right. The place was patched up as best they could in a couple of hours, the front door was repaired and they'd managed to glue at least some of her ornaments back together. With any luck she wouldn't need the video tonight, because he hadn't been able to afford a replacement for that. He'd talk to his boss, see if he could get an advance on his wages. Presumably the thugs had taken it, and the cash in her purse, to make it look like a robbery, which meant he should probably be thankful they'd left the TV. She didn't like to be without her TV. Her friend, Mrs Haskins, was going to come and stay tonight. She was happier with that, she'd said, than putting him out when he was so

226

busy. That was typical of her, trying not to make a fuss. Things happened, she always said, and they just had to get on with their lives the best they could.

So that was what he would do. Carry on, the way she wanted. She could stay in Bethnal Green tonight with her friend keeping an eye on her, while he went home to Romford to face whatever was waiting for him there. It hadn't come in the last two nights, since her place had been done over, but a clearer message was on its way, he knew that, just as surely as he knew what answer he was going to give when it came.

Neela didn't know where they were now, but she hadn't known before. She'd just done as she was told the night they'd left the other place, run quickly and quietly down the stairs to a lorry whose big back doors were open ready for them to get in. They'd been told to take their mattresses and other belongings, but no-one had anything more than the clothes they wore.

This place wasn't very different from the last, just hotter and with nowhere to wash. Trains thundered past and made the walls shake. The machines had arrived earlier, so they could work again now. For three days they'd been unable to do anything but sit around and be afraid. Even Bhanu, who hated everyone and was always nice to Mota Ben, had become quiet. Ekta had stopped singing songs to cheer them all up, because now the songs made them cry.

There had been no chance yet for Neela to go to the men who hurt them. Since coming here no-one had been taken outside at all. In her heart she was glad, for she was terrified of what they would do to her. She wanted the time never to come, even though she knew it would. She'd told Ekta what she meant to do, and Ekta had said she was very brave. Ekta would keep the secret, and try to steer Mota Ben Neela's way when she next came to take someone to the men. Ekta would look after Shaila too, while Neela was gone.

Getting chosen wouldn't be easy when she wasn't beautiful like some of the others, but Ekta said that the men liked them to be young and sometimes fear pleased them too. Neela was just sixteen and she was very afraid.

It was still daylight outside. They could see through the cracks in the boards at the windows, and everything sounded fast. Traffic, trains, footsteps, voices. Some of the women were working on the machines, but there wasn't much to do, so the others were just lying on their beds staring at nothing. Neela was building a house of coloured cotton reels with Shaila. On the bed next to them Ekta was chanting under her breath. They tried hard not to make a noise, because they'd been told if they did very bad things would happen to them.

Suddenly Ekta stopped chanting. Neela turned to look at her, and noticed that the other women were alert now too. Then she realized why. Someone was unlocking the door.

Neela's heart began thudding. When Mota Ben walked in with the man they called the driver Neela knew more fear than could fill the world. When the driver came it was to take them to the men.

Neela's big brown eyes met Ekta's, then watched the older woman as she got up to speak to Mota Ben. Their voices were low so no-one could hear what Ekta was saying, but Neela knew she would be telling Mota Ben that the ugly girl with the marked face was the only virgin left.

Mota Ben glanced in Neela's direction. Neela lowered her head and pulled the soiled folds of her shawl up around her. Sensing something was wrong, Shaila tucked herself in close to Neela's body. Neela's hand covered the top of Shaila's head. She kept her eyes down. She could hear Mota Ben and Ekta still talking. They started walking towards her. Neela was terrified and wanted to be dead. Her heart was tearing through her chest. Big rushes of fear were washing over her, as if she was drowning in a river. Mota Ben and Ekta stopped at the end of her bed.

Neela didn't look up.

Mota Ben reached forward and jerked Neela's face up.

Neela's eyes met Mota Ben's but she lowered them quickly. She wanted to disappear so that Mota Ben could no longer see her. *She was not brave.* She wanted to die here, in this place, not out there where men were going to hurt her.

She swayed as Mota Ben let her go.

'Bring her!' Mota Ben snapped.

Ekta leaned over and took Neela's hand.

'Not her. *Her!*' Mota Ben snarled. She was pointing at Shaila.

Neela's head came up. The other women began muttering. Mota Ben told them to stop.

They fell silent.

Mota Ben turned back and snatched Shaila by the arm.

Neela clung to the child.

Shaila was screaming. So was Neela.

Mota Ben slapped them, and called to the driver.

He came quickly, picked up Shaila's flailing body and put a hand over her mouth.

'Shut up!' Mota Ben hissed at Neela. 'Shut up or you'll never see her again.'

It was early in the evening and gloriously sunny as Laurie passed the flower stall on Bond Street. The huge buckets of lilies made her think of Sherry and how Sherry compared her to the flowers, and then of Sherry's date with Nick. She'd spoken to her earlier, but couldn't remember much about the call now. Actually, she probably could, were she able to make her mind focus, but right now she couldn't.

As she turned off Bond Street into one of the side roads that was home to an exclusive jeweller and several art galleries, she thought fleetingly of Rhona, and Hydra. Though Rhona had called several times this past week, and practically begged her to go, she wasn't going to. She couldn't even bear to think of it now. She needed to be here, close to Elliot, doing something, anything, to get the two of them back together.

Approaching Chris's gallery, she felt her hands clench and wondered if she'd ever been so nervous in her life. She hadn't told Elliot she was coming. She was afraid he'd tell her not to, or make sure he was out when she got there. It was horrible, unthinkable that either would be a possibility

– she could barely grasp the fact that it might be. It was as though they'd suddenly taken opposing sides in a battle that she had no idea how to fight. The very thought of him being the enemy closed around her heart like a fist, pressing in the pain, squeezing so hard she had to stop breathing.

Why, she was asking herself, as she stared at the doorbell, unable to push, was she standing here like this? What had happened to her courage? An hour ago, before she'd got on the train, it had seemed a good idea to do it this way, but now it didn't. She didn't feel right – either about herself and the mental state she was in, or about what she was doing, and why she was doing it.

She took a step back from the doorway and walked a few paces on down the street. It wasn't that she was backing out, it was just that she needed a few minutes to pull herself together. She knew Elliot was in there because Rachel had called to make sure. She'd used the pretext of looking for Chris, who she'd known was at the BBC with Andraya. Had Elliot guessed what the call was really about? He was nobody's fool, so he might have.

Though she was staring at the examples of Andraya's work in the gallery window, she wasn't seeing them at all. She was thinking of the craziness of being too afraid to go and talk to the man she loved, the man she had lived with for two years. She had shared so much of herself with him that she still couldn't make herself believe this was happening. They belonged together. Everything about their relationship was right. They were so attuned to each other that they often knew what the other was thinking. There had been no fight, no misunderstanding, no decline of their sex life. Nothing had been going wrong. So what was all this really about?

Giving herself no more time to think, she quickly turned back to the door and pressed the bell. After what felt like an eternity his voice came over the intercom.

'Elliot. It's me,' she said, hearing a surprising sharpness in her voice. 'Please let me in.'

Seconds ticked by.

She couldn't bear it. He couldn't be shutting her out like this. It didn't make any sense. Angrily she pushed the bell again, just as the buzzer sounded to release the door.

Entering, it was as though she was stepping into a dream, climbing a staircase she didn't recognize, yet knew and was afraid of. Ever since he'd gone her mind had been playing these kinds of tricks. She didn't seem to think the same way any more, or feel, or act. But it was OK. She knew what she wanted to say. Something was going on that he wasn't telling her about, and she'd come here now determined to find out what it was.

He was waiting at the front door as she reached the top of the stairs. Seeing his face, the concern in his eyes, the sadness that shaped his mouth, she almost started to break down. As though sensing it, he reached for her and pulled her into his arms.

'I'm sorry,' he whispered into her hair. 'You shouldn't have had to come here like this. I know it can't have been easy.'

She was overwhelmed by the familiar smell of

him, the closeness of his embrace, the sense of his comfort. This was where she should be. It was where she belonged. 'I don't understand why you won't speak to me,' she said, when she finally had control of her voice. 'What have I done?' As soon as the question was out she regretted it. It was self-pitying and irrelevant, for she knew very well she'd done nothing.

'Come on,' he said, drawing her inside.

The sitting room at the end of the hall was large with high ceilings, sash windows facing the Victorian buildings opposite, and full of paintings either hanging or stacked against the walls. Two elegant sofas flanked the hearth, with an expensive glass coffee table in between. There were several newspapers scattered around, which was typical of any place Elliot was, as was the low-volume TV news coming from a portable set on one of the bookshelves. His laptop was open on a table by a door that appeared to lead into a kitchen, making it look as though he'd been working before she came in; his mobile was next to it, but she couldn't tell whether it was on or off.

'Can I get you something?' he offered, still holding her hand. 'I've got vodka. Or tea.'

'Nothing, thank you,' she said.

It was disorienting her, being here, with him, in a place she didn't know, but he did. She was his guest and a voice inside her was screaming out in protest. They should be in their own home discussing their wedding, or doing the things they normally did with their lives.

Sitting down on one of the sofas, she tried not to be distracted by thoughts of what should or

233

shouldn't be. This was how it was, and this was what she must deal with.

She waited until he was sitting on the sofa opposite, and not allowing herself to be hurt, or read anything into the distance he'd put between them, she said, 'I need to know why you're doing this. I know you're hiding something, so I want you to tell me what it is.'

His eyes remained on hers, showing almost nothing of what he was feeling, as he took some time to think about his answer. In the end he spoke very gently. 'I understand how hard this is, and I know why you're telling yourself there's more to it, but there isn't. I care for you, Laurie. You mean more to me than just about anyone, but . . .' He swallowed. 'I told you the truth the night we broke up. I just don't love you the way you should be loved.'

As pain and denial washed through her, everything she wanted to say, had rehearsed all the way here, was swept clean away. All she knew now was the mounting desperation that was starting to work its way towards panic. 'I don't believe you,' she said shakily. 'I know you love me. I *know* something else is going on.'

He shook his head. 'I'm not lying to you,' he said. 'I wouldn't do that over something that means this much.'

She only looked at him, the expression in her eyes telling him that she still wasn't accepting what he was saying.

'Laurie, if I felt the right way about you, believe me, there's nothing in the world that would make me do this. I swear, there's no story, no undercover operation, nothing at all of that nature that I'm holding back from you.'

Still she said nothing.

'I almost wish there were,' he said, 'because God knows I don't want to be doing this.'

'Then don't,' she said. 'You don't have to. We can go back to the way we were.' Her voice was starting to shake again. 'Oh God, please, Elliot, don't do this. I love you. Nothing feels right without you. You just can't do this.'

'If I married you . . .' he said, then stopped and shook his head.

She waited, hope quickly blossoming in her heart at just those four words, for in the state she was now he could set almost any condition and she'd accept.

'You need to be loved the way you should be loved,' he told her. 'As a woman, not as a friend, or a sister.'

Her face froze in shock. 'Is that how you see me?' she said.

'Maybe not quite like that,' he confessed, 'but the way I feel . . . It isn't what you deserve, Laurie.'

Her eyes showed so much hurt and confusion that he had to look away.

She continued just to stare at him, seeing the man she loved, but hearing a stranger. She lifted a hand to her head, then let it drop again. She didn't know what to say, or do. 'What about you?' she said finally, in barely more than a whisper. 'What do you deserve?'

He shook his head and let his eyes fall away.

'Then what do you want?'

'I don't know. My freedom, I guess. To continue

as I am.' His eyes came back to hers. 'I don't want to be married. I thought I did, but certain things have happened to make me realize I don't.'

'What things?'

'It doesn't matter.'

'Yes it does.'

He shook his head. 'It's not something I want to get into. I just want you to understand that if I thought it was right for us to marry, I wouldn't be doing this.'

'You have to tell me why it isn't right.'

'It's the way I feel. What's going on inside me. I had no idea this was going to happen, and God knows I wish it hadn't, but when I realized . . . When I saw . . .' He stopped, unable to find the right words. 'I guess what I'm saying is it's just not right for us to be married,' he finished lamely.

'Then why don't we simply go on living together?' she said. 'We don't *have* to be married. We can forget about the wedding and go back to the way we were.'

Though he said nothing, his expression showed his answer.

'You don't want that either,' she said.

Briefly he shook his head.

She looked away, sensing that nothing she said was going to change his mind now. If it didn't matter so much, maybe she would give up, but it mattered more than anything, so she had to keep trying. She couldn't just let him go. 'Elliot, please,' she said, her mouth quivering as she turned back. 'We have to work this out. *Please!* There must be something we can do.'

He took a breath and let it go slowly. 'I want us

to still be in each other's lives,' he said. 'We'll be running into each other all the time . . .'

She clasped a hand to her mouth, unable to bear the thought of them passing like strangers, no longer being connected, politely asking how the other was, maybe hearing he was in a new relationship. There was no way of holding the tears back now.

He sat quietly as she wept into her hands, staying remote, feeling her pain as deeply as his own, until, finally, he got up and went to her. 'I know you're not going to believe me now,' he said, pulling her head onto his shoulder, 'but one day you'll thank me for this.'

'Don't say that!' she choked, pushing him away. 'It's patronizing and it's not true. You don't seem to understand how much I love you. It's not just going to go away because you've decided it should. It's here, in me, the biggest part of me. I feel as though you're destroying me, so how the hell do you think I'm ever going to thank you for that?'

Knowing there was no more he could say to convince her, he wrapped her in his arms again and held her tight. It probably wasn't the right thing to do, it would probably have been better to keep his distance, but when she was hurting this much, it was all he could think of to help her.

It was a long time before she finally raised her head from his shoulder. Her face was ravaged, her eyes bloodshot and swollen. 'Never, in all my worst nightmares, did I ever imagine . . .' she said brokenly. She pressed a hand to her mouth in an effort to stop herself crying any more. She couldn't bear it. She just couldn't. 'I don't suppose,' she said, 'you've got any idea what it's like to look at someone, the way I'm looking at you now, and know that you have absolutely no control. That nothing you do is going to make a difference. I love you. Everything in the world that matters to me is in you, but I can't make you feel the same way. You're the one with all the power, because you're the one who isn't in love.' She took another breath, and brushed away more tears. 'What fools that stupid emotion makes of us. It's cruel and vicious . . . I never want to feel it again . . .'

His head went down as his eyes closed. He wasn't handling this well, which was exactly why he hadn't wanted to discuss anything yet. He'd needed to get it straight in his own mind, work out how he was really going to explain everything to her, without screwing it up in this way.

Deciding to try and change the subject he said, 'I thought you were going to Hydra. Rachel mentioned something . . .'

Refusing to be distracted, she took both his hands in hers and looked into his eyes. 'Please tell me you'll give this some more thought,' she said. 'Say that it isn't over yet. You don't have to make any more promises than that, I just want you to understand that I really do love you, and I'll do whatever it takes to make you come back.'

Still looking at her, he lifted a hand to her face. 'I do believe it,' he said, very softly, 'but it doesn't change anything.'

Though she was staring into his eyes he could see that the words weren't really reaching her.

'I'm sorry,' he said. 'I wish I could explain things better. I wish to God I understood them. I just know that I have to let you go.'

For what seemed an eternity her tragic blue eyes remained on his, until finally she freed her hands and stood up. Her face had become very pale now, showing him that inside she was breaking apart, but her voice was steady as she said, 'In spite of everything, Elliot, I love you with every fibre of my being, and that's not going to change.' There was a light of defiance in her eyes as she stared up at him, a challenge that told him she wasn't going to let him go, at least not that easily, and certainly not yet.

Not knowing what else to do, he pulled her into his arms and buried his face in her hair. 'I love you too,' he whispered, knowing he shouldn't.

They stood together for a long, long time, holding each other close, neither wanting to let the other go. In the end she was the one to break the embrace, turning away and walking to the door.

As she opened it he started after her, but when he got there she was already halfway down the stairs. He stood listening to her footsteps, to the slamming of the door, to the sound of her walking along the street, then to the silence that followed.

In the end it was the phone ringing on his desk that reminded him he was still a part of the real world, even though he felt trapped in a nightmare.

'Elliot Russell,' he said gruffly into the phone.

'Hello,' the voice at the other end purred playfully down the line, 'feel like joining us all for dinner?'

239

'Andraya,' he said, his eyes closing as he thought of how it might have been if she'd called five minutes before. But he wouldn't have answered the phone then, so it wasn't an issue. 'I don't think so, not tonight,' he said.

'Oh, now I'm disappointed, and you know how I hate to be disappointed.'

'I'm sorry,' he said. 'This isn't a good time.'

'Mmm,' she responded, 'then maybe I should come over there and turn it into a good time?'

Without answering he clicked off the line, then turned off the phone. Did it make it any better, he was asking himself bitterly, that he'd waited until he was no longer with Laurie to sleep with Andraya? If it did, it sure as hell didn't feel that way.

Chapter Twelve

Sherry was at Laurie's office going through the mail that had piled up over the past couple of weeks. Splitting her time between her own and Laurie's commitments was proving a bigger juggling act than she'd expected, but on the whole she seemed to be coping. Having Nick back in her life definitely helped, for it had fired up her energy to a level where just about anything felt possible. It was as though she'd shaken off heavy boots, cut loose from invisible reins, broken out of a cast to become the happy and carefree person she really was. At least that was how she felt every time she saw him, or whenever he rang.

In between times it didn't take long for her to start fretting about everything from Nick's feelings for his wife, his relationship with this Elaine Sabarito, to whether she'd ever hear from him again, which was insane, because he'd given her absolutely no reason to doubt him. He always called when he said he would, and on the two other occasions she'd seen him since the night they went for dinner – once for lunch and once for a cocktail party at a news magazine – everything had been just fine. So she didn't need to be this afraid of what the future might hold – it was simply the demons from the past trying to scare her into believing that nothing ever really worked out, when sometimes things actually did.

Well, to hell with them, she decided, binning the junk mail, and turning on Laurie's computer she clicked to go online. There should be more information from Rose and the crew by now, who were still in Gujarat trying to locate the head of the snake, as Rose had dubbed that end of the operation. Finding several messages, she read and downloaded them, then opened the 'immigrant' file to start adding her own recent discoveries, the most significant of which was Dr Patel's sudden attack of amnesia. Clearly the good doctor had been got to, which could well be a result of Cribbs and his cronies finding out that the press – i.e. Sherry MacElvoy – was on their tail. It made her wonder how long it would be before they approached her too, a daunting prospect, but since it went with the territory of investigative journalism she wasn't going to allow it to deter her – at least not yet.

'Still no contact from Cribbs or the Ghosh woman?' Nick asked when he called a few minutes later.

'No, nothing,' she answered. 'My guess is, they're playing a waiting game, they won't move until we do.'

'And your next move is?'

'That's what we're meeting about this morning,

so I'll let you know. The order I put in as a fashion buyer is due for delivery tomorrow, so I might call Mrs Ghosh later to see if it's on schedule.'

'You're going to continue with your cover?'

'I'm not supposed to know it's been blown, remember, so for the time being it might be interesting to see what happens if I keep it up. If nothing else it gives me a reason to call, or even go round there. And if they start closing the doors, they've got to know that the investigation will just get tougher, because it'll be taken as an admission that they've got something to hide.'

There was a smile in his voice as he said, 'Watch out Eddie Cribbs, you just don't know who you're dealing with.'

'Oh, I'm sure he's really scared,' she laughed. 'Though he should be, because if we find that he really is bringing women into this country illegally and selling them into prostitution, take it from me, his days are numbered.'

'That's my girl,' Nick responded. 'Stick it to him.'

Still laughing, she said, 'What time's your flight?'

'Two thirty.'

'Are you excited?'

'Even more than Julia is. It'll be her first time in London as a teenager, as she keeps reminding me. I think that's letting me know she's grown up now, so not to get in her hair. It's bad enough that I'm flying over there to get her – not cool, I'm told. But neither Trudy nor I wanted her to do the flight alone.'

'And you get back when?'

243

'In three days.' He gave a sigh, that sounded like a stretch. 'We should have a good time exploring my home town, the two of us.'

Trying not to mind that the number seemed to exclude her, she looked down at her mobile as it started to ring. 'It's Laurie,' she told him, 'I'd better take it.'

'OK. I'll ring when I get to New York. Good luck with it all, and watch out for Cribbs.'

Relieved that he hadn't mentioned anything about Elaine Sabarito again, whom she had no desire to be in touch with now, she rang off and picked up her mobile.

At the other end, Laurie was barely able to get her breath. 'Sherry! Thank God!' she gasped. 'Where are you?'

'At your office.'

'Have you seen the *Express* this morning?' Her hand was shaking as she stared down at a small article tucked away on an inside page.

'No, why?'

'I'll be there in five minutes,' Laurie said, and put the phone down.

Since she was staying with Sherry at the moment, it was indeed only five minutes before Laurie walked in through the door of her office, looking so tense she might snap.

'What is it?' Sherry said, as she dropped the paper on her desk and pointed to the article.

'Read that,' she demanded.

Sherry barely had time to before Laurie said, 'He's sleeping with Andraya Sorrantos.' The words were like a blow, causing her to panic again.

'That's not what it says,' Sherry protested.

'I'm going round there.'

'Laurie no!' Sherry cried, jumping to her feet as Laurie started for the door.

'I have to know what's going on,' Laurie almost shouted, and before Sherry could stop her she'd gone.

Quickly Sherry picked up the phone and dialled Rachel's number.

Forty minutes later Laurie was standing in the street outside Chris's gallery, pushing on the bell to the top-floor apartment. She could hear it, buzzing faintly in the upstairs hall, but the intercom stayed silent. She thumped the door and rang the bell again, and again, shouting Elliot's name, pressing herself to the door as though to force it open. People passing were giving her strange looks, but she was so desperate she didn't care. She just needed to see him, needed to know that he wasn't in there with Andraya Sorrantos.

'Elliot, please,' she sobbed. 'Please let me in.'

'Laurie.'

She spun round to see Rachel getting out of Chris's car, then watched wild-eyed as Chris drove off to park and Rachel took out her keys.

'Is it true?' she demanded, as Rachel came towards her. 'Is he seeing her?'

'All it said in the paper was that he had dinner with us all last night,' Rachel said, trying to exert some calm. 'I was there, Laurie, and I'm telling you, you're leaping to conclusions . . .'

'So where is he now?'

'I don't know.'

Laurie's heart turned inside out. 'So he could be with her?'

'No,' Rachel said firmly. 'Believe me, if there was anything going on Chris or I would know.'

Laurie's eyes were full of doubt as she looked at her, her torment so deep that Rachel groaned with pity and pulled her into her arms.

'I can't bear it, Rachel,' Laurie whispered. 'I just can't bear it.'

'I'm afraid I don't have long,' Anita told Sherry, as she carried their coffees to a table outside the Riverwalk Café. 'I have a meeting at twelve.'

'Me too,' Sherry said. 'Though I don't think Laurie's going to make it.'

'Where is she now?' Anita asked, sitting down.

'With Rachel.'

'And what does Rachel say? Is there something going on?'

'She doesn't think so. She admitted that Andraya comes on strong when she's around Elliot, but she's the same with all men, so she doesn't see any reason to read anything into it. Anyway, as time is short, I'm going to be selfish and cut straight to the reason we're here. What do you think about what I told you the other day?'

'You mean about Nick and his wife, and his relationship with this Elaine woman?'

Sherry nodded.

'Well, for what it's worth,' Anita responded, picking up her coffee, 'it seems as though he probably lied about his feelings for his wife when he met you the first time around. All those excuses, his mother, his religion, his daughter . . .' She took a sip. 'Don't get me wrong, I'm sure he loved every minute of his time with you, but I doubt, from what you're telling me, that he had any intention of breaking up his family because of it.'

Sherry's face was solemn as she nodded. 'So much for our star-crossed romance,' she stated glumly. 'It makes me look such a fool for believing in it all these years, doesn't it?'

'Not really. He obviously had some very strong feelings for you, because he stayed in touch after you split up, and even helped get you started in London.'

'But what about this Elaine woman? I honestly thought, if his marriage did ever break up, that he'd come straight to me.'

'I'd put that down to a combination of things: his mother dying, his wife leaving him, his daughter acquiring a second father . . . He had a lot to deal with then, and I expect this woman was more a distraction than a real passion. It often happens when someone's going through a traumatic time, they get into a relationship that makes no demands, is just easy and accommodating and basically there when they need it, and not when they don't. If this woman is a high-powered attorney she'll have plenty of other commitments, and it was probably an arrangement that suited her too, at the time. Whereas you, and the feelings you two shared in the past, was something he simply couldn't handle when he had so much else going on.'

Knowing just how complicated everything had been back then, Sherry was ready to accept the answer. 'And what about his daughter?' she asked.

'What about her?'

'Well, he hasn't actually said I can meet her.'

'He's probably just assuming it'll happen, which I'm sure it will. When's she coming?'

'They'll be back on Friday for what should have been two weeks but has now turned into six, since her mother's off on some yacht with the rich lover and some superstar friends for the summer.'

'Sounds like she's got it worked out,' Anita commented, unwrapping a biscuit and dunking it. 'Remind me where he's living again.'

'He's renting the basement flat of his cousin's house in Highgate. She, the cousin, has two kids of her own, both teenagers, so it should work out well for Julia. I'm just wondering how often I'll get to see him while she's around.'

'Where there's a will,' Anita reminded her. 'Now, tell me about the bed department? You don't have to go into detail, unless you want to of course, but have you done the deed yet?'

'Actually, no, we haven't. He's being a perfect gentleman. We're just dating, getting to know each other again, though I'm pretty certain it'll happen when he gets back from New York.'

Anita nodded. 'Then remember to heed your own advice, Dear Molly,' she cautioned. 'These are very early days. Don't try to run before you can walk, or more accurately, don't expect too much, too soon.'

Sherry frowned as she thought. 'So you think wanting to be whisked off up the aisle by the end of the month is expecting too much?' she responded, with a perfectly straight face.

Anita laughed, but then was serious again. 'A lot of water has flowed under the bridge since you two first met,' she said. 'Things have happened, you've both changed in ways you're probably not even aware of yet.'

'I accept that,' Sherry assured her. 'But I do know he's the right one. To be honest, I've never really been in any doubt of it, I've just tried to bury it, mainly because I had to. But now, seeing him again, being with him . . . It's just there. We're just . . . *right*.'

'Who are you trying to convince, me or you?' Anita teased.

Sherry smiled. 'Me, probably. I mean it does feel right, but then . . .' She shrugged. 'I have all these doubts.'

'He dropped out of your life once, so it's quite understandable you're afraid he'll do it again. I think it's unlikely that he will, but it takes time to build security in a relationship. So, once again, don't rush things, don't expect too much, and make sure the negative thinking doesn't get out of hand.' As she finished she followed Sherry's eyes to a man sitting alone at a nearby table. 'Someone you know?' she asked.

Sherry shook her head. 'I was just wondering if he might be one of Eddie Cribbs's people.' she said softly. 'I told you they're having me watched?'

Anita's eyes widened with alarm. 'No, you didn't,' she replied.

Realizing she'd made a mistake in admitting it, Sherry said, 'Well they were. They're probably not now.'

Anita wasn't so easily put off, nor was she afraid to be blunt. 'It doesn't make you important, Sherry, to have those kind of people following you.'

Sherry smarted, and flushed with annoyance. 'That's a ridiculous thing to say,' she retorted.

'Is it? I know how much it means to you to make a breakthrough in this field, but those people are dangerous, Sherry . . .'

'I don't need a lecture,' Sherry cut in. 'Now let's just forget I mentioned it.' She glanced at her watch. 'It's time we were going, anyway.'

Anita's expression softened. 'I don't want to part on a bad note,' she said. 'So I'm sorry if I offended you.'

'You didn't,' Sherry responded, still struggling with her anger.

Anita looked as though she wanted to say more, but clearly decided to let it go as she rose to her feet and dropped a tip on the table. 'Let me know what happens with Laurie,' she said, as they parted. 'And with Nick, of course.'

Right at that moment Sherry didn't feel inclined to talk to her again about anything, but she murmured an appropriate response, and giving her the usual kiss goodbye she started back to the office.

When she got there she found a message on the machine from Laurie, excusing herself from the meeting with Barry, and hoping Sherry could cope alone. There wasn't enough time to call and find out how she was now, so she'd do it later, and taking out the notes she'd made for a new strategy on the story, she began to go through them. It was hard to concentrate though, with Anita's accusation still rankling at the back of her mind, and Laurie's distress reminding her of when she'd been in the same state herself. It was awful, terrible, the way rejection could tear you to shreds, turn you into someone you hardly even knew. Without any question it was the worst experience she'd ever had – or certainly one of them. Those cruel feelings of despair and denial, the blackness, the helplessness, the not knowing which way to turn. She just hoped to God she never had to go through it again, because Laurie's nightmare was starting to feel horribly like a sign.

'You're looking very pensive,' Barry commented, coming in through the door. 'Laurie not here yet?'

'Something came up . . . My God, what happened to you?' she cried, seeing his bruised and swollen face.

He shrugged. 'Got caught up in a bit of a scuffle over at West Ham the night before last,' he answered. 'Nothing to do with me, I just managed to cop a boot in the eye and another in the jaw before a couple of me mates dragged me out of it.'

'It looks really sore,' she said. 'Have you put something on . . . ?'

'It'll be all right,' he said impatiently.

Surprised by his abruptness, she regarded him closely and felt a tremor of unease. 'Do you think it had anything to do with Eddie Cribbs?' she asked.

'If it was, they didn't say so,' he replied. 'But it'll be OK. Now let's get down to it, shall we? Any more news on the doctor?'

'Still refusing to take my calls,' she answered, deciding to go with it, for what else could she do? 'Stan's coming over later. He's talking about breaking into the workshop again, to take a look through Karima Ghosh's files. I was also thinking it might be an idea to try befriending someone at one of Eddie Cribbs's clubs, a barman, a bouncer, maybe one of the strippers. They might know something they're willing to tell.'

'So who's going to do that?'

'You?' she ventured.

'You want me to go and chat up some stripper and ask her if she knows about some brothel full of illegal immigrants who her boss is touting for pervs. Yeah, I'm sure I'm going to do that, and I'm sure she's going to tell me.'

'She might if she thought you were a potential client.'

His eyes opened wide. 'You want me to make out I'm a perv?'

Her smile was sheepish. 'I can hardly do it myself.'

He was shaking his head. 'Eddie Cribbs knows who I am,' he reminded her. 'He'll see right through it if I go in there now and start chatting up his birds.'

Deflating as she realized the truth of that, she said, 'Maybe we should get Stan to do it.'

'Stan's too well known around these parts too. What we need is someone totally anonymous, who's never crossed Eddie Cribbs's line of vision before.'

Sherry's thoughts went immediately to Nick, but apart from being otherwise engaged with his daughter for the next few weeks, he just didn't have the right look to be going into that sort of club pretending to be that sort of guy.

'All right, leave it with me,' Barry said

grudgingly. 'I might be able to come up with some-one. It's not going to be easy though, and I hope you got plenty of cash in the kitty, because every-one's going to want paying, including the brass who tips us the wink, if we can even find one.'

'Don't worry, the money'll be there,' Sherry promised rashly. 'Now, after I've called Mrs Ghosh to check on my order, I think I'll pop over and pay the doctor a visit, see if I can find the cause for his amnesia.'

'I can tell you that right now,' Barry informed her. 'The man's got kids. Very powerful weapons of persuasion, are kids.'

Sherry's heart sank. 'I wondered if it might be something like that,' she said bleakly. 'So the ques-tion now is, are those women still getting medical help where it's needed? They surely must be, because they wouldn't be profitable if they weren't intact.' Her eyes closed, as another horrible thought occurred to her. 'He'll regard them as disposable assets, won't he? In other words, damaged goods don't always have to be repaired or returned, do they? They can simply be discarded, especially if no-one even knows they exist.' She looked up at Barry. 'Except *we* know they exist, which is why we've got to find them, before he decides to get rid of them.'

'If he hasn't already.'

'We have to work on the assumption he hasn't,' she responded.

Avoiding her eyes, he said, 'If we stopped look-ing we might actually be doing them a favour. I mean, it's us putting the pressure on that could make him do just what we're afraid of.'

'I understand that, but we can't give up on them.'

They looked round as Stan came in.

'Any news?' Sherry asked.

He shook his head. 'Nothing,' he answered. 'They've vanished into thin air.'

'Neela-*masi*,' Shaila whispered, '*mehne pela ben saathe pacchu nathi jevu.*' I don't want to go with the lady again.

'*Naa, naa,*' Neela answered, stroking her hair as she pulled the little girl's head against her. No. No. '*Havee apene Ba ne sothewa jaiye?*' Shaila asked. Can we find Mummy now?

'*Haa,*' Neela said, her liquid brown eyes gazing blindly into the darkness. Yes.

Long minutes ticked by. Neither of them moved. No sound but the gushing roar of a train as it sped past, and the occasional snore or snuffle from the other women in the room.

'I don't want to go with the lady,' Shaila said again.

'*Naa,*' Neela replied.

As she lay on her mattress Neela could still feel the terror that had filled her the day Mota Ben had taken Shaila. She would never lose that terror. It would be with her for ever, even though Shaila was back now, unharmed. They had taken her to a place and washed her, she'd said, and brushed her hair. Then she had sat in a room on her own for a long time. Ekta said they might have been taking pictures with a hidden camera. Everyone was sure that was what they had done.

Since the driver and Mota Ben had brought

Shaila back Mota Ben had only returned to bring them food and pick up the garments they had stitched. No-one had been taken to the men, so Neela was becoming desperate now to find a way out, before they came back for Shaila again.

The evil Bhanu Ganesh was sick. Her skin was wet with fever and her teeth chattered like stones. Ekta said she must see a doctor, but Mota Ben would not allow it. Neela had thought of pretending to be sick, but now she knew it would do no good.

'Neela-*masi*?' Shaila whispered.

'*Haa*?'

Shaila didn't answer.

Neela held her closer, seeming to draw some comfort from the fragile limbs. They helped her stay strong, even though her heart was in despair.

Chapter Thirteen

'What the hell's this?'

Cheryl looked round from her locker and cast a glance down at the roster. Suzy, the club's so-called star dancer, was looking like she wanted to shove it in Cheryl's face.

'It's your hours for next week,' Cheryl told her.

'Since when did you give me my hours?'

'Since I was put in charge.'

Suzy's ice-blue eyes seemed about to ignite. Her short, upturned nose flared wide and her puffy lips started to quiver. Not much of a looker when she was in that state, Cheryl thought to herself, and turned back to carry on unloading her locker.

'I'm going to talk to Trevor about this,' Suzy snarled. 'I do the rosters around here, and I'm sure as hell not taking any orders from some half-brained tart who's been getting right up my fucking nose since the day she started.'

'You'll need to take it up with Eddie,' Cheryl informed her, as Suzy started to storm out. 'He was the one who put me in charge. He didn't think it was right, one of the dancers telling the others what to do, so he said I . . .'

'You're a dancer!' Suzy seethed. 'Or you like to think you are.'

'Eddie doesn't want me doing it any more. He says I'm too good for it.'

Suzy's face blanched at the insult. 'Too good for it!' she spat. 'I'll tell you what you're too fucking good for, you lame-brained, cock-sucking bitch . . .'

'What the hell's going on in here?' Trevor, the club's manager, strode into the locker room, hands on hips, face on grim.

'If she's going to be doing the rosters, then you can find yourself another star dancer,' Suzy fumed. 'I'm not having some jumped-up little whore . . .'

'All right, don't let's get excited,' Trevor cut in. 'I approved those rosters, so if you don't like them you better take it up with me.'

'But she's not on there, is she? So who the fuck does she think she is now? That's what I want to know.'

'She's Eddie's girl, it gives her certain rights,' Trevor said simply. To Cheryl he added, 'Eddie's driver's waiting outside.'

'Oh, that'll be to take me to the flat Eddie's just rented for me,' Cheryl responded, tossing Suzy a superior little smile. 'Cinnabar Wharf. The big glass buildings, right on the river. I expect you've seen them. Really classy.'

Suzy slammed her eyes shut in anger and tugged open her locker.

'You'll have to come over, once I'm settled in,' Cheryl continued. 'I'll pay you to be the entertainment at the flat-warming party.'

Suzy spun round. 'Tell me, does Eddie's wife know about you?' she hissed.

Cheryl's smile froze.

'No, I didn't think so,' Suzy snarled. 'One word in her ear and you'll be in the fucking river, not on it, so if I were you I'd watch my step around Cinnabar Wharf, Cheryl Burrows.'

'I hope you heard that, Trevor,' Cheryl retorted, hefting her holdall onto her shoulder. 'It was an outright threat. I'll have to tell Eddie, and she'll be lucky now if she hangs on to her job at all, never mind the star position.'

As she stalked out the heady buzz of power lengthened her stride and straightened her back. Like Trevor had said, she was Eddie's girl, and no-one messed with Eddie's girl, as Suzy Big-Mouth Dawson had just found out.

'Do you remember the way?' she said to the driver as he took her holdall.

'Course I do, we was only there this morning,' he replied, dumping the bag in the boot. 'I just had a call from Eddie. He said not to turn up until after seven. He's having a meeting, and he don't want you banging about, moving your stuff in.'

She shrugged. 'That's all right. Gives us plenty of time to go and get my stuff from my mum's.'

It was just before eight when she finally turned up at the luxurious apartment block of Cinnabar Wharf, where the driver helped carry her belongings up to the third floor. 'Meeting's still going on,' he told her, an ear pressed to the front door.

'He said after seven,' Cheryl reminded him, 'so it should be all right to go in now.'

The driver shrugged. 'It's your neck,' he

responded, and leaving her to it he started back down the stairs to where he'd left his car on double yellows.

Using her key to get in, Cheryl gingerly pushed open the door, which led straight into the sitting room. The air was thick with smoke and stank of whisky. It took a moment to pick Eddie out from amongst all the men, but she soon spotted him, sitting on one of the clumpy armchairs that had come with the flat, a big cigar in one hand, a bunch of papers in the other. He seemed to be listening to what someone was saying, but it was hard to tell when he had his back to her.

Not quite sure what to do she waited for someone to notice her and looked around at the pastels on the walls, the shiny hardwood floor, stainless-steel open-plan kitchen set back in one corner, and the floor-to-ceiling picture windows that curved in a half-moon all the way round two sides of the living room. From the balcony outside you could see everything from the three big towers of Canary Wharf all the way up the river to Tower Bridge and that weirdy egg-shaped building just past it. She was going to get some plants and wicker furniture to go out there, and probably some wind chimes too.

Eventually some bloke with not much hair and thick rimmed glasses clocked her, and leaned over to tap Eddie on the arm.

Eddie's weight made the manoeuvre of turning an awkward one. 'How long you been there?' he demanded gruffly.

'Only a few minutes,' she answered timidly. 'I can go and come back again, if you like.'

He was about to tell her to do that, when he seemed to have a change of heart. 'Just get yourself into the bedroom,' he said. 'I'll be in when we've finished here.'

Meekly picking up her holdall she began skirting the backs of the sofas and had just got to the kitchen bit, when Eddie suddenly said, 'Bring us some more whisky. It's in the cupboard over the sink.'

Obediently she went to get the new bottle. 'Shall I pour?' she asked, noticing the three empties on the coffee table and all the overflowing ashtrays.

'No, we can do it. You just come and sit here.'

As he pulled her on to his lap her knees poked out of the rips in her jeans, and his hand circled the bare skin between the top of her hipsters and the bottom of her skimpy white shirt. Though she kept her eyes down, inside she was thrilled by the way he was showing her off, letting everyone know that he trusted her enough to allow her to be there while they talked business.

'So the bottom line,' he was saying, 'is that they want fifty grand for shopping, and another fifty once the goods are bought and loaded.'

'That's about it.'

To Cheryl's surprise, a woman's voice said, 'We must make arrangements to receive the goods. The last batch has been moved to the back-up address. We can't take the risk of reusing the first.'

From beneath her lashes Cheryl sneaked a look in the direction of the voice, knowing from the accent that she had to be some kind of foreigner. She turned out to be an Indian, or something like that, with a big red dot on her forehead and a fancy dark blue sari wrapped all around her.

'We've already got someone on the lookout for new premises,' Eddie was informing her. He turned to someone else. 'Since the Bedford fiasco we should switch to other routes and change our import venues. Get back to me by the end of the week with a list of alternatives.' Then to someone else, 'I want the figures for last month's services.'

'Not a good indicator,' he was told. 'We had to suspend business, remember?'

'Yeah, that's right,' he grunted, and Cheryl felt his hand slip under her shirt on to her breast. 'Fucking press,' he snarled. 'What's the latest on that?'

'I had a call the day before we made the delivery,' the Indian woman answered. 'She was checking it was on time.'

'Was the delivery made?'

'Yes.'

'And nothing since?'

'No, but there is something that concerns me. I've had word from my cousin in Seurat telling me that some British journalists are asking questions about the markets there.'

Eddie didn't look a bit pleased with that information – in fact the hand on Cheryl's left boob closed on it like a vice. She winced, knowing he wasn't actually thinking about her, but wishing he was, because it really bloody hurt.

'Fucking vermin,' someone growled. 'They get everywhere.'

Ignoring the remark Eddie said, 'Is there a connection to this Sherry person?' And before

261

anyone could answer, 'Of course there is, there has to be. It's too much of a coincidence.'

'It hasn't been confirmed yet,' the horn-rimmed man told him, 'but Laurie Forbes's producing partner is out that way.'

'Fuck!' Eddie seethed. 'Has anyone alerted Aseem?'

'Yes. My cousin has been in touch with him,' the woman replied.

Someone's phone rang, which prompted someone else to refill the glasses.

'We've heard back from the Italians,' Mrs Gandhi said when everyone was paying attention again. 'They've seen the girl and they're interested in repeating the same arrangement as before.'

Eddie blinked once or twice. 'Well that's some good news,' he responded. 'But it's only part of the deal. What about the women?'

Mrs Gandhi looked at the bloke with the horn-rimmed glasses. 'Six adults and the child,' he answered.

'Did you tell them the price had gone up?'

'Yes. They're willing to pay. I'm currently negotiating a share in the video sales.'

As Eddie thought he toyed idly, and rather nicely, with Cheryl's nipple. 'Tell them it's all or nothing,' he said finally. 'That way we can get the lot of them off our hands in one go, and be ready for the next shipment.'

'We might want to hold off on the next one until the press stops sniffing around,' the horn-rimmed one suggested.

'Mm, yeah,' Eddie said slowly. 'You could be right there. How're the websites doing?'

'Not bad. I'll have last month's figures for you to look at by the end of the week.'

They went on talking about setting up some new porn websites to add to those they already had, until eventually Eddie gave Cheryl a gentle push to make her stand up. 'Right, let's call it a day now,' he said, standing up too and yawning. 'We'll meet again tomorrow over at the office. Oh, and Perry, see about getting a computer put in here, will you?'

Cheryl looked up and gave him one of her best shy smiles. She'd asked for a computer, and even being as busy as he was, he'd remembered.

He leaned down to whisper in her ear. 'Go and get yourself ready to say thank you the way I like best.'

Knowing exactly how that was she trotted off happily to the bedroom, leaving him to show their guests to the door. This took a lot longer than expected, so her knees were getting quite sore by the time he came to join her.

Elliot's mobile phone was ringing as he walked across the sitting room of Chris's flat to answer the downstairs door. Seeing Laurie's number come up, he let the call go through to the voicemail and spoke into the entryphone.

'Who is it?' he said.

'Guess.'

Recognizing the voice, he released the lock and went back into the sitting room. It wasn't long before the clip of high heels could be heard coming along the tiled hall. He turned to the door and as she appeared his response was immediate. But for the shoes, and the thin coat she dragged behind her, she was completely naked.

'I thought you weren't free this evening,' he remarked as she let the coat go.

'I'm not. I don't have long.'

'Would you like a drink?'

'That's not why I'm here,' she replied. As she came to him he slipped a hand between her legs, put an arm around her and pushed his tongue deep into her mouth. Barely more than an hour had passed since he'd left her, but he was as ready for her now as if he hadn't made love in a month.

Her head fell back, and she pushed her fingers into his hair as he stooped to take each of her swollen nipples into his mouth. His hands moved down over her hips to the ample fullness of her buttocks. He squeezed and pulled, opening her wide, pushing her back against the sofa, until lifting one of her legs high, he dropped to his knees to pleasure her there.

After a while she turned away and started for the bedroom. Casting a look over her shoulder she beckoned him to follow. When he reached her she was pointing at the bed.

'Lie down,' she commanded.

Doing as he was told he lay back and looked up at her, holding her eyes as she unzipped him and took out what she'd come for. She sat over him and they moaned in unison as she sank onto him, taking him all the way in. She raised herself up and did it again – and again, faster and faster, until she was riding him like a horse, bucking and writhing in the force of their thrusts. His hands moved all over her, grabbing, pulling, slapping.

Her hair whipped around her. He spun her onto her back, plunged into her again and pressed his mouth to hers. She clawed and scratched his back, wrapped her legs round his waist, and bit into his skin. He was ramming her so hard he could feel his climax seconds away. He wanted to hold back, but she urged him on.

'I keep the taxi waiting,' she told him.

The words and her fingers on his balls sent him over the edge.

A few minutes later he was helping her into her coat. 'Come with me,' she said, turning to face him.

He looked down into her magnificent eyes. 'You know I can't,' he replied.

'It's just cocktails at . . .'

'No,' he said firmly.

Her eyes narrowed. 'She's going to find out sooner or later.'

He said nothing.

'Come on, Elliot,' she murmured, moving in closer. 'She's a big girl, she'll get over it.'

'You've got a taxi waiting,' he reminded her.

She lifted her mouth to his and he kissed her deeply. 'Will you come to Tuscany when we go?' she asked.

'No promises.'

She smiled silkily. At the door she turned round and opened her coat. 'Just so's you don't forget,' she teased.

He lifted an eyebrow. 'Come back when the party's over,' he told her. 'I'll be waiting.'

The moment she'd gone his conscience flared with a terrible might. He looked down at his mobile, knowing Laurie would have left a message, but unable to listen to it now, or to call her back. He didn't want to go on denying there was an affair, but nor could he bring himself to tell her the truth, that rather than cheat on her with Andraya he'd given her up. That was how irresistible he found Andraya. He'd fought it, had managed to turn away from her on at least three occasions, until he'd realized that whether he slept with her or not, to want her that much meant that he had no right to marry Laurie. Now the question was, how on earth could he tell that to Laurie without causing her any more pain than he already had?

Downstairs in the gallery Rachel was standing stock still in the doorway to the office, staring at the space outside where a taxi had been a few moments ago. She wished to God she hadn't seen what she just had, because no matter how hard she tried, she couldn't think of a single innocent reason for Andraya to be visiting the flat upstairs.

Putting a hand to her head she tried to think what to do. She could hardly feel worse, since it was she and Chris who had brought Andraya into Elliot's life. Dear God, if they'd known, they'd never have done it, no matter how talented the damned woman was. But what the hell was Elliot thinking? Throwing away everything for the sake of . . . for the sake of what? It surely wasn't serious between him and Andraya. Except he'd called off his wedding. He'd totally destroyed Laurie . . . She groaned out loud, for she didn't even want to think about how Laurie was going to take it when she found out. Suspicion was one thing, having your fears confirmed was something else altogether.

In the end, needing to discuss it with someone, she picked up the phone and called Sherry.

'Oh no,' Sherry murmured, when she told her. 'This is going to completely devastate her.'

'I feel so responsible. If only I'd known . . .'

'It's hardly your fault,' Sherry assured her. 'He's the one who's doing all the lying.'

'But what are we going to do?' Rachel said. 'We can't have a situation where we know and she doesn't.'

'Of course not. He has to tell her.'

Rachel looked round as the door opened and Chris came in. 'I've just seen Andraya leaving the flat upstairs,' she told him.

Chris's expression showed more dismay than surprise.

'Did you know?' she asked.

He shook his head.

'Someone has to tell Laurie.'

He immediately looked alarmed.

'I'm not saying it should be you,' she assured him. 'But maybe you could be the one to speak to Elliot, tell him he has to.'

He didn't appear particularly keen to do that either. 'Who's that you're talking to?' he asked.

'Sherry.'

'Isn't Laurie staying with her?'

'She's gone down to her parents for a couple of days. Chris, you have to talk to him.'

He inhaled deeply.

'I'm sorry, I have to go,' Sherry said. 'Nick's going to be here any minute.'

'All right. Let's speak in the morning,' Rachel replied. As she rang off she was still looking at Chris.

'I'm not sure we should interfere,' he said.

'If we don't, it's going to mean lying to Laurie ourselves,' she reminded him. 'Unless *we* tell her, of course.'

At that he could see that there really was no alternative, so he reluctantly turned back to the door and started up the stairs.

'I missed you,' Nick cried, sweeping Sherry straight into his arms as she opened the door.

'I missed you too,' she responded, laughing as he showered her face with kisses. Then his mouth found hers and they sank into a much deeper embrace.

'Mm, that felt good,' he told her, finally letting her go. 'I now feel as though I've well and truly landed.'

'I'm not quite sure how to take that,' she said archly, reaching for his hand. 'Come on, dinner's in the oven. Wine's in the bottle.'

'Hell, I should have thought to bring some,' he groaned, pushing the door closed behind them. 'Well, I did, but . . .'

'It's OK. I know, it's been a frantic two days since you got back. Parenthood is very demanding. So how is she? How was the flight?'

'She's wonderful, jet-lagged, but still determined to go everywhere and do everything this town has to offer. Just thank God for Natasha, my

268

cousin's fourteen-year-old. I wouldn't know where to begin without her.'

Sherry was taking down glasses. 'Is that where she is now?'

'Yep. They're having a sleepover with a couple of Natasha's friends. Guess I'll have to return the favour at some point. Can you imagine me, playing host to a bunch of screaming teenage girls? Here, let me do that,' and taking the corkscrew from her he began to open the wine. 'Now tell me about you,' he said. 'What's been happening while I was away?'

'Nothing that I didn't already tell you on the phone,' she answered, going to check on a saucepan. 'Except there was an interesting development earlier today, in an email from Rose, who's in India . . .'

'Yeah, I remember who she is. Go on.'

'Apparently she's made contact with a local news producer who's involved in the same kind of investigation. There's a good chance this producer can take Rose and the crew to an agency that specializes in trading people. It's set up like a travel-cum-employment agency, apparently, promising to find people work abroad. I've got no idea if it'll give us a link to our women here, or to the traffickers Eddie Cribbs is using, but it will provide us with some vital footage showing where the women have come from, and how they might have been bought and sold in the first place. That's if they manage to shoot it, which is a big if.'

'Then here's to Rose and the conquering of ifs,' he said, clinking her glass.

As they drank, their eyes stayed on each other,

sending all kinds of messages, until putting both their glasses aside he pulled her back into his arms. 'You look lovely tonight,' he told her softly.

'Thank you.'

He kissed her hard, pressing her body to his and pushing his tongue into her mouth. 'I have something to ask you,' he murmured, when finally he stopped to look into her eyes.

'Mm?' she responded.

'I was wondering . . . Kind of hoping, actually, that we might have a sleepover of our own tonight.'

Her eyes lit with amusement, even as a slow burn of desire stole its way through her. 'Oh, I should think so,' she replied. 'Did you bring your pyjamas?'

'I confess, no. But I did bring something else.'

'Oh?'

'It's still in the car. I'll get it later.'

'Intriguing,' she commented, turning back to the stove as the timer chimed.

Closing in behind her he slipped his arms round her waist. 'Mm, smells good,' he said, as she took the lid off a pan. 'What is it?'

'Filets of sole in a white wine and caper sauce. You can make yourself useful and go and cut some chives for the potatoes. They're on the right, as you go out on to the balcony.'

He'd been gone only a few seconds when she heard him say, 'Wow, look at this.'

Following him into the sitting room she glowed with pleasure to see how impressed he was by the candles she'd spread out over the balcony, all along the balustrades, in amongst the flowers, and on the small circular table where they were going to eat.

'It's so romantic,' he said, sliding an arm around her. 'And with Ella on the CD . . . It's just perfect.'

She looked up at him and smiled. 'Chives,' she said softly, and after popping a quick kiss on his lips, she returned to the kitchen.

'So,' he said, when they finally sat down to eat, 'it sounds as though you've more or less taken over this story. Is Laurie involved at all now?'

'Not very much.'

'Do I take it she and Elliot aren't back together?'

Sherry sighed. 'Actually, I've just found out tonight that he's seeing someone else. An artist by the name of Andraya Sorrantos?'

He shook his head, and ate a mouthful of food. 'Never heard of her,' he said. 'How did Laurie take it?'

She pulled a face. 'She doesn't know yet. Chris, a friend, is going to talk to Elliot, tell him he has to break it to her, because none of us wants to, that's for sure.'

'I'm not surprised,' he commented. 'How long's it been going on?'

She shook her head. 'I don't know. But it can't be long, she's only been in the country a few weeks.'

'Mm,' he replied, seeming vaguely baffled. Then, apparently dismissing it, he said, 'The food is delicious, by the way. I had no idea you were such a good cook.'

Her eyes narrowed playfully. 'There's a lot you don't know about me, Mr van Zant,' she responded.

'Oh?' He looked intrigued, and putting down his fork reached for her hand. 'Are you going to tell me?'

'No. I'll let you find out as we go along. But I will tell you this, I'm glad you know about what happened in the past. It's so much easier not having to hide things.'

'Which is something we're going to change,' he told her gently. 'You've got nothing to be ashamed of, and I'm not going to let it carry on holding you back, which I think it probably has until now.'

Her eyes shone with feeling as she said, 'You've made up your mind about that?'

'You bet. And once van Zant makes up his mind, you don't stand a chance.'

Loving the sense of him taking over in a way that felt both protective and freeing, she leaned forward and kissed him. 'I'm glad you're back,' she told him, knowing the double meaning wouldn't be lost on him.

'I'm glad too,' he said.

As they began to eat again, both aware of the wonderful feelings weaving their way around them, she encouraged him to tell her about his short trip to New York.

'Actually, one thing I did was have a talk with my wife,' he told her, picking up his wine. 'She wants a divorce.'

Though on the one hand it might have been exactly what she wanted to hear, on the other she couldn't not be aware that it was the wrong way round. 'Is that good?' she ventured, her mouth starting to turn dry.

He shrugged.

She topped up their glasses. 'Would you take her back, if she wanted to come?' she asked, trying to sound neutral.

'I don't think so. Anyway, it's moot, because she wants to marry her millionaire.'

She took a sip of wine and tried to think what to say next, since the *I don't think so* had thrown her rather. 'What does your daughter say about it?' she asked. 'Does she want her mother to marry someone else?'

Again he shrugged. 'She likes the guy, so I don't think she'll have a problem with it, and I'm not going to do anything to sour it.'

'It must be hard, having someone else in your place,' she said, wondering why she was pursuing this when she'd much rather change the subject.

'Yeah, it is. I miss her, you know, being in the same house, seeing her every day. Well, every day that I'm there. Actually, I miss them both.'

'Still?'

'I guess less now, but . . . Elaine was a godsend at the time Trudy and I broke up. I sometimes wonder how I'd have got through it without her. Which reminds me,' he said, 'I wanted to put you two in touch. I meant to call her while I was there, but time ran out on me.'

'That's OK. There are a lot of lawyers here I can contact who're in the same field, and to be honest, I don't much want to be in touch with your ex-girlfriend.'

He seemed surprised by that, which made her laugh.

'I'm jealous,' she told him frankly. 'She was with you for all that time, when I could have had you.'

273

His eyes sparkled, and leaning towards her, he rested his chin on his hand. 'But you've got me now,' he murmured.

Liking that, she said, 'The question is, what am I going to do with you?'

'Take as long as you like to decide. On second thoughts, don't take too long.'

Laughing, she continued to eat, loving the easy banter that flowed back and forth between them, sometimes flirtatious, sometimes serious, but always with a feel of intimacy that warmed her all the way through.

Finally, with their hands linked on the table, and the candlelight flickering in the breeze, he murmured softly, 'I'm going to pop down to the car, and I reckon by the time I come back we could be about ready for dessert, don't you?'

Her eyes narrowed. 'Would that be a euphemism, by any chance?'

'If you want it to be.'

Her head went to one side as she considered it. 'You go to the car,' she told him, 'and while you're gone I'll serve up the real thing.'

He grinned. 'Tell me that's a euphemism,' he challenged.

'You'll find out when you come back.'

By the time he returned she had arranged more candles around the bedroom and turned on the speaker to allow Roberta Flack's haunting voice to diffuse more romance into the air. The windows were open, the lapping sound of the river drifted in; the bed was low, and scattered with big downy pillows. On one of the nightstands was a strawberry and chocolate dessert.

'Is this real enough for sir?' she asked, as he came to find her.

His eyes were dark with emotion as he gazed down at her, lying amongst the pillows in a cream silk slip and tiny diamond pendant. The candlelight bathed her skin in a warm, amber glow, the scent of lilies perfumed the air around her. 'There's just one thing missing,' he told her, and pulled a bottle of Crystal from behind his back.

Loving the surprise, she watched as he opened it, and was about to suggest she get glasses when the cork exploded and the expensive champagne cascaded all over her.

Shrieking with laughter, she rolled out of the way, and continued to laugh as he sank down beside her, trapped her to the bed with one arm, and began to drink from the bottle. 'Now you,' he said, putting it to her lips.

As she tilted it up he started to lick the champagne from her neck and shoulders. She fell back on to the pillows, loving the feel of his tongue. Lifting his head he gazed down into her eyes, then lowered his mouth to hers for a deliciously long kiss, before he returned to her neck and began moving slowly, tantalizingly, towards the champagne-soaked silk covering her breasts.

'Mm,' he murmured, raising his head and licking his lips. 'You sure taste good.'

'Take off your clothes,' she whispered.

His eyebrows went up. 'What kind of restaurant is this?' he challenged.

'You're about to find out,' and she reached for the dessert.

*

275

It was just after seven in the morning when Sherry woke up to the sound of birds singing and the shower running. Frowning, she looked at the clock, then groaned out loud as she turned on to her back. It had been a long time since she'd last made love, so his passion had left her tender and bruised, and the wine and champagne weren't helping her head. She smiled warmly to herself, though, as she recalled how closely he'd held her, how loving and attentive he had been, as well as playful and demanding. It had been even more beautiful than she remembered, or dared hope, and now she wanted to do it all over again.

Wandering into the bathroom she started to clean her teeth, while watching his reflection in the shower.

'Good morning,' he said, stepping out and wrapping a towel round his waist. 'Did I wake you?'

'I'm not sure,' she answered, meeting his eyes in the mirror as he came to embrace her from behind.

Taking the toothbrush, he began cleaning her teeth for her, until turning her face he put his mouth over hers and kissed her slowly, sensuously, letting his hands move to her breasts.

'Mm,' she murmured, removing his towel. 'I think we should go back to bed, don't you?'

He grimaced an apology. 'I have to go,' he said. 'I promised Julia I'd be home by eight.'

Her astonishment broke out in a laugh. 'I'm sorry,' she said, reaching for her robe. 'Are you saying you told her you were spending the night here? With me?'

'I said I might be, if you were willing.' He was using her toothbrush now to clean his own teeth.

She wasn't quite sure what to make of that. 'So you've told her about me?' she said, realizing how much it would please her if he had.

'Not in any real detail,' he confessed. 'We met, remember, while I was still with her mother. So I told her you're someone who's been a friend for some time, and who I'm now getting to know a bit better.' Replacing her toothbrush, he leaned down to kiss her again.

Though she kissed him back, she was feeling vaguely let down by his answer, for it had a slightly jarring ring of truth about it – or at least of how it had been for him.

'Tell me,' she said, as he started to dry himself, 'you do remember that we made love before? That we were more than just friends?'

His eyes twinkled. 'Sure I remember,' he replied. 'But I've got to tell you, last night was the best.'

Another answer that maybe should have pleased her, but didn't.

'How was it for you?' he teased.

'Oh, definitely the best,' she assured him, and went to turn on the shower.

A few minutes later, as she was in the middle of shampooing her hair, he pulled open the shower door.

'I have to run,' he said. 'I'll call you later,' and touching his fingers first to his lips, then to her thigh, he winked, and slid the door closed again.

Though a part of her was trying to be euphoric, another part was having more success with confusion. There was no doubt that it had been a wonderful evening, or that their lovemaking had been utter bliss, but something was out of kilter, she felt, though try as she might, she just couldn't quite put her finger on what.

Then, once again, just like the few other times she'd seen him, or spoken to him on the phone, she began falling prey to feelings of edginess and unease. This time, however, it was worse, because she'd been so sure that once they'd made love all her niggling doubts would simply evaporate in the afterglow of togetherness.

By the time she went into the kitchen to put on some coffee she was feeling so down that she didn't even pick up the phone when it rang – until she heard his voice on the machine, when she snatched it up.

'Hi, are you missing me?' he said.

'Mm, I think it's just starting to kick in,' she responded, hugging the receiver in close to her neck. 'How about you?'

'I can't stop thinking about you.'

Smiling she said, 'Where are you now?'

'Somewhere between you and Highgate. Closer to Highgate. I had a wonderful evening.'

'Me too.'

'What are you doing for the rest of the day?'

With a small leap of hope that he was going to suggest getting together, she said, 'Nothing much. Just meeting Laurie for lunch and doing some more online research, actually trawling porn sites, would you believe? Saturdays are always pretty quiet. Well, Sundays too, come to that.'

'Lucky you,' he commented.

'Why don't you come and join us for lunch,' she suggested. 'Laurie's dying to meet you.'

'I'd like to meet her too,' he replied. 'But I'm in the hands of a jet-lagged thirteen-year-old today.'

Disappointed, despite knowing that would be his answer, she said, 'Do you have anything special planned, the two of you?'

'Not really. I know there was some talk about the movies tonight, maybe a bit of shopping this afternoon. We'll see when I get home.'

'Well, whatever you do, have fun,' she said.

'I'll try. I'll call again later.'

After she'd rung off she went back to the kitchen, definitely buoyed by the call, though knowing she'd have been happier if she'd been included in a trip to the movies tonight. But his daughter had only been here two days, she needed time to settle in, get used to being with her father, and catch up with her cousins whom apparently she hadn't seen since she was eight. It was all quite a big deal for the girl really, which Sherry fully understood, even though she had to confess to being a tiny bit jealous of all the time she was going to get to spend with Nick. However, knowing how much it meant to him, and totally understanding a daughter's possessiveness of her father, she decided that now might be a good time to heed some of Dear Molly's advice not to rush things, let them happen in their own time, and stop trying to create problems where there really were none.

Chapter Fourteen

A week later Nick was heading into Davey's, the pub-style restaurant on Fisherman's Walk, when he spotted Elliot sitting at a window table, and went over to greet him.

'Why don't you join me?' Elliot said. 'I'm waiting for Laurie, but she's not due till one.'

Deciding he could always duck out when Laurie arrived, Nick offered to top up Elliot's drink, and went to get one for himself.

Thanks to Elliot's obvious distraction, the conversation got off to an awkward start, though for a while it settled into a fluent discussion about an editorial in that morning's *Times*, of interest to them both, since it concerned US foreign policy. Elliot was extremely knowledgeable on the subject, which was no surprise to Nick, but though he seemed perfectly in tune with what he was saying, Nick couldn't help noticing how restless his eyes were, constantly glancing across to West India Quay, or at the door when someone came in. It didn't take a genius to work out that this lunch with Laurie wasn't one he was looking forward to.

After a while the conversation started to falter again. Nick watched Elliot as he stared out at the passers-by, seeming almost to have forgotten he wasn't alone. Then his eyes came back to Nick, and realizing they'd stopped talking, he said, 'Sorry. What were we saying?'

'No need to apologize,' Nick assured him. 'I can leave you to it, if you prefer.'

Elliot had just started to respond when his phone cut him off.

It was hard for Nick not to listen when he was sitting right there at the table, and it soon became clear, from the tone of voice as much as the words, that it was the new girlfriend.

'Yes, I'm here now,' Elliot was saying softly, slightly averting his head. 'You know I do. Yes, even now.' He paused, then started to smile. A moment later he was serious again. 'I don't know how long I'll be. I'll call when I get back to the flat.'

As he rang off he looked up, and from the way his face paled, Nick guessed that Laurie must have arrived. Elliot stood up. Nick turned round, and one look at the beautiful young blonde staring at Elliot with such bleak, haunted eyes was enough to make him wish with all his soul that he could be anywhere else on the planet right now.

'Hi,' he heard Elliot murmur as he pulled her into an embrace. 'Are you OK?'

'Yes, I'm fine,' she answered.

Her gaze moved to Nick as he got up.

He smiled and held out a hand to shake. 'Nick

281

van Zant,' he told her. 'I guess you must be Laurie.'

'Nice to meet you,' she replied, with a smile that didn't quite make it to her eyes. 'Is Sherry joining us?'

'No. I was . . . just passing. Probably time I was going.'

'Please don't leave on my account.'

'Stay and finish your drink,' Elliot insisted.

Not sure how to refuse, Nick sat down again, and watched as Laurie slid past Elliot to sit on the chair next to him.

'What'll you have to drink?' Elliot asked her.

'A lemonade.' She looked at Nick again and tried another smile.

'I'll get it,' Nick said. 'Same again for you?' and hardly giving Elliot time to reply he took off to the bar.

To his dismay, when he returned to the table, the tension seemed to have increased.

'So,' he said to Laurie, trying to keep it nice and light, 'Sherry's been telling me about the story you're working on together.'

'Oh yes, she's being incredibly helpful,' she replied. For a moment it didn't seem she was going to say any more, but then she continued. 'Did she tell you about the trafficking agency the crew in India has tracked down?'

He nodded. 'Yes.'

'Are you using us as a back-up?' Elliot asked her, referring to his own team of researchers.

'No,' she answered, looking at her drink. 'I thought I should probably get used to not having them any more.'

'You don't have to do that. It doesn't have to change.'

'Yes it does,' she responded. She picked up her glass, and looked at Nick. 'I'm glad Sherry's discussing the story with you,' she said. 'I'm afraid I'm not as much help to her at the moment as I should be.'

'Actually, I think she's rather enjoying the challenge,' he assured her, and might have said more, had he not realized that she wasn't really listening.

After a while Laurie turned to Elliot and said, 'How's the book coming along?'

'OK,' he answered. 'I think the first chapter's about done.'

She nodded and looked down at her drink.

Silence fell and Nick could hardly have felt more awkward as he sat there struggling for something to say, while remembering being caught in a similar, horrible scenario himself when he and his wife had first started to converse like strangers. It was hell, suddenly not knowing what to say to the person you'd shared so much of your life with, particularly when you were the one who wanted to go on sharing.

To his great relief a photographer he knew well came in through the door at that moment. 'Ah, there's Colin,' he said, getting up a little too fast. 'I was hoping to run into him. If you'll excuse me.'

'It was nice to meet you,' Laurie said, shaking his hand. 'I'm sure we'll meet again.'

'I hope so,' he responded, meaning it.

'I'll be in touch,' Elliot told him.

Laurie watched as Nick crossed the bar to join

his friend. 'He seems really nice, doesn't he?' she commented, trying to inject some lightness into her voice. 'Very good-looking.'

Elliot nodded.

'Did he talk about Sherry at all? Does it seem like he's serious?'

'He didn't mention her.'

There was a short pause which they suddenly both tried to fill.

'You first,' she said.

'No, you,' he insisted.

'I was just going to say it's made such a difference to Sherry, having him back in her life.' She smiled, awkwardly. 'It's quite a romantic story, really, don't you think?'

'Mm, I guess so.'

'All that time, and now they're back together. Makes you think it was meant to be.'

His eyes came briefly to hers, before moving away again.

'So what were you going to say?' she prompted, hating how nervous and withdrawn he was, and trying not to read anything into it.

He shook his head. 'It's gone now,' he replied.

She looked down at her drink, took a sip, and felt a dozen eyes watching her. 'I wish you'd try a bit harder to make conversation,' she muttered under her breath. 'I came because you said you wanted to talk.'

'Maybe this isn't the right place.'

'Well we're here now.'

He didn't respond.

'I've got the wedding cancellations ready to send out,' she told him after a while, hoping the words would hurt him as much as they had her.

More minutes ticked by.

'So this is us being friends, is it?' she said, her eyes dark with pain in spite of the tartness in her voice.

'Laurie, I . . .'

'You what?' she said when he didn't finish.

He shook his head.

'For God's sake,' she seethed.

She watched him as the muscles in his face tightened, and his hand clenched into a fist. Did it help, knowing that he was hurting too? Maybe, in a way, because it suggested there might be some hope, but then the mere thought of his pain caused hers to increase almost unbearably.

'I only came today,' she said, 'because I thought, hoped, you were going to tell me it wasn't all over . . . That you'd had some time to think . . .' She broke off as his eyes came up to hers.

'There's something . . . something I have to tell you,' he said.

Immediately her heartbeat started to slow. Whatever it was, it was serious, she could sense that, and suddenly she didn't want to know what it was. But what could be worse than the nightmare she was going through now? What could he say that was going to hurt more than anything he'd already said? Maybe he was going to the States for a while, to get away from this, from her. It would be awful, but if it would help him to clear his mind, to sort out what he really wanted, she could bear it. She wondered if it was about Phraxos. Maybe he'd done something during the investigation that was just catching up with him now. She wouldn't care. She'd stand by him, no matter what. If he went to prison she'd visit him every day, and if she went to prison too, then she'd fight from there to clear their names.

There was so much madness crashing around in her mind that she almost didn't hear him as he said, 'I'm seeing Andraya.'

Everything suddenly stopped. She looked at him and blinked. There was no sound beyond the humming in her ears, nothing to see except his face, no breath to take, no words to speak. She couldn't move, she could hardly even think – until like the delayed thunder of an explosion the meaning of what he'd said began to reach her. She could feel herself starting to shake, because she knew. She'd known since the day she'd seen the story in the paper.

'So it was true?' she said, wondering how she managed to get the words out.

He nodded. Her pain was so palpable that he reached for her hand, but she pulled it away.

'How . . . ?' She tried again. 'How long?'

'Not while we were together. I swear nothing happened until after.'

She looked around helplessly. Did that make it any better? She didn't know. All she knew was that she couldn't go any further with this because she was falling apart and people were watching.

'I'm sorry,' he said quietly. 'I wish to God it hadn't happened, but when I started to realize how I felt . . . I couldn't marry you when I was feeling that way about someone else.'

She couldn't listen to any more, because it would make it real, and it couldn't be real, it just couldn't. 'And how do you feel?' she heard herself ask.

'It's not important.'

'Yes it is.'

He didn't answer.

'*I want to know,*' she demanded, slamming a hand on the table.

'I wanted her badly enough to do this,' he replied.

The words sent her reeling. 'Wanted?' she repeated. 'So this is about sex? You've called off our wedding so you could have sex with another woman?'

'The fact I could want it that much . . . It wouldn't have been right to go ahead with our plans.'

'Do you love her?' Her voice was starting to fracture in spite of her efforts to hold on.

'We haven't been seeing each other long.'

Oh God, why hadn't he denied it? Even if it were a lie, he could have said no. 'Who instigated it?' she asked. 'Did she, or did you?'

'Laurie . . .'

'Just answer the damned question.'

'It was something we both felt.'

'She seduced you, didn't she? While you were choosing a painting for me, she seduced you!'

'Not then, later. And she wouldn't have succeeded if I hadn't wanted her to.'

She turned her head sharply away, so unwilling to accept this that she felt like lashing out at him to make him stop. 'You're just a plaything for her, you do realize that, don't you?' she told him, her mouth twisting with scorn. 'You're just another conquest, another notch. She doesn't care about you. She only cares about herself, and how powerful she is as a woman. She thinks she can get any man she chooses, and you, like a fool, have fallen straight into her trap.'

He said nothing.

'Look at you,' she cried, still trying to keep her voice down. 'You're pathetic. I thought you were a man. I always looked up to you, because I believed you were someone who had more integrity, more honesty, more backbone than anyone else I knew . . . But look at you now. You're just a spineless fool with a hard-on for some tart with fake tits and fat ass.'

Still he didn't speak.

She clasped her hands to her head as though to contain the madness. 'Jesus Christ, Elliot,' she blurted, 'I can't believe you're behaving like this! After all we've meant to each other, everything we've been through and dreamed of . . .' Her voice started to falter as the horror of it gripped her anew. 'I love you,' she choked. 'Don't you understand that? Doesn't it mean anything to you, what this is doing to me?'

'Of course it does.'

'Then why are you doing it?'

'I can't marry you when I have feelings for someone else. It would be wrong, and it's not what you deserve.'

'But you don't love her,' she cried. 'You can't. You might think you do . . .'

'I'm not saying I love her,' he interrupted. 'But I do want to be with her.'

She gazed desperately into his eyes, feeling the tearing pain of anger and despair. 'And what about when she doesn't want you any more?' she said. 'What then? Am I supposed to take you back?'

He shook his head. 'No.'

His answer hurt beyond anything, for in that one word he'd confirmed that it truly wasn't just about Andraya. 'You really don't love me, do you?' she said, as stunned as she was broken.

'Actually I do love you,' he responded, 'but . . .'

'No,' she gasped, covering her ears. 'Don't say it. I can't bear it . . . Oh my God, oh my God.' Then suddenly knowing she couldn't take any more, she grabbed her bag and stood up. 'I'd like to get out please,' she said. 'Please let me through.'

For a moment it didn't seem he was going to, but then he stood up to clear the way. 'Where are you going?' he said.

'You don't have the right to ask that question,' she responded. This was hard, so very hard, but she had to keep it together, she just had to. A few more seconds and she'd be outside, walking away, leaving him behind and breaking into a thousand pieces.

'I'll call you,' he said.

She didn't answer, she just kept moving past him, walked to the door, pushed it open and stepped outside into the warm summer day. Breathing was hurting her lungs. She couldn't get any air.

'Oh God, Elliot,' she gulped. Her hands were clenched hard at her sides. She was still moving forward, into the crowds. She needed to run, to get as far away as she could. She had her phone. She should call her mother, or Sherry . . .

She reached into her bag, but the sheer awfulness

of everything was engulfing her, bearing down on her with so much pressure she was almost sinking to her knees. Somehow she kept going. She collided with someone, mumbled an apology, then suddenly, bewilderingly, she felt strong arms going around her.

'It's OK,' Nick said. 'I've got you.'

She looked up. Was this a dream? Nothing was feeling quite real. 'I'm sorry,' she choked. 'I must have tripped.'

'I saw you leave,' he told her. 'I thought I should come after you. Are you OK?'

Still dazed, she nodded. He'd come, but Elliot hadn't.

He glanced back towards the pub and saw Elliot watching from the window. 'Come on,' he said, taking her arm, 'let's get you out of here,' and he began leading her through the crowds to where Elliot couldn't see her any more.

'There you go,' Sherry said, handing Laurie a cup of coffee.

As she took it, Laurie gave a half-hearted laugh. 'I feel like an invalid,' she said. 'All this attention.'

Sherry picked up her own coffee and came round from the kitchen. They were back at Sherry's flat now, after she'd turned up to take over from Nick, who'd called to let her know what had happened. It seemed he'd coped rather well considering he didn't even know the woman he was rescuing, but as Sherry remembered only too clearly, he'd always been good with people, and was a lot less embarrassed by female emotion than most men she knew. He'd gone to meet his daughter now, but would call later, he'd said, to find out how everything was.

'I can't believe Elliot told you like that,' Sherry murmured, sitting in the armchair holding her coffee. 'I suppose there's no good way, but at Davey's!' She shook her head, still hardly able to credit it.

The force of denial in Laurie's heart seemed to be growing. 'It was really good of Nick to come after me like that,' she said, in an attempt to wrest herself from the pain. 'You're lucky to have someone so sensitive.'

Sherry sipped her coffee. 'He was concerned,' she said. 'When he saw you leave . . .' She stopped as Laurie put a hand to her face.

'I'm sorry,' Laurie whispered. 'It just keeps coming over me.'

'It's OK.'

After a moment Laurie lifted her head again and took a deep breath. 'I felt as though I was going to faint, or throw up, when I came out of there,' she said. 'I hardly knew what was going on. God, just to think of everyone watching from the bar . . .' She waited for the awful tide to ebb and gave a weak little laugh. 'I wonder what they're making of it now, me walking out on Elliot, and Nick van Zant coming after me.'

Sherry had wondered much the same thing, though anyone with half a brain would know there was no way Laurie would be interested in anyone else this soon after the break-up. All the same, she wouldn't put it past someone to twist it all around to claim that Laurie had left Elliot for Nick.

'Where is he now?' Laurie asked.

'Nick? He had to get back for his daughter,' Sherry reminded her.

'Of course. I hope I didn't hold him up too much. I kept insisting he should leave, that I'd be OK, but he wouldn't go until you got there.'

Recalling how she'd found them, sitting together on a park bench at Westferry Circus, Laurie's head on his shoulder, his arm around her, Sherry couldn't help wondering how keen he'd been for her to arrive. They'd looked extremely cosy until he'd spotted her coming into the park, when his relief could hardly have been more evident.

'He was telling me how he felt when his wife broke the news to him that there was someone else,' Laurie confided.

Sherry stood up. 'I don't think I need to hear that,' she said, going to stop the balcony door from banging in the breeze.

Laurie's eyes filled with concern. 'I'm sorry,' she said. 'I wasn't thinking . . . I – He's over it now, though. That's why he was telling me, trying to comfort me, I suppose.'

Realizing what a fool she was being, Sherry's expression softened as she turned back. 'He's good at that,' she said, remembering just how tender and supportive Nick had been at a time when she'd needed it most.

'He's a nice man.'

'I think so.'

'He seems very keen on you.'

'Really?' Sherry's pleasure showed. 'What makes you say that?'

'Just the way he looked at you, I guess.'

292

Liking the answer, Sherry returned to the chair and hooked her knees over one arm.

'I wonder where Elliot is now,' Laurie said. 'With her, I expect.' The very idea of it tore through her so painfully that she had to stand up. 'Never in my life have I wanted to kill someone,' she said, going to the window, 'but I do now. I hate her. I absolutely hate her.'

'I can understand that.'

'I hate him too. I detest him for the way he's done this. He's made it so much worse. All the lies . . . Oh God, I can't stand to think of them together,' she cried, clasping her hands to her face. 'I want to tear out my own mind to stop myself thinking about what they're doing . . . If only he'd never told me. I was better off not knowing.'

'But you'd have found out in the end.'

Laurie's laugh was bitter as her head came up. 'Yes I would,' she said, 'except I already knew. That day I saw their names together in the paper. We should always trust our instincts.' She added wryly, 'Dear Molly says always trust your instincts.'

A quick image of Laurie and Nick on the park bench flashed through Sherry's mind again, but she knew in her case it was paranoia, not instinct that was alerting her to take note, and paranoia was always best ignored. 'Dear Molly can be a pill,' she said drily.

Laurie was barely listening. 'He's like a stranger, Sherry,' she said. 'He's turning into someone I don't know. What's happened to him? Why's he doing this?'

Sherry looked at her in dismay. 'I wish I knew,'

she answered, not wanting even to suggest that Elliot might genuinely have fallen for Andraya, for that was definitely not what Laurie needed to hear right now. It probably wasn't something she could cope with, either. It all had to happen in stages, and this was far too early to do much more than agree and listen, and give whatever support she could.

'Thank God Rhona's coming back tomorrow,' Laurie stated. 'You must be fed up with me by now.'

Sherry laughed in surprise. 'Not at all,' she said. 'I just wish it weren't happening.'

'But with you and Nick getting back together, this is the last thing you need.'

'It's not about me, it's about you, and how to get you through this.'

Laurie's hands almost went up as though to defend herself from the meaning of the words, for the very idea of having to get through it not only meant it was real and had to be faced, but that it wasn't going to be resolved the way she wanted. However, she didn't know that for certain. Anything could happen, the phone might ring any minute and suddenly everything would change and they'd be back together.

'Other people don't have the luxury of friends like you,' she said as she returned to the sofa. 'Other people have to pull themselves together and get on with life. They can't just walk out on their jobs, or rely on someone to drop everything and come to rescue them, the way you just did. I don't deserve all this, and I shouldn't be so pathetic. I have to get a grip.' A small light of

294

defiance flickered in her eyes. 'If it's her he wants, then it's her he shall have.'

Sherry smiled inwardly. Just like anger, hope, confidence and courage, defiance would do its bit to hold her back from the pit of despair, but sooner or later she would go there, everyone did, unless Elliot came back, of course, and right now that wasn't looking likely.

'I'm a mess,' Laurie said brokenly. 'I just don't have what it takes . . . I'm obviously not as strong as other people.'

'Rubbish,' Sherry said firmly. 'If you knew what some people do at a time like this, the kind of letters I get in my Dear Molly bag, you'd realize you're coping a lot better than most.'

Laurie's smile was weak. 'That's definitely not how it feels,' she said.

'I know, but you've got to give yourself a chance. It's only just happened.'

Laurie nodded bleakly. 'So how long is it going to last?' she asked.

'At this intensity? A few months, probably not as long as a year.'

Laurie wanted to die. 'Are you serious?' she cried, unable to accept the idea of feeling like this for another minute, never mind a year.

'I'm afraid so. But everyone's different. You might suddenly wake up one morning and think, my God, he did me a favour. Life is so much better without him.'

Laurie almost laughed. 'If I thought that was going to happen then I'd seriously doubt I ever loved him.'

'So would I, if it happened any time soon.' Then

seeing Laurie's face she said, 'I'm sorry. I wish I could tell you it was something you could just pack up and put away, or better still, throw out with the rubbish, but I'm not going to lie to you. Anyway, you know it isn't. You know it's only time that will heal this, but there are certain things you can do to make it easier on yourself.'

'Oh God tell me. Please. Whatever they are, I'll do them.'

Though Sherry smiled, she was reluctant to go into any detail now, when it was all still so raw. 'OK,' she said, 'but they're not as easy to do as they're going to sound. They'll take an enormous amount of will-power and courage, which I know you have in abundance, but just not today. You're still in shock, and while you're in this frame of mind you're not going to believe what I tell you, never mind be able to carry it out.'

'Oh no, you can't do that,' Laurie protested. 'You've got to tell me. I'll do anything. I swear, *anything*.'

Sherry was touched by her trust. 'I will tell you,' she promised. 'And don't worry, there's no rocket science or witchery involved. It's all common sense really. Well, you'll see when we talk.' As she finished she was walking across to the front door to answer the downstairs bell. 'It's probably Rachel,' she said.

'Oh yes, I'd forgotten I called her,' Laurie responded. 'Poor thing, she must have felt dreadful finding out like that, and not knowing how to tell me.'

'Hi, come on up,' Sherry said into the entry-phone, and pressed the buzzer. 'I'm afraid I'm going to have to leave you two here,' she told Laurie, coming back into the sitting room. 'I'm meeting Barry and a friend of his in half an hour, then, believe it or not, I could be going on to a strip club.'

Laurie's eyes widened with surprise. 'You mean one of Eddie Cribbs's clubs?' she said, catching on.

'Yep. Barry's suggested I pose as one half of a couple looking for a threesome. Apparently there's a chance one of the strippers could be persuaded to *parler un peu*, for the same fee as *ménaging à trois*.'

'But won't someone recognize you?'

'No-one there knows me, and they definitely won't when I've got my blonde wig on.'

'You've got a blonde wig?'

'I have now.'

Laurie's eyes closed as she laughed. 'The things we do,' she murmured. 'Is Barry the other half of this couple?'

'No. It's the friend he's bringing to the meeting.'

Frowning, Laurie said, 'Just a minute, I thought Barry was going to find someone to pose as a pervert?'

'He was, but guess what, we don't have any volunteers. No-one, but no-one wants to even pretend they're into anything that might involve children, and frankly who can blame them? In today's climate they're likely to be arrested, tried and convicted before they can even utter the word undercover. Anyway, it's probably better that I try to handle it myself, so let's hope this stripper actually has something to tell.'

297

Laurie nodded agreement. 'Has there been any move on Eddie Cribbs's part to try to block you at all?'

'Surprisingly no, and I don't know if I'm still being watched either, though Stan says we should assume that I am. It's a strange sort of feeling, spooky in some ways, but not quite real in others. Has it ever happened to you?'

Laurie nodded. 'You need to take care,' she warned. 'Criminal gangs, people-traffickers . . . They can be extremely violent . . .'

'I know,' Sherry assured her, 'and I have to confess to a certain fascination with them, because from everything I've been reading they obviously live in a whole other culture, which, in its way, is totally integrated into ours. It's like an otherwise healthy body with invisible cancer cells eating it away. Or a beautiful house with evil masked inside the walls.'

Laurie was regarding her curiously.

Sherry smiled. 'Just taking an objective view,' she told her. 'On a personal level, you're right, I need to take care, and I will. What's concerning me most right now though, is that their failure to act could mean the women have already been disposed of.'

'What does Stan think?'

'He says it's possible, but isn't convinced. I forwarded an email to you this morning, from Rose. I don't suppose you've seen it?'

Laurie shook her head.

'Apparently she's been contacted by a local TV producer in Surat, who's offering to put her in touch with an actual human-trader. It's all highly

298

suspicious, she says, because this producer's also claiming the trader has connections here, but it could prove genuine, so for the moment she's going with it. She'll keep us posted, obviously. In the meantime, we seem to be in a bit of a stand-off situation. Our delivery has been made to the shop we're using as cover. I thought something might happen there, but it all passed off as normal. I called Mrs Ghosh to thank her. She was cool, but polite, much as she was before. And my request to meet with Eddie Cribbs is still being ignored, but I'm planning to pay Mrs Ghosh another visit in the next week or so, to put in a new order. It'll be interesting to see what comes up then.' She turned round as Rachel tapped on the front door. 'In here,' she called.

Rachel's face showed almost as much distress as Laurie's as she hurried into the room. 'Oh Laurie,' she said, as Laurie got up. 'I hardly know what to say. I'm just so sorry . . . I feel so respon-sible . . .'

'Ssh, don't,' Laurie told her, as they embraced. 'It's not your fault. You didn't know it was going to happen. No-one did.'

'But when I found out . . .'

'Please, stop blaming yourself,' Laurie said, having to cut her off because she couldn't bear to hear any more. 'They're adults, two grown people who make up their own minds. There was noth-ing you could have done to stop it – only they could have done that, and they chose not to.'

As she listened Sherry was impressed by the spirit in Laurie's tone, when she must have been feeling like hell right now. It wouldn't last of course, but at a time like this every strong moment was to be treasured.

'Have you seen him, or spoken to him, since I left him at Davey's?' Laurie asked.

Rachel nodded. 'He called a few minutes after you did to let me know he'd told you, and to apologize for putting me in such a difficult position.'

Laurie's voice trembled slightly as she said, 'Well, that was big of him.'

Rachel's eyebrows went up. 'He offered to move out of Chris's flat too, if we want him to.'

'To go where?'

'He didn't say.'

'So did you say he should?'

'I said, as it was Chris's flat, he should speak to Chris, which was a way of stalling, to find out what you'd like us to do.'

Confused, Laurie turned away.

Rachel looked at Sherry.

Sherry shrugged, not sure what to say.

'If you tell him to move out he'll just move in with her,' Laurie said, voicing all their thoughts.

Rachel looked at Sherry again, and this time her eyes conveyed so much unease that Sherry got the distinct impression another blow was on its way. She glanced at the clock, and decided she should leave now, rather than have to make her excuses in the middle of a new crisis.

After telling them to stay as long as they liked, and to help themselves to anything, she packed up her files and took off for Laurie's office. It wasn't that she didn't care what Laurie's next hurdle was going to be, it was more a need to keep on top of this story, which, ultimately, was going to help Laurie a lot more than staying around now to mop up more tears. Besides, she could guess what the issue was: that now the secret was out, Elliot was planning to accompany Andraya – provided Chris and Rachel agreed – to Eduardo Olivieri's villa in Tuscany, before they all flew on to New York. So this really was an awkward situation for Rachel, since she could hardly snub one of Chris's most important artists, nor could she avoid Elliot if he was going to persist in this affair.

There wasn't much doubt that they were going to become a cosy little foursome, and Sherry had to admit that she'd fantasized about her and Nick being a part of the group too, while Laurie got a taste of what it was like to be frozen out as a single. Not that she'd ever dream of actually doing that, it was just one of those despicable little roads the mind travelled before the journey was cut short and genuine affection and human decency continued to steer the course. Much as it had at lunchtime today, when she'd felt that ridiculous surge of jealousy on seeing Nick with his arm round Laurie. She was perfectly OK with it now, because she knew very well that he was just someone who cared about other people. He always wanted to help, or fix things, or come up with some kind of solution, which all too often involved him in more than he was able to give. Since it was a quality she adored, she didn't in any way want him to change it, though maybe she should keep an eye on things there, make sure he didn't get in too deep. When a woman was as needy as Laurie was right now, and he was such a diehard Galahad, an entirely different kind of disaster could be looming – and that was something everyone would want to avoid, most of all her.

Chapter Fifteen

Cheryl was padding about her luxury flat in the cool lace-up crop top she'd got at Miss Selfridge earlier today, and a black Calvin Klein thong. It was late afternoon now and she was starting to get bored. Eddie had gone to Majorca with his wife, to a right fancy-sounding spa that she was going to get him to take her to just so's everyone would know that she got the same privileges as Mrs Eddie; all her mates were busy doing other things today, and even her mum couldn't come over until tomorrow. So here she was, all on her tod, with nowhere to go and no-one to talk to. She supposed she could always go to the club, but the other girls were such bitches, especially now that cow Suzy had roused them all up against her. So if she did go she'd only end up sitting around on her own, watching them all dance, and she'd have to keep telling the punters to get lost and leave her alone, which definitely wasn't her idea of a good time.

Sinking down at the computer, she called up the

solitaire game and started moving the cards. This was bloody boring, but there was nothing on the telly and the neighbours had complained about how loud she played her music. There was no point listening to it unless the place rocked, so screw it, she'd turned it off altogether. If it weren't for Eddie she'd have given them a right mouthful, but he'd been very strict about that – she weren't to cause no fuss with the neighbours, she had to get along with them real nice, and try not to have anything to do with them at all if she could help it.

Anyway, mouthy women weren't what turned him on – nice and meek and malleable was what Eddie liked, so nice and meek and malleable was what she was. She could be an actress, she thought, she was so good at pulling that off. She could make the kind of videos he sold on the Net, though if those actors were actually screwing for real, and from the ones she'd seen it definitely looked like they were, she knew Eddie wouldn't allow it.

She wished she knew how to use this computer properly so she could surf the Net and things, the way Danny had when he'd come over earlier. He was brilliant at it, going all through Eddie's porn sites, showing her what kind of videos and services Eddie's company was offering. Seeing it all had got her really turned on, so she'd dragged Danny and his lovely big dick back into bed for another marathon session.

She hadn't felt one bit guilty about it at the time, after all Eddie had abandoned her for another woman, even if she was his wife. And it wasn't as if she'd gone out of her way to invite Danny over, she'd just said, 'Yes, OK,' when he'd asked if he could come and leave Eddie a message. Plenty of Eddie's people did that, so there was nothing wrong in Danny doing it too, though she had to admit, she didn't usually open the door to the others in a bikini. But it was a hot day, so she'd been outside sunbathing. That was how she'd tell it, if she had to. She probably wouldn't have to, though, because she couldn't see any way of Eddie finding out.

Actually, now Danny had gone she was starting to regret what had happened, because if Eddie ever did find out . . . Well, she hadn't forgotten how he'd threatened to cut Danny's dick off just for mentioning his precious daughter, so God only knew what he'd do if he found out Danny had been poking his girl. And in Eddie's bed too. At one point Eddie had rung up to get his messages, which had been a real turn-on, Danny doing her doggie-fashion while she talked to Eddie on the phone.

Come to think of it, she couldn't remember now if Danny had left his message. He'd shot off in such a hurry, saying he had to meet some bloke, that she hadn't thought to ask what his message was. He could have left it on the computer for Eddie to find when he got back, but she'd better make sure. If anyone had seen him come in here, and there was no message to give, she was going to have some serious explaining to do, especially considering how long he had stayed.

This was starting to feel increasingly like a set-up. However, since she was trapped in the back

305

of Barry's ancient Ford Capri, being driven deeper and deeper into the East End, while his friend Danny, her 'date for the evening', explained why it would be his pleasure to stitch Eddie Cribbs up with the press, she didn't have much choice right now but to go along with it. The Marilyn Monroe wig, however, which was managing to make her look more like Myra Hindley, was so excruciatingly tight she'd just have to discard it until they reached their destination.

'Bastard reckons I don't know what he did to my old man,' Danny was saying, as they sped along the A13 towards Dagenham. 'He told my old lady and me it was the Turks what did it, but we know different. Eddie Cribbs had my dad taken out, because he was in discussions with the Turks to go over with them. Eddie was worried what information he might take wiv 'im, so he had someone wait outside his local one night, then they dragged him off down the railway lines and slit his throat. Nearly took his bloody head off, the bastards.'

Sherry winced, then quickly braced herself as Barry hit the brakes to avoid another car that shot out of a turning in front of them.

'Moron,' he muttered.

'Where are we?' she asked, looking out at the tatty shopfronts and filthy gutters of the high street they'd just turned into. As it was early evening there were still a few people around, though she got the impression it wasn't a place where many ventured out after dark.

'Not far now,' he answered.

Sherry said to Danny. 'So tell me more about the girl we're going to meet. And how do we know we can trust her?'

'I told you, her name's Suzy,' he answered, glancing back over his shoulder and doing a double take when he saw her hair had changed colour. 'I've known her since we was at school. She's a diamond. She'll do anything for me, and she ain't too happy wiv Eddie lately, but you don't need to mention that.'

'Are you sure she knows something that can help us?'

'She says she does, but you'll have to talk to her yourself. She'll want paying, so I hope you got the cash.'

Sherry assured him she did. 'Can't we just meet at her place?' she said. 'Or yours? Why do we have to go to the club?'

'It's what she wants. The way she sees it, if Eddie gets to find out she talked to you, she can say you tricked her by coming to the club with me to set up a threesome. It'll happen in full view of everyone, not that many'll be in at this time of night, and it's the way these things're normally done. She's just safeguarding herself the best way she knows how.'

Though Sherry supposed it had a certain logic, she might have felt happier if Barry was intending to come in with them. But he was just going to drop them off, leaving Danny to make sure she got home all right. Not for the first time on this journey, she was regretting not listening to Nick when he'd tried to talk her out of coming. She needed to know more about these people, he'd told her firmly. It wasn't enough that they were friends of Barry's.

Remembering what Barry had told her when he'd introduced her to Danny, back at the office, she said, 'So you must know this Suzy too, Barry, if you were all at the same school.'

'Not as well as Danny does,' he answered, 'but yeah, I know her. She's all right. A good girl. Here we are. We're here,' he announced, pulling up outside a sex shop.

Fifteen minutes later Sherry was sitting in a darkened booth at the back of the basement club, finding it extremely disconcerting to try and make social chit-chat with a woman she'd just watched take off all her clothes and flaunt herself extremely provocatively in the faces of a few leering men. Not only that, she'd seemed to enjoy it every bit as much as they had, jutting out her buttocks, fondling her breasts, doing many of the things they'd clearly love to do for her. For some reason Sherry had always assumed that women in this sort of work remained aloof, unconnected to what they were doing, but even if some did, it didn't appear Suzy was one of them. Actually, since she was such an accomplished dancer, it seemed naïve now not to have realized she might just enjoy doing what she was good at.

Danny, on the other hand, didn't seem to be enjoying anything. His eyes were darting about all over the place to see who was watching, which, considering how uninterested the sparse audience appeared in anything not on the stage, was becoming annoying.

'So looks like we've got a deal,' the diminutive,

large-breasted Suzy declared loudly, making Sherry start.

Belatedly realizing it was for the benefit of the G-stringed waitress who'd come to clear their table, Sherry couldn't think of anything to say except 'Good.'

'You, me and her,' Danny piped up, as Sherry watched the waitress and wondered what it felt like to strut around virtually naked in front of total strangers. The thought of doing it herself made her shudder – exhibitionism had never been her thing.

'This'll be her first time,' Danny was explaining in a bad actor's voice to Suzy. 'She's never done it with another woman before, i'n't that right?'

Sherry smiled weakly, then actually felt herself blush as the waitress threw her a wink.

'Well Danny's brought you to the right person,' Suzy was assuring her. 'How long have you two known each other?'

'A couple of months,' Danny answered. 'She's pretty hot stuff, aren't you babe?'

As he hugged her Sherry fought the urge to shove him off, and injected a note of coyness as she said, 'Sssh, people will hear.'

The waitress moved on and Danny got to his feet. 'Right, we're going to Suzy's place,' he announced. 'It's not far, walking distance. This is how it's normally done,' he added in a lower voice to Sherry.

'I can't be long,' Suzy told them, checking her watch. 'I'm on again at eight.'

'Do you do this a lot?' Sherry asked, as they climbed the stairs out of the club. 'Slip out between shows?'

Suzy threw back an incredulous look. 'Is she for real?' she demanded of Danny. 'This is what I do, darling. It's me job. You know, just like you slip out for the odd bit of information that gets you a story, I slip out for the odd bit of cash that gets me a living.'

Feeling faintly foolish, Sherry decided not to say any more and followed her outside.

Suzy's flat was on the eighth floor of a high-rise council block close to a main-line station, where the lifts and communal areas were obviously doubling as a toilet and message centre, and stank so badly Sherry had to hold her breath as they went up. Stepping into the flat was like stepping into a flowering meadow after a festering sewer. It was spotlessly clean, delightfully fragrant, stylishly furnished – mostly from IKEA – and was crowded out with bang-up-to-the-minute electronics. The corner bar, which was very Seventies, seemed to offer everything from the humblest mixer to the rarest cognac, and from the look of it Danny was as at home here as Suzy herself.

'So,' Suzy said, bringing a tray of drinks over to the coffee table, 'we might as well get straight down to it.'

For one alarming moment, as she cast aside the sweater she had draped round her shoulders, Sherry thought she meant the *ménage à trois*, but then to her relief she said, 'Remember, nothing I tell you here tonight came from me. Have we got that straight? I never said nothing. Right?'

'Right,' Sherry agreed. Then after a pause, 'So what do you know about these women?'

'You mean the ones he brings in from other countries, right?'

Sherry nodded. 'Most of all, we'd like to know where he keeps them.'

Suzy crunched on an ice cube. 'You been to the workshop on New Road?' she said.

'Yes.'

'Well the women are all upstairs. Not directly overhead, sort of over at the back . . .'

'They've been moved,' Danny interrupted.

Suzy looked surprised. 'Where to?'

'We don't know, that's why we're asking you. I went over to his bird's place today and had a look on the computer there. Nothing.'

Suzy's eyes were wide with disbelief. 'You went over to that flat? The one on Cinnabar Wharf where that slag Cheryl is shacked up? Are you out of your mind? You know what Eddie'll do if he ever finds out you been messing . . .'

'Just shut it!' he barked. 'No-one's gonna know unless you tell them, and I don't think that's gonna happen, do you?'

Suzy's face was taut with anger as she glared at him.

He glared back.

Sherry watched, saying nothing, but noting that Eddie Cribbs apparently had a girlfriend called Cheryl who lived in Cinnabar Wharf. It might come in useful.

In the end Suzy said, tightly, 'So how do you know they've been moved?'

'Because the place has been checked out,' he answered. 'They've gone. We ain't lying, so come on, do you know where they are now?'

'Not exactly, but I could probably find out.'

'How long would it take?' Sherry asked.

'Not sure. This is a very sensitive area we're talking about here, I hope you realize that.'

An understatement if ever she'd heard one, but all Sherry said was, 'Yes, I do, and I'm really grateful for your willingness to help.'

'It's gonna cost ya,' Suzy snapped.

'How much?'

'Five grand.'

Sherry didn't flinch, though she knew Laurie probably would. 'If the information's good enough, then five grand it will be,' she promised.

Seeming satisfied, Suzy picked up her glass and clinked it against Sherry's.

'So tell me what happens to these women,' Sherry said.

'What do you mean what happens to them?'

'Is it true they're being forced into prostitution?'

Starting slightly at the bluntness, Suzy said, 'I don't know if I'd put it like that . . . But yeah, I suppose you're right. It's forced.'

'Is it a special kind of prostitution?'

'What do you mean by that?'

'For example, are they used to service the needs of sadomasochists? Or maybe paedophiles?'

Suzy's eyes darted to Danny, then came back again. 'All I know is they do stuff the rest of us won't do,' she said. 'They're good little earners, I'm told. They're Indian this time, aren't they? They was from Eastern Europe before.'

'What happened to the Eastern Europeans?' Sherry asked.

Suzy shrugged, but she was careful to avoid

Sherry's eyes as she said, 'How would I know? I never get to meet any of them. I just know they're there, as back-up, is what we call it.'

She was lying, Sherry knew it. 'What are you hiding?' she said.

Suzy was immediately defensive. 'Nothing!' she snapped. 'I'm not hiding nothing.'

'I think you are,' Sherry persisted.

'Well, I can't help what you think, can I?'

'What happened to those women?' Sherry said, repeating her question. 'Where are they now?'

'I told you, I don't know. Why would I lie?'

Sherry didn't know, but she was more convinced than ever that Suzy was holding something back.

Suzy looked at Danny. 'You didn't tell me I'd have to get into any of this,' she complained.

Danny said, 'I didn't know she was going to ask, did I? And you was the one what mentioned the East Europeans.'

'For God's sake, what happened to them?' Sherry broke in.

'I don't know,' Suzy said tightly. 'And that's that, all right? I don't know.'

Realizing she'd have to concede defeat, if only for the moment, Sherry said, 'OK. If you won't tell me that, then will you tell me if children are involved?'

Suzy's discomfort was clearly increasing. 'I've heard they might be,' she answered stiffly.

'Can you find out?'

Her eyes bulged. 'Are you out of your mind?' she cried. 'If I start asking those kind of questions . . .'

313

'You can always say you've got an interested customer.'

'Those kind of customers don't come through the club, or not that I've ever known.'

'So where do they come from?'

'The Internet,' Danny answered.

Of course, she should have realized that. 'Do you know the Web addresses?' she asked.

'That was partly what I was hoping to find when I went round to the flat earlier,' he said. 'The porn sites are easy to get hold of, but the specialist ones . . . Nothing doing.'

Sherry turned back to Suzy. 'I take it you're aware that some of these women are being very badly injured by the men you pass on.'

Suzy's manner was becoming hostile again. 'It's why we pass 'em on,' she snapped. 'It's what it's all about.'

Sherry watched her and waited, for she obviously had some kind of conscience about it, or she wouldn't be so defensive.

'The way we see it,' she said finally, 'and Eddie sees it too, is that we're doing society a favour, making sure these sickos are catered for, otherwise they'd be preying on our women and children, wouldn't they?'

Sherry still only looked at her, and wondered when she had ever found it so hard to hide her disgust. That those poor, defenceless women were human beings too was clearly not worthy of consideration here. 'You know who the men are,' she stated. 'I mean the deviants who are inflicting the injuries. You know who they are.'

A quick nervousness sprang to Suzy's eyes.

314

'Yeah, I probably know some,' she conceded, 'but no way am I going to tell you their names. And if you ever quote me as saying any of this, I swear to God you won't be writing anything by the time I've finished.'

'I gave you my word before we started,' Sherry reminded her. 'That won't change. If I quote you at all, it'll be as an unnamed source.'

Danny said, 'Try not to quote her at all.'

Sherry glanced at him, but made no promise. 'The doctor they used, Doctor Patel,' she said, 'he won't speak to us now. Do you know of any other doctor who might be involved?'

Suzy shook her head.

'What about how the women are being brought into the country? Do you know anything . . .'

'We're not getting into that,' Danny cut in. 'We'll help you find the women that are here, but no more. That was what we agreed. Now, is that your phone ringing, or did you do a spot of shopping at Al's before you came into the club?'

Sherry looked down at her bag which was trembling on the ground. Quickly taking out the phone she checked to see who it was, then said, 'Excuse me. I need to take this,' and getting up she walked over to the window and clicked on. 'Hi,' she said softly into the mouthpiece.

'Hi yourself. How's the ménage going?'

'Fine. Pretty good, actually. But can I call you back? I'm still in the middle of things.'

'Oh?' Nick responded. 'Can't wait to hear. What time will you be done?'

'Half an hour.'

'I'm off the hook tonight. Can I come over?'

315

'I'd love that. If you're there before me, talk to the porter, he'll let you in.'

As she rang off, she returned to her chair, ready to pick up where they'd left off, but to her dismay Suzy said, 'I have to get back now. Have you got my money, for tonight?'

Sherry took out her purse. 'Three hundred, is that right?' she said.

'Four.'

Sherry's eyes came up. 'I thought we agreed three.'

'It's just gone up.'

Fortunately she could cover it, but as she handed the money over Sherry said, 'Please don't spring an increase on me again like this. I might not have it the next time.'

'You want the information, you do it my way,' Suzy responded tartly.

'OK. So how do I contact you?'

'You don't. Danny will. Stay away from the club now. If anyone sees you again they might get suspicious.'

Happy to go along with that, Sherry downed the rest of her drink and went ahead of them out of the flat. They were riding down in the lift when Suzy looked her straight in the eye and said, 'Do you really not know what you're dealing with here?'

Sherry countered with, 'Why don't you tell me?'

Suzy's eyes narrowed. 'You don't know, do you?' she said.

'I'm asking you to tell me.'

Suzy shot a glance at Danny, then to Sherry she said, 'If you don't know now, you're gonna, and

316

when you do, you're gonna wish you never got started. That's my prediction for you, and if I'm wrong, you come and see me – if you can – and I'll give you back every penny you've ever paid me, and double it.'

Later, as she recounted it all to Nick, it was the 'if you can' that kept ringing in Sherry's ears.

Neela didn't know where she was going. The streets were dark, the noises and traffic were different from those she was used to. Some people were dressed the same, but not many. A few lay on the pavements or in doorways, huddled in blankets and papers, the way she had back in her own country. They seemed to be sleeping, but one or two cupped their hands hoping for bread or coins. Her thoughts made pictures in her head of the Tughlak Fort where she'd begged with her mother, gazing up at tourists as they came and went. She'd point to her mouth and sometimes someone would toss a coin. Hundreds and thousands of people, bicycles, cars, animals, teemed around the streets. The noise never stopped. Hooting, shouting, barking, screaming, bells, whistles, engines, wheels. It wasn't like that here. There was no music wailing out of the windows, no smells to torment her stomach. There was only the fear that was bigger than the whole of the Tughlak Fort, and twice as deep as the Tapti River.

All kinds of buildings sped past in a blur. Through the tiny gap in the shawl she'd wrapped around her face she tried to read the signs, but nothing made sense and she was too afraid to try any more.

The driver didn't speak to her, but he knew her language. He kept his eyes on the road. She sat in the back, wrapped in her sari, a small, frightened figure, in the midst of an evil world. Silently, desperately, she muttered prayers to Ambamata.

Ekta had said they wanted a virgin and Neela was a virgin. This was her chance and Ekta had sworn to take care of Shaila while she was gone. No-one would take her, Ekta had promised. She would be safe.

Neela hated the place where they were kept like prisoners, but she wanted to be there now. She wanted to be safe on her mattress next to Ekta, holding onto Shaila. Someone was going to do bad things to her. They were going to hurt her and then she would need a doctor. Laurie Forbes knew the doctor, so Neela was praying hard to Ambamata to come in the form of Laurie Forbes to save them, because someone had said that men were going to make a film of them being hurt. And others said they would make a film of them being hurt until they were dead.

Chapter Sixteen

'Well, this is a surprise,' Sherry commented, as she walked into the Grapes to find Nick sitting at a table with Laurie and Rhona.

'It was supposed to be,' he told her, getting up. 'I had a meeting over this way, so I thought I'd drop by the office to see if you were free for lunch. Didn't you say you were going to be there this morning?' he added, after kissing her.

'I did, but something came up.' She took the chair he was holding for her, raising her eyebrows as Rhona mouthed, 'He's gorgeous. Give him to me.'

'I'll get you a drink,' he said. 'What'll you have?'

Looking at Rhona's and Laurie's glasses, she said, 'Are we celebrating something?'

'Rhona's return!' Laurie declared. 'That's what we're celebrating.'

Raising an eyebrow, Sherry said, 'Then a glass of champagne for me too.'

As Nick went off to the bar she turned back to Laurie. 'How long have you all been here? I thought we weren't meeting till one.'

'We weren't,' Laurie confirmed, 'but when Nick came into the office looking for you, I thought rather than hang around there, we might as well come here. So I got on the phone to Rhona, and she came too.'

Sherry was still smiling. 'I didn't realize you were going into the office this morning,' she said.

'No, nor did I, until Rhona brought me breakfast in bed and I realized I couldn't go on indulging in the high life like this. It's time I started pulling my weight and got back to work. I don't think I've actually achieved much, yet, but I will. Oops,' she laughed as she hiccuped.

Sherry cast a glance at Rhona, whose expression appeared deliberately neutral. 'So how is it, being back at Butler's Wharf?' she asked Laurie.

'Only bearable because Rhona's staying with me,' she confessed. 'But let's not dwell on that. Tell me how you got on with the Immigration Crime Team this morning. That is – hiccup – who you were seeing, isn't it?'

'Not the whole team,' Sherry answered. 'How many of those have you had?'

Laurie grinned. 'This is my second, and I haven't eaten so it's going straight to my head. There's an email from Rose, by the way. Have you seen it? Apparently she's actually got two oily creeps, as she calls them – agents for the buying and selling of young females for "Western clients" – to appear on camera. Shadowed, so they can't be recognized, of course, but it's quite a coup, wouldn't you say?'

'I certainly would,' Sherry agreed, smiling up at Nick as he passed her drink. 'Has she managed to come up with any links to our women, by any chance?'

'Not directly, but the important thing is to show how it's done that end, then what happens to the women when they get here, which we can only do if we find them. Linking it all together will be up to the police.'

Though she didn't show it Sherry was surprised, for it wasn't like Laurie to stop before uncovering the entire operation, and it wasn't her, Sherry's, intention now. However, since Laurie was obviously still distracted by the other events in her life, Sherry merely raised her glass and clinked it against those of the others. 'Welcome home,' she said to Rhona.

'Thank you,' Rhona responded. 'Now let's choose something to eat, or you're going to be under the table.'

Sherry turned to Nick as he pulled a chair up next to her. 'So who was your meeting with?' she asked quietly.

His eyes immediately lit up. 'John Burke-Godfrey at the *Independent*,' he answered. 'Would you believe, he wants to put me on staff.'

'He'd be lucky to get you,' she responded. 'But I thought you wanted to go freelance once you moved here.'

'I do. And I probably will, but it's a bit of a boost for the old ego. I might even take him up on it, just until I get settled.'

'Then here's to you too,' she said, clinking his glass. 'Welcome back to Blighty. I always did say John Burke-Godfrey was an editor of extreme good sense and impeccable taste.'

'Elliot really rates him too,' Laurie joined in. 'Actually, he and his wife were coming to the wedding, which reminds me, my mother's sent out the cancellation notices now, so you should be getting yours any day.'

Sherry's heart stirred with pity, for despite the effort Laurie was making to hide it, it had to have been hard for her to sound that casual.

'We've been trying to think of something to do on what would have been the big day,' Rhona told Sherry.

'We should just get drunk,' Laurie declared. 'In fact, as it's only two weeks away we could start now and just keep going.'

'No, we should go somewhere,' Rhona insisted. 'The villa's still free on Hydra.'

'But you've only just come back.'

'So? I can go again.'

'We could go to Bali,' Laurie interrupted. 'I happen to know of a wonderful resort there, and I do believe they've got a vacancy around that time.'

'Are you talking about one of the Amman Resorts?' Nick said. 'If you are, then I've got to tell you, the Ammanpula is one of the most beautiful spots I've ever been. Put it top of your list if you're looking for luxury, peace, everything on tap. The suites have even got their own private pools . . .'

'She knows,' Sherry said quietly. 'It's where they were going on honeymoon.'

Nick's eyes closed. 'Oh God, I'm sorry,' he murmured.

'No, I'm the one who should be sorry,' Laurie

insisted. 'You weren't to know, and I walked you right into it. Please, don't think any more of it.' She attempted a smile.

'I'm voting for Hydra,' Rhona declared, before an awkward silence had a chance to descend.

'I'll second it,' Sherry responded.

'What about Tuscany?' Laurie said.

Rhona threw her a look.

'I had a call from Rachel last night,' Laurie said, turning to Sherry. 'Apparently they're all there now. Chris and Rachel. Elliot and Andraya. Their names ring well together, don't you think? Elliot and Andraya. Yes, it definitely sounds right. And they'd look right together too, wouldn't they? She's about as tall as he is. In fact, I can just see them, strolling hand in hand through the vine- yards, dining in out-of-the-way cafés, sharing a magnificent bedroom in Eduardo's magnificent villa . . .'

'Laurie, don't,' Rhona cut in. 'You're just tormenting yourself and embarrassing Nick.'

'Oh don't mind me,' he came in quickly, before realizing it wasn't quite what he should have come in with.

'Sorry again,' Laurie said, looking at him. 'I'm making a bit of a fool of myself today, aren't I?'

'Not at all,' he assured her.

'Why did Rachel call?' Sherry asked, curious because Rachel surely knew that any call from her right now would be extremely hard for Laurie to take.

'Actually, she was calling me back,' Laurie confessed. 'I needed to know if he really had gone. And he has.' She swallowed some champagne.

'Apparently he asked Rachel how I was. I'd have thought he'd be too busy shagging his Brazilian bimbo to think about me, wouldn't you?'

Sherry glanced at Nick as he said, 'I don't want to get into defending him, but I'm sure he's not feeling too good about what's happened.'

'Well that's a relief,' Laurie retorted harshly, 'because I hope he isn't. I know I'm not. In fact, there should be surgery for this, some way of cutting him out of my life as though he'd never been in it.'

'Now there's an idea,' Rhona responded. 'Why on earth didn't God think of it, pack it all into one removable little spot in the body, like the appendix, instead of right in the middle of the one organ we can't live without.'

'Muscle,' Laurie corrected. 'The heart's a muscle.'

'Whatever. Now come on, let's decide what we're going to eat,' Rhona urged.

After jotting their orders down on a page from Sherry's notebook Nick went off to the bar, while Laurie, still appearing slightly befuddled, tried to focus her mind on anything that wasn't to do with Elliot.

Sensing her need for distraction, Sherry began telling her about her visit to the police that morning. 'If they know anything specific about Eddie Cribbs, or our women, they're not letting on,' she said. 'The most I could get out of them was an acknowledgement that there are thousands of illegal immigrants in this country, and that they're aware some are forced into prostitution, but that's Vice and they're Immigration. So my next stop is Vice.'

'What about the stripper, Suzy?' Laurie asked. 'Any news from her yet?'

'No. I've got a feeling she might be having second thoughts, actually. In fact they both might be her and Danny, because he's not returning my calls and I've left three messages in the past two days. He's spoken to Barry though, who still seems confident they'll come up with the goods. I just hope we find out soon where those women are, because I've had a really bad feeling about it since Suzy wouldn't tell me what happened to the Eastern Europeans.'

'What do you think might have happened?' Rhona prompted.

Sherry shrugged. 'I'm guessing they probably get sold on,' she answered, 'but to whom, and what for . . .' She shuddered.

'How did you get on surfing the Net for the paedophile club?' Nick asked.

Her lip curled in disgust – she'd spent a lot of hours over the past few days looking for that club, and she wouldn't have minded if she never entered that kind of territory again in her life. 'Nothing that in any way leads us to Mr Cribbs,' she told him. 'But my God there are a lot of sick people out there.'

'If it's paedophiles you're looking for, I might be able to help,' Rhona said, looking pensive.

They all turned to her in amazement. 'Are you serious?' Sherry responded.

'I'm not sure. I just remember doing a promotion for a crime psychology book a year or so ago, which included a section on paedophiles. The author did an incredible amount of research. I could contact him, see if there's something he could suggest, you know, how you might find a particular club or ring.'

'That would be great,' Sherry told her, taking out her notebook. 'What's his name? I wouldn't mind reading the book.'

As Rhona spelled out the complicated Polish name, Laurie glanced up at Nick and smiled.

At that moment their food arrived, and after they'd been sorted out with the right meals, knives, forks, bread, ketchup, etc., Nick drew Laurie into conversation about some of the stories she had covered, while Rhona confided to Sherry in low tones how concerned she was about Laurie.

It was hard for Sherry to pay full attention, or even make any comment, while Laurie was sitting right there, not just in earshot, but getting on so well with Nick it was starting to seem as though they'd forgotten anyone else was at the table. She kept reminding herself that of course they'd have a lot to talk about, they were in the same profession, the same branch of it even, but she still wouldn't have minded Nick looking just a little bit less enamoured. It was as though the only person there who had anything of value to say was the woman he couldn't seem to take his eyes off. The woman who was starting to glow in all his male attention. Though she wasn't able to hear much of what they were saying, it all seemed to be about the various stories they'd covered, but at some point the subject obviously moved on, because she heard them exclaim in surprise as they discovered they'd both spent time in the Emirates as children. Then the next she knew they were agreeing on how much they loved Woody Allen's films.

Sherry was a fan of Woody Allen's films too, but, unlike Rhona, she didn't join in the conversation. Nor did she comment on the fact that Nick had never told her he liked Woody Allen, or that he'd spent four of his formative years in the Emirates. It would sound petty if she did, and anyway it shouldn't matter. But it did.

'Are you OK?' Rhona asked quietly as they finally left the pub and stepped out into the sunshine.

'Me?' Sherry replied in surprise. 'I'm fine. Just thinking about all I have to do this afternoon – and regretting the champagne. What are you up to now?' she asked Nick, as he slipped an arm round her shoulder.

'Julia and I have an appointment with an estate agent at three thirty,' he answered, looking at his watch. 'So I guess I should be on my way. I got a lift here, so how do I get back?'

'The station's just along there,' Sherry said pointing.

'I'll come with you,' Laurie offered. 'It'll make a change from taking the river bus.'

Sherry turned to look at her. 'I thought you were back at work.'

Laurie looked startled. 'Oh! I am if you need me,' she assured her.

Rhona laughed. 'Who's the boss here?' she teased.

'Sherry,' Laurie answered. 'Definitely Sherry.'

It was Sherry's turn to laugh. 'I don't think so,' she responded. 'But there's not much to do this afternoon, so I'm off home to catch up on my own work.'

'Good, so that's settled then,' Nick said, more

than ready to take off. 'Shall we go?'

'I'm right with you,' Laurie replied, falling in step beside him.

'Oh hell,' he suddenly cried, and doing a fast about-turn he swept Sherry into an engulfing embrace. 'I'll call you later,' he said, his mouth still very close to hers.

'Are you likely to be free tonight?' she asked. 'Or are you being a parent?'

'I think being a parent,' he answered. 'But things change by the minute.'

Rhona was still chuckling as she and Sherry turned in the other direction. 'He's a nice man,' she declared. 'I like him.'

'I'm sure the feeling's mutual,' Sherry told her. 'In fact I know it is, because he likes everyone. Though he seems particularly fond of Laurie.'

'Because she's your friend. He wants to make a good impression. I think that's rather sweet.'

Sherry smiled.

After a while Rhona cast her a sideways look. 'He's just done Laurie's confidence the power of good, paying her all that attention,' she said. 'It's something she really needs right now.'

'I know,' Sherry responded.

They walked on a little further. 'Are you really as upset as you seem?'

Sherry sighed and shook her head. 'No. Or maybe yes. The trouble is, having lost him once, I'm terrified of it happening again.'

'But surely not to Laurie, when she's going through all that she is?'

'No. Of course not. It's just me. I get too caught up in my own fears.'

328

'Then you need to relax, or you'll make them happen,' Rhona cautioned. 'The mind has that sort of power, and you know it.'

Yes, Sherry did know it, and she wasn't thinking of Nick now, but the other overpowering fear in her life – the one that had lain dormant for so many years she might have thought it was conquered, were it not for those occasional, damnable letters. And now Nick's return, instead of helping to kill it altogether, which was what she'd hoped for, was having the adverse effect of stirring it up all over again.

'Why are you doubting him so much?' Rhona asked. 'It seems to me he could hardly be more into you.'

Sherry finally smiled. 'I suppose if he'd just include me more in his life,' she said. 'Introduce me to his family. I still haven't met his daughter.'

'Hah!' Rhona scoffed. 'That sounds like a blessing to me. All those rampaging hormones and teenage tantrums. *Puhlease!*'

Sherry laughed.

'No, believe me, he's doing you a favour,' Rhona insisted, 'because once she's on the scene, make no doubt about it, it's all going to be about her. In fact, that could very well be why he's keeping you apart right now, he doesn't want her sabotaging his relationship with you – which thirteen-year-olds are prone to, as well you know, Dear Molly.'

Sherry's eyes were dancing as she stood aside for Rhona to go into the building ahead of her. 'Are you staying at Laurie's again tonight?' she asked, as they rode up in the lift.

'No. I'm going to the theatre with some friends.

329

She has to be on her own in that flat sometime, so tonight seemed a good time to start.'

'Tell me,' Sherry said, as the doors slid open and they stepped out onto the landing, 'do you think Elliot will come back?'

Rhona inhaled deeply and shook her head. 'To be honest, I don't know,' she answered. 'He's behaving so out of character these days, it's anyone's guess what he might do.'

Elliot and Andraya were lying on the large bed of their room in Eduardo's exquisite old Tuscan villa, basking in the afterglow of their most recently spent passion. The sheet was kicked aside, their clothes scattered on the floor. Thin bands of sunlight pressed in through the edges of the shutters. The buzz of cicadas, now that Paolo Conte's hauntingly raspy voice had faded from the CD downstairs, was the only sound to accompany the hot, still, afternoon siesta.

'What are you thinking, *meu amor*?' she whispered.

He lifted a hand, put it on her breast and traced the nipple with his thumb. After a while he lowered his mouth and began to suck and gently bite it.

She moaned with pleasure and opening her arms wide rolled on to her back.

Propped on one elbow he lay looking at her again, amused by the way her breasts stayed upright, becoming excited, as he always did, by the sheer size of her nipples.

'Eduardo must be sleeping now,' she commented, after several minutes had passed with no

330

more music coming from the room below. 'It is so peaceful here. I love the afternoons.' She turned to look at him. 'Will you come to New York?' she said.

Surprised by the question, he pressed a kiss to her lips. 'I thought it was settled,' he responded. 'Of course I'll come.'

Her eyes gleamed wickedly. 'I just wanted to hear you say it,' she told him, and drawing his fingers to her mouth she began kissing them one by one. 'I'm afraid you're still thinking of her,' she said after a while. 'If you are I shall be so jealous I will do something terrible to you.'

With a dry laugh he pulled his hand away and rolled onto his back. 'I called Max, my partner in New York,' he said, staring up at the faded ceiling frescos. 'His apartment might be free for us to rent.'

Her eyes took on a dark, sensuous glow as she turned his face to hers. 'For how long?'

'Six weeks.'

She bit into his shoulder. 'What if I get bored with you before six weeks is over?'

'Then I guess one of us will have to move out.'

Laughing, she pulled herself up to sit astride him. 'I am so happy that you are in my life,' she told him softly, watching his hands as they moved over her thighs. 'I feel as though we belong to each other.'

His eyes revealed little as he looked up at her.

'Soon we will belong to New York too,' she declared. 'You will show me all the places that you know, take me to all the galleries and museums. And then,' she added, lowering her voice, 'you will come with me to Rio. I will show you my city. She is like me, dark and beautiful and exciting, full of passion and danger.'

Reaching up, he pulled her mouth down to his and pushed his tongue deep inside. They kissed for a long, erotically charged time, letting their desire build to a point where their bodies needed to join again. But just as he was easing her onto her back, she slipped from his arms and went to throw open the shutters.

The view down over the tiers of olive groves and out to the forested hills beyond was bathed in white sunlight. The air was thick and still with heat, the scent of jasmine drifted from the flowers clinging to the villa walls. She was framed like a portrait, from head to mid-thigh, her nudity exposed to the magnificently rugged scene that spread out before her, her big round bottom waiting for his touch.

Knowing how it thrilled her to exhibit herself this way, he came up behind her, more than ready to perform the role she had now cast him in. Until the moment of her release he could be anyone. She wouldn't know his name, she wouldn't even acknowledge he was there. She would simply lean forward to rest her hands on the window ledge, continuing to absorb the view as he entered her from behind and took her so hard that all the golden flesh of her body would ripple with the force, and the power of her orgasm would be swallowed into the densely wooded hills in the distance.

Half an hour later, sated and now still, they lay

together on the bed, limbs loosely entwined, her head on his shoulder as she slept. His body was still damp with the sweat of exertion, though his heartbeat was steady now, his muscles less tense. He inhaled the musky scent of her hair, and felt the whisper of her breath on his skin. There was nowhere else he wanted to be, just here, with her, bound in the magnetism that made it impossible for them to resist each other, a long way from reality, untouched by the heartache he'd left behind.

As she stirred and turned her head away, he glanced down at the lustrous thickness of the hair she'd left spilling over his shoulder. Lifting it to his lips he absently kissed it. Then, sitting up, he leaned over to kiss the hair between her legs too. He could use his tongue now to bring her awake, but instead he got quietly up from the bed and slipped into his clothes.

To his surprise, when he walked outside into the long, shady bower where an hour ago they'd all been eating lunch, he spotted Rachel sitting at the far end playing with Charlie, her eight-month-old son.

'Couldn't sleep?' he said, going to join them.

Seeing him, Charlie promptly exposed his two bottom teeth in a delighted grin.

'That's Charlie's new game, isn't it?' she answered, playfully shaking her son. 'It's called let's wake up when everyone else goes to sleep.'

'I guess everyone keeps telling you how much he's like his father,' Elliot said, allowing his fingers to be pulled back as far as Charlie could make them go.

'Mm, but I almost wish they wouldn't.'

Elliot's eyes came up in surprise, then, realizing why she wished it, he said, 'It's a reminder that you still miss him?'

She nodded. 'It's only been a year since he was killed, and now, having Charlie . . . It hurts a lot that he'll never know his father.'

'Is Chris going to step into that role?'

'He already has, but we're agreed that Charlie will always know who his real father *was*,' she gasped as Charlie lunged forward, almost landing himself on Elliot's lap.

Taking him, Elliot bounced him around and made him laugh, until he was ready to return to his mother.

'I don't have to ask if you miss Laurie,' Rachel said, trying to sound neutral. 'You and Andraya are inseparable, it seems.'

Not rising to the slight edge in her voice, he said, 'I'm sorry if I'm making this awkward for you.'

'I wasn't actually thinking about me,' she responded.

His eyes met hers for a brief moment, then he looked away to the tangled mass of plumbago that all but masked the stone steps leading down to the pool.

'I know it's none of my business,' she said, 'but I think you're making a terrible mistake.'

He didn't reply.

'You and Laurie are so right for each other.'

He turned to look at her. 'I don't want to offend you,' he said, 'but I'd rather not discuss it.'

Stung, as much for Laurie as for herself, she pressed her lips to Charlie's blond curls, and

334

struggled to push her thoughts in another direction. She couldn't fight Laurie's battles for her, and trying to make him feel bad for the way he was behaving wasn't going to get anyone anywhere either. 'Chris mentioned you're thinking of coming to New York with us,' she said, putting Charlie down on the ground to play. 'That it might even be a permanent relocation. Is that the plan?' She didn't add, *have you told Laurie yet*, though she wanted to, because God knew she didn't want to tell her.

'Possibly,' he said. 'I wouldn't mind the change, and I think Andraya's going to fall in love with the place.'

Rachel's heart turned over. With a remark like that there really could be no doubting how serious he was about the woman. 'What if she wants to stay living in Rio?' she asked. 'Would you go there?'

He looked amused and shook his head. 'It has to be London or New York, she knows that and she's OK with it.'

'Just as long as you're together?'

He didn't answer.

'My, my, my,' Andraya drawled, sauntering towards them in an extremely sexy bikini. 'This looks very intimate. Can anyone join in?'

Elliot stood up, went to meet her and took her hand.

She chuckled softly with her lips against his, then looking past him to Rachel she said, 'Please forgive me, but I need to have him all to myself for a while. I'm sure you understand.'

As they walked back into the house Rachel

glanced down at Charlie and felt another wave of sadness sweep over her, for Elliot had just left her with nothing at all to pass on to Laurie that Laurie in all her lifetime would ever want to hear.

Chapter Seventeen

It was evening now, and Sherry was still waiting for a call from Nick after he'd left the pub earlier with Laurie. Of course, she knew better than to listen to the voices in her head, and the suspicion they were planting, but as the minutes ticked on and the phone still didn't ring, it was getting harder and harder to ignore them.

She opened the French doors and stood on the balcony, breathing in the scent of the flowers and watching the fast, gentle flow of the river. Water, jasmine, fear, jealousy. It was all too strong a reminder of the past. A garden, a pool, the night air, distant voices. She'd never imagined finding herself in this place again, but it was happening, and though she knew she was creating it, she couldn't make herself stop, for the images were growing bigger and clearer, the voices were getting stronger, drawing her back and back . . .

Quickly she turned inside and closed the door. Taking a breath she let it out slowly, then started as the phone suddenly cut into the silence.

She stared at it, willing it to be Nick, but it was Laurie's voice that spoke into the machine. 'Sherry? Are you there?' she said. 'Will you pick up, if you are?'

Relief got her reaching for the receiver. 'I'm here,' she said. 'Are you OK?'

'Can you come over?'

'Sure. Is everything all right?' What a stupid question – Elliot was in Italy with another woman, and they were just thirteen days away from when they should have been getting married. How could she possibly be all right?

Laurie's voice was fractured with pain as she said, 'I need to know what I have to do to get through this. If you don't tell me I honestly think I'll go mad.'

'Of course,' Sherry said softly. 'I'll be there as soon as I can,' and feeling dreadful for even thinking Laurie might have been spending the evening with Nick, she put down the phone, picked up her keys and left the flat.

How many times, she wondered, as she ran down the stairs, had she made this errand of mercy before? Too many to count. Too many not to know what to do. She just hoped Laurie was ready to deal with it, for it was still very early days. Though Sherry didn't doubt Laurie's inner strength, getting to grips with the pain and learning how to handle it was really expecting far too much of herself at this stage. However, if anyone could do it, Laurie could, and if she did, it would be yet another reason to admire her, as if there weren't enough already.

*

As Laurie prepared drinks and a snack in the kitchen Sherry stood in the sitting room, letting her eyes wander across the high, vaulted ceilings, the white brick walls, the Oriental-style balustrades of the mezzanine, to the dramatic river view. By anyone's standards this could qualify as a dream home, she was thinking to herself. From the custom-made Italian furniture, to the exquisite Kashmiri silk carpets, to the curve of the staircase and modern paintings that hung on the walls, virtually everything had been chosen or created from a design Laurie and Elliot had worked on together. It was no wonder Laurie was finding it so hard to be here alone, so much of them and who they were, as individuals and as a couple, was wrapped up in the place, it had to be close to torture.

Turning as Laurie came round from the kitchen, she watched her set down a tray of iced lemonade and crudités, knowing it was unlikely either of them would eat much, but at least she'd persuaded Laurie to do without alcohol. It was an easy trap to fall into at a time like this, but it only ended up making everything seem ten times worse.

'I shouldn't have drunk so much at lunchtime,' Laurie said, turning her sore, tired eyes to Sherry.

She looked so vulnerable that Sherry didn't hesitate to draw her into an embrace, almost as though she were a parent comforting a child. In a way that was the role she was going to play for the next couple of hours, that of a parent, or an older sister, who could pull on all the experience she'd had at doing this, helping to get someone past the worst of the pain.

'I'm sorry,' Laurie said. 'I feel so wretched. I should be able to handle this better, but I just can't seem to. I keep tormenting myself with images of them together, and the worst of it is, they seem so right for each other.'

Sherry watched as she covered her face with her hands, as though to close out the images. 'You can tell yourself anything you like,' she said, 'it doesn't necessarily make it true.'

Laurie inhaled, then dropped her hands. 'Thank you for that,' she said, and went to sink into one of the big, downy cushions that were scattered around the coffee table. Now was the time to tell Sherry that she'd spent the afternoon with Nick, but she knew she wouldn't because she didn't want to distract Sherry from the reason she was here.

She looked up and forced a smile. 'Lemonade?'

Sherry watched as she began to fill two glasses.

'Now you're here,' Laurie said, 'I'm starting to feel embarrassed about my inability to cope again. I'm a grown woman, successful, in full health, with so much else going for me . . . I shouldn't be falling apart like this.'

Understanding the need to underestimate what she was going through, Sherry let the comment go and helped herself to an olive.

'Actually, I can be going along just fine,' Laurie continued, 'getting on with my life as though everything's OK, no tears, no hysteria, no panic, then suddenly it's as though all the breath has been knocked out of me. I feel so utterly incapable of dealing with anything, and so terrified of spending even one evening alone, that it's as though I'm going to be swallowed up by it all and never make it out the other side.'

Sherry nodded. 'I know what you mean,' she said.

'Then please tell me how to make it stop. I'll do anything. *Anything*. I know you said it won't be easy, but whatever it is, I need to try.'

'OK,' Sherry said, 'but I'm afraid an escape, which is what you're basically asking for, isn't the answer. You have to go through it. It's the only way you'll get past it.'

'Oh my God,' Laurie murmured, her eyes glazing as she picked up her glass. 'My dad said virtually those words after Lysette's funeral. "The only way past this is through it," he said.' Her face was paler than ever as she looked at Sherry. 'I don't want to go there again,' she whispered. 'Surely to God I don't have to. He's not dead. It's not the same. He might come back, so can't you just tell me how to cope with these next few weeks without driving myself insane?'

Seeing no reason to point out that days, weeks, years, it didn't really matter, the pain still had to be got through, not around, Sherry said, 'Actually, it is the same inasmuch as they're both forms of loss. But it's true, what's happened with Elliot is going to have a very different outcome to what happened to Lysette, whether he comes back or not.'

'Do you think he will?' Laurie said, sounding as pathetic as she looked.

'If it's right, if it's meant to be, then yes, he will.'

It was enough of a straw for Laurie to cling to. 'It is meant to be,' she said decisively. 'I know it. I feel it. We belong together.'

341

'Then he will come back, but I don't think it's going to happen tonight.'

Laurie's face fell. 'No. Tonight he's over there with her, screwing her into oblivion, no doubt.' Her pupils dilated as she gazed at Sherry. 'Do you think he loves her?' she asked. Then with a quick shake of her head, 'You don't have to answer that. Just tell me how to stop tormenting myself like this. How the hell can I turn off the pain?'

Touched by the naïvety in her trust, Sherry said, 'Well, I guess first you should brace yourself, because what I'm about to say isn't going to be what you want to hear.'

Laurie swallowed. 'OK. I'm braced,' she said.

'Then you need to begin by going right into the very heart of the pain, letting it take you over so completely that it isn't possible to feel anything else. Let it own you as much as you own it. Let it become you.'

Laurie's face looked pinched. 'What happened to putting it out of my mind, keeping myself busy with other things?' she protested. 'That's what everyone else is telling me to do.'

'You can do that, but those are avoidance tactics. They won't take you through it, they take you around it, which is a bit like skirting the scene of an accident and not stopping to help. What's there, what's happened, needs to be dealt with, and in this case you're the only one who can do it. If you skirt round it the injury will take a heck of a lot longer to heal. So you need to go right up to it, face what's happened and do what's required to bring about a cure.'

Laurie was still looking very unsure. 'Please tell

me this isn't some kind of California cult thing,' she said. 'A New Age version of a hair shirt. Because I've never heard of having to get yourself all wrapped up in the pain before.'

Sherry smiled. 'That's because you've never had to deal with a broken heart before, nor have you had any therapy on how to cope with loss. Ask Anita, or anyone in her profession, they'll tell you it's never a good thing to avoid or ignore what you're feeling. It has to be faced, so that's what I'm trying to help you to do.'

Laurie's eyes began moving about the room. 'I suppose,' she said, 'the reason I don't want to face it, or go right into it, as you put it, isn't just because it hurts so much, but because it'll make it real. I'll have to accept then that he really has gone.'

'Which he has,' Sherry responded as gently as she could. 'And what you're doing is causing yourself a lot more pain than necessary by resisting the fact that things are going in a different direction to the one you planned. As far as you're concerned this isn't how it's supposed to be. You had it all mapped out. You'd bought the apartment, booked the wedding, were all set for happy ever after, and now suddenly you've been thrown right off course. You're not in the driving seat any more. Life's not conforming to your dreams.'

'You're not wrong about that,' Laurie muttered drily.

'The point is,' Sherry continued, 'whether you like it or not you really are on another track now, and the longer you resist the reality of that the harder you're going to make this for yourself.'

Laurie sat quietly, aware that what Sherry was

343

saying made sense, but that didn't make it any easier to accept or to act on.

'To quote one counsellor I knew,' Sherry said, '"Resistance is a self-inflicted form of torment, which is why you need to let it go." It's a waste of time, and no matter how hard you fight you'll never win, because if it's meant to happen, it will. Life, God, Fate, the Universe, call it what you like, is in charge here. It's making up the rules, deciding on the journey, and you just have to trust that you'll be taken to where you need to go.'

Laurie's whole body was stiffening, for the very idea of going anywhere without Elliot wasn't one she could welcome at all. 'But what if I don't want to go on the journey? What if I think it's wrong?'

'Well, to begin with you're already on it, so the point is moot, and anyway, you don't have a choice. All you can decide is whether you go willingly, or fight all the way. Whichever, it's still a journey you have to take and you'll make it a lot easier on yourself if you accept that.'

'What about fighting for him? Other people fight, and they win.'

'Only if they're supposed to. And fighting takes a lot of different forms. The most effective is actually to let go, which I know doesn't sound like a fight at all.'

'It sounds more like giving up.'

'Which in a way it is, because you'd be giving up the resistance. If you fight to get him back, in the sense you mean it, you'll just be forcing it, and usually, if you force it, it'll just fall apart again anyway. So give him the space, or whatever it is he needs right now, because if you don't you're

344

resisting again. And the more you resist the more he'll try to break free.' She paused to let that sink in. 'Let him do what he feels he has to,' she said, 'while you concentrate on what's right for you. I know at this moment you think it's him, but it might just not be. It could be, by the time you come out the other side of this, you won't even want him any more.'

Laurie's expression showed how hard she found that to believe.

'More resistance,' Sherry told her gently. 'Believe anything, because anything's possible.'

Liking the tiny ray of hope that offered, Laurie said, 'So let's make sure I'm getting this right – I have to stop trying to control things and trust whatever's out there to come through with what's right, because it knows and I don't. And meanwhile, I submerge myself in the pain of it all until I can't stand it any more.'

'That's the point at which it will start to lessen.'

Laurie was looking extremely depressed. 'So just how bad does it get?' she asked after a pause. 'What should I expect?'

Sherry hesitated.

'Oh my God, it's that bad!'

'I once heard someone describe it as passing through the Valley of the Shadow of Death, but before you get up and walk out on me it helps to remember that you pass through, you don't stop and pitch a tent. You'll always be moving forward, even without trying, towards that proverbial light at the end of the tunnel.'

'But it's really that dark?'

'It's the pits. You'll become consumed by worthlessness, self-pity, anger, hopelessness, hatred, all the dark emotions you can think of. Nothing will ever have felt so bad. You'll be totally alone.'

'Give it to me straight,' Laurie muttered drily.

Sherry smiled. 'I'm only putting it like that so you'll remember, when you're there, that you're not the first to experience it, and you won't be the last.'

'I still can't say I'm liking the sound of it too much. I mean I can feel all those things without sticking them right in me like knives.'

'Here's how life's going to look if you don't deal with this properly now,' Sherry said. 'The pain will continue to hang around, casting a shadow over your life in ways you might not even be aware of – lack of belief in anything good, failure to trust on any level, a general cynicism and fear that chips away at you until you forget how to enjoy the smooth and open roads when you're on them, because you're always too worried about what might be around the next bend. Whereas, if you confront it now, really go through it, you'll set yourself free from all that negativity and fearful behaviour.'

Laurie said nothing, and Sherry watched the paleness of her face as she struggled with the enormity of what was inside her, knowing very well that it was the bitter conflict between resistance and reality.

'How do I actually do it?' Laurie said eventually. 'I mean get myself right into it.'

'You just do it. Whenever you're feeling ghastly and that you simply can't bear it any more, stay with it. Don't run away. You've heard of fight or flight?'

'Yes.'

'Well this is it. You don't take flight by throwing yourself into work, or TV, or a good book, you stay and deal with what's there to be dealt with.'

'You mean, stay in the moment?'

'Exactly. Try not to look at the big picture, or work out the meaning of things. Just accept what's happening to you now, feel it, then let it go.'

'Just like that? Feel it, then let it go?'

'Believe me, once you've felt it, it won't be that hard to let go. It's avoiding it that makes it hang around.'

Laurie sat staring into space, thinking everything over until finally she had to admit that in spite of believing what Sherry was telling her, she was still resisting it all. She didn't want this to be happening, she didn't want to let Eliot go, and she definitely didn't want to make any kind of journey without him, particularly not the one Sherry was promoting. 'So how many times do I have to make this trip down into Happy Valley?' she asked glumly.

'As many as it takes. The first is definitely the most difficult, and with any luck that might turn out to be all you need. You won't know until you do it. But once you have, you'll start seeing, within days, how much easier it is to cope when you're not resisting. And the fact that you're doing it for yourself is what makes all the difference, because thinking Eliot, or anyone else, can do it for you is just giving your power away at a time you need it the most.'

'But Elliot could make a huge difference if he came back.'

'If that happened,' Sherry said, 'you'd have other emotions to deal with that would be equally important and probably no less disturbing, considering the reason he left and what he's been doing since. But what we're doing now is dealing with "what is" rather than "what if".'

Laurie turned to gaze towards the window and the darkening sky beyond. It wasn't that she was doubting anything Sherry was telling her, it was simply that she just couldn't conceive of ever being willing to let Elliot go, nor could she fully accept that she had no control over what was happening.

In the end she turned back to Sherry and looked at her kind, familiar face in the fading light, the lively, gentle blue eyes, the delicate nose, the large, appealingly imperfect mouth. 'How on earth do you know all this?' she said. 'Was it just the experience with Nick?'

'And losing my parents.'

'Yes, of course, I'm sorry,' Laurie responded, wondering how on earth Sherry had coped, for she knew that to lose her parents now, on top of losing Elliot, would be an end for her. She really wouldn't be able to go on.

'I found painting helped,' Sherry told her. 'It was when I created the little collection I have in my flat. I had so much anger and fear and violence in me at the time. I felt I'd been cheated by the world and nothing was ever going to go right again, so what was the point to anything. I was ready to damage or destroy whatever came into my life. I wanted to punish everybody and everything for what had happened to me. I was having counselling, but I still couldn't get rid of the anger. Then my aunt bought me a set of paints and an easel and suggested it might act as a kind of escape valve. I won't go into what I was like at that time, a madwoman I expect, shut up in my uncle's garden shed raging and cursing and just letting it all go. I had to get rid of it somehow, and that definitely helped. I'm told some people write it all down, while others turn up the music, or cook, or dig the garden, or climb to the top of a mountain and scream. Whatever it is, we all find what works for us in the end.'

Laurie suspected in her case it would be listening to opera, but already she was shrinking from the very thought of hearing just one bar. It was so much a part of her and Elliot, had played such a vital role in their relationship, especially in an intimate sense, that nothing in the world could induce her to put herself through it now.

Her eyes drifted for a while, then feeling suddenly restless, as an image of Elliot and Andraya flashed into her mind again, she got up and went to sit at the foot of the stairs. A few minutes later she wandered over to the window and stared down at the river. 'I know you said you got all this from therapy,' she said, finally turning back, 'but there's more to it, isn't there? There's something else.'

Not sure whether she was more surprised or shaken by the question, Sherry reached for her lemonade and drank, just to give herself some time. 'You're right, there is,' she said finally, putting the glass down and staring at it. 'There was a woman I used to know, in California. She taught me most of what I've told you tonight. She was someone who'd had her heart broken so many times and had tried so many ways to get over it . . . She consulted everyone, therapists, Buddhists, faith healers, priests, shamans, New Age spiritualists, you name it, she'd either read the book, gone for private counselling, or undertaken some pilgrimage to seek guidance on how to overcome the hurt and devastation and move past it.'

She paused for a moment, having to swallow the lump in her throat as she recalled the look of the woman, the sound of her voice, her scent and the bittersweet memory of her tears. 'She was beautiful,' she said. 'Kind to a fault, generous, and one of the saddest people I ever knew. It used to break my heart sometimes just to look at her. I even used to feel her pain. I'd hold her hand and it was as though it flowed from her all the way into me. It was always the same man who broke her heart. She just couldn't stop loving him, though God knew she tried. No-one could ever have tried harder.'

'Who was she?' Laurie said softly, certain she already knew the answer.

As Sherry's eyes came up to hers, a tear trickled on to her cheek. 'My mother,' she said.

'What's your name?' he asked for the third time. 'You must have a name. Why don't you tell me what it is?'

Neela's large brown eyes peered at him through the slit she had made in her veil.

'Do you understand English? Do you know what I'm saying?'

She stared at his round white face. His head, where there should have been hair, gleamed in the lamplight; his grey, bushy beard grew up to his ears. He was putting on his clothes, tucking his shirt into his trousers and pushing his feet into sandals. This was the second time she'd been brought here. She wasn't a virgin now. It had hurt a lot and she'd bled, but it wasn't enough to need a doctor. He hadn't hurt her enough this time either.

He came to kneel in front of her and tried to take her hands. The veil fell, exposing her face. Quickly she grabbed it to her again. When he was doing those things to her, and her sari was on a chair with his clothes, she kept her eyes tightly shut and pretended he couldn't see her. Like this it wasn't possible to pretend.

'How old are you?' he asked.

His eyes were the colour of dead leaves. He smelled of sweat and soap.

'Do you understand anything I'm saying?'

She only looked at him, still afraid even though it was over, and wanting to cry and cry and cry.

He put a hand to his chest. 'I am Daddy. Da-deee.'

She lowered her eyes.

Suddenly his fist crashed into the side of her head. 'Daddy! Do you hear me?' he snarled.

Neela curled herself tightly into a ball.

'Filthy whore!' he hissed. 'How many men have you fucked today?' He grabbed her veil and pulled it tight round her throat. 'Answer me!' he growled. 'Tell Daddy you're a whore.'

Neela was choking, gasping for air. Her fingers clawed helplessly at his.

He punched her again and again, banging his fists into her face and body, kicking her and throwing her to the floor. She was tangled in her sari. She couldn't get up. She clutched her arms round her head and brought her knees to her chest.

He stood over her. She could hear him breathing and doing something else, but she was too terrified to look.

'Get up!' he snarled. 'Get up.'

She stayed where she was, shaking, whimpering, silently praying. Maybe he was going to hurt her enough now so she would need a doctor. She thought of Shaila to give herself strength, and held her breath.

'Get up!' he snarled again, and grabbing her hair he hauled her to her knees.

He used his belt to beat her, bringing the buckle down in a fast, cruel torrent of blows. 'You're a bad girl,' he kept saying, over and over. 'A bad, bad girl.'

Pain seared through her body. Her skin was torn open. She gulped and begged and tried to get free, but there was nowhere to go. She was locked in this room. He could do anything to her and no-one would stop him. Please God don't let him kill her, or Shaila would be all alone.

Laurie was in the office, throwing herself into work with the kind of energy she hadn't had for too long. It wasn't that she was ignoring Sherry's advice to absorb herself in the pain rather than avoid it, she was quite simply feeling much more positive about everything this morning. Elliot had left a message last night saying he wanted to talk

352

when he got back to London today. Of course she might be fooling herself here, but there was no denying the affection in his tone, or the very strong feeling in her heart that they were going to get back together. This Andraya thing was just some kind of aberration, the kind anyone could fall prey to, at any time, even someone like him who was normally so in control of his emotions. Everyone said he was acting completely out of character, so it wasn't just her, trying to make excuses, he really was in the grip of something that was stronger than him.

But it would burn itself out. That sort of obsession always did.

She was just overcoming the sinking nerves that followed her calculation of how long it was before Elliot returned, when the door suddenly flew open and Sherry stormed in, looking so angry that Laurie actually drew back.

'I can't believe,' Sherry raged, her eyes flashing with fury, 'that you would spend virtually an entire day with Nick *and his daughter* and not tell me.'

Laurie had no chance to respond before she raged on.

'I was with you all evening, all *night*, talking about Elliot, doing everything I could to help you, and all the time you failed to mention a single word about the fact that you'd spent the entire afternoon with Nick. Why would you do that? What's the matter with you?'

Laurie's heart was thudding with guilt. She should have known Sherry would find out, indeed she was a fool to have kept it from her, because she'd obviously just made it ten times worse. 'How did you find out?' she asked, amazed that Rhona might have broken her confidence.

'From Nick. How the hell do you think? He didn't seem to consider it a guilty little secret that had to be kept from me, whereas you obviously did.'

Laurie was shaking her head. 'No, it wasn't like that,' she protested.

'Then why didn't you tell me? For God's sake, I spent all that time with you, I came over as soon as you needed me, and you didn't even have the decency to tell me that after you left the pub that day you went flat-hunting with Nick and his daughter.' Another surge of outrage swept through her. 'You do realize, don't you, that I –' she slammed a hand into her chest, 'have never met his daughter. I haven't even been invited to his home . . .'

'I didn't go to his home,' Laurie cut in. 'We got the tube to Green Park where we met his daughter and her cousin . . .'

'I know what you did,' Sherry seethed. 'He told me. Last night, when we were having dinner. "Oh, I think I might have found a flat," he says. "That's good," I say. "Where?" "Regent's Park," he answers. "The one we saw when Laurie was with us." He'd assumed, you see, that you'd told me. But you hadn't, and I'd like to know why. What are you hiding? What's going on in your head, that you'd keep something like that from me? Are you intending to use Nick to make Elliot jealous, is that what you're thinking? Because if that's what you're up to . . .'

'Sherry, stop!' Laurie barked, getting to her feet. 'Just stop. You're blowing this out of all proportion and jumping to conclusions that are totally wrong. Now please, just calm down and let's talk about this sensibly.'

As Sherry glared at her, Laurie could feel herself starting to shake. Her emotional reserves were too drained to deal with this well, but she had to try, for she certainly did owe Sherry an explanation, she just hadn't expected to deal with it quite like this, or today.

At last some of the heat started to fade from Sherry's temper. She pulled out Rose's chair, sat down and folded her arms. 'OK,' she said tightly, 'let's begin with how you came to go with Nick that afternoon. Was it your idea?'

Laurie sat down too and took a breath. Whichever way she answered that question she knew Sherry wasn't going to like it, so her only option was to stick with the truth. 'No,' she said. 'It was his. He felt sorry for me. I was in a dreadful state, as you know, and I was terrified of going back to the flat on my own. I probably even said as much, which would be what prompted him to ask if I'd like to go and look at flats with him and Julia.'

Sherry winced at the use of Julia's name. It seemed so cosy, which it was, now they'd met. More anger suddenly welled up in her, but somehow she managed to suppress it.

'I really am sorry I never told you,' Laurie said. 'I know I should have, but I suppose the truth is, I was only thinking about myself that night. You were being so understanding and helpful about everything that I didn't want to talk about

355

anything else. I know how selfish that is, and it's no excuse, or not an acceptable one, but I was so fixated on Elliot and what I could do to get him back, or get over it . . .' She looked at her friend helplessly. 'Sherry, I don't know what else to say,' she told her softly, 'except I'm truly, truly sorry.'

Though Sherry's hostility was lessening, she wasn't anywhere close to being able to forgive. 'That still doesn't explain why you went,' she pointed out. 'You knew very well how I'd feel about it, yet you went anyway.'

'Because I didn't want to be on my own,' Laurie reminded her. 'Not because I was trying to make Elliot jealous. That thought never even entered my head. Why would it, when he'd have no way of knowing?'

'He would if you and Nick started seeing each other. These things get around very quickly, as well you know.'

Laurie's eyes widened with shock. 'Sherry, why are you doing this?' she cried. 'You know how I feel about Elliot, so how can you even think I'd be interested in another man right now? More to the point, how could you think I would do that to you?'

'You said yourself how fixated you are on your own problems,' Sherry pointed out. 'You'd do anything to get Elliot back, and if you thought that would do it . . .' She shrugged. 'It makes perfect sense to me.'

'Put like that, it might,' Laurie responded, 'but it's so not the case that if I thought you really meant it I'd seriously take offence. Sherry, Nick is crazy about you. He's not interested in me, or anyone else . . .'

356

'Did he tell you that?' Sherry interrupted, still bristling, but preparing now to be mollified.

'Not in those words, but it's obvious. Rhona says it too. We can all see it, so why can't you?'

Sherry started to answer, then stopped. It was time to back off this now and she knew it, but she'd been so damned incensed since he'd told her, had managed to work herself to such a pitch that she'd have gone round to confront Laurie last night if he hadn't been staying . . .

'What did you say when he told you?' Laurie asked tentatively. 'Have you had a row about it? Please tell me this hasn't come between you.'

Seeing the genuine anguish in her eyes, Sherry finally let the fight go. 'No,' she answered, with a sigh, 'I didn't say anything. I couldn't, because I was afraid I'd sound very much like I probably sound now – insanely jealous and beyond all reasonable discussion.'

'So he doesn't even know you were angry?'

'He might. I froze him out a bit after he told me. Well, what was I supposed to do, carry on as though it was all right, when it wasn't? He knows he's never invited me to meet his daughter, so he's got to know it would hurt to find out that you had.'

'You need to talk to him about this,' Laurie said decisively. 'If it's bothering you that much, and it clearly is, you should ask why he hasn't let you meet his daughter. If there's some reason . . .'

'It's too soon,' Sherry cut in. 'That'll be the reason. It's making too much of a statement.'

'Why don't you let him tell you that?'

'What's the point, when I already know?'

Laurie looked at her, not quite sure whether she fully believed that or not.

'I mean that would be the reason he'd invite you and not me,' Sherry explained. 'It's OK for you to meet her, because you're just a friend. With me, we're getting into a whole other area, and if she's as possessive of him as most girls her age . . . Did she seem possessive to you?'

'A little,' Laurie answered, knowing it was what she wanted to hear, even though it wasn't strictly true. 'She was certainly bossy,' she added. 'There's no doubt she's got him right round her little finger.'

'What was she like with you?'

Laurie shrugged. 'Polite. Not really very interested, but I don't expect I was the best company that day. To be honest, I'm not even terribly sure which flat he's talking about.'

Sherry was smiling as her eyes started to drift. 'I can remember what a tyrant I was with my father at that age,' she said, almost to herself, 'and how malleable he was too. Anything I wanted . . . He just didn't know how to say no. It was all about guilt, of course.' Her eyes came back to Laurie's. 'He was away such a lot . . . In Nick's case it's the same, he's always been away a lot, and now there's the marriage break-up . . .' She took a deep breath and let it out slowly. 'I guess I just have to accept that she comes first.'

'For a while, anyway,' Laurie responded. 'Once you've met her and the two of you get along fine, it'll all be different.'

'I hope so. I just wish it was already happening, that we were established enough for me to suggest he come and live with me – or that we

358

find somewhere together.' She frowned suddenly. 'Why would he want somewhere in Regent's Park, do you think? It's hardly convenient for where he needs to be.'

'I've no idea,' Laurie answered. 'To be near his family, maybe?'

Sherry was on the point of saying, *what about me*, when she decided that she really did have to back off now, for even she could hear how obsessive she was becoming. And it wasn't about obsession, it was simply about needing to know that she featured in there somewhere, even if it wasn't in the number one position. 'Maybe,' she echoed, lightly, 'and what does it really matter? He's going to be in London, we're seeing each other regularly, and I'm just a paranoid madwoman who doesn't deserve any friends for going off at you the way I just did. I'm sorry.'

Laurie smiled. 'Completely forgiven,' she assured her, and deciding it would probably serve them best to drop the subject now and get on with some work, she said, 'OK, if you'd like to help yourself to coffee, we can start going over where we're up to with the story.'

As Sherry wandered into the kitchenette, Laurie turned back to her computer to begin sorting through the research she'd been systematically downloading for the past hour. There was a lot, and she wasn't entirely sure whether it was information Sherry had already accessed – she'd found no trace of it in Sherry's typed-up notes, but maybe she just hadn't had time to update the file yet. Or, more likely, considering Sherry's lack of experience in putting a TV programme together, she hadn't realized that this kind of background was needed. Laurie would work up to it though, wanting to be clear on where the investigation was before moving it forward.

'Have you been in touch with Karima Ghosh again yet?' she asked as Sherry came back.

'I'm going over there later to place another "order".'

Laurie was frowning. 'How do you think that's going to be useful?' she asked.

Sherry prickled. 'I'm getting the lie of the land again,' she replied. 'I want to see how she behaves towards me now she knows who I actually am.'

'Has she mentioned it?'

'No. At the moment the charade continues.'

Laurie glanced down at the file again. 'What about Stan?' she asked. 'What's the latest from him?'

'He's meeting me later to wait outside the workshop while I go in.'

'And Barry and his friends?'

'I've had a text from Danny asking me to call him at six tonight. Maybe we'll get some news then. I've also got an address now for Eddie Cribbs's girlfriend in Cinnabar Wharf.'

'Have you spoken to her?'

'No. Barry advises strongly against it, until he can get more information on who she is exactly, and how she's likely to respond.'

'Do the others know her? Danny and the stripper?'

'Yes, but I thought they were more valuable just concentrating on where the women might have been moved to.'

'Do you think they actually know?' Laurie asked bluntly. 'Or are they just conning us out of our money?'

Sherry's voice was tight as she said, 'Let's see what Danny comes up with this evening, shall we?'

Laurie nodded, and began to read on. 'OK. We need to start shooting some footage,' she said decisively. 'We want exteriors of the workshop, the club, possibly the flat in Cinnabar Wharf. General views of the East End, particularly women in Indian garb. We also need some background on similar cases, which is what I've been doing this morning. There are two police operations of particular interest, Operation Twins and Operation Reflex. The first involved the cracking of a child pornography ring, and the second was an investigation into a people-smuggling network, most specifically from the Indian subcontinent.'

Sherry listened and sipped her coffee.

'We need to start lining up some interviews with the officers involved in these cases,' Laurie continued. 'If we can get someone from the Serious Sex Offenders Unit that would be great. Rhona says they're not always terribly forthcoming . . .'

'Rhona?'

'She spoke to the author she mentioned,' Laurie explained. 'I'll call him myself, later, he could be worth interviewing too.'

'What about finding out where the women are?' Sherry said, clearly smarting that she hadn't contacted the author herself yet. 'I thought that was our priority?'

'Of course it is, but we need to explain, with visuals, how they got where they are, and what's been happening to them. Obviously we're never going to get any footage of what the men are doing to them, and even if we did we couldn't show it, so we have to have people talking about it.'

Sherry regarded Laurie expressionlessly and listened in silence as she went on to outline a rough programme sequence, indicating where Rose's material from India would intercut with their own from the East End. 'I don't know if you've seen the email from Rose this morning,' she was saying, 'but it turns out that the local TV producer and human-trader are both on the level. She's interviewed the trader already, and he's given her a map of possible routes that are being used to get human cargo to this country. Have you contacted anyone from Interpol? They could be extremely useful on this, if they want to be.'

'No,' Sherry answered shortly.

'I've got a contact in Brussels. I'll give him a call, then one of us should go over there to talk to him. Of course this is all going to change as we go along,' Laurie said with a smile, 'but it helps to focus us on what we actually need, so that we don't waste time going off on tangents that get us nowhere.'

'So would my undercover role as a buyer qualify as a tangent?' Sherry enquired smoothly. 'I only ask because I don't want to waste my time going over there if it does.'

'You should keep the appointment now you've made it,' Laurie assured her. 'It's just a pity you can't take a hidden camera in with you, but at this stage I think the risk would be too great.'

'Isn't that for me to decide?'

Laurie regarded her carefully. 'Let's do it without for now,' she said. 'We can always reassess later.'

'OK,' Sherry responded, getting to her feet, 'now you're here to plug all the holes I've left, I should be on my way to meet Stan.' As she reached the door, she turned round. 'Isn't Elliot due back today?'

Laurie's insides went to jelly. 'Late this afternoon,' she replied. 'I'm hoping he'll call.'

'I'm sure he will,' Sherry responded, and left.

Dismayed by the abrupt departure, Laurie looked out of the window and watched her pass by. She'd been afraid of something like this, and blamed herself entirely. Just stomping in and seizing back the reins, when Sherry had put so much into the story, had been totally insensitive, to say the least. She'd have to think of a way to make up for it, and while she was at it, it might be a good idea to apologize about Nick again too. On second thoughts, it was probably better to leave that particular subject alone now. She didn't want Sherry blowing up at her like that again.

'It was pretty heavy,' she said to Rhona on the phone later. 'You should have seen her. She's *so* sensitive where he's concerned. And so insecure.'

'Mm, I'd noticed,' Rhona responded. 'It's like we're seeing another side to Sherry Mac now he's back in her life.'

'That's what men do to you,' Laurie commented.

'Turn you into another person. God knows, it's happening to me.'

'Any word from Elliot yet?'

'No, nothing. But don't let's talk about it. Tell you what, don't let's even think about it.'

Chapter Eighteen

Sherry could feel Karima Ghosh's eyes boring into her back as she rifled through a rack full of cheap tweed jackets. She'd love to know what was going through the woman's mind, whether she was intending to up the stakes and challenge Tara Green's identity, or if she was at all fearful that Sherry might be about to spring something unexpected on her. Maybe she was planning something even more foul than her breath to get rid of Sherry altogether – which was why Stan was keeping watch from across the street.

The phone rang and Karima turned to pick it up. She spoke in a language Sherry couldn't begin to understand, though her tone was unmistakably sharp, angry even, and when she rang off her face seemed more bitter than ever.

'I trust your last order was satisfactory,' she suddenly snapped.

'Oh, very,' Sherry responded, moving on to a short rack of sheepskin-lined leather waistcoats.

She pulled one out, and was surprised to see it wasn't half bad.

'These are very much in demand,' Karima told her, impatiently.

'I'm sure,' Sherry replied with a smile. Though her own manner was calm, beneath the surface she was as agitated and distracted as Karima appeared to be, though for very different reasons. She turned back to replace the waistcoat, giving herself a moment to refocus her thoughts, for this situation needed her full attention.

After talking it all through with Stan and Barry over the past few days she'd been quite clear about how she was going to play this meeting, then suddenly last night, boomph, it was gone, blasted out of the picture by the bombshell Nick had dropped that Laurie had gone flat-hunting with him and Julia. And now there was the added distraction of this morning's scene, which, OK, might have set her mind at rest about Laurie's intentions towards Nick, but had done virtually nothing to explain what his intentions might be towards Laurie. True, he was just the type to take pity on a female in distress, but the fear that there was more to it was flaring up again now. This anxiety, combined with the way Laurie had so tactlessly pointed out what was missing from the research, made it extremely difficult for her even to care why she was here, never mind concentrate on what she, Stan and Barry had worked out.

She picked up the waistcoat again and reminded herself forcefully that she must think only of the women they were trying to find. Their suffering was far worse than hers – the two couldn't even begin to compare. It was hard to keep a passion going, though, for women she'd never met. However, their future, their very lives, could depend on her now, so she owed it to them to summon up the strategy she'd prepared with Barry and Stan and bring this to some kind of head.

'What if I were to order six hundred of these?' she enquired, turning back to Karima. 'In each size, from ten to sixteen. That would be, let me see . . .'

'Two thousand four hundred,' Karima supplied frostily.

Sherry was impressed. 'You're very fast,' she remarked.

Karima's pinched face rejected the compliment. 'That's a very large order for one small boutique,' she commented.

Sherry's smile was pleasant. 'I think I mentioned during my last visit that we were merging with a high street chain,' she said. 'It hasn't gone through yet, but it's looking likely. So I'm interested to know how your workshop would cope with an order that size.' She was wandering over to look through Karima's office window to where the machinists in the room outside were resolutely keeping their heads down as they got on with their work.

'I would have to make some enquiries and get back to you,' Karima told her. 'But maybe you would be happier placing your order abroad. You'll find the rates much more competitive than anything we can offer here. I'd be happy to make some recommendations.'

Yes, I bet you would, Sherry muttered to herself. 'I might take you up on that,' she said. 'But in the meantime, why don't I take four in each size? I'm sure your workshop can cope with that.'

'We are very busy at the moment,' Karima told her. 'I would be unable to guarantee delivery.'

'But you don't know when I require them.'

Unfazed, Karima said, 'Our order books are very full. We have commitments taking us to early next year.'

Sherry allowed her surprise to show. 'You must be the envy of the East End rag trade,' she said, 'because from what I hear most other workshops are counting themselves lucky to get one order on the books, whereas you seem to be telling me you're so overloaded you can hardly cope.'

'We are very popular with our customers,' Karima responded tartly.

Sherry looked out of the window again. 'All those machines unmanned when you're so busy,' she said. 'Amazing.'

'We have adequate staff to meet our demands.'

Sherry's eyes reached her at the very instant she realized her mistake.

'All those unemployed cutters and machinists,' Sherry said, digging her point home. 'And all these idle work tables and machines. Why on earth wouldn't you be willing to fulfil my order? I could take it elsewhere and my hand would be snatched off.'

'You are most welcome to take it elsewhere,' Karima snorted. 'We do not need your business.'

Sherry's eyebrows shot up at the rudeness, but her response was swift, and charged with meaning.

368

'Oh, but I think you do,' she said, and held Karima's sharp, hostile eyes with her own.

At last the woman was thrown, for she clearly didn't know how to react. Sherry wasn't entirely sure where to go either, for she was way off what they'd rehearsed now, and still boiling with all her other resentments. She was aware she should be treading more carefully, but this snotty, corrupt little woman, put together with Laurie's attitude this morning, was starting to irritate her to a point where she couldn't give much of a damn about anything.

'I'll tell you what,' she said suddenly, 'why don't we cut the crap going on here? You know exactly who I am and why I'm here, so let's get down to what this is really about.'

Karima's face twitched with shock. 'Forgive me,' she said stonily. 'I don't know what you're talking about.'

'Well, first off,' Sherry said, battling to keep her voice steady, 'there's Daya, the girl *you* took to Doctor Patel, and where exactly she might be now.'

'I am told by her family that she has returned to India.'

'Do I look like a fool?' Sherry hissed.

Karima's piercing eyes were turning to slits as her nostrils flared.

'Where are those women?' Sherry demanded.

'I have no idea what you're talking about.'

'You're not even a good liar,' Sherry told her.

'I'm afraid I must ask you to leave.'

'I will leave when I'm good and ready. I want to know where those women are, and you're going to tell me.'

369

'I don't know anything about any . . .'

'I'm sure you're aware that holding people against their will is an imprisonable offence, and probably the very least of your crimes where those women are concerned,' Sherry cut in.

Karima's pocked face was tight with anger. 'If you are so certain that criminal actions have been carried out on these premises, may I ask why you have not contacted the police?'

Sherry's eyebrows rose. Mrs Ghosh wasn't only fast, she was smart. 'As a matter of fact, I have spoken to the police,' she responded. It was both a lie, and not a lie, for she had spoken to them, just not specifically about these women.

'Then I can only assume that the police thought you as foolish as I do,' Karima said hotly. 'Or I'm sure they'd have contacted me.'

Sherry was about to shoot back another acid reply when she decided she'd gone far enough – probably too far, so it was time to retreat. 'Don't be surprised if they do,' she warned, and picked up her bag. 'Before I go,' she said, turning as she reached the door, 'I want you to give a message to your boss. Tell him he's not going to get away with this. He has my word on it, he *will not get away with this*.' And turning on her heel she stalked out of the room.

As she emerged on to New Road Stan came jaywalking through the traffic to join her. 'How did it go?' he demanded, falling in beside her. 'Did she let on she knew who you were?'

'She knows,' Sherry confirmed. Now she was outside she wasn't sure she wanted to admit to how far she'd gone.

370

'So what happened? D'you place another order, or what?'

'Actually no. What I did was tell her I know exactly what she's up to, that I want to know where those women are, and I also sent a message to Eddie Cribbs telling him he wasn't going to get away with this.'

'Yeah, right,' Stan grunted with a chuckle.

'I'm serious.'

He stopped walking. 'Tell me you're not,' he said. 'Tell me that was a joke.'

She turned to look at him, more unnerved than she wanted him to know. She'd behaved stupidly and she knew it – not just that, she wouldn't be the only one to pay, because the women almost certainly would too.

'If you've delivered a threat to Eddie Cribbs,' Stan said, 'then you're gonna need someone watching out for your back every minute from now on.' He shook his big head in despair. 'You're a silly girl, Sherry Mac. A very silly girl. Blokes like that don't mess about when it comes to protecting themselves, and they've got more ways of doing it than you'll ever know. Jesus Christ,' he growled, looking like he wanted to shake her. 'Does Laurie know anything about this? Did she know you were going to do that?'

Sherry walked on angrily, wanting to scream at him that it was Laurie's damned fault she'd done it, because if Laurie weren't angling in on Nick, or trying to make her look inadequate as a reporter, she'd have been able to concentrate on what she was doing, instead of being thrown around all over the place by what move Laurie might make next on Nick, or Nick on Laurie. So don't blame her for what had happened, blame them. *No, not them, because that paired them together* and she couldn't have that, she just couldn't.

Blame Laurie because she was the one who'd got her involved in this story, when it suited her, and now it didn't any more, she was trying to make her look stupid in an attempt to get her out. Well to hell with that. This was her story now, she was the one who cared about those women, who'd gone undercover to find them, who was leading the hunt to track them down, and she was the one who was prepared to risk her life to save them. So Laurie Forbes could just go back to her broken heart and cancelled wedding, while she, Sherry, consulted *her boyfriend* Nick on how she should proceed from here.

'Oh!' Cheryl exclaimed, coming in the front door to find a stranger sitting on the sofa. 'Didn't know no-one was in here. Eddie around, is he?'

'He's in the bathroom,' Barry replied, getting to his feet.

'Oh. Right. So who are you?'

'Barry. Barry Davidson.'

Putting her head to one side she gave him a frank once-over. Not bad. Quite tasty, actually, in a Phil in *EastEnders* sort of way. 'Got some business with Eddie, have ya?' she asked.

'That's right.'

She nodded, then stuck out her hand. 'I'm Cheryl. Nice to meet you. Got a drink?'

Barry glanced down at the table where two glasses of Scotch and soda were sitting, barely yet touched. 'Thanks,' he said.

'Right. Well, I suppose I'll leave you to it,' and picking up her shopping bags she sauntered on through to the bedroom, glad she had the real low-waisters on to give him a good view of what Eddie had and he didn't.

She was just dropping her bags on the bed when Eddie came out of the bathroom. 'What are you doing here?' he grunted. 'I thought you was shopping with your mum.'

'I was, but she went to get her hair done, and then I was missing you, so I came back.'

'You didn't even know I was gonna be here,' he told her, enjoying the feel of her as she slid her arms around him.

'You said you might,' she reminded him, testing to see if her fingers would meet behind his back. They did, just. 'Who's the bloke in there?' she asked. 'Don't think I've seen him before.'

'He's no-one. Just a bloke.' His hands were moving up under her T-shirt. 'So what d'you get, something nice?' he asked.

'I'll give you a show when he's gone, if you like.'

He grinned. 'Then we'd better hurry up and get rid of him,' he responded, and giving her boobs a hearty squeeze he returned to the sitting room.

'So where were we?' he said to Barry, sinking into his favourite armchair. 'Oh, that's right, you were about to tell me something I already know.'

Barry's face showed his discomfort.

Eddie picked up his drink. 'So here we are, on our regular Wednesday meet,' he said, 'and all you can tell me is your friend Sherry Mac's paid a visit to Mrs Ghosh.' He took a large mouthful of Scotch.

'Now, why do you think I wouldn't already know that?' he continued. 'Do you reckon Mrs Ghosh would have kept it to herself, is that what you were afraid of?'

'No,' Barry answered, sounding as strained as he felt.

'Then what?' Eddie prompted. 'What have you really come here to tell me? There's got to be something, so don't hold it in. You'll feel a lot better once it's out.'

Barry cleared his throat and took a breath. He was thinking fast, but nothing was happening. Apart from Sherry's blow-up with the Ghosh woman, he just couldn't think of anything that would satisfy the fat bastard, while enabling him to hang on to what was left of his integrity.

Eddie sighed and drank some more. 'Tell me, how's your old mum doing these days?' he asked chattily.

Barry blanched.

Eddie looked at him.

'Yeah, she's good,' Barry answered.

'Get the new video and DVD, did she?'

Barry nodded.

'What was that?' Eddie said, cupping a hand to his ear. 'Thanks? Did you say thanks? No problem, son. Least I could do. I was very upset to hear what happened. Let's hope nothing like it happens again, with her having a weak heart, and all.'

Barry stared grimly down at his drink. He could tell him more, he could tell him a lot, in fact, but he hated the bastard so much he'd rather cut out his tongue – if it weren't for his mum.

'You're wasting my time,' Eddie told him, glancing up as Cheryl emerged from the bedroom. 'Oi, scat,' he barked. 'Stay in there till I tell you to come out.'

Obediently she retreated, closing the door and sighing with boredom. She'd only wanted to go and play a game on the computer, that wasn't too much to ask, was it? It weren't as if she was interested in what they was talking about, and anyway she could hear from in here, so there wasn't a lot of point sending her out, was there?

Flopping down on the bed, she put her hands behind her head and stretched out a leg. Idly she wondered who this Sherry Mac was. It was a name that seemed to be cropping up a lot lately, and from the odd snippets she'd caught it seemed Eddie weren't too happy with her. Poor cow, he weren't someone to be on the wrong side of, as well she knew, which was why she always did everything he said. No fuss, no anything, just give Eddie what he wanted, keep him happy, then he'd keep her happy too. Which reminded her, she ought to thank him again for giving her friend Marianne a job at the club. She was a really beautiful girl, Marianne, not too tall, but with great tits, a tight little ass and lovely coal-black skin. The punters liked black, and since Marianne was such a fantastic dancer as well as being different and exotic, Cheryl didn't think she was going to have too much trouble getting her promoted to the star attraction.

She smiled happily to herself. That would put the bitch Suzy's nose well out of joint. She might even try to be there to see her face when she found out. In fact, this was definitely a better idea than getting her fired, she decided. Demotion, Suzy, you bitch. How's that feel while your boss's girlfriend's swanning it around her classy flat on the river?

She jumped suddenly as the phone rang next to the bed.

'Get that!' Eddie called out.

Picking it up she repeated, verbatim, what he'd told her to say when answering this line. 'Hello? Can I help you?'

'Is Eddie there?' a smooth, nasal voice demanded.

Recognizing it as Perry's, she said, 'He's in a meeting. Can I take a message?'

'Yes, tell him the Italians are good for it all. The deal's done. We got what we wanted.'

'OK, I'll tell him. Anything else?'

'I've got the dates, if he wants them,' he replied. 'And details of the new trade routes we talked about.'

'I'd better write it down,' she said. 'Can you hang on? I'll get a pen.'

Pulling open the bedroom door she got the all-clear to come in, then went to rifle through a kitchen drawer. She was replaying it all in her mind, so not really listening to what Eddie was saying to the bloke, Barry, as he showed him out the door. Something about him being a good lad for telling him this Sherry Mac had a contact inside Eddie's organization.

'It's vital you get the name, Barry, my son,' Eddie told him, slapping him on the back, 'because we definitely don't like two-timers, now do we? Know what I mean?'

Barry did, only too well, and was in no doubt it was as much a threat to him as it was to Suzy and Danny, whose names he hadn't actually revealed, but he knew it was only a matter of time before he was forced to. As he walked off down the hall he felt so depressed that if it weren't for his old mum he might just have gone and chucked himself in the Thames.

'*Ba*. Go to *Ba*,' Shaila whispered, looking pleadingly up into Ekta's face.

'Ssh, she is sleeping,' Ekta told her.

Shaila turned her big eyes to Neela's swollen face. The cuts weren't deep, but the bruises were dark and livid.

Ekta thought what a child Neela looked. She thought too how courageous and strong she was, for she didn't complain, nor did she cry in front of Shaila. She didn't want to frighten her little niece, who'd lately started to call her *Ba* – mother.

Her injuries, though painful and still raw, had not been severe enough for Ekta to insist on a doctor, though she'd tried. 'Mota Ben,' she'd said, 'please you must get her some help.'

'No!' Mota Ben had replied.

Mota Ben was possessed by evil spirits. She'd even let her own spy, Bhanu Ganesh, suffer with no doctor until she died. They'd taken her body away, Ekta didn't know where to. Bhanu was no good for the men, she was too old and too ugly so there was no reason to save her life.

Ekta knew she was too old for the men too. Her husband had sold her for ten thousand rupees, enough to buy opium to soothe the pain of his teeth. The opium would have run out long ago, and she hoped his pain had driven him to such madness that he had thrown himself in the river and drowned. If she had a river she would throw herself in and drown. She would take Neela and Shaila with her, because they were going to die here anyway.

It was late in the day, but two girls were still working the machines. Mota Ben had brought the material yesterday. She wanted the new garments by tomorrow. Because they hoped to keep in Mota Ben's favour, the two girls had volunteered straight away. If Mota Ben liked them, they thought, maybe she wouldn't send them to the worst of the men. But Ekta knew there was no favour to be had with Mota Ben. No matter what the girls did, they were doomed.

Hearing Neela stir, Ekta turned and watched her eyelids flutter open.

Seeing she was awake Shaila strained towards her, so Ekta let the child go.

'Hello, Shaila*beta*,' Neela whispered, stroking the girl's hair.

Shaila settled in beside her, clinging to her sari that was still blood-stained and ripped. Mota Ben had left material for Neela to make herself a new one – she'd need it for her next visit to a m..n. Ekta had already made it for her, because Neela was determined to carry on until they let her see a doctor. In her heart Ekta was very much afraid that they would let her die first.

Minutes and hours ticked by. The sun faded, darkness came.

In the middle of the night Ekta woke to the

sound of whispering. It was Mota Ben with someone Ekta had never seen before. He was short,
with a beard and clothes that reeked of men's
perfume. He spoke in English, but with an accent
Ekta had never heard. It was too hard for her to
understand, and too dark for her to see all of his
face.

She lay very still as they walked through the
shadows until they reached Neela's mattress.
Ekta's heart stopped beating. She prayed to
Ambamata that they wouldn't take Neela again.
It was too soon. She needed time to heal.

Gingerly turning her head she saw that Neela
was still sleeping. Then suddenly she wanted to
scream, for Mota Ben was pulling Shaila up by the
arm.

Shaila's terrified eyes were bright like stars in
the darkness. '*Ba*,' she murmured. '*Ba*.'

The man's face was close to the child's. He
jerked her head back to get a better look. Then,
turning to Mota Ben, he nodded.

Ekta didn't care what happened to her now.
They would have to chop off her hands before she
let them take Shaila. She watched, waited, then
tears flooded into her eyes as Mota Ben and the
man started to walk away. They hadn't taken
Shaila tonight, but Ekta knew beyond any doubt
that soon they would. Shaila was the prize, the
treasure for which they would pay many fortunes.
She was being sold to the highest bidder, Ekta
realized that, and soon the winner would come
to take her away. There was nothing Neela could
do to stop them. There was no doctor to help them
now, Ekta realized that too, and though she was

little more than a child herself, Neela was too old to go in Shaila's place.

Ekta lay staring blindly into the darkness, her heart sinking like stones in a river as she listened to Shaila quietly sobbing. Ekta had never killed another living soul, but she knew now that in order to save Shaila from the men, that was what she must do.

Chapter Nineteen

Laurie was so nervous she couldn't even sit down. Elliot was on his way over, and though she'd tried everything to make herself relax, she couldn't. She just paced around the flat, wringing her hands, going over and over what she was going to say, how he was likely to react, and what she would say then. She was sure she'd thought of everything by now, though of course he was bound to come up with the very thing she hadn't prepared for, it always happened like that.

Feeling as though she was going mad, she took herself off to the mirror to check how she looked again. She'd been ready for over half an hour, having finally decided on the white semi-transparent blouse he'd always found sexy, an over-the-knee skirt she'd rushed out and bought specially, a tiny white G-string with matching transparent bra that she'd picked up during the same panicked spree, and gold strappy sandals. She'd tidied the bedroom and put clean sheets on the bed, just in case. The very thought of it sent more nerves shuddering all the way through her. Did she really have the courage to try and seduce him? Would he even find her attractive now, after experiencing such a sexual powerhouse as Andraya? Oh dear God, what was she going to do if he turned her down? But he wouldn't. This was going to work out, so she was just going to cancel all the negative thoughts, summon what was left of her confidence and put *La Bohème* on the CD ready to play.

After doing that she went to the kitchen to start mixing their favourite cocktail – Absolut Mandarin Cosmopolitan. She got as far as filling the shaker with ice before deciding it was too obvious. So she went to the fridge to make sure there was wine. Of course there was, not only had she already drunk a glass, she'd bought plenty earlier when she was shopping for the dinner she was supposed to be cooking tonight. She'd invited Rhona, Sherry, Nick and her adored gay friends Andrew and Stephen, who'd just come back from a South African safari. Everyone had understood completely when she'd called around five to tell them she'd finally heard from Elliot, who'd been back for two days now, so dinner was off. No-one had even cautioned her to play a little harder to get, probably because they knew she was too afraid he'd go off to New York without seeing her at all to start playing games now. And Sherry had sounded quite relieved, since it meant she could fly over to Brussels tonight to meet the Interpol officer, rather than get up at the crack of dawn tomorrow.

Fortunately the atmosphere between her and

Sherry wasn't quite so tense now, though it had turned pretty explosive again after Sherry's visit to Karima Ghosh. Not because Laurie had come down on her as hard as she'd have come down on herself had she screwed up like that, but because Sherry, obviously expecting an almighty row, had leaped straight to the defensive by shouting at her, not realizing at first that the showdown wasn't happening. Nor was she being thrown off the story. Everyone had bad days, Laurie had reminded her, and God knew she, Laurie, had made her own share of mistakes. She was hardly going to penalize Sherry for something she might easily have done herself, considering her own distractions.

Anyway, it probably wasn't as big a disaster as it seemed, and once tonight was over they'd find a way to make it work for them, rather than against them. Until then she just couldn't think about anything else.

She glanced at her watch. Ten minutes to go. He'd be late though, he almost always was. Her stomach reacted to another wave of nerves and she had to run back to the bathroom. When she came out again, were it not for the fact that she'd already had one drink, she'd have gone straight to the fridge. Maybe she should get down on her knees and start praying instead, for it truly felt as though her entire future was at stake tonight – and actually, it was.

She wanted to spend the rest of her life with Elliot, she was in no doubt about that, she wanted to marry him, have his children, share his dreams and do all the things they'd planned. In her heart she was convinced he still wanted it too, so somehow she had to persuade him that nothing had changed, he'd just lost sight of where they were going for a while. She didn't blame him for what was happening now, anyone could be blinded by Andraya's dazzling charms, and though she wished every disfiguring disease and mental derangement on the woman, she was prepared to put it all behind her as long as Elliot was too.

Knowing it couldn't possibly be as simple as that, but not prepared to go any deeper, she suddenly caved in and went back to the fridge. Just a mouthful, no more. She had to have something, or she was going to drive herself crazy, especially now the dread that he was only coming to collect more of his belongings, or to discuss selling the flat and dividing their assets, was forcing its way back in. But no! He'd said he wanted to talk, and that wasn't talking, it was . . . leaving.

She gulped down the wine, then snatched up the phone as it rang. It would be Rhona with a last-minute good luck.

'Hi,' he said, 'it's me.'

Laurie's heart stopped beating. 'Hi,' she responded. 'Where are you?'

'Something's come up. I'm afraid I can't make it.'

Her eyes grew wide as the world seemed to turn itself in on her. She'd set so much store by this, had truly believed there might be a chance they would get back together. 'Why?' she said, her voice sounding strangely cracked and almost shrewish. 'What came up?'

'It doesn't matter.'

384

'What's so important that you suddenly can't come, when three hours ago you could?' she demanded.

He didn't answer.

'It's her, isn't it?' she snapped, as the blood began rushing to her head. 'She won't let you come. She's afraid of what might happen between us.'

'Laurie . . .'

'You said you'd be here at eight,' she raged. 'I want you to come over here now!'

'I'm sorry, I can't.'

'*Why?* Just tell me why.'

'It'll only upset you.'

'You don't think I'm that already? For God's sake, Elliot! What's the matter with you? How can you just call up at the last minute like this and tell me you're not coming?'

'I'm sorry,' he said. 'It couldn't be avoided.'

'I'm not hanging up this phone until you tell me what the hell is going on.'

There was a pause, then he said, 'Andraya's . . . There's a dinner at the British Museum tonight. Andraya's one of the guests of honour. Chris was going with her, but something came up for him and she doesn't want to go alone.'

Laurie's heart was folding over in pain – everything inside her was starting to collapse. Andraya came first. He was doing this for Andraya. Suddenly she wanted to run and run, or scream and rant. This was all wrong. He didn't belong to Andraya, he belonged to her. They were supposed to be getting married at the end of next week, and this was happening instead. She put a hand to her

385

mouth to stop the hysteria exploding out of her. She turned around, walked to the window and turned back again.

'Are you still there?' he said.

Her voice was laced with anger, threaded with despair. 'So what you're saying,' she said, 'is I don't matter? After everything we've meant to each other, the years we've been together, you're just dropping me now to go and be with her?'

'We're not together now,' he reminded her gently. 'If we were, it would be different, but we're not.'

That hurt so much that Laurie just wanted to die. Again she covered her mouth to prevent herself crying out. It was as though everything was dissolving, turning into nothing, disappearing, disintegrating, dying. There was so much she wanted to say, such a lot she needed to make him understand . . . Then she heard herself speaking, saying words she didn't mean, using them as though they could hurt him back. 'If she means so much, why don't you take her to Bali?' she spat. 'It would be a shame to waste it.'

His silence shocked her as she suddenly realized what it meant.

'Oh God, Elliot,' she cried, 'please tell me you're not going to do it. *Please*. You can't take her there.'

'No, of course not,' he responded. 'But maybe you should go. Take Rhona, or Sherry.'

'Are you out of your mind? Do you seriously think I could go there now, without you?'

There was another silence.

'Elliot, why is this happening?' she begged, starting to cry. 'I don't understand it. One minute you love me, we're together and happy, the next we're not getting married and my whole life is falling apart. How did that happen? What did I do?'

'You didn't do anything,' he told her. 'I wish it wasn't happening either.'

'Then stop it. Please. I love you.'

He was silent again.

'She's just using you,' she cried. 'She's a slut, a whore, a talentless piece of dirt.'

'Laurie . . .'

'Don't you dare defend her!' she cut in. 'I don't want to hear . . .'

'I'm sorry, I have to go,' he said. 'I'll call you tomorrow.'

'Don't bother,' she screamed. 'Don't call me ever again! Just drop dead, the pair of you. Just fucking drop dead.'

As she slammed down the phone her whole body was seized by sobs. They came wrenching out of her, loud and desperate, filled with hatred and despair. She pressed her palms to her head. She couldn't bear this. She just couldn't. It hurt too much. She had to find a way of making it stop. Anything. Please God, anything to make it stop.

Turning to the fridge, she yanked open the door and splashed more wine into a glass. She drank it down, then sank to her knees, holding herself tight as she sobbed and sobbed. She hated and despised him. She never wanted to see him again. That he could do this to her, treat her as though she didn't matter at all . . . It was too awful. Too painful. It was tearing her apart and every day it was just getting worse.

387

'Please, Elliot, please,' she cried, letting herself fall against the cabinets. 'I love you, please don't do this.' She covered her face with her hands, still gasping his name, and Rhona's and Sherry's, anyone who might help her make this go away. She thought of Sherry's advice, to stop resisting and go with it, let it drag her into its hideous depths. But she couldn't. It was impossible. She *had* to resist it. Oh God, she had to speak to Sherry. She had to stop her going to Brussels and make her come here instead.

After dialling Sherry's number she wiped the back of her hand over her face, pushing away the tears and panting for breath. Images of him, putting the phone down just now then turning to embrace Andraya, were tormenting her. She could see their love, feel it, even smell it. It was like a living force bearing down on her as though to destroy her.

Almost screaming as she got Sherry's machine, she quickly tried her mobile. *Please, Sherry, answer. Please. You've got to tell me what to do.*

Only the voicemail there too.

As she rang off she felt as though she were drowning. She took a deep shuddering breath. It didn't help, so she took another and another. She held on to the counter top as if to keep herself upright, and eventually, tentatively she managed to lift her head as the worst of it seemed to subside. She turned to stare out at the sitting room, and imagining him there she almost buckled with the pain again. But she forced herself forward, taking herself round to the CD. Though every instinct told her to run, to escape this nightmare any way she could, if Sherry was right – and everyone said she was – the only way she was ever going to truly get past this was to face it and go all the way through it.

When she got to the CD she felt the tears rising up fast again. Was she really going to force herself to listen to the very opera they'd first made love to? Did it really make sense to put herself through so much torment? Already the dread of it was overwhelming her, for she could see the candlelit garden in Mexico where it had happened, the villa where they'd stayed after the first story they'd covered together. It had been so beautiful and romantic, so perfect that the mere thought of it now caused infinitely more pain than she could bear. She knew that to hear the music, to listen to the doomed love of Mimi and Rodolfo, playing out to its tragic denouement, was going to half-kill her.

Steeling herself, she picked up the remote, closed her eyes and prayed silently to anyone or anything that was listening to give her the strength to get through this. It was madness, self-torment taken to its extremes, but if going right to the heart of her pain was the way to get her out of it, she would find the courage to do it.

She took a breath, put her finger on the Play button, and was about to press down when some-one knocked on the front door.

It made her jump, even confused her at first, as she turned to look at it. Then with a wild leap of her heart she realized it must be him. He'd put his car in its usual space and had taken the lift up. Yes, it had to be him. No-one else could get in.

The deflation of her hope was as quick as the rise. It couldn't be him, he'd never have got here so fast. It must be a neighbour. She didn't want to talk to anyone, or not someone she barely knew. Whoever it was knocked again. She looked down at the remote in her hand, and abruptly threw it on to a chair. She didn't care if it made her a coward, she couldn't do it. She needed to know who was there, just in case it was him.

At the door she stood on tiptoe to peer out through the security glass. Whoever it was had their back to her. Then he turned round and she blinked in astonishment. Nick? What was he doing here?

Feeling only relief that she didn't have to be alone now, she pulled open the door.

'Hi,' he said, brandishing a bottle of wine. 'Sorry I'm late. I came in behind someone down . . .' He stopped suddenly as he registered the signs of distress. 'Are you OK?' he asked.

'Yes, uh, I'm fine. Sorry. Didn't you get the message?'

'Message? Oh God,' he groaned. 'My cellphone's on the blink. Don't tell me, the party's not on, and obviously this isn't a good time. I'll just go. Sorry. Pretend I was never here.'

'No! No. It's OK,' she said, almost grabbing him. 'Please, come in,' and she stood aside for him to pass. 'Elliot was supposed to be coming,' she explained. 'That's why I cancelled the dinner.'

He turned around.

'He stood me up,' she said, with an attempt at a laugh. 'Well, not stood me up, exactly. He had a more pressing engagement.'

Sighing and shaking his head, he reached for her hand. 'I'm sorry,' he said. 'This is a terrible time for you. Are you sure you don't want me to go?'

'I'm sure. As long as you don't mind putting up with me again.'

He smiled. 'Come on, let's crack open this wine,' he responded.

In spite of knowing how Sherry would disapprove, of the wine and him being here, she led him through to the sitting room. A few minutes later they were sitting cross-legged on the cushions around the coffee table, carrying on with the bottle she'd already opened, with his in reserve.

'I feel such an idiot now,' she confessed. 'I got all dressed up . . . Look at me. I thought . . .' She swallowed and shook her head. 'I don't know what I thought. Well I do, I just don't want to admit it.'

'You look lovely,' he told her.

She smiled in disbelief. 'With mascara all over my face and my eyes all puffed up like doughnuts? I don't think so.'

'Well, OK, I guess you wouldn't want to use this particular look to run for Miss Universe,' he conceded, 'but I'm not one of the judges, so don't mind me.'

She gazed down at her drink, feeling grateful to him for being here, but not quite able to respond to his humour. She drank some more wine in the hope it might buck her up, but it didn't. The weight of Elliot's call, of where he was now, and the fear that he really might never come back, was still pulling her down and down. 'Is it possible for him just to feel nothing now?' she said, looking up at Nick. 'After everything we meant to each other . . . Can he have changed that much in so short a time?'

He shook his head. 'I doubt it. It's just a defence mechanism we men have, block it out and pretend it's not happening. It comes in particularly handy when guilt's involved – and I'm pretty sure there's a lot going on here.'

Her eyes went down again. She didn't want Elliot to feel guilty, she just wanted him to feel the way he used to. 'It sounds as though he really loves her,' she said bleakly, and put her hands over her face, unable to stand the truth of her own words. 'I'm sorry,' she gasped. 'This must be very embarrassing for you . . .'

'Don't worry about me, I've seen tears before,' he assured her. 'I've even shed a few.'

She sighed and shook her head. 'The world is full of tragedies and every one of them is worse than mine,' she said. 'So I should stop feeling sorry for myself and get over it.'

He smiled. 'You wouldn't be human if you could do it just like that,' he responded. 'What you're going through now hurts, a lot.'

She looked at him, registering his dark, sensitive eyes and gentle mouth. She was glad he was here, and wouldn't think now about how she was going to explain it to Sherry. Instead she raised her glass to his. 'I think we should drink a toast to everyone in the world who's hurting,' she said.

'To every last one of them,' he agreed.

They drank, and she watched quietly as he topped up their glasses. 'Sherry says I shouldn't resist the hurt,' she told him. 'She thinks I should accept what's happening instead of trying to fight it.'

'I'd say Sherry's a very good person to listen to when it comes to matters of the heart,' he replied. 'She had a lot of practice with her mother, too much, in fact – it meant she saw first-hand what worked and what didn't. Then, after coming through what she came through, on a personal front . . . Well, let's just say you can be sure she'll do everything she can to stop it being as bad for you.'

Feeling almost sobered by such nobleness Laurie picked up her glass and drank. 'How did you two meet, exactly?' she asked.

He seemed surprised. 'Sherry's never told you that?'

She shook her head. 'I just know it was around the time her parents died. Did you know them?'

'Uh –' His eyes dropped to his glass. 'Not exactly,' he answered.

She frowned. 'What does that mean?' she prompted.

'It means her father was already dead when we met,' he said, 'and her mother . . .'

'I thought they died in a plane crash,' she interrupted. 'That's what Sherry said, that they were killed in her father's plane.'

He inhaled deeply.

'That's not it?'

He shook his head. 'No, but I think I know where that came from. A couple of months before it all happened, John, her father, lent his plane to a friend to fly up to San Francisco. It crashed on the way back, killing the friend and his wife.'

Starting to feel more than a little light-headed, Laurie said, 'So what happened to her parents?'

His eyes returned to hers. 'Sherry's mother isn't dead,' he told her. 'In fact, she's very much alive.'

Laurie blinked. 'I don't understand. Why does Sherry say she's dead, if she's not?'

'I guess it must be her way of coping,' he answered. Then, after a pause, 'Her mother's in prison.'

Laurie's eyes dilated. 'In prison?' she echoed. 'What for?'

'For murdering Sherry's father. Sherry and I met when I went to LA to cover the trial.'

'Oh my God,' Laurie murmured, pushing a hand through her hair. 'I had no idea. This is terrible. Poor Sherry. I hardly know what to say. Does she ever see her mother?'

He shook his head. 'No. It's one of the real tragedies of what happened, because they were very close. Bluebell. That's what they used to call her mother.'

'But why won't she see her?'

'She won't discuss it. Not even with me. But it can't have been easy seeing your own mother shoot dead the father you adored.'

'It's unthinkable,' Laurie muttered. She turned to look at him, still lost for words.

'I don't think you should mention anything to Sherry,' he cautioned. 'She obviously doesn't want people to know, or she'd have told you herself.'

'No, of course not,' Laurie responded.

They sat quietly for a while, absorbed in their own thoughts, until noticing their glasses were empty, he said, 'I think we need the other bottle now, don't you?'

She nodded, distractedly. 'So you got her through the trial?' she said, when he came back.

'Actually, our month together was immediately after the trial,' he replied, pulling the cork. 'We didn't really meet during it.'

As he sat down and refilled their glasses her eyes followed his movements. He was such a nice man, she was thinking, so easy to talk to and be with.

'Now tell me about you,' he said, clearly wanting to change the subject. 'How did you get into this business?'

Reluctantly she tore her mind away from Sherry, only to find her spirits sinking again as she considered his question. 'It's too tied up with Elliot,' she answered, having difficulty focusing her eyes on her glass.

'Then tell me about him.'

She looked at him in surprise.

'You never know, it might help,' he said, not sounding particularly convinced by it himself.

With a laugh she said, 'If you knew what you were asking . . . I swear, I'd be a blubbering wreck by the end of it. Or worse, you'd probably be dragging me out of the gas oven.'

'Ah, but I'm not just a good listener, I'm also good at rescuing women from gas ovens,' he declared.

She tried a smile but it didn't quite happen. 'No,' she said, shaking her head. 'I can't do it. I can't talk about him. I can't even think about him, except I never think about anything else. To tell you the truth, I'm probably losing my grip. I'm all right now, talking to you, but really I'm a mess. I'm no use at the office, I can't do anything here, I'm avoiding my parents, putting upon my friends . . . I live in total terror of him never coming back . . . I can't face the fact that I've still got that day to get through at the end of next week. I'm so delusional, so in denial that I keep allowing myself to believe it'll actually happen, and we will get married. If only I could take something, then wake up and it would all be over.'

She drained her glass and held it out for more. 'We can't go on like this,' she said, 'avoiding each other . . . I'd go round there, but I don't want to bump into her. There are things to sort out, such as what we're going to do with this flat. I can't afford it on my own, and I'd rather set fire to it than let him bring her here.'

She drank again, and swallowed down hard in the hope it might keep her tears back. 'I told him tonight to take her to Bali,' she said, her voice starting to falter. 'You know, I think he actually considered it. It's where we were going on honeymoon. Can you believe he'd even think about taking her there? All the time I'm imagining them together. I can even tell you what they talk about, how they both look in the nude, the erotic picture they make, their bodies so perfectly in tune . . .'

'Hey, hey,' he said, coming to sit next to her and drawing her into his arms. 'You don't have to do this.'

'I don't know how to stop,' she wept, resting her head on his shoulder. 'It haunts me, day and night. They're there when I get up and they're still there when I go to bed. I'm obsessed by them. They're going to New York next week – that's where he'll be when we should have been getting married. Oh God, Nick,' she gasped, 'it's all gone so terribly wrong and I don't know what to do.'

'Ssh,' he soothed, whispering into her hair. 'It'll be all right. I promise. You'll get through this. Meanwhile, don't be too hard on yourself. Lean on your friends, pour it all out, let them be there for you, the way you'd be there for them.'

Her eyes were closed, her cheek was pressed against him. It was so comforting being held like this, and the sound of his voice, vibrating softly in his chest, made her feel safe. With all her heart she wished he was Elliot. If he were, oh God, if only he were . . .

'I think I'm drunk,' she confessed in a whisper.

'It could have something to do with the wine,' he responded.

She smiled blearily and lifted her head.

He looked down into her eyes, and brushed the hair from her face. 'Still not quite going to make it as Miss Universe,' he told her softly.

'That bad?'

He nodded. 'But beautiful too.'

Her eyes rested on his mouth, then moved away as the desire to kiss him stole up on her. It was only the closeness she wanted, and she couldn't use him like that, or do it to Sherry. She cleared her throat. 'Would you like some coffee?' she offered, staggering slightly as she tried to get up. 'Or something to eat? Oh my God, you came for dinner. You must be starving.'

'An understatement,' he assured her. 'What do

you have? I'll make it, while you go and freshen up.'

Liking his bluntness she took his hand and led him out to the kitchen. After showing him where everything was, she made her way upstairs to wash her face and straighten her clothes. When she got to the bedroom and remembered what she'd hoped for tonight, she almost sank to her knees and howled. Instead she turned abruptly away, toppled into the bathroom and turned on the light.

The mirror pulled no punches. She looked dreadful, and not even a quick clean-up of the mascara and brush of the hair could hide the redness of her eyes, or the blotches on her cheeks and neck. Her ribs ached from so much sobbing, and her heart felt like a hot burning stone, but at least on the surface she was slightly more present-able by the time she'd finished. Though it crossed her mind to change into something marginally less revealing, it seemed a rather redundant concern when she'd been sitting there pressed against him just now, her skirt riding high on her thighs and her breasts almost visible through the double layers of transparency.

Checking her reflection again to see just how transparent, she decided that the very faint hint of dark nipple was OK, because he probably wouldn't notice anyway, and if he did, he'd be too polite to mention it, or even to look for very long. Actually, it was quite exciting her to think of teas-ing him like this, it made her feel powerful and attractive, like a woman who could win a man over instead of one who had just been left to feel worthless and unloved.

As she walked back down the stairs she saw him in the kitchen and felt a surge of resentment towards him for being in Elliot's place. But it wasn't his fault he wasn't Elliot, or that Elliot had chosen to leave her for someone else. It had nothing to do with him, and at least, unlike Elliot, he was here, caring about her and how she felt, doing everything he could to help her deal with the wrenching awfulness of rejection – not out there somewhere running round at the beck and call of someone whose ass was bigger than Sugar Loaf mountain.

'Hi,' he said, as she joined him. 'Omelette OK? Smoked salmon, chives and a green salad on the side.'

'Sounds delicious,' she responded, wondering if she'd be able to eat.

Without thinking she picked up the nearest wine glass and drank some more. 'I'll get the cutlery,' she said.

They carried the food back to the coffee table, returning to the cushions they'd been on when he'd moved round to sit next to her. This time, as they talked, mostly about him now, she was more aware of her skirt riding up, exposing her thighs, and maybe even offering a glimpse of her panties. She didn't attempt to pull it down, even wriggled slightly to make it go higher. She became fascinated by his hands and imagined them on her legs, smoothing their way up under her hem, circling her waist . . . Picking up her glass she drank again. Her head was swimming with fantasies and wine. She felt unable to speak without slurring her words, and anyway she was afraid of what she might say.

She tried to eat, but the fork felt too heavy to lift. The sound of his voice seemed oddly distant, not connected at all to what was going on. She drank more, then hung her head.

'Are you OK?' he said gently.

'Yes, yes, I'm fine,' she assured him, looking up. 'I just . . .' Her eyes went to his.

He smiled and returned her gaze.

She looked at his mouth again and was about to turn away when he caught her gently by the chin. 'No more wine,' he said softly.

She shook her head. Then almost before she knew it she was pressing her mouth against his.

He kissed her back, tenderly, sliding a hand into her hair, down over her neck and up again. She put her arms around him, willing him to touch her anywhere, all over, under her clothes, everywhere, but he just went on kissing her, until finally he gently eased her away.

'I'm sorry,' she said, dropping her eyes, 'I shouldn't have done that.'

Using his fingers to tilt her face up, he smiled down at her. 'I did it too,' he reminded her.

As she looked at him she could feel her desire turning into a pressing need. 'Please don't tell Sherry,' she whispered, though whether she meant about the kiss, or what she hoped was going to happen next, she didn't know.

'Is that why you stopped?' he asked.

She nodded, then shook her head. 'I don't know. Isn't it why you stopped?'

He inhaled deeply and reached for her hand. 'I don't want to take advantage of you while you're in such a vulnerable state,' he told her.

400

She looked at their hands. 'What about Sherry?' she prompted. 'Surely it's because of her too.'

'Sherry and I,' he began, and glanced away. 'Well, I'm very fond of her . . . In many ways she's a wonderful person . . .' He stopped and looked back at her.

'It's OK, you don't have to tell me,' she said. 'It's between you and Sherry, and I don't want to know something she doesn't.'

In response he squeezed her hand.

After a while she said, 'You've had too much to drink to drive home.'

He merely continued to look into her eyes.

'There's a spare room if you'd like to stay,' she told him.

His eyebrows arched. 'I don't think I could control myself, being under the same roof.'

She swallowed, started to speak, then raised his hand to her throat. 'Please stay,' she said in a whisper.

He took a breath, and afraid he was going to say no, she started to unbutton her blouse.

'I want you to make love to me,' she said. 'Please.' She was unfastening the front clasp of her bra. 'Just tonight,' she whispered, lifting his hands to her breasts. 'Don't say no, Nick. Please don't say no.'

Chapter Twenty

Sherry picked up her supermarket bags and walked outside into a clammy, overcast day. The forecast was for thunder tonight, then sunshine again tomorrow. She'd like to think it was a metaphor for her life. She'd call Nick tonight, they'd have a damned good row about why he hadn't been in touch, then tomorrow he'd send flowers and all would be well.

Two days had passed since she'd visited Brussels to interview the Interpol agent, and the only time she'd spoken to Nick was when *she'd rung him* to say she was back. He'd stayed on the line a matter of minutes, saying he was in the middle of something and he'd call back. There was still no word.

There was no excuse. He *knew* he'd told her he'd call, and he *knew* he hadn't, so what had suddenly changed his mind about her? Unless there had been some kind of accident. His daughter might have been hurt, or he might. Maybe she should show some concern and find out if he was all right.

If he was, and he didn't want to speak to her, that was OK, she could just hang up and get on with her life.

Were it only that simple!

What advice would Dear Molly give? Dear Molly would say, 'You're giving him all the power, and that's not good. It shouldn't matter that he hasn't called for three days, at this stage of a relationship it's no time at all. So get on with your life, or better still, get a life.' And that would work if their relationship were as simple as a new romance, but it was a far cry from that. They had a history. They were connected in a way that went beyond the mundane level of heart and mind, they were on a life journey that had destined them to be together. Though she could see that quite plainly, she understood that maybe he couldn't. He was still cluttered from the breakup of his marriage and now moving back to England, starting a new life, having to deal with his daughter . . . He had a lot going on, whereas she was much clearer in her life and in her outlook. She was also a woman, and women usually caught on much faster to these things than men.

'Stop doing this to yourself,' both Rhona and Anita had told her. 'Just call him. If he's not interested any more you'll soon know, and better to find out now than later.'

Clearly they didn't understand. Maybe they'd never really been in love. Nick van Zant meant more to her than anything or anyone else alive, and now he was back in her life, she couldn't just let him go. He wasn't someone she could simply cut off from, or replace with some stranger she

403

had absolutely no desire to know. He was the person who understood all the pain she had suffered, was bringing love back to the emptiness she'd been left with, healing the wounds that were still open and raw.

As she descended the steps on to the river path the first drops of rain began to fall. Remembering she'd left her French doors open, she quickened her pace. By the time she reached the gym the rain had vanished and the sun was out again. Anita would probably be doing her workout at this hour, but though Sherry longed for some advice, she kept on going, feeling an inexplicable need to get home.

She was just crossing the footbridge behind her apartment block when her mobile started to ring. She put down her shopping, and seeing it was Laurie, she clicked on. 'Hello, stranger,' she said, nestling the phone on her shoulder so she could pick up her bags and carry on walking. 'Are you still at your mother's?'

'No, I'm back in London now,' Laurie answered. 'Sorry I didn't call before. It's been, well, a difficult few days.'

'Rhona told me how he let you down the other night. I'm sorry. Have you spoken to him since?'

'No.' There was a pause, then Laurie said, 'How are things with you and Nick?'

'I'm not sure,' she answered. 'I haven't heard from him since I got back.' Her heart thudded hard as the coincidence of not hearing from either of them suddenly flared horribly in her mind. It made her feel sick and light-headed, until she managed to push it away again.

'Why don't you call him?' Laurie suggested, echoing everyone else.

'I might. Later.' Needing to get off the subject, she said, 'Did you read my notes from Brussels yet?'

'Yes. They're very informative. We need to get some maps made of the smuggling routes the Interpol guy gave you. Did he agree to be interviewed on camera?'

'He said he would.'

'Good. What news on the stripper?'

'Barry said she's got cold feet, so I don't think we should rely on her now.'

'But we don't have any other lead,' Laurie pointed out, 'and after your showdown with the Ghosh woman there's a good chance they'll be moved again, or sold on, or whatever he does to get rid of them, so we need to start speeding this up.'

'I'll call Barry as soon as I get home,' Sherry promised, deliberately not going on the defensive. 'I met someone from the Vice Squad this morning,' she continued. 'She wouldn't go into detail, but apparently there's an extremely involved and widespread undercover operation going on concerning forced prostitution. I asked if Eddie Cribbs was involved, but she wouldn't confirm or deny it.'

'Did you tell her about the women we're looking for?'

'Yes. She accepts they probably exist, but Vice's focus in this instance is on the pimps and perverts, as she put it, who should lead them to the women.'

'Then it'll be interesting to see what comes of

405

it,' Laurie commented. 'Let me know if there's anything I can do, won't you? I'm your able-bodied assistant on this.'

Knowing this was a sop to her ego, Sherry's smile was weak. 'I will,' she said. 'Actually, what are you doing now? Would you like to come over for dinner? We could discuss our next moves.'

'I'd love to, but I'm meeting my godmother at seven. She's been really worried about me since all this blew up . . .'

'I didn't know you had a godmother. That's nice.'

'She's my mum's best friend. They were at school together, so she's more like family. Do you have a godmother?'

'No. There's just me these days. And Aunt Jude, of course, my dad's sister.' She allowed a few seconds to tick by, then, bracing herself, she said, 'I don't suppose you've seen or heard anything from Nick yourself, have you?'

'Me? No,' Laurie answered. 'Nothing.'

Sherry could feel herself turning cold. The response had been too quick, and held no conviction. 'OK,' she said lightly. 'I'm just about to go in the door now, so I'll have to ring off. Talk to you later,' and she abruptly ended the call.

As she rode up in the lift she could already hear Rhona's voice, telling her to stop being ridiculous. Laurie was still far too involved with Elliot even to be looking at another man, least of all one who was in a relationship with such a close friend. And if anyone in the world knew what it was like to be betrayed right now it was Laurie, so no way would she do it to Sherry. Of course Rhona would be right, and Sherry was in danger of becoming paranoid, but even so, the suspicion had taken root and it wasn't going to be easily plucked out.

After dumping her shopping in the kitchen she turned back to close the front door, and was just coming through again when her heart suddenly jolted in shock. There was someone standing on her balcony – a man, whose face she couldn't see because the sun was behind him.

She said nothing, only stared at him. An appallingly neutral voice in her head was reminding her that she'd always known someone would come, that it had only ever been a matter of time. She could feeling herself starting to shake as her two worlds collided. She hadn't expected it to be now – nor, for some reason, had she expected a man.

'Hello, Sherry,' he said. 'It is Sherry, I take it.'

The cockney accent threw her. She blinked, drew a breath, then suddenly realized she had it wrong. This wasn't someone stepping out of her past, like a corpse rising up from a grave, this was someone from Eddie Cribbs. The situation was no better, yet it was slightly easier for her to breathe.

'I think we need to have a little chat,' he said, stepping into the sitting room.

Though her limbs were still weak with fear, she managed to walk forward, keeping her eyes on his face, until it was finally visible. Though she'd never seen Eddie Cribbs she knew this man, with his strangely scarred face, was too young to be him in person.

'I've got some advice for you,' he told her, sliding his hands into his pockets. 'You can take it or leave it, but if I were you, I'd take it.' He flashed a quick smile. 'It's not a good idea to keep going on with this snooping around you've been doing,' he said. 'Let's say, it's not in your own best interests.'

She stared at him, pale-faced and silent.

'We know you've got secrets,' he told her amicably, 'and we respect that. Everyone has some kind of business they don't want no-one else poking around in, and a mother who's a murderer isn't something anyone would want advertised, now is it? Particularly not when that mother's somewhere she can be got to nice and easy.' He tapped the side of his nose. 'Know what I mean?'

After a pause she gave a brief nod of her head.

'Good. I'm glad we understand each other,' he said, 'because we don't want anything turning nasty, now do we?'

She made no response.

'No, course we don't,' he answered for her. 'So you just let all this go now, like a good girl, and we'll forget you and your mother ever existed.'

As the door closed behind him she ran to the bathroom and threw up. There was no food inside her, but the bitter bile of fear just kept on coming. Deep down inside her a child was screaming for her mother, wanting to save and protect her, to push it all away and pretend none of it had happened. The voices in her head were chattering, faster and faster, her father, her mother, strangers swarming all over the house . . . She had to make them stop. She just had to. She wasn't in that house. It was all in the past where it couldn't hurt her any more. But it could, the man who'd just come here had proved it.

She'd have to call Laurie, tell her she couldn't go on with this project. Though she passionately wanted to be the one to find those women, she was too scared now. But what excuse could she give? She thought of Nick and suddenly realizing she had a good reason to call him, she rinsed out her mouth, dried her face and ran back to her desk. To her surprise and relief he sounded pleased to hear her.

'How are you doing?' he said. 'I was about to call you.'

'I've just had a visit from one of Eddie Cribbs's people,' she said breathlessly. 'He's telling me to back off . . .'

'Did he hurt you?'

'No. He just said I . . . I don't want to tell you on the phone. Can you come over?'

'Sure. I'll be there as soon as I can.'

Rhona was shaking her head and looking at Laurie in incredulous dismay.

'I didn't mean it to happen,' Laurie cried, throwing out her hands. 'I was drunk. Elliot had just let me down . . .'

'I'm not having a problem getting the picture,' Rhona assured her. 'I'm just wondering what the hell we do now. I take it Sherry has no idea.'

'For God's sake, no! I mean, I don't think so. How could she? I can't imagine he'd tell her.'

'Probably not. And she'd certainly have mentioned it if he had, so I guess we can safely assume she's still in the dark.' Her eyes narrowed as something else occurred to her, and treating Laurie to a curious scrutiny, she said, 'I know this isn't very likely, but is it . . . Well, is this something that might go somewhere? I mean, do you have any feelings for him?'

'Rhona! I don't know how you can even ask. It's just something that happened. It was one night – on the rebound.'

'What about him? Does he have feelings for you?'

'Of course not. I don't think so. He . . . Oh God, I don't know. I just wish it had never happened.'

'Well you certainly will if Sherry ever finds out. Now, tell me again what he said about her mother. I can still hardly believe it. In prison for murder. No wonder she never talks about her. Let's hope it doesn't run in the family, eh?'

'That's not even funny. Now, please, can we concentrate on what's really at stake here?'

'Well, you have to admit, she is a little odd, especially where Nick's concerned.'

'Rhona!'

'Sorry.' Then, after a pause, 'Are those flowers from him, by any chance?'

Laurie looked at the simple but beautiful bunch of lavender-tinged pink roses. 'Yes,' she answered. 'As a matter of fact they are. I threw the card away, just in case, by some horrible fluke, Sherry ever got hold of it.'

'What did it say?'

Laurie blushed. 'To Miss Universe,' she mumbled.

Rhona's eyes lit up.

'It was a joke,' Laurie cried. 'Something that . . . Look, never mind that. It doesn't mean anything, what I want to know is what the hell am I going to do?'

'Has he called at all?' Rhona persisted.

'Only once.'

'And he said?'

'That he doesn't want to rush me, that he understands about Elliot, so he'll leave it for me to call him, should I ever want to.'

Rhona looked impressed. 'So he does have feelings for you,' she declared. 'Did he mention Sherry?'

Laurie shook her head.

Deciding to take a moment to think, Rhona strolled over to the huge picture windows, where she gazed up at the traffic to-ing and fro-ing over the bridge.

'There's something else,' Laurie told her quietly.

Rhona turned round, eyebrows raised. 'That's not enough?' she responded.

'Actually, it's part of the same thing. It doesn't make it any better – I suppose it makes it worse, in a way.'

'I'm intrigued to know how that's possible.'

Laurie slanted her a look, then thinking it might be easier if she wasn't actually in eye contact for this, she turned aside as she said, 'When we woke up in the morning, we . . . Well, I expect you can imagine, I felt really bad. I couldn't believe he was there. It was awful . . . I wanted him to go straight away . . . I told him he had to . . .'

'You ended up doing it again,' Rhona interrupted.

Laurie stared at her miserably. 'It still didn't mean anything,' she insisted. 'It was just a comfort thing. I was upset, and he wanted to make me feel . . . well, better, I suppose.'

'I'm sure Sherry'll understand completely if you put it like that,' Rhona remarked.

'Don't,' Laurie snapped. 'Sarcasm's not helping. We're supposed to be working together, for God's sake, and I can hardly bring myself to speak to her on the phone, never mind look her in the face. She thinks I'm with my godmother tonight. I couldn't go over there. I'd feel such a hypocrite. And she hasn't heard from Nick. He's stopped calling her. Oh God, if he ends their relationship now, because of me,' she cried, clasping her hands to her head. 'This is all such a mess, and it's his fault. Elliot's. If he'd come that night, none of this would have happened. What am I saying? If he hadn't got the hots for that fat cow . . .'

'I think,' Rhona said, coming to a decision, 'that we need to get you out of the way for a while. Call Sherry, tell her she can take over the story completely – it's what she wants, then you and I will disappear off to Hydra and stay there until the wedding and honeymoon period are over.'

Though Laurie took a breath to protest, she hesitated, as it actually didn't seem such a bad idea. It was certainly preferable to facing Sherry right now, and it wouldn't exactly be leaving her in the lurch, because Rose was due back any day. And she was so deeply dreading being here, in London, in this flat, while he was in New York with Andraya, on the very day they should have been getting married – no, she couldn't do it, she just couldn't. She had to be somewhere else too. 'How soon can we leave?' she said.

'I'd say right away,' Rhona replied, with a smile, 'but I've just agreed to a two-day tour with an author next Monday and Tuesday. So do you think you can keep yourself in check for another week?'

'One day I'll find your jokes funny again,' Laurie responded. 'But it's not going to be today.'

Nick was sitting with his elbows resting on his knees, staring down at his drink as he thought over what Sherry had just told him. Sherry was perched on the arm of a chair inside the French windows, gazing out at the thunderous sky, and vaguely registering the first fat blobs of rain dropping into the river.

She was much calmer now. It had taken a while, but eventually she'd realized that to remain in a panic would be just about the most disastrous course she could take. Level-headedness and reason were vital if the situation was going to be resolved with any degree of success, though the fact that Laurie had called half an hour ago to ask her to take the story over completely had complicated matters considerably. However, it was only until Rose came back, and as Laurie wouldn't be leaving until the middle of next week she shouldn't be in charge for long.

She glanced over at Nick. The fact that he was here, taking it all extremely seriously, was as heartening as his arrival, when he'd appeared genuinely concerned and relieved to see that she really hadn't been harmed. He'd even drawn her into his arms and held her as affectionately as he always did, which she hadn't attempted to resist, since the issue of two days with no call seemed a petty grievance in the light of what was happening now.

413

'So you didn't tell Laurie anything about the visit?' he said eventually.

'No,' she answered. 'I couldn't. She'd just said she needed to get away from London with the wedding coming up, and in the circumstances I could hardly tell her she had to stay.'

'When is she going?'

'Next Wednesday or Thursday, I think.'

'What's she doing until then?'

'She didn't say.' Her heart was thudding, her mouth turning dry, for it was starting to appear that Laurie's movements were of more interest to him than what was happening to her.

He lifted his glass and drank. 'I think you'll have to back off now,' he told her. 'I don't see any alternative.'

'You mean just pretend those women don't exist? Walk away and leave them to their fate?'

'Laurie's around for another week,' he pointed out, 'then Rose is back. It's their programme, and if they knew what you were . . .'

'Don't even go there,' she cut in. 'I'm not telling Laurie about the visit, or my mother, I don't want her to know anything.'

He was watching her closely. 'So you are concerned about your mother?'

Her eyes flashed. 'Of course I am. How could I not be?'

'You have no contact with her . . .'

She turned sharply away. 'That's got nothing to do with it,' she snapped. 'We're talking about Laurie, and if she did take back control she'd be facing the same threat.'

'Not exactly the same.'

414

'No. But Eddie Cribbs isn't going to be any happier about her digging around in his affairs than he is with me.'

Sighing, he pulled a hand over his face and thought some more.

'Would you like something to eat?' she offered after a while. 'I've got plenty in.'

'No, it's OK. I'm fine.'

'It's no trouble,' she assured him, getting up. 'I'm hungry myself, so I'll fix a salad.'

As she began preparing the food he came to stand the other side of the counter. 'You could always go to the police,' he suggested.

'With what? I've got nothing to give them until I know where those women are, or I can at least prove they exist.'

'They'd have to check it out.'

'Eddie Cribbs is not going to take kindly to having the police swarming all over his business, and it if happens right after one of his henchmen paid me a visit . . .'

'Then you should at least put Laurie in the picture.'

Her eyes remained down, masking her annoyance that they were back to Laurie again. 'No,' she replied firmly. 'I think we need to consider this as though she's already gone to Hydra.'

Turning away he walked over to the windows and stared up-river in the direction of Tower Bridge.

She carried on washing and chopping the salad, throwing it all into a bowl ready to toss. Though she was glad to have his input, and would always value his advice, she'd been hoping he'd offer to take the story on with her. It would be a great grounding for them as a couple, professionally and personally, and she couldn't imagine for one minute that Rose, when she returned, would object to having him on board. The question was, how to talk him round when he seemed so determined to honour his commitment to his daughter?

Finally she carried two cold chicken salads to the dining table, then went back for the wine. 'I think we should change the subject now,' she said, as they sat down. 'We can sleep on it, see how it looks in the morning.'

He didn't object, nor, to her relief, did he seem to balk at spending the night.

'So, what's been happening with you?' she asked chattily, draping a napkin across her lap. 'How's Julia?'

'Still loving London. Her mother's afraid she'll want to come and live here.'

Sherry's eyes widened. 'Is that likely?' she responded, not liking the idea too much. 'I mean, would it work?'

'I don't think so. I travel such a lot, or I will when I get back to it, but if she set her heart on coming, I guess I'd find a way.'

Sherry picked up her fork and started to eat. Did she want to become the stepmother of a teenage girl? Or share him with an adolescent who was always going to have first call? Not at all, but if it was important to Nick, which obviously it was . . . No, she still didn't like it. It would get in the way of their careers, and what if they had children of their own?

'I think I should tell you,' he said, picking up

416

his glass, 'that Laurie already knows about your mother.'

She froze.

His eyes came to hers.

'How? Who told her?' she said.

'I did.'

Her mind was reeling. He'd told Laurie about her mother. He and Laurie had discussed her and her mother. Her appetite had gone, her ability to think was in shreds. Then quite suddenly she shut it down, closed it out, as though it were a blast of music that could just be switched off. 'It's OK,' she said with a brittle smile, 'you don't have to explain.' She didn't want to hear it. If she didn't allow him to say the words they wouldn't exist. And if she didn't allow herself to form the thoughts, they'd have no power. Everything was all right, he was here, helping her to solve this dilemma . . . He wasn't with Laurie, and Laurie was going to Hydra . . .

Putting down his fork he reached for her hand.. 'You've got nothing to be ashamed of,' he said gently. 'You don't need to hide it from people who care . . .'

'I just didn't want anyone to know,' she responded, pulling her hand away. 'But it's all right, it doesn't matter.'

'I'm sorry,' he said.

Sherry drank some wine then continued to eat. She wondered why Laurie hadn't mentioned it when she'd called earlier, then realized she couldn't, without admitting she'd heard it from Nick. She wasn't prepared to think any further than that because she didn't want to know when

Laurie had been with Nick, in case there had been another occasion besides the one she already knew about. Nor did she want to know why they'd been discussing her. It didn't matter, it really didn't, so she was just going to let it drop.

'The first thing I thought,' she said, gazing at the candle flame, 'when I saw someone standing there, was that he'd come to take me back to LA.' She looked at Nick and saw his surprise.

'You don't have to go back,' he reminded her.

'The curious thing was,' she continued, almost as though he hadn't spoken, 'I realized, when I saw him, that I'd always thought it would be a woman who'd come. I wonder why I thought that.'

'No-one's going to come,' he assured her. 'Why would they?'

'Why indeed,' she said, and gave him a smile.

They continued to eat. Silence wrapped itself around their thoughts, though she knew they were about the same woman – women, because it wasn't just her mother, it was Laurie too . . . She felt a peculiar stirring inside as it occurred to her how, all those weeks ago, Laurie's wedding invitation had turned up in the same mail as what she'd later learned was her mother's suicide note. The co-incidence seemed to be taking on some signifi-cance, though in what way it was impossible to say. It was just there, striking her as extremely curi-ous that neither event was going to come to fruition. She considered mentioning it to Nick, but it seemed too sinister, too strange and elusive.

By the time they'd finished eating the rain was coming down fast, bouncing off the balcony and splashing into the room. Nick got up and went to close the windows. The phone rang, and hearing Barry's voice Sherry picked it up.

'Have you spoken to Danny?' she asked.

'Yes. Suzy says the women are still here, but she's having trouble finding out exactly where.'

'Are you sure she's on the level?' she pressed. 'Or is she just planning to rip us off for more money?'

'The easy answer to that is don't pay till you get what you want.'

'And when's that likely to be?'

'Danny reckons by the end of the week. He says something's about to go down that'll push Suzy off the fence.'

'Then let's hope it does.'

As she rang off she turned to Nick. 'It seems we could know where the women are as early as this weekend,' she told him.

His tone was sombre as he said, 'And what then?'

She shrugged. 'I'll try to get in there with a camera.'

'What about the risk, not just to you and them . . .'

'I'll need an interpreter to come with me,' she said, cutting him off. 'Stan might know someone. I'll call him tomorrow.' Smiling, she sauntered towards him and linked her hands behind his neck. 'It's so cosy with the rain outside and us and the wine in here, don't you think?' she murmured.

Though his mouth responded warmly enough to hers she was aware that he wasn't putting his arms around her. She pressed herself harder to him, and let her head fall back to gaze up into his eyes. 'You don't think Eddie Cribbs'll send another visitor tonight, do you?' she said, feigning concern.

He shook his head. 'I doubt it.'

She smiled. 'Well, even if he does, I've got you here to protect me, so I won't worry too much,' and after kissing him again she took his hand and led him through to the bedroom.

Chapter Twenty-One

Suzy was madder than hell. This was absolutely the last time she did her act in this joint. Not for ten thousand quid a pop would she ever work this dive again, with that bitch Cheryl out there gloating over her pathetic little triumph of getting her best friend Marianne put top of the bill.

Well that was OK, let Marianne have the spotlight – why not, she was good, the punters liked her, and not for a minute did Suzy hold any of this against her. Dumb cow, probably didn't even know she was being used to score points. So no, let her get up there and jiggle it all about for all she was worth. She'd be off again in a few months, up the West End, or to some sleazy men's club somewhere abroad. They all went in the end, it was only Suzy who'd ever stayed, loyal and true, until that slag Cheryl had come on the scene.

Well, fuck 'em. She didn't need 'em. She had her special punters, they'd come with her wherever she went, and while she was at it she'd rip off a couple of the other girls to come too. Just no way was she staying here to be humiliated by the likes of that little whore. She was off. Out of here.

As the music ended she peeled off her G-string, twirled it twice and flicked it straight into Cheryl's face. Everyone laughed and applauded, except Cheryl. After curtseying demurely, Suzy gave a cheeky little wave to her admirers and disappeared behind the screen, the sunniness of her smile turning to an instant thunderstorm.

She was surprised to find the changing room empty, and hoped for Cheryl's sake that she hadn't got rid of everyone with the idea of coming back here to rub her face in some more of her shit, because Suzy was just in the mood to deal with her now. In fact, she'd like nothing better than to get hold of that tart's rat-tail hair and pull every last strand of it out of her stupid fucking head. And that was just for starters, because what she'd like to do to the rest of her had a lot less to do with baldness than with total annihilation. To her disappointment, though, it was Trevor who swaggered in as she pulled open her locker door, and Trevor who made it clear he'd told the other girls to scram.

'Come on, Suze,' he said, sinking down on the chair next to her place. 'Don't leave like this. Marianne's not going to last. You know that. You'll be back on top before you know it.'

'As long as Eddie's in that bitch's knickers,' she spat, not caring who heard her, 'there's no place for me here.'

'Course there is. You're just getting things out of perspective. Your pay isn't being cut. No-one's interfering with your punters. It's just Marianne gets top billing. So what? Where's the big deal?'

'If you don't understand, Trevor,' she snorted, pulling on her jeans, 'I'm not going to explain. You can dock my pay to the end of the week.'

'That's generous considering it's Friday.' He waited for her to laugh, but nothing doing. 'Look, I'm not going to do that,' he said. 'What I'm going to do is try and persuade you to stay here and keep us all happy, the way you always have. The place won't be the same without you.'

'I'm not closing up shop,' she informed him tightly. 'If you still want your nooky, you know where to find me. I just won't be here no more.'

'What about my manager's discount?' he joked, giving her a wink.

She turned her back, not wanting him to see how much she'd like to slap his face. That was all those bastards ever cared about, where they were going to get it and how much they'd have to pay. They were all the same, whether they married the girl, took her out for dinner, bought her flowers, set her up in a flat somewhere – it was all just variations on the same theme. Well, fuck him, his discount days were over. He could have stood up for her over this, but no-one ever crossed Eddie, did they? God forbid anyone should ever even think about crossing Eddie. Well, it was a pity that slag out there didn't think about that before she started messing with someone who had ten times more brains, and a lot more friends.

'Before you go,' Trevor said, as she started towards the door, 'Eddie wanted me to tell you not to think about taking any of the punters with you. Or any of the girls. If you do . . .' He shrugged. 'Just don't do it.'

With the blood boiling in her veins Suzy tore open the door and stormed down the corridor to the back exit. That was it! That was absolutely fucking it! There were so many ways she could get her revenge here and if he was too much of an asshole to see it, then he – and that bitch he was screwing – deserved everything they had coming. And boy were they going to get it now, the pair of them, right where it was going to hurt the most.

Neela was panting for breath and clinging tight to Shaila. Her eyes were wide with terror as she stared at Ekta, whom the other women were holding down. Ekta had lost her mind. Evil spirits had come into her and made her try to smother Shaila with a pillow.

Ekta's eyes were bright, drool ran from the corner of her mouth. She was looking at Neela. 'It's better for her this way,' she rasped, still trying to get her breath too. 'They can't hurt her then.'

Neela continued to stare. She didn't know what to say, she was too shocked and afraid to move.

'They came while you were gone,' Ekta told her. 'Tell her,' she implored the others. 'They took photographs,' she said to Neela. 'They made her stand . . .' Distress choked off her words. 'There,' she said, trying to point. 'They made her stand there. You know why they did it. We all do. Neela *laddali*, it's better for her this way.'

Neela's gaze moved to the other women's faces.

They were still holding Ekta, but everyone was watching her. To her horror Neela could see they agreed. She should let Ekta do this terrible thing in order to save Shaila from the men.

A single tear rolled from her eye and fell on to her cheek. She thought of what had been done to her that morning. Then her head went back and she let out an animal-like howl of anguish. '*Madaad karo*,' she cried despairingly. '*Hamune koi madaad karo*.' Help us. Please, somebody help us.

'Are you sure you're all right?' Anita said, concerned by how distracted Sherry seemed.

'Yes, I'm fine,' Sherry answered, dragging her eyes from the window. 'Sorry. What were you saying?'

'I was just wondering how it was all going. I haven't heard from you in over a week, so I thought I'd come and find out how you are. If it's not convenient . . .'

'No, it's fine. Everything's fine.'

Anita waited. 'So, have you seen Nick?' she prompted.

'A couple of days ago.'

'And?'

'Have you spoken to Laurie at all?' Sherry suddenly asked.

Anita frowned in surprise. 'No. Why would I?'

'I just wondered, that's all.'

'Is she all right?'

'Yes. I think so. As all right as she can be.'

Anita glanced at her watch. 'I have to go in a minute,' she said, 'but I can meet you for a drink at six, if you'd like to get together.'

'Oh, no, I can't. I've got too much work on. But thanks.'

After seeing Anita out Sherry returned to her desk and sat staring at nothing. It was late in the afternoon and she had a Dear Molly deadline to meet, but her mind was too full of everything else. She'd have liked to confide in Anita, but it was so hard to know where to get started. Maybe if Anita had asked about her mother . . . But why would she? As far as Anita was concerned there was no reason to.

Rhona hadn't mentioned it either when she'd seen her earlier, though surely Laurie would have told her. Except Laurie was so wrapped up in her own life that maybe she hadn't given Sherry's mother a second thought. Sherry usually didn't either, unless she could help it, but since Nick had confessed to telling Laurie all about her, she'd hardly been able to think of anything else.

Her mind went back to three nights ago. He hadn't wanted to stay, not really, so she'd used his conscience to make him. They'd made love, but he'd only been there in body – in his mind he'd been elsewhere. She had no way of knowing if he'd been thinking of Laurie, or even pretending Sherry was her, but she was afraid he was.

If only Rhona had been able to put on a better show when she'd confronted her, maybe then she wouldn't be sitting here, frozen in the dread of Laurie and Nick being together even now. But Rhona's denial just simply hadn't had the right ring of truth.

'Heavens, Laurie can't even think about anything except Elliot,' she'd more or less scoffed.

'It'll be a long time before she gets involved with anyone else.'

'Yes or no?' Sherry persisted. 'Do you think there's anything going on between her and Nick?'

'Sherry, you know the answer, so I'm not even going to go there.'

She'd skirted the issue, and they both knew it. 'So why is she avoiding me?' Sherry had countered.

'She's not. I don't know why you're saying that.'

'I know they've seen each other. I think it was the night Elliot should have gone round there.'

Rhona's eyes widened. 'What makes you say that?'

'It's just a feeling I have.'

'Well, if he did, I know nothing about it.'

Sherry might have believed her had she not then gone on, unprompted, to say, 'I don't know why you're doing this to yourself. You've seen him since, haven't you? He came over and spent the night. Everything was all right then – wasn't it?'

Sherry had only nodded in response, but of course it hadn't been. She didn't want Rhona to know that though, she didn't want anyone to. She just wanted to go back to a time when everything was all right, even though she couldn't actually think when that was.

Nick hadn't been in touch since he'd left the next morning, and she was certain now that he wouldn't be again. Which meant that somehow she had to make herself accept that he didn't feel the same way she did. He might have, if it weren't for his ex-wife Trudy, and his ex-girlfriend Elaine, and his new love, Laurie. He'd allowed other people to distract him, not realizing that with her he could have had something so special, so unique he would never have needed anyone else. Why hadn't he understood that? It had always seemed so plain to her.

Maybe she'd got it all wrong about him. Maybe he wasn't the man she'd always believed him to be. He obviously hadn't been thinking about her all these years, longing to get away from a love-less marriage so he could be with her. He'd been happy with his wife until she'd left him. Then instead of rushing out to find Sherry, he'd moved in with another woman whom he'd spent a whole year with, presumably not giving a second thought to Sherry, whose life was on hold for him.

And now? What was going on now? Was he falling for Laurie, or was she just someone else who needed rescuing, the way Sherry once had? Maybe that was how he operated: find a woman in distress, take advantage, then leave as though it had never happened.

How could he be so like her father without her noticing it before?

She shifted restlessly. It was exactly how her father had seduced his starlets – search out the vulnerable one, ply her with champagne and promises of stardom, then, when she held no more interest for him, he returned to his wife. And all the time her beautiful, delicate and devoted mother just carried on loving him with all her heart and forgiving him with all her soul. It hadn't been hard to understand why, for he was the easiest man in the world to love, and no-one, not even Sherry or her mother, could ever be in any doubt that, in spite of everything, he loved his wife above all other women, with the possible exception of his daughter, whom he sometimes claimed to love even more. And throughout her life Sherry had never loved anyone as much as she loved him. Ever since she could remember he was their world. Her mother came alive when he was at home, and when he wasn't there, they just waited for him to come back.

Nick wouldn't come back. Not because of Laurie, or because he didn't love or care for her, but because, in his heart, he was guilty of the very prejudice she'd always feared: if the mother was a murderess, maybe the daughter could be too.

She didn't blame him for feeling that way, she even understood it, she'd just believed he was different. With him she'd thought there could be a chance, a way of putting it all behind her so that the sacrifices would have been worth it. That could still happen, if she were able to convince him how vital he was to her in so many ways.

Reaching for the phone she dialled his mobile number. To her surprise, for she'd expected him to avoid her, he answered.

'Hi. I was just thinking about you,' he said, sounding pleased to hear her.

So like her father, always warm and friendly, no matter who was calling or what it was about. 'I have a question,' she told him. 'Please answer me honestly. Is there something going on between you and Laurie?'

The beat before he answered was answer enough, but she waited, having to be certain, needing to hear him say it. 'Not exactly,' he finally replied. 'But I won't lie, I'd like there to be.'

'Have you slept with her?' she asked.

He was silent.

'You have, haven't you?'

'Sherry . . .'

'It's OK. That's all I need to know. Goodbye,'
and she rang off.

She got up from her desk and walked out to
the balcony to begin tending her flowers. She
wouldn't be like her mother and let them die
while she waited for the latest passion to burn
itself out. She would keep them alive, because she
didn't want anything in her life to die ever again.
It would of course, she knew that, because everything did − relationships, friendships, hopes,
dreams, in the end everything turned to dust.
Ashes to ashes, dust to dust. She pictured herself
standing at her father's graveside. She was overwhelmed by a longing for him that could have
filled an ocean and reached to the sky. She wished
she knew how to keep everything alive, but she
didn't. It was all going to die, everything and
everyone. There was only ever one end, and that
was to die.

Suzy sat half-turned in the passenger seat, looking at Danny. With no make-up on her face and
her hair scrunched into a bun she seemed so
youthful and fresh it was hard to credit what she
did for a living.

They'd been parked on this cobbled, lamplit
street for a while now, knowing they were in the
right place and that all they had to do was just go
and drop the note off and it would be over, but

so far neither of them had made a move to get out of the car.

'Remember, you drove me here,' she said, breaking the silence.

He threw up his hands. 'What, you think I'm going to tell someone?' he cried.

'No. I just want you to remember, we did this together.'

'Just fucking do it,' he said irritably.

Suzy's fingers closed more tightly on the note. 'How are we going to get paid?' she demanded. 'I don't have no job no more, remember?'

'Barry's going to take care of it. Now, just go.'

She was on the point of getting out when something else occurred to her. 'I know what Eddie had done to your old man,' she said, turning back, 'but as far as I know he's always been good to you . . .'

'Yeah, like fucking threatening to chop off my dick if I as much as look at his daughter.'

'You better hope he never finds out you poked that little slag,' she warned.

'You got a way with words, Suzy, anyone ever tell you that?'

'So what are you going to do if this finishes him?' she asked. 'You're on a nice little earner, so why would you want to screw it up now?'

'I got other things happening,' he told her. 'And you can come wiv me if you just get out of this bollocsing car and deliver that note.'

Suzy was watching him carefully. 'Where are you going, Danny?' she asked. 'Where's the next stop, after Eddie?'

He flicked her a glance, then continued staring ahead.

'You're not talking about the Turks are you?' she said. 'Please tell me you're not talking . . .'

'I might be, but then again, I might not. Now, you just go and do what we're here to do, and then we'll drive somewhere else and have a little chat.'

Tearing her eyes from his face, Suzy turned to look up at the moonlit façade of Dunbar Wharf. Somewhere in there Sherry MacElvoy, she of the cheap blonde wig and book full of questions, was presumably sleeping. No nightmares, Suzy hoped, because she'd quite liked the woman in spite of her bossiness. Even if she were submerged in some kind of Jungian weirdness, she'd have a nice surprise waiting for her when she woke up in the morning, presuming an anonymous note containing a secret address was still something she wanted.

Laurie was much calmer waiting for Elliot this time than the last. She wasn't sure why, because her feelings hadn't changed. She still missed him and wanted him back in her life almost more than she wanted to breathe, yet there had been no frantic preparations in the hour leading up to his arrival. She wasn't wearing expensive underwear in the hope of seducing him, nor was there a CD on the player waiting to bring back precious memories. She didn't even stop for a last-minute check in the mirror as she went to open the door.

She wondered if it had something to do with allowing herself finally to hit rock bottom last night, to take that flight without wings, that horrible descent into the deepest, darkest despair she

432

had ever known. Nothing in her life had ever felt that bad. She had found herself imprisoned by the bleakest, cruellest part of her mind, where nothing could exist, not even the tiniest flicker of hope, or whisper of a prayer. It was as though there was no point to life, nothing that followed and no God to care. She'd looked through old photos, listened to their favourite operas and reread his letters. She'd wanted to destroy everything and still wasn't sure why she hadn't.

In the cold light of day she wondered how effective or wise it had been to make herself suffer so much, though she couldn't deny that she'd woken up this morning feeling slightly different from the way she had before. It was hard to put into words how different, except she had just gone through an entire day without experiencing a single attack of the awful, heart-wrenching panic that made it seem impossible to go on.

The big test, however, was going to be when she opened the door.

She wasn't afraid, though she had to admit she was nervous. She wondered if he was too. How strange it was to think of him standing outside his own home, waiting to be let in.

His back was towards her. Seeming to sense rather than know she was there, he turned round. As their eyes connected the jolt in her heart dismayed her, for it was far worse than she expected. His dark, glowering features were so familiar, everything about him was so known to her that every part of her seemed to yearn towards him. Didn't he feel it too? Could he really stand there, gazing into her eyes, and feel nothing at all?

'I hope I'm not late,' he said.

She shook her head and stood aside for him to pass. 'I'm not going anywhere,' she told him.

He didn't attempt to kiss her, even in a friendly way. In four days they would have been getting married, and now they couldn't even embrace.

They walked along the short hallway together, past their studies, into the sitting room.

After a difficult pause she said, 'Can I get you a drink?'

'Only if you're having one.'

Deciding she would, she left him standing there and went to the kitchen. She wondered what he was thinking as he looked around. Did he have any regrets, was it painful for him too?

She started as she almost dropped the glass she was holding. He turned at the sound.

'OK?' he said.

'Yes, fine.'

They smiled politely.

'I'm sorry about last week,' he told her, sliding his hands in his pockets as he came to stand at the counter.

She wondered how true that was, and if it would be any truer if he knew what had happened as a result. Would he be jealous if she told him about Nick? She never would, for he might think that made it all right for him to be with Andraya, and nothing would ever make that all right.

'Rachel tells me you're going to Hydra,' he said, as she pushed a glass of wine across the counter top.

'On Thursday,' she confirmed. 'The same day as you go to New York, isn't it?'

434

'We go on Friday,' he said.

The 'we' hit her hard. Had he really needed to say that? Couldn't he just have said 'I'?

'Cheers,' he said, raising his glass as she came round to join him.

She raised hers too, then went to curl into one of the big armchairs. 'You can sit down,' she told him.

He perched on the edge of the sofa, looking as uncomfortable as he obviously felt.

As she watched him she knew both anger and longing. She remembered the hell of last night, and wondered what he would say if she told him about it. 'So,' she said, 'here we are, the week before the wedding that's not going to happen.'

His eyes went down. Her words had stung, she could tell, but when he looked up again all he said was, 'I sent your father a cheque to cover expenses . . .'

'He got it, thank you, but there was no need. We just haven't quite figured out what to do with the dress yet.'

To her surprise, he continued to look at her. 'How are you?' he asked. 'You look good.'

'I'm great, thanks,' she replied. 'I won't ask how you are, that's more Andraya's concern now than mine. Did you have a nice time in Tuscany, by the way?'

Leaning forward he put his glass on the table, and linked his hands.

'Do you make love to opera, when you're with her, the way you did with me?' she asked brightly.

His expression closed down, telling her he didn't appreciate the question.

Well that was too bad, because she didn't appreciate anything about this, but she was having to live with it anyway, so he could too.

'How long are you going to Hydra for?' he asked.

Refusing to be distracted, she said, 'Does that mean you do make love to opera? The fact that you didn't answer – is that a way of avoiding a lie?'

'I don't see how discussing my life with Andraya is going to be helpful here,' he responded.

'Then please tell me what is,' she invited, 'because I'm at a complete loss to know what else we have to discuss. Unless, of course, you're finally facing up to the fact that something needs to be decided about this flat. Or maybe you've come to get your diamond ring back. As you can see, I don't wear it any more, but I'm sure if you take it to a good jeweller he can alter it to fit any old fat finger.'

'The ring's yours,' he said quietly. 'I bought it for you.'

She turned her head away. She wasn't going to think about how he'd surprised her with that ring. It was one of the happiest moments of her life, and happy memories weren't going to help her right now.

'I'd like you to keep it,' he said.

She turned back. 'Oh really? Well, that's a shame isn't it, because I don't want it. You see, I was under the impression that it was given as a token of love, a sealing of the fact that we were going to get married, so that makes it about as

436

worthless now as the man who gave it to me, wouldn't you say?'

His only answer was to look down at his hands.

Several seconds ticked by, and she could feel herself getting more and more worked up. 'Elliot, why are you here?' she demanded in the end.

He took a breath, then let it go, slowly, deliberately.

'I need to tell you now,' she jumped in, suddenly afraid of what might be coming, 'that if you're thinking about moving Andraya in here then it'll be over my dead body.'

'But we do need to talk about what we're going to do with the flat.'

'We have to sell it,' she said shortly, and thanked God that he couldn't see what was going on inside her.

He looked around, his eyes travelling from the view to the paintings they'd chosen, to the kitchen they'd designed, and on round to the stairs that led up to the bedroom where they'd slept and made love. Everywhere there were signs and mementoes of who and what they were, photographs of holidays, framed posters of headlines, treasures they'd picked up on their travels, books they'd bought for each other, CDs and DVDs of their favourite music and films.

'You've made it look wonderful in here,' he told her.

'We did it together,' she reminded him. Then with a shrug, 'But it's just a flat, there are others, and I'm sure Andraya will create a magnificent home for the two of you somewhere. Do you have anywhere in mind? Rio? São Paulo? A little love nest on the Amazon? You could become your own South American correspondent.'

Not rising to the sarcasm, he said, 'We might stay in New York.'

Her face immediately drained. The thought of him being so far away was almost as bad as the thought of him being with somebody else. She couldn't bear it, she didn't want to go on with this conversation, because clearly nothing was going to change his mind and no matter what she said she just ended up being hurt even more.

'Rose is back from India on Friday,' she stated suddenly, taking a sip of wine.

Though he obviously knew that the return had been scheduled for Rose and the rest of the crew to make the wedding, all he said was, 'How's it gone out there? Have they got what they went for?'

'I think so. Rose seems quite happy with it. I'm not really involved any more. Sherry's taken over my end.' She looked up as the phone started to ring. Ordinarily she wouldn't have answered, but feeling the need to escape him, if only for a moment, she reached for the receiver.

'Laurie? It's Nick,' the voice at the other end told her. 'I know I said I'd leave it for you . . .'

'It's OK,' she interrupted, feeling a strange light-headedness coming over her, as though some part of this was happening in a dream. 'How are you?'

'Great. How are you?'

'I'm fine.' She glanced at Elliot, then away again.

'Listen,' Nick said, 'I know you're going to Hydra on Thursday and I was hoping . . . Well, I've got a couple of friends out there who run a small boat-charter business . . .'

'I'm not carrying any drugs,' she joked feebly.

He laughed. 'No, it's not that. I was just thinking, I want to take Julia somewhere for a week or so, and if it was OK with you . . . I mean we don't have to meet up or anything, but I haven't seen these guys for years, and . . .' He laughed again. 'I'm behaving like a teenager here. I want to see you again, and I'd love us to get together there, but if you feel it's an intrusion . . .'

'No, it would be lovely,' she told him, not having the faintest idea whether she meant it or not. 'What about Sherry? Is she coming with you?'

There was a moment's silence. 'Actually, Sherry and I . . . Well, let's just say she understands now that it's not going anywhere between us.'

Laurie put a hand to her head. This wasn't what she wanted to hear. Not after what had happened between them. 'You know, I'm really not sure what kind of company I'll be . . .' she said.

'Don't worry about that,' he interrupted. 'We'll have a good time, all of us. I'll make sure of it. Now I'm going to go and break the news to Julia. She'll be thrilled, she really took to you, you know.'

As she rang off Laurie was still dazed by the call. She looked at Elliot and wondered when she was ever going to make sense of her life again.

'I came here to offer to buy you out of the flat,' he said bluntly. 'But now I'm here . . .'

She felt herself crumbling inside. Was there no end to this? It just seemed to go on and on and on. The woman had her man, her future, her dreams and now she wanted her home too. And he had been prepared to give it to her. 'What's happened to you, Elliot?' she said quietly. 'Just who have you turned into?'

Looking as uncomfortable as she intended him to feel, he downed the rest of his wine and got to his feet. 'I need to take some more clothes,' he said. 'Is it OK if I go and get them?'

'No,' she responded, 'it isn't. You can leave now, because frankly, I just want you out of my sight.'

As he walked to the door it took every ounce of will-power she had not to run after him. It didn't seem to matter how much she loathed and despised him, she still couldn't stop loving him, though God knew she was going to try. From now on she was going to do everything in her power to free herself from this stranger, because he wasn't worthy of her any more, not worthy at all.

Chapter Twenty-Two

It was Wednesday afternoon. The anonymous, handwritten note that had been pushed under Sherry's door late on Friday night was still sitting on her desk, where it had been since she'd picked it up early on Saturday morning. From the description the porter had given of the woman who'd delivered it, it could only have been Suzy, so the address must be where the women were being kept.

Since receiving the note Sherry had spent the time mainly thinking, but also practising with a handheld camera and talking to the interpreter Stan had found. For herself she had reached the conclusion that her life simply couldn't go on like this. The truth had to come out, and if the answers that had been steadily revealing themselves to her over the past few days could be made to work, then, in the next few days, everything, but everything, would be resolved.

She'd just made a phone call to a lawyer. Her hand was still on the receiver, shaking slightly, while her eyes remained fixed on the note. The risk she was readying herself to take was enormous, and could easily backfire, but she was determined to go through with it anyway, because the way forward from here had been shown to her with such clarity, such obviousness and simplicity, that even if she wanted to, she couldn't ignore it. All that was going to happen now was meant to be. She was in no doubt about that, or it wouldn't have come to her in the way it had, or at the time it had. One way or another everyone was going to be taken care of – the women in captivity, the men who had put them there, Karima Ghosh, Laurie Forbes, Nick van Zant, Sherry MacElvoy and her mother, Isabell MacEvilly.

The beauty of her plan was that no-one would be harmed by her hand, for never again could she take a human life. Her father's face haunted her every minute of every day – the shock in his eyes the moment he'd realized what she'd done, the disappointment that had turned to understanding as he'd finally slumped to the ground. She would never forget, nor ever forgive, either herself or her mother, for it was her devoted, self-sacrificing mother who'd denied her the punishment she deserved and taken the blame for a crime she hadn't committed.

Wrapping her arms around herself, Sherry walked to the window and stared out. The tragedy of their existence was burning through her with a power she hadn't known in so long. No-one had listened to her back then, though God knew she'd confessed enough times. They'd all believed she was trying to save her mother, when it had been the other way round. In the end, half-demented with frustration and the need to punish her mother as well as herself, she had sworn never to see Isabell again until she was prepared to tell the truth. She would let her rot in that prison and never visit her once. She would destroy all her letters and ignore all her calls. She would change her name, her job, even her country. She had ruined her mother's life, taken from her the only man she'd ever loved, or ever would, and her mother wouldn't allow her to pay.

Had any mother ever loved a daughter more? Had any daughter ever suffered more for that love?

She didn't know, but she could guess, that her mother's suicide threat had been to let her know that she would go to her grave with the truth, rather than see her daughter lose her freedom. *So please come, my darling. Please don't let this estrangement continue when we're all each other has now.* She could hear her mother saying it, even see the beseeching look in her eyes. Those eyes, so like her own, large and blue, full of kindness, yet tinged with pain. Always pain and the fear of when it would begin again. That was why Sherry had done what she had – she just hadn't been able to stand seeing her mother hurt any more. In her mother's view that made her guilty, not Sherry, because she should have hidden her pain, not shared it with a child who would feel it too. But Sherry had been an adult by then, and her father's affairs had made her feel as though he was betraying her too. How could he say he loved them above anyone, or anything, then disappear for days, even

weeks at a time with a stranger who was sometimes even younger than Sherry? Why would he
want to spend time with anyone else, when he
could be with them? His flower girls, as he'd called
them.

'We're the Liliaceae family,' he used to say.
'Mummy is the bluebell, because they're her
favourites. You're the lily because you always smell
so good and I'm the onion that makes you cry.'

She could hear his voice now, deep and soft,
and as filled with unhappiness as it was with love.

'I'm truly blessed by my flower girls,' she'd
heard him telling a friend on the phone on that
fateful night, 'but Bluebell's depressions . . . The
highs are as frightening as the lows now. I just
don't know how to handle her any more. I've
stayed with her all these years, but living with
someone like her, it's not a marriage, it's . . . I don't
know what it is. I only know that she's sick. She
needs help and as long as I'm here she won't get
it. She depends on me, it's like she can't exist without me, and I've got to tell you, there are times
when it feels as though she's sucking the lifeblood
right out of me. Don't get me wrong, I love her, I
always will, but I'm no good for her, and I don't
want to sacrifice any more of my life. Since I met
Jane I've realized what it is to be with a real
woman. All the affairs, the girls, they were escapes,
a bid to try and stay sane. This time it's different.
I just have to find a way to break it to Bluebell. I
considered asking Lily to do it for me, but that's
the coward's way out. She might be an adult now,
but we're still her parents, and I know this is going
to be a blow for her too. Knowing her, she'll move

444

back into the house to take care of her mother, but if she has any sense she'll make poor Bluebell get the help she needs, which is what I should have done years ago.'

Maybe if her mother hadn't been listening too things wouldn't have gone the way they had, but seeing the fear and devastation in those childlike eyes, then listening in the privacy of their pool house to how she hated herself for what she'd done to her husband, how she deserved to suffer for ruining his life, had just been too much for Sherry to bear. If he left for good her mother's life would be over. She would go into a decline and never come back. Sherry couldn't let it happen. She had to stop him.

Her intention, in those crazed few minutes when she went to get the gun, was to kill them all, her father, her mother and herself. They would die together, and be bound in eternity for ever. But after she pulled the trigger, and saw her father looking back at her with his shocked, then understanding eyes, she just hadn't been able to do it again. For several seconds she and her mother had merely stood there, frozen in horror as they stared down at him, watching the life draining out of him, until his eyes closed for the last time. Then, quite suddenly, her mother had grabbed the gun and fired two more shots. They weren't the shots that had killed him though, it was the one Sherry fired that had done that.

Next to her the phone started to ring. She looked at it and blinked. Coming back to the present, she found her thoughts going instantly to Nick. She knew it wouldn't be him, but it was hard to stop the hope, even though it died almost as quickly as it came to life. Her next thought was of Laurie. Hatred welled up in her, triggering every violent impulse she had.

Each time she pictured Laurie's face now, she wanted to crush it. She'd had several calls from her over the weekend, but hadn't returned them. She'd never speak to Laurie again. She'd slept with Nick. No friend should ever do that to another. There were no excuses, no way it could be forgiven. But it wasn't only about Laurie and Nick, it was about her and her mother. It was about justice and following the right path when it opened up, even though she was afraid of taking it. It was about the women secreted away at that scribbled address and doing what she could to rescue them. She just prayed that one or two more nights of abuse wouldn't make a difference after so many.

Hearing Stan's voice, she lifted the receiver and cut into his message. 'I'm here,' she told him.

'Good. Right. I've checked out the address you gave me, and it's where they are all right. No way of getting in unless we bribe the guard. It already cost me a ton for him to admit they was there.'

'How much for us to get in?' she queried.

'He's asking for a grand and he don't want to be nowhere around when it happens. So we got to give him some notice – and cash upfront.'

'I can have it in an hour,' she told him. 'Can you take it to him?'

'No prob.'

'So when do we go in?'

'No point hanging about. Let's go in tonight.'

So soon. She hadn't expected it to happen for at least another day. 'OK,' she said. 'I've got the camera. Call the interpreter and I'll meet you both at the office at seven. Oh, and listen. Don't mention any of this to Laurie. If she knows we've found the women she won't go to Hydra, and for obvious reasons she needs to be away this weekend.'

'Gotcha,' Stan replied. 'See you at seven.'

After ringing off Sherry checked her address book and dialled the number of the New Road workshop. Karima Ghosh's recorded voice came down the line asking the caller to leave a message. Sherry waited for the beep, then said, 'This is Sherry MacElvoy. Please inform Mr Cribbs that I will be at his apartment in Cinnabar Wharf tomorrow morning at ten. It would be a good idea for him to be there too.'

Mota Ben had never told them before what was going to happen, but this morning when she had come, her eyes full of hate, her voice ladling bitterness, she had told them about the men who were going to make films. She had taken much pleasure in describing what kind of films – the kind that would show them being tortured in many violent and terrible ways, until they were no more.

But not Shaila. Something else was going to happen to Shaila, but Mota Ben wouldn't tell them what.

Now Shaila was clinging to Neela, her tiny body trembling with terror every time a sound came from the stairs outside. The other women were quaking too, staring at the door, or praying, or weeping in each other's arms.

Neela watched them. Ten terrified and helpless faces. Ten spirits trapped inside their weak female bodies. There was nothing they could do to save themselves. They were at the mercy of Mota Ben and strangers who were going to abuse and torment their innocent flesh until their spirits could hold on no longer.

Her gaze moved to Ekta. Ekta's head was down, but Neela knew she was praying for guidance and strength. Earlier she had offered the women their only way out. She would help them, she'd told them, and those who didn't want to do it must find it in themselves to help too. She was waiting now for each of them to come to a decision. Neela had already come to hers – she would ask Ekta to put the pillow over her and Shaila's faces together, so that their spirits would be released at the same time. She couldn't ask yet, because Shaila was holding on too tight, and she didn't want the child to hear.

One by one the women began to get up from their mattresses to go and whisper in Ekta's ear. After a while they talked openly, because it became clear that no-one wanted to stay, they all wanted Ekta to help them to go. Ekta was a very brave woman to be able to do this, Neela was thinking, but what would happen to Ekta herself? Who would be left to put a pillow over Ekta's face, if Ekta did it for everyone else?

Later, when Shaila was finally sleeping, Neela whispered her question to Ekta.

Ekta's face was sad but strong as she said, 'I will find a way for myself. After I have helped you all it will be easy to follow.'

'I will do it with you,' Neela told her. 'I will hold their hands and pray to the Lord Shiva to speed them on their way.'

Ekta lifted a hand to stroke her face. *'Bahoo merbani,'* she whispered. Thank you.

One of the women started to wail. *'Naa, naa.'* No. No.

Ekta and Neela looked up, then they heard the sound too. Something was happening outside the door. The sounds were different from those they were used to. They didn't know what they were.

Neela returned swiftly to her mattress and scooped Shaila into her arms. Ekta came too, and huddled in front of them to shield them from harm. The other women clung to each other, whimpering and moaning. Had they come already? Was there going to be no time to set themselves free?

Neela was daring to hope a miracle was happening. Maybe it wasn't the men, maybe it was someone sent by the gracious and forgiving Lord Shiva to save them. But then the door was opening, and seeing the woman with a camera Neela, like the others, began to scream.

Laurie was on the mezzanine of her flat, holding the phone as she stared blankly out at the night. After waiting for Sherry's recorded message to finish, she said, 'Hi, it's Laurie. I was hoping to speak to you before I leave in the morning, so if you get this message *please* call me back. I'll be up quite late, or you can get me before nine in the morning.' She paused, wanting to say more, but a voicemail wasn't the way to do it, so she hung up and went back to her packing.

A while later she was sitting on the edge of the bed wondering if she should try Sherry again. It was too much to hope that they might be able to clear the air over Nick, particularly now he'd decided to go to Hydra too – which hopefully Sherry knew nothing about, or their friendship really was doomed. She just didn't want to go away without finding out how the story was progressing. As the producer it would be highly irresponsible of her to do that, and under any other circumstances she'd be storming round there now to find out what was going on. Knowing how sensitive Sherry had been lately, though, and how badly she had handled things herself, she wasn't at all sure what she should do.

In the end she phoned Rhona, who was finally back from her author jaunt around London. 'It's all such a mess,' she complained. 'I don't want her to think I'm interfering, or that I don't trust her, but surely she realizes I have to know what's going on.'

'You're presuming she's avoiding you,' Rhona responded, 'but actually, she's not in.'

'Are you sure?'

'There are no lights on. I'll go and knock if you like. Or I can check with the porter to see if he saw her going out.'

'Try the porter. I'll hang on.'

As she waited she could hear Rhona speaking on the intercom, and the porter's voice telling her Sherry had gone out around seven.

'So where is she now?' Laurie wanted to know when Rhona came back on the line. 'It's gone eleven.'

450

'You sound like her mother. Maybe she's out with Nick.'

'I wish, but he more or less told me it was over, and besides he's taking the ten o'clock flight to Athens, so he's already gone. Have you seen her at all in the last couple of days? I've lost count of how many messages I've left.'

'I saw her this morning, briefly. She was on her way to your office.'

'Did she mention anything about the story? Or about Nick?'

'It was just a quick good morning. We were both on our way out, going in opposite directions. Does she know Nick's going to Hydra?'

'I hope not. I'm sure he wouldn't tell her. To be honest, I wish he wasn't.'

'You don't have to see him once we're there.'

'It's a small island, so it'll be hard not to.' She sighed wearily. 'I don't seem to have a proper grip on anything right now,' she said, 'so I guess I should just take myself off to bed. If you do happen to see her, make sure she calls me back.'

A few minutes later the phone rang, and praying it was Sherry she grabbed it up. 'Hi, Sherry?'

'No. Rachel.'

Laurie deflated, even as her heart twisted, for Rachel was just one removed from Elliot. 'I was hoping you were Sherry,' she told her.

'Sorry to disappoint you. I was just calling to wish you *bon voyage* tomorrow.'

'Thanks. I suppose I should be wishing you the same, for Friday.'

'There's a chance we have to delay until Saturday,' Rachel said. 'An interested client who's

451

only in town for the next two days. Have you heard anything from Elliot?'

'Not since I threw him out. Has he mentioned it at all?'

'No, but I wouldn't expect him to. Something's up though, because he did one of his disappearing acts last night.'

Laurie's heart skipped a beat. 'Do you know where he went?'

'Not a clue. He's back now, but whether he's managed to calm Andraya down yet is anyone's guess. She's convinced he was with you.'

Laurie sank down on the bed and tried to think. 'Is he still going to New York?' she said.

'As far as I know. Put it this way, he hasn't cancelled.'

'Do you think he's likely to?'

'I'm afraid only he knows. I just thought you'd like to know that things might not be quite as rosy as they seem between those two.'

Though it was exactly what she wanted to hear Laurie suddenly felt very tired. 'You know, right now I couldn't care less what's going on between them,' she declared. 'I've been too hurt, it's too confusing, and I desperately want to make contact with Sherry.'

'Then I hope she calls,' Rachel said, and after wishing her a warm good night she rang off.

Though it was well after midnight by the time Laurie finally went to bed, there was still no call from Sherry, and when she tried again in the morning the answering machine was still on.

'She's been out all night,' she told Rhona, when she called at seven to wake her up.

452

'No, I heard her come in, around one. Sounded like she watched TV for a while, so she's probably still asleep.'

'Can you go and knock? Make sure she's all right?'

A few minutes later Rhona was back on the line saying, 'She's fine. Apparently she went to some magazine party, and was too wired to sleep when she got home so she put on a video. She said to have a good trip and to forget everything here, it's all in hand.'

'Maybe I should just give her a quick call.'

'Maybe you should just do as she says and have a good trip.'

As Laurie rang off she was picturing Sherry in her apartment, probably wrapped in her dressing gown and bleary-eyed from not enough sleep. What was she thinking, Laurie wondered. How was she feeling? Without speaking to her it was impossible to know, yet she didn't imagine Sherry would confide in her anyway. She wanted to ask her about the women, if there had been any news, but even that was feeling like an intrusion now.

Hating what was happening, on every level, Laurie picked up her suitcase and began to struggle with it down the stairs. She desperately wanted to stay here and retake control of the programme, but she couldn't think how to do it without offending Sherry, or disappointing Rhona. If only she didn't have such a guilty conscience about Nick she was sure she'd know how to handle this, but right now it was clouding everything.

She had no idea how much Sherry knew, but the way she was ignoring her calls had to mean she knew something, so was it wise to leave her programme – or more importantly, the fate of those women – in the hands of someone who must hate her? Instinct was telling her she shouldn't, but were her instincts to be trusted right now?

She didn't seem able to think straight about anything, but at least she knew Rose was flying back on Friday, by which time the dreaded wedding day would be about to dawn and there was absolutely no way in the world Laurie wanted to be in London for that.

Though the time spent filming the women last night would remain forever in Sherry's mind, and had upset her beyond anything she could ever have expected, this morning she was resolutely refusing to allow her emotions free rein on what she had seen. If she did, they would drag her into a quagmire of pity and confusion that simply wouldn't help her now. She needed to stay aloof, completely detached from that nightmare prison on the upper floor of a derelict engine shed between the East London gas works and an abandoned rail depot.

The hysteria that had greeted them as they'd prised open the door had taken a while to calm down. Just thank God they had employed an interpreter who was blessed with a level head, or the entire mission would have been doomed. The woman with the camera meant them no harm, he'd rapidly, but soothingly explained, she wanted only to take pictures, then she would come back to set them free. Sherry wondered now if their terror of a camera was a cultural inheritance, or if they'd already been exploited that way? Maybe she should have asked the interpreter, but he'd had his work cut out reassuring them that she really would come back.

She knew now that there were ten women in there, most of them no more than twenty, if that, and one small child. Whether this was Daya's daughter she had no idea, but it didn't matter, she still had to be rescued, as did all the others. The young girl holding the child had begged her to take the child now, but Sherry had to refuse.

'We *will* be back,' she'd made the interpreter promise as they left.

'When?' the girl had wanted to know.

'Soon. Very soon.'

One or two more nights surely wouldn't make a difference when they'd already suffered so much.

Now, even though she couldn't stop herself being haunted by those faces, or the unimaginable helplessness that afflicted them, she still wouldn't allow herself to be turned from her goal. She needed to focus on the next step, which was to put the videotape she'd shot into an envelope, together with two typed pages detailing everything the police would need to know should anything go wrong.

That done, she sat down at her computer to type out a brief set of instructions for the lawyer, telling him that if more than seventy-two hours passed before she returned to collect the envelope, it should be opened and appropriate action taken.

After printing the letter out she glanced at her watch. Still only nine fifteen, so plenty of time to feed and water the plants before she dropped into the lawyer's office on her way to Cinnabar Wharf, where hopefully Eddie Cribbs would be waiting.

'If this is a joke, Perry, my son,' Eddie Cribbs was saying into the phone, 'I'm not laughing.'

'I wish it was a joke,' Perry responded. 'But I'm afraid it's not.'

Eddie took the drink Gentle George was handing him. 'So what happened?' he wanted to know. 'How the fuck did the cops even know what plane the nonces was going to be on?'

'We're just starting to get wind of what they're calling Operation Comet,' Perry answered. 'According to the first news broadcast, a couple of minutes ago, the police have been working on this for months. Whether it's just us they're focusing on, or if it's part of something wider, we don't know yet. All we do know right now is our clients were arrested the minute they set foot in the country.'

Eddie fixed George with his flinty eyes and spoke to both of them as he said, 'I told you the kid should have been sent to Italy. It was a mistake letting them come here. Boy, was it a fucking mistake.'

'We don't know the damage yet,' Perry said. 'It could be they'll keep their mouths shut and not let on where they were going. Or who they've been dealing with.'

'Don't be obtuse, Perry. The cops must already know that or the Eyeties wouldn't have been arrested, would they?'

'Not necessarily. If they knew, they'd have come here first.'

Spotting Cheryl putting her head round the

456

bedroom door Eddie growled, 'Get the fuck back in there until I tell you to come out.' As she disappeared he said to Perry, 'Talk to Karima. We've got to get those bimbos moved.'

'To where?' Perry asked.

'How the fuck do I know? Just find somewhere.'

'But, Eddie,' Perry protested, 'only one of the Italians actually knows where they are, and he's not amongst those arrested. He's being taken care of, even as we speak, so I say keep the women where they are. If we start moving them around now we're going to end up with an even worse situation than we've already got.'

'He's right,' George said, able to hear. 'We got to keep cool. Don't do anything now that might draw attention.'

Eddie was glaring at him as he said to Perry, 'They were paying me a hundred grand for those women, and twenty for the kid. Have we got any of it?'

'No,' Perry replied. 'But we have to forget that now.'

Eddie's face turned even darker. 'I take it that website's off the air,' he growled.

'Already done,' Perry assured him.

Eddie sniffed and started to pace. 'I don't like it,' he grumbled. 'I don't like it one bit. First we got this fucking reporter ringing up demanding to see me this morning, and now the Eyeties are arrested coming in through the airport. So what's going on here, Perry, my son? Have we got someone grassing us up, because that's how it's fucking looking to me?'

'I admit, it could be the case,' Perry responded.

'Well you better get on it, boy, or we're all going on a journey we won't want to be taking.' He looked round as someone knocked on the door.

'It'll be Douglas with the cash you wanted,' George reminded him.

'Let him in,' Eddie snarled, looking at his watch. 'The reporter's due in ten minutes, keep her waiting outside when she gets here, let her know I don't appreciate being told what to do and where to be. Meantime,' he continued to Perry, 'fuck keeping those bimbos where they are. Put the emergency plan into operation right now. I don't want any trace of any one of them left. Do I make myself clear?'

'Crystal, Eddie,' Perry assured him. 'Absolutely crystal.'

A warm, welcome breeze was drifting aimlessly over the hillside, wandering like a tourist through the narrow cobbled lanes and quaint little archways, around the gleaming white houses with their red tiled roofs and clinging bougainvillea, moving up towards the rustic stone terrace of Rhona's family villa, where she was lying alone, next to the pool. The view down to the azure bay, where luxury yachts, ferries and tour boats were gliding in and out of their moorings, was as spectacular as it was soothing. Inside the shady living room, however, where Laurie was framed in an open window with vivid flowers tumbling from a long, terracotta pot, neither the view nor the sluggish heat of the day were helping to ease her tension.

Her foot tapped impatiently as she waited for her call to go through. It was beautiful here, but torture, when she was feeling so wretched for walking out on her responsibilities and so desperate to know why Elliot had disappeared on Andraya two nights ago. *Please God let there be a rift. Please, please, please God.*

At last she heard a ringing tone at the other end of the line, followed, to her unutterable relief, by Stan's gruff voice saying, 'Yup!'

'Stan! Thank goodness,' she cried. 'Where have you all been? What's happening over there?'

'Nothing special,' he answered casually. 'Why, what's up?'

'I've been trying to get hold of Sherry for days. Do you know where she is?'

'Yeah, she's gone to a meet with someone this morning, back around lunchtime, she said. I'll get her to give you a call.'

'What about the women? Have you made any progress? Do you need me over there? I should be there . . .'

'What for? We got it all taken care of. No need for a panic.'

She took a breath. Was that how she sounded, in a panic? 'Have you heard from Rose?' she demanded.

'Not yet. She's not due back till tomorrow.'

'So no delays?'

'No delays.'

Laurie flinched as a cannon in the bay boomed.

'Having a nice time over there, are you?' Stan enquired.

'Trying to,' she answered. 'Just finding it a bit difficult to switch off.'

'Give it a few more days,' he counselled.

'Always takes a while to wind down, when you goes on holiday. We'll keep you posted if we need to, but everything's fine over here.'

'OK,' she said. 'Thanks. And don't forget to tell Sherry to call.'

After ringing off she wandered back out to the pool and went to perch on the low stone wall to gaze down over the jungle of wild shrubs and hibiscus that spread like a carpet between their villa and the one below. She could hear the sound of a donkey's hooves approaching, the jangle of its bell and murmured song of its rider. A butterfly came to land on the valerian next to her, a gecko darted back from the edge of the pool.

'Everything OK?' Rhona asked, putting up a hand to shade her eyes.

'I think so,' Laurie answered, turning to her. 'I spoke to Stan. He told me not to panic.'

Rhona laughed. 'Then let's hope you listen to him,' she said, sitting up. 'What time are Nick and his daughter coming?'

'In about half an hour, which means we should think about getting dressed.'

'If it weren't for the daughter I'd stay like this,' Rhona responded, admiring her own nudity. 'But you look good in that bikini. Why cover it up?'

Casting her a wry look, Laurie lifted her legs and lay out along the wall. Talking to Stan had helped ease her conscience over the programme, at least to some degree, though it still hadn't done much for how she felt about Sherry. Nor had it even begun to address what might be going on with Elliot and Andraya. However, there really wasn't anything she could do about any of it right now, and with the sun feeling so good on her skin, and the prospect of a rift between Elliot and Andraya warming her heart, she decided to lie there just a little bit longer and try not to think about how disloyal she was being to Sherry for looking forward to Nick's arrival.

Chapter Twenty-Three

Sherry's eyes followed Eddie Cribbs's to the bearded giant seated on the chair adjacent to his own. It was the man who'd checked her for recording devices when she'd arrived and kept her waiting downstairs for over ten minutes, though he hadn't introduced himself, so she had no idea of his name. The same went for the sullen-faced individual in the corner, who was apparently paid to sit glowering in the background, like some token mute from a James Bond rip-off.

Likening this scene to a movie was working well for her, because certainly nothing about it seemed real. It could have been a scene from one of the bad – or even good – scripts that had come and gone from her father's study over the years. The gangster boss and his henchmen, and the heroine fighting to save the helpless victims he had in captivity. However, the script was about to take a radical turn from the norm, and even now, as she sat here with it all running around in her mind, she wasn't entirely sure she'd find the courage to go through with it.

As Cribbs's eyes came back to hers her heart gave a thump of unease. She'd just told him the address of where the women were, and that she had video footage of them, taken last night, stamped with the date.

'And you say this video is with a lawyer now?' he said, linking his fingers.

She nodded. 'That's right.'

'So you brought me no proof of its existence?'

'No. But I've just told you the address, so even if there weren't a video, which there is, I clearly know where the women are.' Telling him about the lawyer was, she hoped, her insurance for getting out of here.

His piercing eyes were fixing her so hard that after a while she felt herself starting to sweat. 'All right,' he said gruffly in the end, 'so what's the deal? You obviously want something from me, or you'd have gone straight to the police with what you've got.'

Not allowing herself even a moment's hesitation, she said, 'There's someone . . .' She cleared her throat. 'There's someone I'd like you to . . . get rid of.'

At that Cribbs's left eyebrow rose. 'And by get rid of, you mean what, exactly?' he said.

Sherry's insides were like water. Could she spell it out? Could she actually say the word that was buzzing wildly in her head now?

'All right, I think we both know what you mean,' Cribbs said, 'so who is this someone?'

'Her name is Laurie Forbes,' she told him. 'She's a reporter.'

He nodded. 'I know who she is.'

'She's on Hydra at the moment,' she added.

He turned to the man next to him. Neither of them spoke, but some kind of communication seemed to pass between them. In the silence that followed she could almost hear her heart banging against her ribs. 'And here was me thinking,' he said, sounding vaguely amused as he turned back, 'that you and Laurie Forbes was friends. Or colleagues at the very least.'

She didn't reply, merely stared at him with unblinking eyes.

Cribbs tilted his bulk forward and picked up his drink. 'So she's in a place called Hydra,' he said. 'Now where in the fuck is that, if you don't mind me asking?'

Having to clear her throat again, she said, 'It's a Greek island. Roughly a two-hour ferry ride from the mainland.'

His fleshy bottom lip jutted forward. 'As it so happens, we got a lot of friends in Greece, haven't we, George?' he said.

George nodded his bovine head.

'I'm intrigued to know,' Cribbs went on, settling himself more comfortably, 'why a nice girl like you would be making such a request. Not that I'm saying we can't help you, you understand, I'm just interested to know what's behind it all.'

'It's personal,' she answered, her breath so tight in her chest it was hard to speak.

'Yeah, well, it usually is,' he grunted. 'But it's OK, if you don't want to tell us your reasons you don't have to. What you do need to tell us though, is why we should trust you. I mean, we could do as you're asking, and what's to stop you going straight to the cops anyway?'

Though she was prepared for the question, her bravado was faltering badly. Even so, her voice sounded perfectly steady as she said, 'You know where my mother is.'

'Ah, yes, your cranky mother,' he said. 'I was momentarily forgetting. Bluebell. Wouldn't want no harm to come to her, I suppose.'

Sherry shook her head.

'And if you don't get out of here, this lawyer you've left the tape with has instructions to open it?'

She nodded.

He mulled it over. 'So,' he said finally, 'we do as you ask and pop off Laurie Forbes, you give us the videotape, then we all go merrily on our way and forget we ever knew anything about each other?'

Again she nodded.

He inhaled deeply. 'Well, that all sounds fine and dandy,' he commented, 'which it would be, if you was the only one what knew about the women. But you're not, are you? Someone had to have told you where they was, so what we need to sort out now, is who.'

'I'm afraid I can't reveal my sources,' she replied.

'Gentle George here could make it so's you can,' he suggested, helpfully.

Her eyes darted nervously to the big man.

Cribbs watched her and waited. In the end he was the first to break the silence. 'You got past my guard and filmed these women,' he said. 'Now I want to know how you managed it.'

'Bribery,' she replied.

His expression was loaded with scepticism. 'Of course bribery,' he responded. 'But who helped you? You couldn't have done it on your own, so who else is involved?'

'No-one. I did it alone,' she told him. 'I bribed the guard and went into the building.'

Sighing, he shook his head. 'I reckon you're spinning me a few Tom Peppers here, Sherry Mac,' he said, 'but all right, let's leave that for the moment and go back to Laurie Forbes. Apart from the fact that you and her have had some kind of a falling-out, which I've only got your word for, by the way, how do I know you haven't told her about this video? Convince me this isn't some kind of a set-up you two journo-lists are cooking up.'

'It isn't,' she replied.

'Just like that? It isn't.' He sipped his drink, glanced at George, then settled more comfortably again. 'Tell you what,' he said, after some minutes of deliberation, 'here's my offer: you tell me who's been helping you, and I'll see to it that your friend doesn't use the return part of her ticket from that Greek island. Now how's that for a deal?'

Sherry's mouth was turning dry. He really was going to do it, and she really was going to tell him what he wanted to know – she was just having trouble mustering enough conviction to support the next lie.

'Let's put it this way,' Cribbs said, 'you won't be walking out of this room until you tell us who helped you and I don't have a lot of time.'

'It was Karima Ghosh,' she stated, amazing

466

herself by how credible she'd managed to sound.

Cribbs's eyebrows reached for his hairline as he turned to George. 'Now that does surprise me,' he commented. 'That surprises me a lot.' He turned back to Sherry. 'You sure you're not telling me a tall one here?' he challenged.

'You asked, I've told you,' she replied, calmly, in spite of the erratic beat of her heart. Then reaching into her bag she pulled out a sheet of paper and stood up. 'Here's the address Laurie Forbes is staying at,' she told him. 'The method and actual planning I'll leave up to you.'

'Well that's big of you,' he declared, appearing faintly amused.

'I'd like it to be carried out by the end of the day on Saturday, if possible,' she said. 'If it isn't the video will go to the police. You'll find my number on that piece of paper. Once I've heard from you to confirm it's done, I'll bring you the tape.'

'You're not giving us much time, Sherry Mac,' he grumbled.

Without answering, she picked up her bag and walked to the door. No-one said anything. She couldn't quite believe they were allowing her to leave this easily. Was that it now, had she really achieved what she'd come here for?

'George, see the lady out,' Cribbs said.

George immediately got to his feet, yanked open the door and after making sure she was on her way down in a lift, returned to the flat.

Outside in the street Sherry took several gulps of air and started to shake uncontrollably. She had no idea if Cribbs would really do as she'd asked, but it had certainly sounded as though he would,

467

so instead of standing here, half-paralysed by the shock of it, she should focus on getting back to Laurie's office now, so that she could carry on with what needed to be done next.

Back in the flat George was helping himself to a Scotch. 'So what are you going to do?' he said to Cribbs, who'd already refreshed his own glass.

Eddie was looking thoughtful. 'If she's got a videotape, my son, and I do believe she has, then I'd say she's got us by the short and curlies.'

'But we've got access to her mother. She ain't going to do nothing when we can get to her.'

'How do you know that? She ain't never seen her in all this time. Could be she don't give a flying fuck what happens to the old bird, is just making out like she does.'

George still wasn't happy. 'But Laurie Forbes is press,' he reminded him. 'You know we don't go after press, if we can help it.'

'When needs must,' Eddie responded.

George regarded him over the rim of his glass. 'So do you want me to get hold of Nico in Piraeus, or what?' he said.

'It won't hurt to have a little chat,' Eddie replied. 'Whether he can pull it off by Saturday though . . .' He shrugged and downed his Scotch. 'This isn't turning out to be a good day, George,' he sighed. 'Not good at all. The cops have got the nonces, our reporter friend knows where the women are, and now the little tart is jerking my chain in a way I don't like one bit.' He began refilling his glass. 'Reckon it's time to cover our asses and fuck off out of here,' he decided.

'What about Karima Ghosh?' George said, speed-dialling Nico's number.

'I'll get Perry to make sure she's taken care of. He'll know what to do.'

'You're not going to talk to her, check it out first?'

'No time, George,' he replied. 'Get rid of all the evidence, that's what we need to do, and that includes the Berkeley what just walked out of here.'

'But what about the tape?'

'I admit that's a problem,' he conceded, taking the phone as George held it out. 'We'll find a solution. Nico, my friend, how are you?' he called down the line. 'Long time no speak. Course it's me, who the fuck else did you think it was? Can you hang on a minute?' He put a hand over the mouthpiece and said to George, 'Get yourself on over to my house and tell my missus to start packing. You know what other arrangements to make. I'll meet you at the boat by five.'

After George had gone he put his request to Nico, listened patiently to the string of expletives when Nico learned how fast he had to move, then agreed to pay double the going rate if he managed to pull it off.

'Right,' he said to Dougie as he put the phone down, 'you go and bring the car round, old son, while I take care of the silly bitch in the bedroom.'

Cheryl gaped at Eddie in astonishment. 'What was that for?' she cried, holding her stinging cheek. He'd never hit her before and she still couldn't quite believe he'd done it now.

'Take what's yours and get out of here,' he told her, going to the window to see what the kerfuffle was on the river path below.

'But why? What's happened? Where've I got to go?'

'I don't give a fuck where you go. Just get yourself out of here.'

Confused, and starting to feel afraid, she went to put her arms around him.

'Get your hands off me,' he growled, knocking her out of the way.

She gasped and crashed back on the bed. 'Eddie, what is it?' she cried. 'What have I done?'

He stared down at her, disgust contorting his fleshy features. 'What have you done?' he repeated, advancing on her. 'I'll tell you what you've done. You poked another man in *my* fucking bed, that's what you've done, you dirty little whore,' and grabbing her up by the hair he whacked her again.

'I don't know what you're talking about,' she wailed. 'I never poked anyone, except you. Honest, Eddie. I wouldn't do that . . .'

'Shut the fuck up,' he snarled. 'I don't want to hear it. I just want *you* out of here, and you can tell your boyfriend, Danny with the great big dick, you tell him from me, he's a dead man.'

'Eddie, no! You . . .'

'And if you know what's good for you, keep looking behind you, you *dirty* little whore.'

As he slammed the door behind him Cheryl picked herself up from the bed, limp with fear and trembling like a jelly. She had to call her mum. No, first she had to call Danny. How the fuck Eddie had found out she had no idea, but

470

from everything she'd heard today, he was in no mood to start messing around. If he said Danny was a dead man, then he meant Danny was a dead man.

Not bothering to take even half her clothes, she stuffed a few in a bag and crept gingerly out of the room.

Eddie was on the phone, so she managed to get past without being seen.

Out in the hall she pressed the button for the lift, and in her haste to get in she collided with Happy as he stepped out. 'Oh Happy, sorry,' she mumbled. She looked up at him. 'Eddie's really mad,' she told him. 'He's just chucked me out.'

'He tell you he knows about you and Danny?' he asked.

She nodded. 'Who told him? How did he find out?'

'It was that bloke Barry Davidson,' he answered. 'He got it from Suzy, who must have got it from Danny. Now if you know what's good for you, scram. There's a lot going on round here today, and if you ask me, you've got a lucky escape.'

Her face was streaked with mascara, her cheeks and one eye already starting to swell as she stepped out into the street to look for a cab. There were never any round here, so she'd have to call, but first she had to ring Danny.

'Oh fuck, where are you, where are you?' she wailed when his phone just rang and rang. 'I'm going to kill that bitch Suzy. I'm going to tear her limb from fucking limb.'

Putting her phone away, she tottered off down

the street, hefting her bag, still sobbing and swearing. In the back of her mind she was thinking about what she'd heard, because her mum had always told her make sure you listen, and remember what's important, because you could never have too much knowledge in the bank. Well, she reckoned it was important he was going to Spain on account of some nonces being arrested. Nonces was child molesters, she knew that, so this was bad. Then there was that Sherry woman who'd come in telling him she knew where some women were and asking him to off her friend. Some fucking friend she was. She'd recognized the name as well, because it was that poor cow whose bloke had chucked her when they was supposed to be getting married. Wonder what her horoscope was looking like for the month.

Anyway, none of that mattered right now, what did was getting hold of Danny – or killing that bitch Suzy. She'd call a cab first though, to take her home to her mum, then she'd ring Danny from there.

Sherry was back at Laurie's office, updating the files ready for Rose's return. Though outwardly she appeared calm, inside she was a seething mass of emotions. She wondered what Cribbs was doing at this moment, if he'd already contacted his Greek friends. What was Laurie doing over there on Hydra, apart from grieving for the wedding that now would never be? Where was Nick? He might even be with Laurie, but she didn't dwell on it, because though it hurt, it made no difference now.

Scrolling down to the end of the file, she typed

in the name and phone number of the lawyer who was holding the videotape they'd need for the programme, then the address of where the women were being held. After hitting the save button, she turned off the computer and gathered up her belongings ready to leave.

She took a long, last look round, knowing she'd never see the place again. She could have felt sad if she'd allowed it, but she merely turned away and went to let herself out of the door. After locking it, she put the keys back through the letter box and started down the street towards her flat. In a way she hoped Nick was with Laurie, for if he was, it would add even more justice to the punishment of her unforgivable betrayal.

Laurie and Rhona were laughing as Nick, much to his daughter's embarrassment, attempted to converse in terrible Greek with a waiter whose English was fluent.

'*Dad!*' Julia muttered under her breath, her eyes darting around to make sure no-one else was listening.

'What about this one?' Nick suggested, presenting his daughter to the waiter. 'She's yours for fifty roubles and a female donkey. Now how's that for a deal? Are you shaking your head. OK, no donkey and fifty roubles.'

'Dad, they use euros,' Julia said, rolling her eyes in Laurie's direction. 'He's not with us,' she informed the waiter. 'We've been trying to lose him all day, but he just won't go away.'

'Ah ha, now isn't that the truth?' Nick smiled. 'Ever since Adam turned up, first thing this

473

morning, she's been doing her damnedest to dump me. Her own father, and she'd rather be off with some hunk of a sixteen-year-old who doesn't even have the decency to be blighted with spots like most kids his age.'

'And who's Adam?' Rhona wanted to know.

'The son of the friends we're staying with,' Nick told her. 'He goes to school in the States, and just flew in for the summer holidays.'

'So, you're glad you came now,' Laurie said to Julia.

'I was until he started behaving like an idiot,' she replied, her pretty, fresh face not quite able to scowl away the laughter.

To the waiter, Rhona said, 'Just bring us margaritas all round.'

'Oh, cool,' Julia responded.

'Lemonade for the child,' Nick called after the waiter.

'I'm going to whack you,' Julia threatened.

'I think you would too,' he decided, looking at her. 'Don't you think she seems the type?' he demanded of Laurie. 'Those eyebrow and nose rings, the tattoo on the arm, the spiky black hair – she's blonde really, you know.'

'I remember,' Laurie assured him.

'Did she ask permission to turn herself into a gothic nightmare? Did she hell. Is she going to get it from her mother? Sure as hell.'

Laughing, Julia leaned against him, and snuggled into the arm he put round her.

'So tell us more about Adam,' Rhona encouraged. 'Cute, is he?'

'Very,' Julia assured her. 'He said he'd take me

474

to a disco tonight, if Father will allow it.'

'Absolutely out of the question,' he told her.

Julia looked at Laurie, and grinned as Laurie winked.

They were sitting outside a crowded café, right on the port, almost close enough to touch the nearest luxury yacht. The noise and bustle were enveloping them as stiflingly as the hot humid air, and every now and again a chorus of shrieks and laughter greeted the jarring and deafening explosions from the port cannons.

'What is that all about?' Laurie groaned as yet another went off.

'Oh it's probably some religious day,' Rhona told her, getting up to go to the Ladies. 'St Wilberforce, or someone like that. Just be thankful it's not Greek Easter. They fire them all day and all night for the entire weekend – and the whole island just goes party, party, party. '

'We need to come at Easter,' Julia informed her dad.

He was about to respond when a large, elderly woman with a big friendly smile and disposable Kodak elbowed past Rhona, saying, 'Excuse me, excuse me. I see you laughing and you look so happy with your family. Do you mind, I take a photo?'

Laurie started in surprise as she realized the woman was talking to her. Happy? How deceptive appearances could be, she thought, as Nick reached across the table for her hand.

'Click away,' he instructed.

Julia leaned back against him, while Laurie made herself sit in closer, not wanting to dampen the light-heartedness with unnecessary corrections. What did it matter if the old woman thought they were family? They'd never see her again, and it was sweet of her to want a photo of strangers, just because they looked happy.

'Say cheese,' the woman called in her throaty Greek accent.

They all smiled, and the woman's finger went down. At the same instant a cannon went off. Laurie almost jumped out of her skin. A group at the next table cheered and applauded. Someone suddenly turned the music up loud. Nick and Julia started laughing at something, and a man behind them leaped up on the table to dance.

Laurie looked round to say goodbye to the old woman, but she was already disappearing into the crowd. The margaritas arrived and Rhona came back. Then Nick's friends and their son turned up and more chairs were squeezed round their table. Plates of tsatsiki and calamares started to arrive. They all ate and drank, bantering with each other as the sun beat down on the canopy overhead and the lean island cats came to beg like dogs.

It seemed strange, Laurie was thinking, the way she was able to submerge herself in the mood of the moment, even though a part of her felt she was in the wrong place with the wrong people. But where was the right place now, and who were the right people? Tomorrow would have been her wedding day, but she would be here, thousands of miles from Elliot, with a man she barely knew, whose charm was like an elixir, and yet whose very presence filled her with guilt.

'I think we should all go to the disco tonight,' Nick suddenly decided.

'Yeah! That's a great idea,' Julia cried. 'Then I'll actually get to go.'

'You'll come too, won't you?' he said, looking at Laurie and Rhona.

'Of course,' Rhona assured him. 'I love to dance. So does my friend here, don't you, my friend?'

Laurie looked at Nick and felt some of the warmth drain from her smile. 'Yes,' she replied, not wanting to spoil the moment.

She'd make her excuses later, when they'd returned to their separate villas for siestas. It wasn't that she didn't want to go, because a part of her did – certainly it would be a lot better than sitting at home thinking about what she would have been doing on the eve of her wedding, if Elliot hadn't changed his mind – but she was very much afraid that more drink, a late night and dancing would conspire with her sadness to throw her into bed with Nick again. Not that he'd made a single gesture or comment to push her in that direction, but the chemistry was there, she could feel it, and was certain he could too.

'Rhona threatened me with physical violence if I didn't come,' she told him later, while dancing in his arms, 'but I feel as though I'm using you to hide from the pain, and that's not fair to you, or to Sherry.'

'I admit, I feel bad about Sherry too,' he responded, 'but if the feelings aren't there what am I supposed to do?'

Wondering if that was how Elliot talked about her, she said, 'Hurt her as little as possible,' and her eyes went down as she realized the hypocrisy of what she was saying.

Tilting her face to his, he kissed her gently on the mouth. She wasn't sure she wanted it to continue, but she made no attempt to pull away. She was thinking of Elliot and what he might be doing now. It hurt, unbearably, but though it felt wrong, being in the arms of another man, she pushed herself in closer to Nick and felt his desire. She imagined him making love to her the way he had before, and became torn between longing and despair. Then she thought of Sherry, and was again racked with guilt. She started to pull away, but asked herself, what purpose would it serve to turn back now? The damage was already done and she really didn't want to be alone tonight.

Barry was sitting in his parked Fiesta shouting into the phone. 'Sherry! Where are you?' he cried. 'I've got to talk to you. Please pick up if you're there.'

He waited, sniffing and banging a fist against the gearstick.

'Sherry,' he said. 'There's been an accident. Suzy and Danny . . .'

'I'm here,' she said, coming on the line. 'What about Suzy and Danny?'

As the horror of what had happened swept over him again he ducked his head and dropped it against the wheel. 'They've been killed, Sherry,' he said. 'I just had a call. Danny's car was totalled. They're both dead.'

He waited for her to respond, but there was no sound from the other end of the line.

478

'Did you hear me?' he demanded. 'Are you still there?'

'Yes, I heard you. What happened? Do you know?'

'They said it was a lorry. The driver fell asleep at the wheel, is what they're saying. He's in hospital now, all cut up, but the point is, Sherry, I told Eddie Cribbs that Danny was poking his girlfriend and now Danny's dead.'

'Why did you tell him that?' Sherry cried.

'I had to. He was threatening my mum. He wanted information on you, so I had to give him something.'

'What did you tell him about me?'

'Nothing. Just stuff he already knew, but he was having none of it. So I ended up telling him about Danny and Suzy.'

Sherry took a breath. 'Look, Barry, I'm really sorry about what's happened, but it sounds like an accident. If the driver's in hospital too . . .'

'It's my fault,' Barry sobbed. 'Don't you understand that?'

'No, I don't. And I'm afraid I don't have time for this now. I have to go. Sorry,' and the line went dead.

Barry stared at the phone in disbelief. 'Bitch!' he seethed, as he clicked it off. 'Cold, stuck-up fucking bitch.'

Dropping his head against the window, he stared helplessly up at the sky and wondered what fucking good came out of trying to do right in the world, because as far as he could see none ever did.

*

479

Cheryl's mother drew back from her net curtains, where she'd been clocking the new people moving in opposite. More Asians, but they was generally a lot politer than the bloody crack-head whites you got around here, so she weren't complaining.

'Mum! Are you listening?' Cheryl wailed. 'What am I gonna do?'

'You stay on the right side of the press, that's what you do,' her mother answered, lighting a cigarette. 'You always get on the right side of them whenever you can, and here's your chance.'

'But Danny's dead, Mum. They might come after me next.'

'That's why you've got to forget about him now, girl, and look after yourself. Eddie's already in Spain with his wife, so he ain't thinking about you, is he? And no-one need ever know it was you what tipped off the press. You don't have to give your name. Just tell 'em what you know and hang up.'

'Well that's clever, innit? How am I supposed to get on the right side of them if they don't even know who I am?'

'You wait and see what happens,' her mother responded through her teeth. 'If it all works out right for the press girl, Laurie What's-her-name, you let them know it was you who tipped 'em off and saved the day. They'll be eating out of your hand, my girl, you mark my words.'

'But I still don't know who to call. We already tried her programme, and no-one's answering.'

'What was the bloke's name?' her mother demanded. 'The one she was supposed to be marrying?'

'I don't know. Russell something, I think.'

'Elliot Russell! That's him. That's who you've got to speak to. He's really big. Get on the right side of him . . .'

'But he just chucked her, Mum! What's he going to care that someone's going to try and off her?'

'Try not to be stupid all your life. Just pass me that directory. If we can't find anything in there, I'll call Jim, up the newsagents, he'll know how to get hold of the bloke.'

Elliot looked at the phone, not at all sure he'd just heard correctly. 'Run that by me again,' he said to Murray, his office manager.

'I don't know who she was,' Murray told him, 'she wouldn't give her name, but she's claiming Eddie Cribbs has put a contract out on Laurie and it's going to happen on a Greek island. Those were her exact words, then she hung up. I've tried calling Laurie, and Rhona, but their mobiles are out of range. That's why I'm calling you, to get the number at the villa.'

'I don't have it, but Sherry will.' He could feel the blood draining from his face, the tightness of his hand as he held the phone.

'I've tried Sherry. No answer, but I've left messages all over. And for Rose. Their flight was delayed so they didn't get back until the early hours . . .'

'Send someone round there to wake her up,' Elliot barked.

'Someone's already on the way.'

Elliot was thinking fast, too fast. 'They must have found those women,' he said. 'Shit, where the hell is Sherry? Is there a contract on her? There must be.'

'Someone's on the way over there too,' Murray told him. 'I'm ringing round trying to get word on Cribbs's whereabouts. I just thought I should let you know, and find out if you had a number for the villa.'

'You're damned right you should have let me know,' Elliot raged. 'I should have been the first person you called.'

'You would have been once,' Murray reminded him.

Only too aware that today should have been his wedding day, and how dimly even his own staff viewed his break-up with Laurie, Elliot snapped, 'Get me on a flight to Athens. I'm going over there.'

'From New York it's going to take . . .'

'I'm still here, in London,' Elliot cut in, not bothering to explain that their departure had been delayed. 'Call me back with the flight details,' he said, and hung up just as Andraya came twirling into the bedroom.

'What do you think?' she crooned, her arms spread wide for him to get a full view of the extraordinary black dress she'd just had fitted by the designer in the sitting room. He'd never seen anything like it. It was quite possibly one of the sexiest garments ever created, but not for the first time lately, he was failing to rise to the occasion.

'Isn't it divine?' she purred, coming towards him. 'Don't you just love it?'

'I'm afraid something's come up,' he responded tersely, grabbing her hands as she started to

482

embrace him. 'I'm taking the next flight to Athens.'

Her eyes opened wide with shock. 'What can possibly be so important . . .' Then it registered. 'It's her, isn't it?' she hissed. 'She's in Greece. Well, over my dead body are you . . .'

'I don't have time for this,' he told her, attempting to push past.

Her eyes flashed with outrage as she spun him back. 'You're coming to New York with me!' she spat.

He stared down at her. 'I'm not going anywhere with you,' he said and easing her firmly aside he moved on into the bedroom.

Fury contorted her features as she stormed after him. 'How dare you speak to me that way!' she seethed. 'You are with me now, not her! She is nothing, *nothing*.'

He was hauling a bag from an overhead cupboard and didn't bother to reply.

'We are going to New York tomorrow,' she shouted. '*You* are coming to New York.'

Still he said nothing as he began gathering things from the bathroom and stuffing them into the bag. He was just zipping it when something extremely hard hit him on the side of the head.

'Don't you dare ignore me!' she screamed, throwing the painting down. 'You are not walking out on me, do you understand? I am *not* letting you go.'

'Andraya, please, just get out of the way,' he said, forcing himself to remain calm.

'You are not going anywhere,' she raged. 'You are staying here . . .'

He moved towards her.

'You are staying here,' she growled, banging her fists into him as he tried to pass by.

Grabbing her wrists, he pulled her round behind him then pushed her down on the bed.

'Aaaaagh!' she screamed, throwing herself at him as he made to pick up his bag. 'You are not walking out on me! No-one ever walks out on me . . .' She gasped as he pushed her on to the bed again. She glared up him, her eyes flashing demonically, then thrusting her hips forward she locked his waist with her legs and started to pull him on top of her.

Grabbing her ankles, he wrenched himself free, and shoved with all his might, so that she backward-somersaulted off the edge of the bed to land upside down with her legs over her shoulders and naked bottom jutting up in the air.

'You bastard,' she screamed, her voice muffled by her own chest and hair. 'You lousy, fucking bastard.'

Seconds later he was descending the stairs to the gallery. 'Rachel!' he shouted, throwing open the door.

'What is it?' she cried, appearing from the office. 'What on earth was going on upstairs?'

'It doesn't matter. Do you have the number of Rhona's villa?'

'No. Why? What's happened?'

'Nothing. I don't know. Have you spoken to Sherry?'

'Not in the last few days. Elliot! What's going on?'

'I'm going over to Hydra,' he told her. 'I won't be coming to New York . . .'

484

'Elliot, for God's sake! Has something happened to Laurie?'

'I don't know,' he answered. 'Just keep trying Sherry, will you? And we need the number of that villa.'

Chapter Twenty-Four

Nick was sitting on the villa wall, gazing out at the spectacular view that was so clear today it made the distant hills of the Peloponnese, over on the mainland, appear much closer than they actually were. The sea between shimmered like crystals in the sunlight, the rocks that towered either side of the port and rose up behind the villa like avenging gods seemed almost as though they would melt in the heat.

Looking round as he heard someone coming outside, he shifted along the wall to make room for Laurie to sit down. 'How are you feeling?' he said.

'Strange. A bit hung-over and a bit disoriented. Time differences help, I'm finding.'

He smiled.

'Did you get hold of Julia?' she asked.

'She's gone sailing with Adam.'

'Did she mind that you didn't go back last night?'

'I don't think so. She's too wrapped up in her

own crush to concern herself with mine.'

Laurie flushed and looked down at her hands. 'Nick, I . . .'

'It's OK,' he told her gently. 'I know it's too soon. I shouldn't have said that.'

Forcing a smile, she brought her eyes to his. 'You're a wonderful man,' she told him. 'Whatever happens in the future, I'll always remember you for this.'

His eyebrows went up, but he said nothing, as he turned to look back at the view.

Following his gaze she found herself thinking of how he'd come to Sherry's rescue in her time of greatest need. It was no wonder Sherry had fallen so hard, if he'd been as sensitive and caring as this – she could easily fall herself, were she not so incapable of detaching herself from Elliot. Earlier she'd remembered a funny little cartoon she'd seen once, that had depicted a woman sitting on a train, while her heart, still attached to her by a spring, was on another train waiting alongside it. As the two journeys began the trains moved along parallel tracks so the heart was always in the woman's view and always at the same distance from her. But after a while the tracks started to move away from each other, and the further apart they went, the more the spring stretched – until finally, unable to resist the woman's need of it, the heart allowed the spring to carry it back to her, leaving the other train to go on its way. Maybe it was saying that the woman had finally reined in her heart, rescuing it from a journey it had stubbornly insisted on going on even though it had been told it wasn't wanted. Whatever, the message was still the same – the woman and her heart couldn't live without each other.

It saddened her greatly that the cartoon had come back to her on what should have been her wedding day. It seemed to be telling her that she and Elliot were on separate tracks now and she should take back her heart because it was hers, not his. She couldn't help wondering again, as she had all day, what he was doing now, if he was thinking of her at all, or blocking her totally from his mind.

'Rhona still sleeping?' Nick asked.

'Mm. Too much wine at lunchtime again.'

He smiled and batted away a fly. 'Feel like taking a walk?'

It was too hot, but she was restless enough to want to do something rather than just sit here.

'There's a beautiful cemetery up at the top,' she said. 'I'll show it to you, if you like.'

'A cemetery,' he said, with no small irony. 'What better to cheer us up?'

Laughing, Laurie said, 'I'll leave a note for Rhona, or she'll be sure to worry.'

Karima Ghosh was standing at one of the boarded-up windows, staring at the chinks in the wood as though she could see through the dazzling cuts of light. She had been here for almost twenty-four hours, tricked into this prison by a guard who had pushed her inside and locked the door. She knew exactly what it was about. The Italians had been arrested, no-one knew what might come of it, so all the evidence had to be destroyed. And she was part of the evidence.

There was no comfort to be gained in standing here planning her revenge on a man she'd only ever shown loyalty to. He was long gone. He cared nothing for her. To him she was no different to the pig-women she was locked up with – in his eyes they were all dark-skinned, foreign, and disposable.

She'd always known this day would dawn, which was why she was finding it so hard to forgive herself for not realizing before they came that it was here. She'd spent years preparing for it, planning an escape route, banking money offshore, arranging a new identity for herself and purchasing an insignificant home in a remote part of India. But instead she was here. There was no escape. This was how it was all going to end, not in her beloved homeland where she might finally have found a sanctuary for her troubled soul, but here, in the way she'd always dreaded. Ever since she was a child, and had watched her mother throw herself on her father's funeral pyre, she had lived in morbid terror of fire. Suttee was outlawed, her mother should never have done it, but she had and Karima had never forgotten it. It was when she had started to hate the world.

Turning round, she found the Neela girl's eyes on her again. That child saw too much. She understood what was going on here, even if the others didn't. Karima hated her. She couldn't wait for the flames to devour those hideously knowing eyes.

The others were all talking about suffocation, because they still thought the men were going to come. There were moments, though, when they believed they might be rescued. What difference did it make? They were all going to die anyway, so let them suffocate each other. She'd take pleasure in watching them, and never would she stoop low enough to ask them to suffocate her too – not even when the flames came. Her glance flicked to the Neela girl again, and in those unnervingly watchful eyes she saw her own lie.

Elliot was on the point of telling the cab driver to speed up when his mobile rang. Seeing who it was he clicked on immediately. 'Rose. Thank God.'

'Where are you?' she said.

'In a taxi, on my way to Heathrow. Do you have the number?'

'Yes. I've just spoken to Rhona . . .'

At last someone had made contact. 'Is Laurie OK?' he barked.

'The last Rhona knew she was fine. She's out for a walk at the moment, with Nick van Zant.'

Elliot was thunderstruck. 'What's *he* doing there?' he demanded, an image of the two of them outside Davey's suddenly flashing in his mind, and shocking him even further.

'I really wouldn't know,' Rose responded smoothly, 'but since Rhona's informing the police, and Nick's with Laurie, I think we can presume she's in safe hands. So it seems there's no need to postpone your trip to New York, after all,' and with that she rang off.

The tall iron gate in the wall creaked into the hilltop silence as Laurie pushed it open and stepped into the cemetery garden. Nick was behind her, moving equally slowly in the heat after their climb up through the meandering lanes and gleaming whitewashed houses. There was no-one about, the air was quite still, and the sky stretched in an endless swathe of blue out to the far hills of the Peloponnese.

'It's so peaceful here,' she whispered, as they wandered over the gravel towards the nearest white marble tombstones.

'Beautiful,' he replied. Then after a beat, 'Why are we whispering?'

She laughed softly. 'Look,' she said, stopping in front of an elaborately decorated grave. 'It's so small. I wonder what the lettering says. According to the dates he or she was only eight years old.'

'It was a he,' he told her, leaning forward to ease some flowers aside. 'There's his picture.'

Laurie's heart stirred as she looked at the cheek-ily smiling face. 'I wonder what happened to him,' she said.

Nick squeezed her hand and turned to walk on, winding a path through the exquisitely sculpted Greek crosses and cherubs, admiring the urns bursting with flowers and the brass lanterns and chalices for burning incense and candles. Reaching the end of a pathway he stood between two towering conifers and gazed out at the view. 'They might be dead,' he said as Laurie joined him, 'but they've got one of the best spots on the island.'

Laurie gazed out to the tranquil yet dazzlingly vivid blue sea and sky, up over the giant grey rocks with their sparse coating of gorse and trees, and back down to the tiny specks of houses huddled in the bowl of the bay. It was as still as a painting, as sharp as a photograph. Nothing moved, except the sunlight on the water.

'No boats, no people,' Nick murmured. 'No birds. No sounds.'

'Because all sane creatures are taking a siesta,' she responded, looking back as she heard the jangling of a donkey bell. She smiled to see a young priest in a tall black hat and black robes riding side-saddle along the track towards the cemetery wall. He gave a friendly wave, so she waved back and watched as he dismounted and came in through the gate.

'I keep meaning to ask Rhona what the difference is between Greek Orthodox Christianity and our own,' she said, as the priest disappeared into the shady gloom of the church.

Nick was about to answer when the sound of running water made him turn round. A woman in a black headscarf was rinsing her vases under a tap. 'I didn't realize anyone else was here,' he remarked.

'Maybe she was praying inside the church.'

They watched the woman carry her vases to a grave, then kneel down to arrange the flowers she'd brought.

'Do you feel as though we're intruding?' Laurie whispered.

'I'm not sure,' he replied, looking around. 'Cemeteries are strange places. Beautiful, but scary.' He winked, and taking her hand he led her to stand in front of a big old family sepulchre.

'Whenever I look at these,' she said, 'it makes me think of waking up to find you've been buried alive.'

'That wouldn't be a good start to the day,' he commented.

Laughing, she strolled on to the next grave, which was barely visible beneath a blanket of white lilies. The scent made her think of Sherry and wonder what she was doing now. Hearing the tread of Nick's footsteps on the gravel, moving along to another grave, she recalled their love-making last night and again this morning. When she was with him she could lose herself totally in the pleasure they shared, and she felt a tremendous affection towards him for understanding what she needed and being generous enough to give it. It wasn't serious for her though, which made what she was doing to Sherry so much worse. How selfish she'd become in her heartache, how shallow in the use of her friends.

'What are you thinking about?' Nick asked, coming to slip an arm round her shoulders.

'Sherry,' she answered.

He made no reply and she wondered how troubled his conscience was too.

'I need to go back to London,' she told him. 'I have responsibilities there, and I can't do this to Sherry any more.' She turned to look up at him. 'I know you say you don't have the right feelings for her, but that doesn't mean she doesn't have them for you, or make what we're doing right.'

'Excuse me,' a voice called from behind them.

They turned round to see the woman in the black headscarf coming towards them, the sunlight behind her.

Nick squinted as he tried to make out her face. 'Isn't that who took the photo, down at the café?' he said.

'I think it is,' Laurie replied, starting to smile.

'Hello,' she said, as the woman drew closer.

'I see you here,' the woman said, beaming with delight. 'I remember you and I want to show you the picture I take. I have it here.' She was reaching into a big black canvas bag.

'Already?' Laurie commented, impressed. 'That was quick.'

'Boom, bang,' the woman chuckled.

Laurie frowned, then laughed as she realized she must be referring to the cannon that had gone off as she'd taken the picture. Glancing up at Nick she murmured, 'Can't wait to see this.'

His eyes were narrowed with amusement as he watched the woman search. Then a quick flash of light drew his attention to the church.

Laurie was about to take the photo from the woman when suddenly Nick's hands slammed into her. At the same instant a deafening explosion rang out round the hillside.

Laurie was falling back. Pain shot through her side.

Nick started for the church. The old woman threw herself against him.

As they struggled Rhona came in through the gate shouting Laurie's name.

Nick swung round.

The old woman broke free and started to run.

The priest was ahead of her, black robes flying, as he dodged through the tombstones.

Laurie blinked up at the sky.

'Are you all right?' Nick said, dropping down beside her.

She winced as she struggled to sit up.

'Oh my God,' Rhona gasped, running up to

them. 'Are you hurt? Don't try to move.'

'She's OK,' Nick said. 'Her shoulder hit the gravestone as she went down.'

Laurie gave a shake of her head, still dazed by the shock of it. 'What the *hell* was all that about?' she demanded.

'Are you sure you're all right?' Rhona persisted.

'Yes. What are you doing here?' She looked at Nick. 'I can't believe that just happened. Who was she?'

'I've called the police,' Rhona told them, 'with any luck she won't get away.'

Nick was looking in the direction the woman had taken off in, and seeing the priest lifting her over a fence he said, 'He was the one with the gun. I saw him come out of the church . . .'

Suddenly registering Rhona's words, Laurie said, 'You've already called the police?'

'I got a call from Rose, about fifteen minutes ago,' Rhona explained. 'Apparently Eddie Cribbs is behind this.'

Laurie gaped at her, until suddenly realizing what it must mean she began struggling to her feet. 'Sherry's found the women,' she declared. 'Has anyone spoken to her? Is she all right?'

'Apparently they're trying to find her,' Rhona answered. 'Rose has all the details.'

By the time they got back to the villa shock had set in, causing Laurie to shake uncontrollably as she spoke to Rose on the phone. 'But someone must have heard from her,' she cried. 'She has to have called someone, so where the hell is she?'

'We're all on it,' Rose assured her. 'The police are here now, at her flat. There's no sign of a break-in, but they're searching the place to see what they can find.'

'What about Barry and Stan? Have you . . . ?'

'I've left messages for both. Apparently the porter saw her going out this morning. She was carrying a heavy bag, so there's a chance someone tipped her off and she's gone into hiding.'

'Oh God, please let that be true,' Laurie murmured.

'I have to go,' Rose said. 'As soon as there's any news, I'll call you back.'

Laurie put the phone down and went to pick up the whisky Rhona had poured her. 'I should never have left,' she said. 'It felt wrong. Oh God, if anything's happened to her . . .'

'Let's not start jumping to conclusions,' Rhona cut in, glancing over her shoulder as someone thumped on the door.

'I'll go,' Nick said.

Laurie's eyes went to the phone as it started to ring. Please let it be Sherry, or at least someone letting them know she was all right.

Being the closest, Rhona picked it up. 'Yes, she's here,' she said into the receiver, her eyes moving to Laurie. 'She's fine. I don't know. I'll ask her,' and putting a hand over the mouthpiece she said, 'It's Elliot. Do you want to talk to him?'

Laurie felt suddenly dizzy. He was the last person she'd expected to hear from. Did he know what was happening? Was that why he was calling? Or had he remembered today should have been their wedding day? She looked round as Nick led two uniformed policemen into the room.

Rhona put the phone back to her ear. 'I'm sorry,'

she said, 'she's busy right now.'

Laurie watched as she hung up.

Rhona grinned and gave a satisfied waggle of her eyebrows.

Nick was struggling with his Greek to introduce the officers.

Taking pity, Rhona came to his assistance.

Laurie looked at the phone, willing it to ring, then reaching for it, she said, 'I'm sorry, I have to speak to Rose again.'

'It's only been five minutes,' Rose reminded her, when she asked if there was any news yet.

'What about the women? Have you turned up anything to say she found them?'

'Nothing so far, we're still trying to get into her computer. I just had a call from Barry though.'

'And?'

'He doesn't know where she is, but he says . . . I think you'd better brace yourself for this, apparently the two people he put her in touch with, the ones working for Eddie Cribbs, were killed in a car crash last night. All the evidence says it was an accident, but considering the timing . . .'

Laurie sat down heavily on the chair behind her. 'He's killed her,' she mumbled. 'Eddie Cribbs has . . .'

'We don't know that,' Rose cut in. 'Barry spoke to her last night. He said she sounded a bit strange, which could mean . . .'

'That someone was there with her.'

'Laurie, stop doing this to yourself. Whatever's happened to her, we're going to find her.'

'I'm coming back,' Laurie said. 'As soon as we've dealt with the police here, we'll be on our way.'

Karima couldn't understand why it hadn't happened yet. The emergency procedure had long been in place, she knew it almost to the letter. Whichever building was being used would be burned to the ground. Everything and everyone inside must perish. There would be no way of identifying the charred remains of the bodies, because they belonged to non-people. They simply didn't exist. Nor was there any kind of paper trail to lead anywhere but the London Borough of Tower Hamlets, who owned the derelict two-storey shed. Burning it down would probably do them a favour, and in less than a week everyone but the insurance company would have forgotten it even existed.

So why hadn't anything happened yet?

She'd been here for more than two nights now, and voices were starting to jabber in her head. The stench all around was as nauseating as the pig-women themselves, the air was clogged with it, the corner where they relieved themselves steamed with it. Flies swarmed in through the cracks in the wood. The floors and mattresses crawled with more bugs and vermin than any normal human being could stand. The pig-women had started to eat the bugs. There had been talk of catching the rats and eating them too. Most of the talk, though, was of the woman who'd said she'd come back to rescue them, but still hadn't. They were at last beginning to understand that she never would. They'd been left here to die. Some thought it would be of starvation, since no-one had brought food for days, others were still terrified of being given to the men.

Earlier a vote had been taken. They'd all agreed that rather than wait and suffer, they'd take their own lives while they still could. All that remained to be decided was when. Karima, or Mota Ben as they called her, hadn't been part of the vote. It was as though she wasn't there. No-one even looked in her direction, but she could feel their hatred. It burned all the way into her, like flames, the flames that would eventually devour them all.

She'd never known hunger before, didn't understand the tricks it played on the mind. It gnawed at her now, as the rats gnawed at the filth. She watched them and felt their ugly teeth chewing her insides. She was ready to grab anything from any one of the pig-women now, and stuff it into her own mouth before they could stuff it into theirs. She imagined doing it and her stomach heaved even as it craved.

The filthy child cried constantly with hunger. The Neela girl soothed her and watched Karima with her demonic eyes. Karima noticed she rarely spoke to anyone, but she saw everything and understood more. She knew Mota Ben had been sent here to perish with them. Maybe the others knew too, but only the Neela girl watched her, seeming to sense her fear.

The day moved on. Karima dozed for a while. When she woke the small bands of light that forced their way in through the boards were fading, and the women were gathered around the older one, Ekta. Something was up, she could tell by the tension in the putrid air. Her first thought was of rescue – that the pig-women's deluded prayers for the mysterious woman to return had in some way been answered. Then, through the gloom, she saw what they were doing, and understood with a terribleness beyond all terribleness that they were deciding the order in which they were going to die.

Some were crying, some prayed and some were utterly silent. Their eyes appeared huge in their gaunt, haunted faces, their saris too copious for their fleshless bones. No-one spoke to her, it was as though they had forgotten she was even there. They wouldn't put her out of her misery, they would leave her to starvation or flames.

She watched in horror as the first woman lay down and Ekta put a pillow over her face. Someone else was holding the Neela girl's child, while Neela held the hands of the woman about to die. Everyone was praying. The air seemed to fill with fear and choke with sorrow. It took a long time. The woman twitched and fought. The others held her down, while Neela pressed her own weight onto the pillow with Ekta's.

Finally it was done, and everyone gazed in disbelief at the corpse. It had seemed so hard, yet now so easy.

The next woman lay down. She blessed Ekta, then gave Neela her hands as the pillow covered her face. It was the same process, she twitched and fought, but then she panicked and managed to throw them off. The instinct to live was as great as the will to die. For a while everyone sat quietly. Some were panting, others were quietly sobbing. Eventually the woman summoned her courage and lay down again. This time they were able to hold her until finally the twitching and resistance stopped.

The third woman peeled herself from her friend's arms and lay down. Death came more quickly and quietly to her than to the others.

The fourth woman took a long time to pray. No-one hurried her, just waited until she was ready to go.

The fifth woman broke down and begged for mercy. She had lost her courage, she wanted to live.

Karima continued to watch, huddled in her corner, stupefied and terrified as one by one the women were released from the prisons of their bodies and baleful surroundings.

By the time Neela and the child lay down, Karima's panic had grown to such a pitch that her mouth was spurting gibberish and her ears were filled by the roar of flames. She was a child again. The crowd was praying, the procession moved on. Her tiny mother was in her arms. Fire was raging up, huge red and yellow tongues, coiling around them like snakes. She could smell her flesh burning, feel it melting from her bones. She was tearing her hair. Saliva foamed from her lips, snot bubbled from her nose, excrement from her bowels. She was going to die in the fire.

Suddenly she leaped up, grabbed the Ekta woman's pillow and lay down with it over her own face.

Neela's eyes went to Ekta, then to Mota Ben's quivering limbs. Shaila's fingers were digging painfully into Neela's neck. Terror had struck the child dumb and turned her into a vice.

Ekta looked at Neela and Neela gave her consent. Mota Ben could die first.

There were only three other women still alive, and each one of them came to throw her weight over Mota Ben's pillow, eager to be a part of this evil woman's death.

Suddenly Mota Ben didn't want to die. She raged and fought. Her body twisted and contorted. The women's hatred overpowered her, their weight seeming to increase in their resolve to end their tormentor's life.

After Mota Ben was dead the women kicked her body across the floor, back into her corner. One of them rammed her head against the wall, as though she were still alive and could feel it. Another lifted her sari and urinated all over her.

When the excitement was over and adrenalin started to wane, Neela returned to her mattress and lay down with Shaila again. Ekta came to stand over them. Neela's heart was full of sadness. She had come to love Ekta and didn't want to leave her to die alone.

'Ambamata, Jagadambe, Mother of the Universe,' Ekta whispered as she lowered the pillow, 'with your kindness we have all happiness and with your blessing no fear at all . . .'

Neela listened and clung trembling to Shaila. Now the moment was here, the will to live was strong. 'We are going to be with Mummy,' she'd told Shaila earlier. 'Mummy is waiting for us.'

The darkness was horrible, the sensation terrifying. Everything in her began a fight for air. Her hands lost the struggle to stay still, her legs rose up to protect her. Shaila fought too, and started to scream. She broke free and fled into the darkness.

Ekta looked into Neela's eyes.

Neela understood. They would have to set Shaila free first.

When it was over Neela held her niece's thin, lifeless body in her arms and lay down with her. Her eyes were dry, her heart shed the tears of a thousand lifetimes.

Ekta was very tired, had little strength left. The other women came to help her, terrified now, as they realized there might be no release for them.

In the end Neela went peacefully. When they took the pillow away there was no need to close her eyes, as there had been with some of the others. Neela's were already closed.

Too weak now to help anyone else, Ekta began winding her sari around her neck.

The others watched her and started to wail.

They were still wailing as Ekta hanged herself from a beam. Then one by one each of the remaining women hanged herself too, and all became silent and still on the upper storey of the rail shed.

Minute after minute ticked by. The dangling bodies ceased to sway, the only movement in the room was the rats and flies. Tiny threads of moonlight wove through the darkness. The colourful saris were like flowers, adorning the bodies they covered. Matted strands of once glossy black hair fell over once beautiful faces. Silken lashes curled from unmoving eyelids. Some lips were parted, others weren't. A hennaed hand rested limply against a pillow, another was almost touching the hand of a friend. One tiny foot lay twisted towards the other. A rat climbed on to a mattress, hunted round then scurried off again. Everything was quiet. No one would abuse them again. They were

503

free now. No-one could ever harm them again.

Outside a train thundered by, and somewhere in the distance a dog barked.

After a while a car pulled up outside and some people leaped out.

Laurie reached the green wooden doors first and began to thump. Rose and the crew were right behind her, not a camera in sight.

'Stand back,' Stan ordered.

Moments later he'd broken the lock and they were charging up the stairs.

'Hello! Hello! Is anyone in there?' Laurie yelled when they reached the door at the top.

The silence from within chilled her heart. She turned to Rose, then to Stan. 'Are you sure it was here?' she said.

'Give me a hand,' he said to the two guys from the crew.

The door finally burst open. The foul stench assailed them, almost pushing them back. Beams of torchlight began whizzing around the room.

'Jesus H. Christ,' Stan muttered.

'Oh my God, no,' Laurie gasped in horror. She was staring at Ekta's wide-open eyes.

Rose was pushing her way through. 'They can't all be dead,' she cried, skimming her torch over one lifeless form after another.

Immediately everyone threw themselves into action to begin checking. 'Oh God, here's the child,' Laurie cried, lifting Shaila's little body.

'Let me,' Stan said, easing her aside.

Laurie turned instantly to the young girl next to her. 'Please, God, please, please,' she muttered, feeling for a pulse.

'I think this one's still with us,' one of the crew suddenly shouted from his side of the room.

A moment later Rose cried, 'This one is too.'

'And this one,' another voice cried.

Finding a faint flickering in Neela's wrist, Laurie immediately began thumping her chest and blowing air down her throat. 'Come on, come on,' she urged. 'Please. *Please!*'

Stan was still working diligently on the child, concentrating on her to the exclusion of all else.

'It's all right. It's all right,' Rose was saying to someone. 'Don't be afraid. We're here to help. Gino, call the police,' she shouted to one of the crew.

'Already done,' he responded.

Neela's eyes started to open. Laurie hurriedly gave her more air. 'Stay with me,' she murmured. 'Please. Don't go.' She blew again and again, then peered down at Neela's face.

Neela was looking at her.

'Oh yes,' Laurie sobbed ecstatically. 'You're here. Oh thank God,' and clutching the girl in her arms she held her so tight that Neela started to choke.

'I'm sorry. I'm sorry. Are you all right?' Laurie gasped.

Neela still only looked at her.

'I'm Laurie Forbes,' Laurie told her. 'We're here to help you.'

After a moment Neela whispered, 'Ambamata.'

The wail of emergency sirens was coming in from the distance.

'Shaila,' Neela said.

Laurie looked at her helplessly. 'I'm sorry, I don't understand,' she said.

505

Neela turned her head towards the child.

Realizing now, Laurie said, 'Stan, have you got her? Is she still here?'

'I'm not sure,' he puffed.

'Oh please God, please, don't let her die,' Laurie begged, tears streaming down her cheeks.

Stan kept at it, pumping the fragile chest, and breathing air into the tiny lungs.

By the time the ambulance arrived Shaila was responding, as were most of the others.

It was the early hours of the morning before Laurie finally walked out of the police station to find Rhona waiting in her car.

'The others have gone home,' Rhona told her as she slumped into the passenger seat. 'But Stan's still in there.'

'Let's wait,' Laurie said, so exhausted she could feel it to the very core of her bones.

Rhona reached into the back seat and produced two flasks. 'Coffee, or brandy?' she asked.

Laurie didn't even hesitate. 'Both.'

As Rhona poured Laurie rubbed her hands over her face, then let her head fall back. 'Was I really still on a Greek island this morning?' she murmured. 'What day is it?'

Rhona checked her watch. 'It's two o'clock, so it must be Monday.'

Laurie took the cup Rhona was passing, but didn't drink straight away. 'As long as I live I'll never forget what we saw tonight,' she said, her voice scratchy with tiredness and emotion. 'Can you imagine how bad it must have been? What they must have suffered to do that to themselves.

What is it like to feel so helpless, so devoid of hope? Five women *dead*.'

'But the child made it,' Rhona said gently.

Laurie nodded. 'Thank God.'

'What'll happen to them now?' Rhona asked after a while.

'You mean after they're released from hospital? God knows. It's too soon to tell. Social services will take over, I expect.'

'What about deportation?'

'No way,' Laurie responded. 'I just won't let it happen, unless it's what they want, of course. Tell me,' she said, turning to look at Rhona, 'why on earth didn't Sherry get them out the minute she knew where they were? OK, shoot the video, but why leave them there?'

'I guess only Sherry knows the answer to that,' Rhona said, as Stan got into the back of the car.

'Why didn't Sherry call the police?' Laurie said, turning round to him. 'What did she say? Why did she just leave them there?'

'She told me she *was* going to call the police,' he answered. 'She said she was going to do it the minute she got home.'

'So what happened?'

'I dropped her off, back at her flat, and that was the last I heard from her. I presumed she'd done it, until Rose called to ask if I knew where she was.'

Laurie and Rhona looked at each other. 'Someone must have been waiting in her flat when she got in,' Laurie said. 'They must have taken her somewhere. Or . . .' She shook her head, unable to put her worst fear into words.

Rhona started the engine, and after driving Stan home she took Laurie back to her place to spend the night.

Early the next morning Rose called, waking them up. 'Jet lag,' she explained, when Rhona complained it was only six o'clock. 'I need to speak to Laurie.'

Rhona carried the phone through to where Laurie was already sitting up in bed. 'What is it?' she asked.

Rhona shrugged and passed her the phone.

'Laurie, I'm at the office,' Rose told her. 'I've just opened my computer and found a note from Sherry tucked away in one of the files.'

Laurie's heart was thudding with dread. 'What does it say?'

'She's telling me to get in touch with a lawyer who apparently has the footage she shot.'

Frowning, Laurie said, 'Does she say why she gave it to him?'

'No. She just gives his name and phone number, and says that's where we'll find it.'

Laurie's mind was racing. 'She must have given it to him for safekeeping and gone into hiding,' she said, swinging her legs off the bed.

'That's what I thought,' Rose responded, 'until I read the last line. It says, "I'm sorry about Laurie, but I had no choice."'

Chapter Twenty-Five

The road to the prison was endless, and dusty. Either side of it there was nothing but dull, flat terrain baking in a heat that allowed little to survive. Though Sherry had always known it was in the middle of a desert wasteland, two hundred or more miles outside Los Angeles, she'd had no way of knowing, until now, just how desolate and isolated a place it actually was. It seemed to symbolize how far she had cast her mother from her life, and to think of her being here all this time made her ache and cry inside. As she drew closer the yearning she felt seemed to grow stronger, as though she were about to have a severed limb reattached. Had it been left to wither too long? Was it possible for it to regain its power?

Aunt Jude had called ahead to make the arrangements, then Sherry had spoken to someone at the prison last night, who'd confirmed she could come today for no more than an hour.

The prison was in sight now, a loose hexagon of long, low buildings inside a high barbed-wire fence. In spite of being modern, to her mind it still managed to emanate as much menace and austerity as a Victorian gaol, and a hostility that almost seemed to stain the air around it.

Visitors were directed where to go by a sign at the gate, and by a uniformed officer who checked her ID. She drove slowly over the scorched tarmac and speed bumps. There was hardly anyone around, just an officer walking from one building to the next, and a couple of blue-overalled prisoners wheeling a cart towards a basketball court. She wondered which one of the buildings her mother was in. Did they all have different functions and she was allowed in only a few? What kind of relationships had she forged with the officers and other women? Was she afraid of them? Did they treat her badly? What kind of life had her own daughter condemned her to?

As she got out of her hire car Sherry felt the heat engulf her like a fire. Inside she was sick with dread and with each second that passed it was getting worse. She wondered how her mother was feeling now, as she prepared, for the first time in seven years, to see the daughter who'd refused all contact with her since she'd sacrificed her own freedom so Sherry could keep hers. Had there ever, she wondered, been any moments of regret or bitterness during all this long time? Had she ever been tempted to confess what had really happened on that terrible February night? Looking around her now, Sherry couldn't imagine there being no regrets or temptations at all, for the bleak isolation of the place and forbidding nature of the fences were in themselves enough to fill anyone with despair. To imagine her beautiful, gentle mother locked away here, month after month, year after year, was too terrible to contemplate for more than a moment.

There were more security checks, forms to fill in, directions to take. Finally she was led towards a small, wooden-fenced area that contained picnic benches, climbing frames and sandpits. She thought of their garden back in LA and all the fun they'd had as a family over the years. The three of them on trips to Disneyland and Universal Theme Park. Special nights at the Hollywood Bowl. Watching her parents dance on the deck of her father's sailboat. Afternoon parties at their Bel Air home for Sherry's friends, or agents and celebrities. Days at her father's office when she'd felt as though he was the most important man on earth. She wondered if he could see any of this now. Was he looking down on his flower girls as they came together for almost the first time since his death? And if he was, how did he feel about the part he had played in bringing them to this?

When she reached the park the guard who'd escorted her let her in, and closed the gate behind her. She walked forward a couple of steps, then turned round to watch the guard go. Her eye was caught by a solitary figure, standing about a hundred feet away, outside one of the wretchedly characterless buildings. Though it was hard to tell at this distance it felt as if she was watching her, then with a jarring thud in her heart she realized it was her mother. Isabell MacEvilly. Bluebell.

As she began walking across the yard to the

511

park Sherry watched her, a slender, dark-haired woman in blue prison issue whose very approach seemed to be filling up her life. She moved with the same grace Sherry remembered, for she was every beautiful symphony ever written, a Strauss waltz, a Mendelssohn concerto, a Venetian barca-role, a playful nocturne. She was a Byzantine beauty with an aquarelle romance. She was a swan, a doe; a hummingbird at dusk, a sparkle of dew at dawn. She was everything that made the world a truly magical place.

She was very close now, and Sherry's heart was so full she couldn't breathe. Tears ran down her cheeks. Sobs shuddered through her body. She never had, and never could love anyone more than this woman, who had given her life, not once, but twice. No matter the time, the distance or the pain, they were still connected in every way and it would never change. How could she ever have thought it would?

Her mother's hand was on the gate, her eyes still on her daughter. She was smiling with such happiness that Sherry just couldn't bear it. As her hands covered her face her mother's arms went round her.

'It's all right,' her mother whispered.

Sherry wept as though her heart would break. The smell, the touch, the voice, everything about this woman gave meaning to her life. She realized now that nothing had made any sense without her, nor ever would. She couldn't understand why she'd cut her off the way she had, when she should have known she couldn't survive without the oxygen of her mother's love.

'I'm sorry,' she said, over and over. 'I'm so sorry.'

'Ssh. You're here now. That's all that matters.'

Sherry looked into her face, her eyes probing deeply, searching for signs of what she must have suffered during these past seven years. And they were there, in the deepened lines around her eyes and tighter set of her mouth. She was like a delicately perfumed soap that had been scoured with a brush – still fragrant and beautiful, but marred. Or a dainty Japanese fan painted with thorns instead of lotus blooms. A perfect garden that had been roughened by a storm. All the horror and sorrow were there, lurking in the shadows of her hyacinth eyes, but mainly they were hidden now behind the joy and relief of seeing her daughter again.

In a way it was difficult to believe so much time had passed for, in spite of the almost indiscernible flaws, she hardly seemed to have aged, except the skin under her eyes was looser and there was grey in her hair. She was wearing it short now in a neat, elfin cut which suited her. She still had freckles on her nose, and a beautifully slender neck that Sherry always wished she'd inherited instead of the freckles. Her skin was tanned and more leathery than it had been, her hands less elegant, and more work-worn, but her lovely, infectious smile was as radiant as ever.

'You've hardly changed,' Sherry told her in a voice still thick with tears.

'You have. You're even more beautiful.'

Sherry spluttered a laugh, and they held each other again, almost oblivious to the baking sun, as they allowed all the emotions of the last seven years to surface at last.

'We should go into the shade,' her mother said finally. 'Over there, under the tree.'

They walked hand in hand to the tree and sat down on a bench. Everything was so still they could almost have been the only people alive, in a wilderness that was so strange it might not even have been earth. 'It's like a dream,' her mother said, as though reading Sherry's mind. 'I've imagined this every day, seen it all in my mind a thousand times, and now, at last, here you are.'

As guilt flooded through her, Sherry took her hands. 'I've missed you,' she said.

'I've missed you too. We have so much to catch up on. I want to hear . . .'

'We don't have long,' Sherry cut in gently, 'and there's something I have to tell you.'

'But first you must tell me how you are,' her mother insisted, gazing into the same deep blue eyes as her own. 'Aunt Jude sends me news from time to time, so I know you live in England now and you're a reporter, but what's your life really like? Do you have lots of friends? A special boyfriend, maybe? Tell me about your home. Do you have a garden? Did you bring any photos?'

Sherry shook her head. 'I didn't think of it,' she confessed. 'I left in a hurry. Mum, I have . . .'

Isabell's eyes were brimming with love. 'You always did call me Mum,' she said, seeming to sink into the word as though it were balm. 'Never Mom. I liked that.'

'You used to make me,' Sherry laughed. 'It was your way of making us stay English.'

514

Isabell was laughing too. 'Is it wonderful being back there?' she said. 'I don't suppose you remembered it very well, you were so young when we left. But we used to visit a lot. Daddy always loved to go home, didn't he?'

It was such a natural and affectionate way to speak of her father that instead of resisting, Sherry found herself going with it. 'And when we got there he could never wait to come back,' she said wryly.

Isabell clapped her hands in joy. 'So typical of him,' she cried, 'always wanting to be somewhere he wasn't. "We're Americans now," he used to say. "Can never go back there and live."'

'Then Christmas would come round,' Sherry continued, 'and suddenly we'd find ourselves swamped in so much nostalgia, having to listen to what real Christmases were all about, with snow and roaring log fires and stockings hanging over the fireplace . . . Do you remember how we used to scour British magazines for country houses to buy? "This time next year," he used to say, "we'll be back in Blighty, where we belong."'

Isabell's eyes were shining with love. 'And now that's where you are,' she said, stroking Sherry's cheek. 'You're even losing your American accent.'

Sherry's smile started to falter. 'Do you still miss him?' she whispered.

Her mother's eyes rose to the heavens as she seemed to drink in the very stillness of the air and pristine blue of the sky. 'I talk to him all the time, in my mind,' she said, 'and I feel him all around me. Do you feel him too?'

Sherry shook her head. 'He won't be there for me . . .'

'Nonsense. He's there. He always was, and he always will be. You just have to let him in.' She smiled and her eyes started to twinkle again.

'Do you know what you're reminding me of now?' Sherry said, needing to get off the subject of her father, at least for a moment. 'How we always used to dress up for parties. Birthdays, Halloween, Thanksgiving, Easter, whatever the occasion we always found ourselves something outrageous and different to wear. My friends used to call you the world's coolest mom. Do you remember that?'

Isabell was nodding and smiling as she became immersed in the memories too.

'They always loved it at our house,' Sherry said, feeling the sadness start to overwhelm her, for it was true, they had all loved to visit the MacEvillys, but only during the times her father was in town and coming home every night. When he was off with one of his floozies, no-one came. Sherry would hear the girls chattering at school about poor Mrs MacEvilly being sick again, as though the terrible depressions were her mother's fault, and not brought on at all by her father going away.

'Tell me about you,' Sherry said, tucking her mother's hair behind one ear. 'What do you do here? How do you fill your days?'

Isabell's eyes lit up again. 'Let me see,' she said, tilting her head to one side. 'I write and I think and I pray. I've become quite religious now, you know, even more than before. I've put myself into God's hands and I know He's taking care of me. He's taking care of you too, you know.'

Sherry tried to smile and found she couldn't, because she knew it wasn't true. No-one was taking care of either of them, they couldn't be, or they wouldn't be here now and she wouldn't have had to do what she had to put it right. 'What else do you do?' she asked softly.

'Well, in a more practical sense, I do some land-scaping, over at the other side. You can't see from here and they won't let me take you over, but there are three greenhouses where we grow flowers. Lots of them, delphiniums and hollyhocks and bluebells of course. And I have a special little section for lilies. That's mine, no-one else touches that. I sit there looking at them sometimes, and that's when I can feel you and Daddy the most.'

Tears were welling in Sherry's eyes again. 'What else do you grow?' she asked, a small sob shaking her voice.

'We have some vegetables. Onions, of course. I have to grow them because of Daddy. He'd be upset if I left him out. And we've had a very good show from the artichokes this year.'

Sherry dashed the tears away and swallowed hard. 'What about friends?' she said. 'What are the other women like?'

Isabell waggled her eyebrows. 'Not always the kind you'd like to meet,' she responded with a wryness that made Sherry smile. 'There is some-one special though. Her name's Charlotte. We share a room.'

Sherry's heart turned over as she wondered if special meant what she thought. If it did she was jealous, because she didn't want another woman to be so close to her mother. Yet it must be so

517

terribly lonely here, so hard for Isabell to live without any love at all, that maybe Sherry should feel grateful to this Charlotte instead of resentful. At least she was providing her mother with something, comfort, tenderness, release from tension, maybe even protection, which was so much more than Sherry ever had. 'Why . . . ?' She cleared her throat. 'Why is Charlotte here?' she asked, trying to keep the picture she had of Charlotte as benign and feminine as she could.

'For the same reason I am,' her mother answered. 'She killed her husband.'

Sherry's heart contracted and her mouth turned dry. She looked into her mother's face and wondered what she was feeling now, what was really going through her mind. She seemed so gentle and untouched by the words, it was impossible to tell. 'But, Mum, you didn't kill yours,' she said softly. 'You know that . . .'

'Ssh, now,' Isabell chided. 'We went through all that at the time. You didn't kill Daddy, sweetheart. I know you think you did, but it was me . . .'

'Mum, *please*, don't do this any more,' Sherry implored. 'I know how much you love me, so I understand why you're doing it, but you have to stop. It's already been too long. You shouldn't be here. You've lost everything because of me. I'm the one who should be paying.'

Isabell's voice was perfectly calm as she said, 'Sherry, darling, I know you mean well, but really, I'm not going to let you take the blame for something you didn't do. You shouldn't even be thinking that way. I'd hoped you'd stopped by now . . .'

'Mum, listen,' Sherry urged, squeezing her

518

hands, 'I know you've had a long time to alter the facts in your mind . . .You probably had to, to make this more bearable, but it doesn't matter how often or how convincingly you tell yourself you did it, it still doesn't make it the truth. Daddy's not here any more because of me. Not because of you. It was me who fired the shot that killed him . . .'

'No, dear. It was the shots I fired . . .'

'Mum, please. You're not responsible. I am. You'd never have fired the gun at all if I hadn't, and you know it. So you don't have to stay here any longer. You can go home, because once they know the truth, they'll set you free. They'll have to.'

Isabell was shaking her head. 'You really haven't read any of my letters, have you?' she sighed. 'Aunt Jude told me you threw them away, just like you said you would, but I always hoped you might take a peek at one or two.'

Not sure how to respond, Sherry merely looked at her adorable, almost childlike face and wondered just how much damage had been done over the past seven years. If she'd read the letters maybe she'd know. 'She said you'd threatened to kill yourself in one,' Sherry told her softly.

Isabell nodded and allowed her gaze to drift. 'It's true, I did,' she said. 'It was a very bad time. They happen – they can't not when you're in a place like this. Mostly it's all right though, you just go through the motions, get on with it, do what you can to make it as tolerable as you can. Charlotte helps. It's nice to have a friend. But sometimes it's just too hard, especially when you've got no-one who comes to visit. Charlotte's son and his wife come every two weeks. She lives for those visits, talks about nothing else for days. Oh, please don't take that as a criticism of you, sweetheart, I understand why you took your decision, really I do. It just hasn't always been that easy to live with. A few friends used to come, back at the beginning, but it's a long way to drive, and when they finally understood that I really wasn't going to sell the rights to my story, they gave up trying to persuade me and stopped coming. Then month after month began dragging into year after year and the only contact I had with the outside world was with your Aunt Jude. As Daddy's sister I often wonder how she found it in her heart to forgive me, but she always was a very special woman. She said once that she thought I was a saint for putting up with the way he was, but he had a lot to put up with in me too, all my moods and depressions, it can't have been easy. They give me medication now so the swings aren't quite so bad, but I still go down from time to time. I write to you a lot then, letters I never send, because they're too dark and they'd frighten you. But when I feel better I write to you again, happier and chattier letters, and I talk to you all the time in my mind, with Daddy, as though the three of us are together. I tell you about my day and my dreams. About the different women here, whether they're Picassos or Lautrecs – there's one woman I swear modelled for his Prostitute, except she's too young, of course. There are rabbits and lions, hyenas and snakes. Sherbert lemons and Hungarian goulash. I tell you all about the sonatas from Chopin and rusty church bells. We used to have such fun making up those descriptions, didn't we? Turning people into animals, or trees, or music, or food. Anything we chose. I thought if I went on doing it, in my mind and in my letters, you'd start sharing it with me again.' She sighed and seemed to drift as she shook her head. 'You really meant what you said, didn't you? You wouldn't come again until I told them the truth.' Her eyes came back to Sherry's. 'But I can't do that, darling. I just can't. Not your truth, anyway.'

Sherry started to protest again, but her mother carried on talking.

'It was a terrible letter to send,' she said, 'but I couldn't help it. It was all I could think of to make you come. Emotional blackmail of the very worst kind. If you don't come, I'm going to kill myself. I even tried to do it, and ended up being punished. Six weeks in solitary confinement. I only moved back to my room a few days ago.'

Dizzied and sickened by the images her mother's words had created, Sherry said, 'How are you now? Do you still feel the same?'

Isabell smiled and suddenly laughed like a girl. 'You need to ask,' she said, putting her hands on Sherry's shoulders. 'As soon as I knew you were coming, everything changed. The sun came out, and music started to play. The world became somewhere I wanted to be again.'

Sherry wrapped her in her arms and held her as though she would never let her go. Just to see her joy, hear her laughter, was enough to make her want the world to stop now, because it was never going to be this good again. This was the very best they could ever hope for now. 'They're going to set you free, Mum,' she told her. 'You can go where there's always light and music. Where you can grow your flowers again, and write your stories and dress up for parties. You don't have to stay here any more. You're going to go back to the life that should always have been yours. The one I stole from you . . . No, listen, please,' she insisted as her mother started to protest. 'You're going to tell them the truth, Mum, because I've done something to make sure you do.'

Isabell's eyes were confused, then became wary as she said, 'I don't understand. What could you do?'

'I've killed someone else,' Sherry said.

Isabell blinked, then smiled as though Sherry had made some kind of joke. 'It's true, Mum,' she said. 'Not with my own hands, but I'm as guilty as if I did it myself.'

Isabell's eyes were starting to dilate. 'Tell me this isn't true,' she whispered. 'Oh, Sherry, you . . . No,' she was shaking her head. 'I know it can't be true.'

'It is, Mum. I arranged for someone to be killed. She's someone who deserved to die anyway, because she was my friend and she betrayed me.'

'Sherry, what are you saying?'

'Even if it doesn't happen,' Sherry continued, 'I'll be guilty of conspiracy to murder, which is the same as if I'd carried it out. I did it to punish her, and to make you set yourself free, because you can't go on doing this to yourself, Mum. I have to pay for my sins. We have to face that, both of us, together. I'll have to go to prison now anyway, so let me go for what I did to Dad too.'

Isabell's shock was too great for her to respond.

'I'm sorry,' Sherry whispered. 'I wish I hadn't had to do it this way, but . . .'

'Who?' Isabell broke in. 'Who was she, this friend?'

'Her name's Laurie Forbes. No-one you know.'

'But what did she do to you, darling? How can you say she deserved . . .'

'To die?' Sherry finished for her. 'She deserved it because she stole Nick from me. Do you remember Nick?'

Wide-eyed, Isabell shook her head.

'Yes you do. He's the journalist I met during your trial.'

'Oh yes. Very handsome. Blond. Tall . . .'

'And married.'

Isabell blinked.

'He never lied about it,' Sherry told her. 'I always knew, the trouble was I fell for him anyway. I was like the girls who fell for Dad, the ones who used to call up in the middle of the night, or come round to confront him. I never did anything like that, but I was still like them. I fell for a married man without even thinking about his wife. The difference was, when he said he couldn't leave her I accepted it and let him go. I didn't run after him, the way all those girls used to run after Dad, but I wanted to. There was something special about him, something that set him apart from everyone else, I felt it as soon as we met. It was as though he was meant to come into my life, we were meant to be. But we only had a month together before he had to go back to his wife. It was awful. I felt as though

I was losing everyone. First Dad, then you, then him . . . It was a horrible time. Horrible, horrible.'

'Poor Sherry. My poor darling,' Isabell murmured, squeezing her hands.

'But then, a few weeks ago, he came back,' Sherry continued brightly. 'It was like a miracle. All that time we'd been apart I kept telling myself I wasn't waiting, that my life wasn't on hold for him, but I knew I was never going to meet anyone else to compare with him. And then, there he was, and from the minute we saw each other I just knew, in my heart, it was destiny, or fate, or some greater plan that we know nothing about that had brought us back into each other's lives. I was convinced it was all going to work out this time. He was no longer married, he was moving to London, he seemed as happy to see me as I was to see him. It all seemed so perfect. He even knew about you and Dad, so I didn't have to pretend, or try to hide anything. I told myself if we were together then maybe everything would finally start to make sense, you wouldn't have given up your freedom for nothing, I would have a real life with someone to love and who loved me. I could tell you about him, we could come to see you, and maybe, in some small way, to see us happy, and even perhaps with a family, you would feel the sacrifice had been worthwhile.'

'It would have been,' Isabell told her, already looking afraid of what was coming next.

'But it didn't work out that way,' Sherry said. 'He didn't love me. It turned out I was just someone he'd known once, and was happy to know again for a while. We had what I guess he considers a fling, until he met my friend Laurie. It just didn't seem fair. He was the only man I'd ever really wanted, and he wanted *her*. Then other things started to happen, not directly connected to them, but close enough and in such a way that made me realize . . . Well, it was as if something somewhere was telling me that though you and I had cheated the system, we couldn't go on cheating life.'

Isabell's eyes were dark with pain as she absorbed the words and clung even harder to Sherry's hands. 'But you don't know if she's actually dead, this friend?'

'She probably is, but I already told you, it doesn't matter. Before I arranged it, I gave a letter to a lawyer confessing to it all. I expect the police will have seen the letter by now, but they won't know where to find me, not immediately anyway. It gave me the chance to come here and tell you that it's time now for you to go home. You can't do anything to change this, Mum, you can't make it better this time, or take the blame yourself. It's done. I did it, and I want you to be there, in England, to visit me, the way I should have visited you. If you stay here, you won't be able to do that. We might never even see each other again.'

Shock and heartache were pushing tears from Isabell's eyes. 'Oh Sherry, Sherry,' she moaned, pulling her into her arms, 'my darling, don't you understand? They won't believe me now. Even if I told them what really happened they won't admit they've made a mistake and had the wrong person locked up all these years. It's not how it works.

There's no justice or fairness once you're this side of the system. No bargaining or . . .'

'But you have to try,' Sherry insisted, pulling back to look at her. 'You at least have to try. Please tell me you will. They're going to make me leave any minute. I don't want to go without hearing you promise to try.'

'I can't, darling . . .'

'Mum, you have to. *Please*. There's no point both of us paying for what only one of us did. Not like this. I don't have a choice now, but you do. Please get yourself out of here. Come to England. Start a new life. We'll see each other as often as we can. You might even find someone else to love. Mum, *please*. If you ever do anything for me in your life again, make it this. Understand how your suffering is mine. Your punishment is mine. Your incarceration is mine. It's not yours, Mum. It's mine. So let it go. Please.'

Isabell's heartbeat was racing as the force of Sherry's will seemed to swamp her. 'I don't know,' she said, still confused. 'What if . . .'

'No! There are no what ifs. I'm going to prison, Mum, no matter . . .'

'But what if your friend isn't dead? What if no-one ever gets to find out . . .'

'I already told you, there's a letter. The police are probably already looking for me.'

Isabell's agitation was increasing as she pressed her palms to her cheeks. 'I need some time to think, Sherry. I wasn't expecting anything like this. Oh God, I don't want to believe it's true. You can't have done something so terrible to your friend.' She stiffened as a voice shouted, 'MacEvilly. Time's

526

up.' The guard was standing at the gate, impatiently waiting for the prisoner to respond.

Isabell quickly clasped Sherry in an embrace. 'Come again, please,' she wept. 'On Saturday. That's the visiting day . . .'

'I don't know if I'll still be here. If I can I will, but if not . . . Mum, give me your word, you'll call a lawyer and tell him what really happened.'

'Oh Sherry!'

'Your word, Mum. Please. I have to have it.'

Her mother looked at her and a whole world of love and pain seemed to brim from her eyes. 'OK,' she said finally. 'But only when . . . When I know for sure that your friend is . . .'

'MacEvilly,' the guard growled.

'I'll write,' Sherry told her, as they walked to the gate. 'Tonight. I'll tell you everything that happened. I'll . . .'

'Let's get out of this heat,' the guard snarled.

'Yes, write, darling,' her mother said, giving her a final hug. 'And come if you can. Saturday. I'll pray you're still here.'

As her mother went through the gate and began walking away with the guard Sherry stood where she was, watching the familiar, beloved figure in blue and feeling her heart breaking apart. The sense of helplessness and despair was so overwhelming in those moments that there didn't seem any point to going on. She had no idea when, or even if, she'd see her mother again, and she was suddenly terrified now that she never would. She wanted desperately to run after her, to beg the guard to take her in too, but everything in her was frozen, crippled by guilt,

527

torn apart by grief, so she could only stay where she was and keep her eyes on her mother's precious dark head until she finally disappeared from view.

Chapter Twenty-Six

Though Laurie had known of the letter's existence since yesterday, after she and Rose contacted the lawyer, it was only a few minutes ago that Detective Inspector James, who was leading the hunt for Sherry, had called to inform her that he was about to fax it over.

'Is anyone with you?' he'd asked.

'Yes, Rose. My partner.'

'Then I suggest you let her read it at the same time,' he'd cautioned.

Now, as the fax came through, Rose picked it up from the machine, made a copy and passed it to Laurie who was sitting at her desk.

They read in silence, first about the note Suzy had left at Sherry's flat, then about the videotaping of the women, then about Sherry's call to Karima Ghosh to set up a meeting with Eddie Cribbs. As she reached the part that concerned her, Laurie's heart began a hard, dull thud.

'. . . I am now about to go and meet Eddie Cribbs at Cinnabar Wharf,' Sherry had written. 'It is my *intention to ask him to arrange Laurie Forbes's death in return for the videotape I have made of the women he is forcing into prostitution. The videotape and address for the women is enclosed with this letter. Should Laurie Forbes already be dead by the time this letter is opened, and it is my hope that she will be, I wish it to be absolutely clear that it was at my request that Eddie Cribbs, or one of his contacts, carried out the murder. I want her to die as a punishment for her betrayal. It is also my hope that Eddie Cribbs and others will be arrested for their part in her murder, as well as for the imprisonment and inhuman treatment of the women they have trafficked into this country.*

'Lastly I would like it to be fully understood that my mother did not kill my father. I am one hundred per cent responsible for his death, and my mother knows this. She has suffered long enough for a crime she did not commit, and now, in doing what I have, I hope that I will be able to set her free and pay for his murder myself, even though it might turn out that it is Laurie's death that ensures this . . .'

At that point Laurie stopped reading. She couldn't focus any more, the words were too blurred by the force of the shock.

Rose looked up, her face almost as white as Laurie's.

Neither of them spoke as Laurie left her chair and went to look out of the window. At the end of the street was the smart mustard façade of Dunbar Wharf, where Sherry's flat was on the second floor, next door to Rhona's. She'd spent a lot of time at that flat, especially lately. She'd come to know Sherry well, or thought she had. Her fondness had grown along with her respect, for

Sherry's kindness and loyalty, her humour and unfailing support. Throughout all this dreadful time with Elliot Sherry had been there for her, had never once let her down . . .

'Are you all right?' Rose asked.

After a beat Laurie nodded and swallowed hard. 'I think so,' she answered. 'I just . . . I was just thinking of what a good friend she's always been to me. We didn't know her long, eight months maybe, but in that time she proved over and over just how much she cared. And how do I repay her? By sleeping with the only man she ever loved. This is what *I* pushed her into doing.'

'Laurie, for heaven's sake, I hope you're not going to start blaming yourself,' Rose scolded. 'No matter what went on between you and Nick, nothing can excuse what she tried to do . . . What she's *already done*, because by her own admission she killed her father.' Rose looked at the letter again, as though to make sure that was what she'd read, for it still hardly seemed credible.

Laurie seemed to be only half listening. 'She was so lonely,' she said. 'I don't think I ever realized that quite as much as I do now.'

'You welcomed her into your life. You opened doors for her . . .'

'I betrayed her,' Laurie interrupted. 'That's what she says in the letter, and she's right. She'd never have done this if I hadn't slept with Nick.'

Understanding that she needed to take a firm line, Rose said, 'Laurie, I'll remind you again, there's still her father, and the fact that she could actually go to Eddie Cribbs and ask him to have anyone killed, never mind you, shows that in some fundamental way she is flawed. You can't be responsible for that. You just can't.'

Laurie turned round, her eyes still showing how shocked and guilty she was feeling.

'Did you hear what I said?' Rose demanded.

Laurie nodded, but her gaze was drifting again. 'I wonder where she is,' she said. 'Has Eddie Cribbs done away with her, in spite of their bargain? He's fled the country now, so he won't be concerned about the videotape. Or is she going to turn up in California, the way the police think?'

'We won't know until they call,' Rose replied, looking at the phone as it started to ring.

Laurie watched and listened as Rose answered. 'Oh hi, Elliot,' she said, her eyes going to Laurie. 'I'm fine thank you. Yes, she's here . . .'

Laurie shook her head and held up a hand, in a blocking gesture.

'. . . but I'm afraid she doesn't want to speak to you.' She paused, then said, 'Yes, I'll tell her. I don't think she'll come though. We've just had a bit of a shock, about Sherry.'

'Rose, no,' Laurie protested.

Rose continued to tell Elliot about the letter. When she'd finished she looked at Laurie again. 'He wants to come over,' she said.

Laurie shook her head. How could she deal with him now, when she barely even knew how to deal with herself?

'She doesn't want you to,' Rose told him.

As Rose rang off Laurie's heart was twisting with longing to see him, and with anger and so much confusion that she had no clear idea how she really felt.

It was late in the afternoon when Detective Inspector James called again, this time to inform them that the Beverly Hills police had just escorted Sherry to Los Angeles airport, where she would soon be boarding a flight to Heathrow.

'We'll be there to pick her up when she arrives tomorrow,' he told Laurie.

'Had she been to visit her mother?' she asked.

'Apparently, yes.'

Laurie put a hand to her head, unable even to imagine how difficult and painful it must have been. 'Is there any chance I'll be able to see her?' she asked.

'Frankly, after that letter, I'm surprised you'd want to, but no, at least not right away. She'll be up in front of the magistrates in a couple of days. There's not much doubt she'll be remanded in custody, but if you still want to, you might be able to grab a few minutes with her then, presuming she's willing. Other than that, it'll be a prison visit.'

As Laurie put the phone down she covered her face with her hands and wondered whether she felt more like crying, or just slipping away to another existence. 'I wish there was something I could do to help her,' she said, after telling Rose what the inspector had said.

'Come on,' Rose said, going to put an arm around her. 'Let's go and get ourselves a stiff drink. We could more than do with one. Then, instead of worrying about Sherry, I think you should decide what you're going to do about Elliot, because you can't keep on avoiding him.'

*

Two days later Laurie and Anita were shown into a small, soulless room at the back of Tower Bridge Magistrates Court, where Sherry was already sitting at an empty table. Her lawyer was standing to one side, talking quietly into the phone, apparently informing the person at the other end that Sherry had been remanded in custody and would be transferred in the next few minutes to Holloway Prison.

Sherry's face was pale and tight, though it showed little of the fear Laurie had been expecting. There was more a hint of wariness, and perhaps a slight confusion. During the short proceedings she'd kept her head lowered, looking at no-one in the court, not even the magistrate when he had pronounced his finding. Yet now she didn't seem to be balking at eye contact at all, as she looked first at Laurie, then to Anita.

'I've told them I'd like you to do the psychiatric assessment,' she said, almost curtly.

Anita looked uneasy. 'I'm afraid I'm not qualified,' she responded, sounding as wretched as she felt. 'But I can definitely refer you.'

'OK. Whoever you judge best.' She moved her gaze back to Laurie. For what seemed an eternity she merely stared at her, saying nothing, only seeming to find her presence curious, or perhaps even intrusive. 'They said you wanted to see me,' she eventually stated.

Laurie nodded, but now she was here, faced with a Sherry she barely recognized, her friend's warm, familiar self seemingly possessed by a hard, cold stranger, she was no longer sure what she wanted to say.

Sherry waited, giving her no help at all.

'I just want you to know,' Laurie finally managed, 'that I'm sorry.'

Sherry blinked once or twice, then looked away. 'Are you still seeing him?' she asked bluntly.

'No. It was never . . . It was a mistake. It shouldn't have happened.'

'But it did, and you knew how much he meant to me.'

Laurie's eyes were wide as she looked at her.

'Is it forgiveness you're waiting for now?' Sherry asked.

Laurie shook her head.

'Then what?'

'Nothing. Except . . . I forgive what you tried to do to me.'

Sherry's expression remained stony. 'Does Nick hate me now?' she asked, her eyes flicking to Anita, then back again.

'I don't think so.'

'What does he say about me?'

'He's concerned. We all are.'

'Where is he now?'

'I'm not sure,' Laurie lied, not wanting to admit that as far as she was aware he was still on Hydra, for she had no idea if Sherry even knew he'd been there.

Sherry turned to Anita. 'I want to stay in touch with him,' she told her. 'As a therapist, would you say that was a good idea?'

Anita looked taken aback. 'I'm not sure,' she answered cautiously. 'We'd need to discuss it, and, I suppose, find out if he's willing.'

535

'Would you do that for me?'

'Of course.'

'Tell him I forgive his betrayal. He's a man, so he's weak. My father was the same. I always forgave him too, until the end.' She turned back to Laurie. 'My only regret in all this,' she said, 'is that I didn't kill the woman he was going to leave my mother for. If I'd done that, he'd still be with my mother and she would never have spent seven years in prison paying for my crime.'

Understanding what she was saying, that she'd chosen to punish Laurie, not Nick, so that she could continue to love Nick, and maybe even keep him in her life, Laurie made no response.

They all looked up a moment later as the door opened and a court official came in, followed by a uniformed prison officer.

'Time to go,' Sherry's lawyer said, ending his phone call.

Sherry stood up.

Anita started to cry and put her arms around her. 'I'll come to see you,' she promised. 'As soon as I can.'

As Sherry embraced her, her eyes stayed on Laurie, but she said nothing as she let Anita go and turned to walk ahead of her lawyer and the others, out of the door.

Laurie and Anita travelled in silence back to Laurie's office.

'Do you have time to come in?' Laurie said, as the cab pulled up outside. 'For some reason it feels wrong for us just to part now, as though none of it mattered.'

Appearing relieved that Laurie felt the same

way she did, Anita climbed out after her and tried to insist on paying the fare.

'It's already done,' Laurie said, and telling the driver to keep the change, she stood aside as he drove away. 'I wonder if she's at the prison yet,' she said, staring down the street towards Dunbar Wharf, where Sherry's flat was on the second floor.

'She was so different,' Anita remarked. 'So unlike her normal self.'

Laurie looked down at her, and on impulse gave her a hug. 'I'm glad we went,' she said. 'I don't know if she is, but I think it was good that we did.'

'Will you keep in touch with her?' Anita asked.

'I'm not sure. It's too soon to tell, and if today was anything to go by, I don't think she wants me to. Will you?'

'Yes. I'm sure I will.'

Laurie smiled. 'Come on, let's go inside,' she said.

As she pushed open the door she was about to start introducing Anita to Rose when she suddenly stopped. The last person she'd expected to see, perched on the edge of a desk, was Nick.

'I didn't realize you were back,' she said, collecting herself quickly.

'I flew back last night,' he replied, coming to embrace her. 'How did it go at the court?'

Laurie turned to Anita. 'Have you two met?'

Anita shook her head and held out her hand. 'I'm guessing you're Nick,' she said.

'This is Anita, a good friend of Sherry's,' Laurie informed him. 'And this is Rose, my partner.

537

Sherry's been remanded in custody, as we expected,' she told them.

'How was she?' Nick asked. 'Did you manage to talk to her?'

'Yes. It's hard to say how she was. She seems very . . . detached.'

'She wants to stay in touch with you,' Anita told him.

He looked surprised, and uncertain.

'You don't have to decide now,' she said.

'What else did she say?' Rose asked.

As Laurie started to fill her in, she could feel a slow exhaustion creeping over her. These past six days, since the bogus priest on Hydra had tried to kill her, had passed in what felt like a fog of unreality. Even now, as she struggled with the inner weight of guilt and sorrow, she could still barely make herself accept it, nor was she seeming to connect with all the pain that had come before. It was as though it had happened to someone else, in some other world that was only tangential to her own. She thought of Elliot, the turning upside down of her life, the devastation of her dreams, the sheer awfulness of cancelling her wedding. Yet, in spite of his betrayal, there was no denying, in her weakened, vulnerable state, it was to him she longed to turn, his strength she wanted to carry her, his love she needed to see her through.

As the others continued to talk, she glanced at the phone and fought the urge to call him. Now wasn't the time. There was too much that needed to be said, too much to try to understand, and far too much to forgive. She still wasn't sure she could

538

do it, and being as drained as she felt now, it would be pointless even to try.

'One of Detective Inspector James's people called while you were gone,' she heard Rose saying. 'They think they know who the old woman and priest are who tried to shoot you.'

Laurie blinked, and gave a vague sort of smile at the bizarreness of what was being said, as though it were merely some kind of joke.

'Apparently they're mother and son from some gangster-type family on the Greek mainland,' Rose continued. 'They can't prove anything yet, but according to the Greek authorities it's not the first time they've staged this kind of double act.'

Aware of Nick watching her, as though concerned to see how she would respond to this reference to what had happened, Laurie merely shrugged. Right now none of it seemed real, so there was nothing for her to feel.

Nick rose to his feet. 'I should be getting off to the airport to meet Julia,' he said, glancing at his watch. 'She's flying in complete with the devastating Adam, I'm told, so love's young dream comes to London where Dad can pick up the bills.'

Laurie got up and walked to the door with him. 'Does it sound weird to say I actually miss her?' she said, as they stepped outside and looked down the road towards Sherry's apartment. 'I just can't seem to get my head round the fact that she's not going to be there any more.'

'What's happening to the flat? Do you know?' he asked.

'Not yet. Rhona's taking care of the plants and everything else right now. It seemed a shame to let them die. All her belongings are still there, it's like she's just popped out and will be back any minute.' Sighing, she leaned against the wall and shook her head in confusion. 'I wish I knew what to feel,' she said. 'On the one hand I'm appalled by what she tried to do to me, but with everything that's happened to her, and still is happening to her . . . It's hard not to feel sorry for her.'

'I know,' he replied, still staring at the distant entryway, where he'd pressed the bell to Sherry's flat many times, never dreaming any of this was in store. 'I wish I'd handled things a bit better when we broke up,' he said. 'Both times.'

'There's never an easy or even a right way to end a relationship,' Laurie said softly.

For a moment he seemed to want to respond to that, until his expression relaxed into a quirky sort of smile that she guessed was covering a question about Elliot. 'I should be going,' he told her. 'I'll talk to you later. Will you be here, or at home?'

'Probably still here,' she answered, accepting his brief kiss on the mouth, and after watching him get into his car she walked back into the office to find Rose holding out the phone.

Knowing instinctively who it was, Laurie almost stepped back. Then, realizing that she didn't want to go on avoiding him now, she took the phone. Going into the small screening room next to the kitchen, she said, 'Hi. How are you?'

'That's what I want to ask you,' he replied.

'I'm OK. Still a bit shell-shocked.'

'I'd like to see you.'

Her eyes closed as she thought of how many times she'd said that these past weeks, though

540

nowhere near as calmly. 'Yes, we need to sort things out,' she responded. 'Why don't you come here, tomorrow? We can take a walk down to the river?'

'What time?'

'Two?'

'I'll be there,' and he rang off.

By the time Elliot arrived the following afternoon Laurie had spent the evening with Rhona, talking it all over, then had managed to track down Rachel in New York to make sure Andraya was there, and that the relationship really was over.

'Oh, it's over all right,' Rachel had assured her. 'I don't know the exact details, but it was loud and acrimonious and no surprise at all to anyone who'd seen him with her over the preceding days. He'd started looking at her as though she'd just dropped in from another planet, like he couldn't understand what she was doing there and wished she'd get out of the way. I'm going to tell you this, Laurie, he deeply regrets what he's done. I know that without him even having to say it, though he has actually admitted it to Chris, and the day he thought you were in trouble, on Hydra, it took him all of a split second to dump Andraya. He was on his way to the airport when Rose called. I expect she told you.'

'Yes, she did.'

'Look, God knows none of this has been easy for you,' Rachel continued, 'and to be honest, I don't know how you forgive what he's put you through, but if you can, I think you should at least try.'

'You sound like Rhona,' Laurie informed her.

'We both want what's best for you, we think you and Elliot are made for each other, but that's us. What matters is you, and what you think. Ultimately the decision has to be yours.'

'Of course, but you're presuming he wants to come back. The day he told me about Andraya, he implied that even if their relationship didn't work out, he still didn't want ours. And now, to be honest, I'm not sure if I do either.'

For once he wasn't late, parking his car outside the Grapes and crossing the street to the office. Laurie was alone when he walked in, feeling faintly queasy with nerves, but reasonably calm. As she looked up her heart immediately tightened. He was standing at the door, as tall and imposing as ever, and even glowering at her in the way he couldn't help, though maybe this time she could detect a hint of uncertainty in his notoriously uncompromising eyes.

Before either of them could speak, the door to the screening room opened and Rose emerged with two of the crew. Laurie watched as they greeted Elliot warmly. They all knew each other well, and she could only feel grateful that their brief, but interested exchange about the recent trip to India covered what might have been an awkward encounter.

Aware that they still hadn't greeted each other, she picked up her bag and started to the door. 'Shall we?' she said, looking at him.

After saying goodbye to the others he followed her out into the sunshine, and fell in beside her as they started across the cobbles to where a gate allowed access to the river.

'It sounds as though you've got quite a programme on your hands,' he remarked.

'I think so,' she responded, relieved to have something else to talk about for a while. 'Whatever else Sherry did, she certainly got some stunning footage of the women. Put together with the material Rose managed to get in India, it could turn out to be one of our most effective programmes to date.'

'Where are the women now?' he asked, standing aside for her to go through the gate ahead of him.

'Two are still in hospital, the others are in the care of social services. We're keeping a close eye on them, making sure the authorities treat them right. Considering the kind of news coverage they're getting they should be OK.'

'How long were they in captivity?'

'We think about six or seven months. By the time they were found, to quote the detective in charge of the case, they'd passed their sell-by date. In other words, they were filthy, scared out of their wits, even damaged beyond use, and not one of them a virgin any more, so they were about to be sold on to a bunch of Italians for snuff videos.'

Elliot remained silent as the horror seemed to sully the very air her words fell into. 'Thank God you found them,' he murmured.

'The credit goes to Sherry.'

He took a breath. 'What news on Eddie Cribbs?' he asked, as they arrived at the river wall and stopped to gaze out at the view.

'He's on the Costa del Sol, apparently. But he's as good as finished. He'll never be able to come back to this country, and if I have my way he'll never be able to go out in public in Spain. I'm in discussions right now with the English newspaper for the region to give away a free video of the programme with each of ten thousand copies of their November issue, so everyone, but everyone will know who that man is and how he's made his money. If nothing else, it'll turn him into a prisoner in his own home, with his wife as the gaoler.'

Elliot's smile was wry. He'd always loved her sense of justice, and passion for a story, and listening to her now reminded him of how much he'd missed it. 'And Sherry?' he said. 'What news on her?'

'Since I saw her, at the magistrates court, nothing. I'm still not sure what to do, whether to stay in touch with her, or not.'

'You'd want to, considering everything?'

She threw him a quick glance. 'I have to look at the part I played in pushing her into it,' she replied, unsure how much he knew about Nick, so going no further than that for now.

He said nothing, merely watched a speedboat roar past, his expression as inscrutable as ever.

'How's your book coming along?' she asked, breaking the silence at last.

'Slowly,' he admitted.

More time passed quietly by, and this time she could feel them finally moving closer and closer to the reason they were there. It had to be faced, and she was ready to do it, but that didn't quell the wretched nervousness inside her.

'The estate agent's been to value the flat,' she told him in the end. 'I don't think we're going to make our money back after everything we put into it, but the price she's suggesting seems fair. Someone's coming to see it tomorrow. Cash buyers, I'm told, so it could happen quite fast.'

For a long time he merely continued to watch the river traffic, keeping his thoughts to himself and seeming to close her out in a way only he could. Then, he turned to look at her, and for a moment, when she saw his expression, she almost wanted to stop him saying whatever was in his mind.

'I know I've screwed up badly,' he said, sounding more strained than she'd ever heard him, 'and I can't even think of the words to use to tell you how sorry I am. All I know is whatever I have to do to make this up to you, I'll do it.'

Since the night he'd left this was all she'd wanted to hear, all she'd thought about, all she'd prayed for. Yet now, as she looked at him, searching the familiar features she'd always loved so much, hearing the echo of his voice, sensing his sincerity, she could feel no stirring of the elation she'd expected.

'Is it too late?' he said gruffly.

She shook her head. 'I don't know,' she answered truthfully. 'Maybe. I just know it isn't that easy.'

His eyes stayed on hers, and for the first time in all this she could really see his pain. 'Because of Nick?' he said.

She felt a stab of anger. 'No,' she retorted. 'It's about you and what you've done, for God's sake. Don't you understand that? Don't you have any sense of how much you've hurt me, what I've been through these last two months? What my parents have been through, too. I can't pretend none of it happened, Elliot. We can't just go back to the way we were, as though it doesn't matter that you called off our wedding so you could screw someone else. Or that you told me you didn't love me. It doesn't all come right again just because you've decided you don't want your Brazilian whore any more. It doesn't work like that. You've done a lot of harm, not only to me and my parents, but to our relationship, and frankly I don't know if it can be repaired. Right now, I actually don't think it can.'

He looked almost as though he'd been struck, though he surely couldn't have imagined she'd respond any other way.

'I understand how you feel,' he said, 'and I only wish I could explain what happened, why I did what I did, so we could at least try to work things out. I've spent a lot of time thinking these last few days, asking myself questions, trying to find answers, but all I can tell you is this, it was like an aberration, a compulsion, a need to break out, not just from you, from everything. Maybe it all stemmed from the Phraxos thing, the guilt and impotence I felt over that. I hated myself for taking that money, you know I did. I should never have let them pay me off . . . No, listen, please,' he said as she started to turn away. 'I know how weak all that sounds, that it doesn't even begin to excuse what I did. I'm just saying it probably played a part in it. What the hell else was going on in my head, I just don't know.'

'Andraya!' she reminded him bitterly. 'I think

she was going on in your head, don't you? Or at least some other part of you.'

'It's true, I wanted her,' he admitted.

'Badly enough to call off our wedding,' she added tightly.

'I couldn't marry you when I wanted another woman the way I wanted her,' he said, his lips turning pale with the strain. 'It seemed dishonest, disloyal. It wasn't what you deserved. I loved you too much to do it to you.'

'Oh please!'

'It's true. I never slept with her while we were still together . . .'

'And that's supposed to make it better?'

'Obviously it doesn't.'

'No, Elliot, it doesn't. Nothing's going to excuse what you did, or the way you handled it.'

His face was taut as he registered the words. 'I'm not trying to excuse myself, I'm trying to explain,' he said. 'I lost it there, for a while. It was as though I'd come unhinged. It happens. People act out of character, and I just wasn't seeing straight. I told myself all kinds of things that make no sense at all now. I thought I didn't love you, that I couldn't if I could feel that way about Andraya. I told myself we weren't doing the right thing, that I wasn't worthy of you, which I guess this proves I'm not . . . There was so much crap going round in my head. I can't even begin to explain it, but if you want me to go and get help to sort myself out, I'll do it. Anything, if you'll just say you won't give up on us without at least giving us one last chance.'

Though she was listening, and in a way feeling

547

for him, her heart still wasn't softening. 'But what about trust, Elliot?' she said. 'What kind of relationship can we possibly have without trust?'

'I admit it's going to take time to rebuild,' he replied. 'But I swear, I'll never do anything like this again.'

Her eyes remained steely and unrelenting as she looked up into his. She didn't doubt he meant what he was saying, now, today, but she meant it too. There could be no relationship without trust, and she just didn't know if she could ever feel it again.

After a few minutes she shook her head and looked off towards the pier. 'There's no getting away from the fact that you've spent these past weeks with another woman,' she said. 'You made me cancel our wedding. You told me you didn't love me . . .'

'It seems insane to me now that I could ever have thought that,' he interrupted.

Hearing the turbulence in his voice, she turned back to look at him again. 'Words are fine,' she said quietly, 'they can mean a lot, but in the end it's actions that count, and I can't just forget what you've done. I don't know if I can forgive it either.'

She saw him swallow, and couldn't help feeling sorry, for she knew how dreadful it was to see everything that mattered slipping away. 'You say you don't know,' he responded. 'Could that mean that maybe there is a chance? Given time?'

She didn't answer.

'Can we at least not shut the door completely?'

Still she didn't answer.

'Tell me what you want me to do, and I'll do it.'

She was tempted to remind him that was how she'd felt when he'd left, and he hadn't given her a chance, but why do it? Scoring points like that now would just be petty and vengeful, and anyway, he knew what he'd done. 'This isn't easy for me to say, Elliot,' she told him solemnly, 'but as far as you're concerned something in me died over the last few weeks. I'm not sure exactly when it happened, but I do know that the fact you could have done what you did . . .' She took a breath to cut off the self-pity. 'I've lost a lot of respect for you, and without that there's no relationship worth having.'

His expression was hard to read, but she knew her words had hurt him deeply. 'Would you consider some kind of trial period?' he asked with small hope in his voice. 'See if there's something there we can at least work on.'

After looking at him for some time she started to shake her head. 'I don't know,' she answered, realizing she didn't have it in her to crush him completely. 'I'll have to think about it.'

'Then can we take the flat off the market while you do?' he asked. 'You go on living there, and I'll still pay my share until . . . Well, until we come to a decision.'

'Where will you go?'

'I'm sure Chris will let me carry on using his flat.'

'Isn't that where you were with Andraya?'

'I'll find somewhere else,' he said immediately.

She turned away again, gazing upriver in the direction of their flat, though it wasn't visible from where they were standing. In a way it was like their relationship, there, but just out of sight. However, it wasn't going to be anywhere near as easy as just taking a river taxi or a train to find it again, and if, despite everything, she didn't love him so much she wouldn't even want to try.

'I have a suggestion,' he said, after a while. 'I'm not sure how you're going to take it, but would you consider coming with me to Bali? Before you say no,' he went on hastily as she turned to him in amazement, 'please just think about it. There are still two weeks left, and maybe it would do us both some good to get away, give us a chance to talk, to see if we think there is a way of sorting things out.'

Still stunned by the very idea, she only managed to say, 'I'm very busy with the programme . . .'

'You always were going to be away right now,' he reminded her.

'That's true, but . . .' She caught her breath, and looked away. Bali? Now? The two of them, after all that had happened? It had never crossed her mind he'd even think of it, let alone suggest it. It was crazy. It didn't feel right at all, and yet . . . 'I'm not going to deny that we need to talk,' she said finally, 'but I don't know if I'm ready to go any further than this yet. I need some time to decide who you really are, because looking back now, I think I idolized you, maybe even more than I loved you. You were my hero, the one person I could always count on. You meant everything to me, and in my eyes at least you could do no wrong. I guess now I'm finding out that you're human after all, with as many failings and weaknesses as the rest of us. Maybe it's a lesson I needed to learn, but I still can't tell you our relationship can be saved.'

His eyes were bleak as he said, 'Then just tell me this, do you still love me?'

'I think you know the answer to that, but it's not enough. I'm sorry, it's just not.'

'It could be a start though.'

Again she turned to look upriver towards their apartment.

'The beginning for us last time,' he said, 'happened in a moonlit garden in Mexico. Maybe we could make a new beginning in Bali.'

She didn't answer, nor did she look at him.

'There's a flight at ten in the morning,' he told her. 'I've reserved us two seats. If you decide you don't want to come I'll cancel them, but I still won't give up. I want you back, Laurie. I don't care how long it takes, or what I have to do.'

Turning round, she lifted a hand and put her fingers over his lips. They were going in circles now, and to stay here any longer would just be prolonging the agony for them both. 'I'm going back to the office now,' she told him. 'I'll call you later with my decision.'

As she started to walk away her heart was aching for him, knowing how hard he was going to find these next few hours waiting for her call. It was giving her no pleasure to be putting him through this, even though many would say he more than deserved it. Maybe he did, but they didn't love him as much as she did, so they wouldn't care how he felt. Probably because she did, and because underneath it all she might just not be ready to give up on him completely, she

551

turned around and, walking backwards, quoted a line of Mimi's from *La Bohème*, '*Sei venisse con voi?*' Suppose I come with you?

It took a moment, then, recognizing the words, he gave a response from Rodolfo. '*El al ritorno?*' And when we return?

'*Curioso.*' Wait and see.

As he started to laugh she turned away again, not wanting him to think it was an answer. '*Sappi per tuo governo, che darei perdono in sempiterno,*' he called after her. For your future guidance, I would be constantly forgiving you.

Unable to stop herself laughing at the misquote, she left it there for now and carried on walking.